THE RATING GUIDE TO LIFE IN AMERICA'S FIFTY STATES

G. SCOTT THOMAS

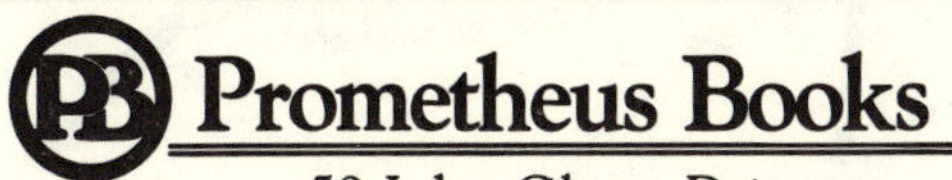
Prometheus Books
59 John Glenn Drive
Amherst, New York 14228-2197

WASHINGTON
MONTANA
NORTH DAKOTA
OREGON
IDAHO
SOUTH DAKOTA
WYOMING
NEBRASKA
NEVADA
UTAH
COLORADO
CALIFORNIA
ARIZONA
NEW MEXICO
TEXAS
ALASKA
HAWAII

NEW HAMPSHIRE
MAINE
VERMONT
NNESOTA
MASS.
NEW YORK
WISCONSIN
RHODE ISLAND
MICHIGAN
CONNECTICUT
NEW JERSEY
PENNSYLVANIA
IOWA
DELAWARE
OHIO
MARYLAND
INDIANA
ILLINOIS
WEST VIRGINIA
VIRGINIA
MISSOURI
KENTUCKY
NORTH CAROLINA
TENNESSEE
SOUTH CAROLINA
ARKANSAS
GEORGIA
MISSISSIPPI
ALABAMA
LOUISIANA
FLORIDA

Published 1994 by Prometheus Books.

 Inquiries should be addressed to Prometheus Books, 59 John Glenn Drive, Amherst, New York 14228-2197, 716-691-0133. FAX: 716-691-0137.

98 97 96 95 94 5 4 3 2

Library of Congress Cataloging-in-Publication Data

Thomas, G. Scott.
The rating guide to life in America's fifty states / G. Scott Thomas.
p. cm.
Includes bibliographical references.
ISBN 0-87975-938-0 (cloth) — ISBN 0-87975-939-9 (paper)
1. Quality of life—United States—States. I. Title.
HN60.T49 1994
306'.0973—dc20 94-22550
CIP

Printed in the United States of America on acid-free paper.

Contents

Introduction: Ranking America 9

Glossary of Important Terms 23

1 History 25
European Settlement 26 / Statehood 28 / Historic Places 30 /
Historic Natives 32 / Presidential Candidates 34 /
Scores and Grades 36

2 Terrain 39
Ocean Shoreline 40 / Inland Water 42 / Forests 44 /
Rangeland 46 / Elevation Variation 48 / Scores and Grades 50

3 Natural Resources 53
Farm Marketings 54 / Timberland 56 / Nonfuel Mining 58 /
Crude Oil Reserves 60 / Coal Reserves 63 /
Scores and Grades 65

4 Resource Conservation 68
Water Usage 69 / Petroleum Consumption 71 /
Natural Gas Consumption 73 / Electricity Consumption 75 /
Renewable Energy 77 / Scores and Grades 79

5 Environment 82
Superfund Sites 83 / Toxic Emissions 85 /
Drinking Water 87 / Waste Generation 89 /
Environmental Spending 91 / Scores and Grades 93

6 Health 96
Life Expectancy 97 / Major Causes of Death 99 /
Family Doctors 101 / Specialists 103 / Hospital Costs 105 /
Scores and Grades 107

7 Children and Families 110
Birth Weight 111 / Infant Mortality 113 /
Births to Single Teens 115 / Children in Poverty 117 /
Marriage Stability 119 / Scores and Grades 121

8 Female Equality 124
Women in Poverty 125 / Employment Opportunities 127 /
Women in Business 129 / Women in Government 131 /
Violence Against Women 133 / Scores and Grades 135

9 Racial Equality 138
Minority Population 139 / Income Disparity 141 /
Housing Disparity 143 / Minority College Graduates 145 /
Minority Businesses 147 / Scores and Grades 149

10 Housing 152
Housing Costs 153 / Rent 155 / Housing Age 157 /
Housing Size 159 / Property Taxes 161 / Scores and Grades 163

11 Education 166
High School Dropouts 167 / High School Graduates 169 /
Standardized Tests 171 / College Students 173 /
Education Spending 175 / Scores and Grades 177

12 Applied Intelligence 180
College Graduates 181 / Doctoral Degrees 183 / Patents 185 /
Research and Development 187 / MacArthur Fellows 189 /
Scores and Grades 191

13 Arts 194
Arts Funding 195 / Theater 197 / Dance 199 /
Entertainers 201 / Museums and Galleries 203 /
Scores and Grades 205

14 Communications 208
Telephone Service 209 / Cable Television 211 /
Broadcasting Stations 213 / Newspaper Circulation 215 /
Library Spending 217 / Scores and Grades 219

15 Sports 222
High School Athletes 223 / College Champions 225 /
Olympic Athletes 227 / Professional Champions 229 /
Spectator Seats 231 / Scores and Grades 233

16 Recreation 236
Park Visitors 237 / Fitness Centers 239 /
Movies and Videos 241 / Shopping 243 /
Restaurants and Bars 245 / Scores and Grades 247

17 Business 250
Gross State Product 251 / Economic Growth 253 /
Manufacturing Productivity 255 / Retail Trade 257 /
Service Sector Strength 259 / Scores and Grades 261

18 Personal Finances 264
Per Capita Income 265 / Income Growth 267 /
Unemployment 269 / Poverty 271 / Upper Incomes 273 /
Scores and Grades 275

19 Public Safety 278
All Crimes 279 / Violent Crimes 281 / Police Presence 283 /
Public Safety Spending 285 / Prison Population 287 /
Scores and Grades 289

20 Transportation 292
Road Mileage 293 / Motor Vehicle Deaths 295 /
Pavement Condition 297 / Public Transit Usage 299 /
Airline Service 301 / Scores and Grades 303

21 Politics 306
Voter Turnout 307 / Electoral Votes 309 /
Presidential Election Trends 311 / Political Party Competition 313 /
State Legislature Turnover 315 / Scores and Grades 317

22 Government 320
State Taxes 321 / State Debt 323 / Government Employees 325 /
Government Units 327 / State Constitution Length 329 /
Scores and Grades 331

23 National Relations 334
Federal Spending 335 / Population Influx 337 /
Domestic Travel 339 / *Fortune* 500 Companies 341 /
Student Migration 343 / Scores and Grades 345

24 International Relations 348
Foreign Employers 349 / Export-Related Jobs 351 /
Foreign Born 353 / Agricultural Exports 355 /
Overseas Population 357 / Scores and Grades 359

25 Future 362
Population Density 363 / Projected Population Growth 365 /
Projected Job Growth 367 / Projected Income Growth 369 /
Future Political Power 371 / Scores and Grades 373

Conclusion: States of the Union 377
National Results 377 / Regional Results 381 /
Size Group Results 385 / The Report Cards 389

Sources 567

Introduction:

Ranking America

H.L. Mencken believed, first and foremost, in the power of words. He skillfully used the English language as a weapon, skewering thousands of politicians, prohibitionists, tent preachers, businessmen, lawyers, chiropractors, countries, cities, and institutions during his reign as America's best-known and most influential newspaperman.

"I am not a constructive critic," he once admitted.

No one was safe from the harsh sting of Mencken's linguistic fury. He condemned government as "organized exploitation . . . the implacable enemy of every industrious and well-disposed man." Those who ran the government, of course, were beneath contempt: "A politician has no actual principles. He is in favor of whatever seems to him to be popular at the moment."

As for the poor, suffering voters? Mencken offered no sympathy. Some of his sharpest rhetoric was reserved for what he called the "booboisie," the average Americans who, in his view, cared little for social justice and even less for books and education.

"No one in this world, so far as I know—and I have researched the records for years, and employed agents to help me—has ever lost money by underestimating the intelligence of the great masses of the plain people," he wrote. "Nor has anyone ever lost public office thereby."

An exasperated critic finally asked Mencken why he continued to live in a country where he found nothing to praise. The journalist had a ready answer: "Why do men go to zoos?"

It is for the impact of his writing—sometimes bitter, often amusing, always provocative—that Mencken is remembered as we enter the twilight of the twentieth century. But another of his qualities deserves to be noted here. Mencken truly understood the power of numbers, a knowledge that inspired him to make an interesting proposition in the September 1931 issue of *American Mercury,* the magazine he edited.

"So maybe it will be possible, by examining certain tables of statistics, with the 48 American States (to which, of course, the District of Columbia should be added) ranged in order, to find out which of them tend toward the top of the heap and which toward the bottom," he wrote. "Statistics, to be sure, are not always reliable, but we have nothing better, and we must make as much of them as we can."

Thus began Mencken's pioneering attempt to rank America. He and his sidekick, Charles Angoff, collected more than 100 statistics for each state. Some were straightforward—murder rates, miles of roads, numbers of college students. Others were intriguingly esoteric—values of mineral deposits, newspaper circulations, numbers of natives in *Who's Who in America.*

Mencken being Mencken, his study had a peculiar bent. It was titled, "The Worst American State." This was no search for quality, no attempt to exalt the finest of the United States. It primarily was a quest to identify the dreariest part of what Mencken called "the dun and dour Republic."

American Mercury dutifully published dozens of tables along with its editor's running commentary in three consecutive editions. Mencken wrapped up the series in November 1931, happily asserting that Mississippi deserved the title of worst American state. He gave less attention to Massachusetts, which finished at the top of his quality-of-life rankings.

This venture into demographics merely confirmed Mencken's basic beliefs. States in the Northeast, the region he considered the most sophisticated, generally held the top positions on his statistical scale; southern states, so often the object of his scorn, were clumped at the bottom.

"The richer states, on the whole, are also the most cultured," he concluded, "and not only the most cultured, but also the healthiest and the most orderly."

Several authors have followed the statistical trail that Mencken blazed. Perhaps the most notable was John Gunther, whose bestseller, *Inside U.S.A.,* was published in 1947. Gunther traveled to all 48 states, interviewing public officials and business leaders and just generally storing observations. "I like the direct eyes-and-ears approach," he wrote. "I have to feel, hear, see."

Gunther did not intend to rank the states, but he devoted considerable space to chronicling what set them apart. "Every state has its own particular and special flavor," he insisted. Differences could be extreme, even between neighbors. "Utah is the most staid and respectable of states," he wrote. "Nevada is, by common convention at least, the naughtiest."

But Gunther found that personal observations could take him only so far in his efforts to describe a nation as large and diverse as America. He relied on numbers to an unusual extent to drive his case home. That was evident from the first time a copy of *Inside U.S.A.* was opened. Out spilled a large, folding chart with column after column of statistics for each state, everything from population and land area to the numbers of lynchings and rural homes without toilets.

The text itself was packed with figures. The reader learned within the first three pages how many doughnuts Americans consumed, how many people held life insurance, how many governmental units had been set up, how much money was bet at race tracks, how many Roman Catholics there were, how many different sizes of women's shoes were available, and how many World War II soldiers had venereal diseases.

Charts and lists of numbers often occupied full pages of *Inside U.S.A.*, under such headings as "A Garland of Statistics"; "Statistics, Sex, and Segregation"; and "Kansas Has Statistics Too." Gunther prefaced one of his numerical digressions this way: "The state of Utah can offer statistics as impressive as any in the union."

The torrent of numbers gradually washed away the author's resolve. He began offering his own informal rankings on p. 910. "The worst-bossed state is Tennessee or New Jersey; the least-bossed, Washington or Arizona," Gunther announced. "The best-governed state is probably New York, and for the worst just blindfold yourself and stick a finger anywhere below the Mason and Dixon's line."

He proceeded quickly to his impressions of the places with the best views, smoothest railroads, least visible signs, quietest streets, crudest newspapers, and best draft beer, all spilling out in a staccato burst of sentences. The long paragraph finally ended in a small gap of white space.

"So now, at last," Gunther wrote, no doubt gasping to catch his breath, "we come to the end of this long, detail-choked and multicolored journey."

America's Building Blocks

The stories above deserve our attention for two reasons. One, of course, is Mencken's theory—innovative in the precomputer age—that a statistical formula could pinpoint the nation's worst (and best) states. The other is Gunther's underlying belief that numbers could help identify the qualities that make each state unique.

These twin ideas are the foundation for this book. We will use statistics, as Mencken did, to determine which states offer the highest and lowest quality of life today. But we will do more than just put together a ranking from no. 1 to no. 50. We also will point out the strengths and weaknesses of every state, as Gunther did, showing what is interesting and surprising about each.

That's not to say that this book merely updates the work of those two distinguished authors. A close look shows that some of their research methods don't fit our purposes, so must be discarded or modified.

Emphasizing the negative was as natural for Mencken as breathing, but our primary focus will be on the positive. We will point out the bottom states in each category, of course, but those at the top will receive more attention. Nor will we accept Mencken's advice about including the District of Columbia in our rankings. The nation's capital is a city, not a state. There is no way it can be fairly compared with states that have a balance of urban, suburban, and rural areas.

Gunther's book was highly personal, based as it was on interviews and on-the-scene observations. There is no denying that *Inside U.S.A.* was compelling and insightful, but we have no intention of copying its style. Our rankings will be based strictly on the numbers, so that residents of Massachusetts, Mississippi, and the other 48 states can see exactly why they received the grades they did. We will remove personal bias from the process as best we can.

The stakes, after all, are high. Americans love to compare states, often in heated tones. Who hasn't sat around with friends in a college dorm or an army barracks or the lunchroom at work, arguing about who comes from the best place?

You know the kinds of questions that spring up in these sessions. Who has the best drivers—Rhode Island or Connecticut? Who has the best athletes—Alabama or Georgia? Who has the best schools—Wisconsin or Michigan? Who has the best state parks—Oregon or California?

Who knows?

One way to find out is to do what Gunther did. Hit the road for three or four years, and see for yourself. But who could afford to do that? And who would believe you when you came back with your final judgments? Your friends would just accuse you of turning up evidence to support your own views. And the argument would begin anew.

The better way to resolve these disputes—if indeed they ever can be truly resolved—is with numbers. The Census Bureau churns out a steady flow of statistical reports on the 50 states, covering everything from population and per capita income to average property tax levels and the number of businesses owned by women. Other government agencies and private firms fill in the gaps, quantifying almost every aspect of daily life. These reports will be our tools, making it possible for us to dispassionately rate the quality of life in each state.

That's all well and good, you say. You admittedly want to know where your home state ends up in our final standings. But, you ask, wouldn't it be more useful to rate *metro areas*? States are passé these days, aren't they? Everybody knows that this is the age of metropolitan media markets.

Consider this question in response. Do you really think of yourself as a resident of a *media market*? Of course not. Nor does anyone else. Nobody at those all-night dorm sessions ever said, "The place I live, the Albany–Schenectady–Troy, New York, Metropolitan Statistical Area, is far superior to where you live, the Modesto, California, Metropolitan Statistical Area." But you can bet there were arguments about the relative merits of New York and California. Plenty of arguments.

That's because there are so many great rivalries between states. New York–California is a perfect example; those two have been bickering for 50 years over which has more power. But that's just one among hundreds of never-ending disputes: Kansas–Missouri over their common border, Michigan–Ohio over college football, South Dakota–Minnesota over the best place to do business, Utah–Colorado over water. And on and on. (See the following pages for a state-by-state list.)

These are not arguments between markets. It's not just people in Salt Lake City lining up against people in Denver. It's bigger than that. It's state against state, all of Utah against all of Colorado.

It is possible to rate metropolitan areas, of course; you can find interesting books on the subject. But they miss the larger point. We aren't a nation of media markets, no matter what some demographers might say. It's not the United *Markets,* it's the United *States* of America.

States are the building blocks of this country. They still have the power; they still set policy in most fields. A metro area has little or no control over income taxes, school funding, prisons, expressway maintenance, colleges, or public assistance programs. Localities in many states must receive permission from the state government before they start building a stadium or jail or major road. Then they usually go right back and ask the state to fund the project.

And let's not forget that America is much more than cities and suburbs. It is also small towns and wide-open rural areas. The latter aren't included in metro areas. But everyone—big city and tiniest village alike—is part of a state.

So if you're looking for a new place to live, or if you're simply curious about how your current home stacks up against the rest of the country, you need to take the broad view. Don't focus on individual markets; look at entire states. That's the level that reflects all of America's nuances.

"However real the nationalizing and leveling power of mass communications, of centralized government and corporate power, each of the 50 states remains a unique blend of history and peoples and economy and politics and natural environment, unduplicated on this continent or anywhere in the world," wrote Neal Peirce and Jerry Hagstrom in 1983's *The Book of America.* "To experience the world of Massachusetts or Texas, of Vermont or Arizona, of Florida or Oregon, is to live and move in strikingly different places."

This book will use statistics to illuminate those differences, eventually revealing the best states of America. And yes, the worst ones, too. Perhaps we'll even settle an argument or two along the way, though we shouldn't hope for too much. Mencken himself recognized decades ago that no matter how precise the ratings might be, the states are unlikely to ever stop quarreling.

"Perhaps these disputes are destined to go on forever," he wrote, "as they have been going on in Europe for centuries."

The Disunited States of America

USA Today catalogued the feuds between states in its July 23, 1990, issue.* A few items might now be dated, but the list remains a good sampling of interstate rivalries. Some of these disputes are humorous; others are deadly serious:

ALABAMA: Mobile boasts the United States' first Mardi Gras, in 1702, much to the chagrin of New Orleans. Alabamans also claim prettier, cleaner beaches than Florida.

ALASKA: Oklahomans and Texans who cashed in on the Alaskan pipeline left hard feelings. A popular bumper sticker reads: "Happiness is an Oklahoman leaving Alaska with a Texan under each arm."

ARIZONA: Beat California in the U.S. Supreme Court for rights to water from the Colorado River.

ARKANSAS: Jokingly notes that if not for Mississippi, Arkansas would rank last among the states in education, housing, and other measures of wealth.

CALIFORNIA: Boundary disputes with Nevada date to the 1863 "Sagebrush War," which included shootings and injuries.

COLORADO: Ribs Nebraska as place for "flatlanders and cowboys."

CONNECTICUT: Fuming over just-passed New York commuter tax.

DELAWARE: Resents Pennsylvania's mocking border signs proclaiming, "America starts here."

FLORIDA: Resents, but needs, northern tourists and retirees who've fueled the state's booming economy.

GEORGIA: Lost U.S. Supreme Court fight with South Carolina for ownership of Barnwell Islands in the Savannah River.

HAWAII: Fierce competitor with Florida and California for sun-lovers' dollars.

IDAHO: Dismayed over confusion with Iowa; mail often goes to Boise, Iowa.

ILLINOIS: Squabbling over Ohio River boundary with Kentucky. Illinois fishermen now must buy Kentucky licenses.

INDIANA: Also fighting with Kentucky over control of the Ohio River.

IOWA: Fighting with Illinois over proposed "Avenue of the Saints" highway, which would connect St. Paul, Minnesota, and St. Louis. Both want the highway to run through their state.

---

*Copyright 1990, *USA TODAY*. Reprinted with permission.

KANSAS: Argues with Missouri over the shifting Missouri River border.

KENTUCKY: Louisville residents make fun of huge city clock in neighboring Jeffersonville, Indiana, which can be seen only from Kentucky.

LOUISIANA: Serious football rivalry between Louisiana State University and University of Florida.

MAINE: Regularly claws at New Hampshire over minimum size of lobsters caught in coastal waters.

MARYLAND: Miffed that farmland runoff (chemical fertilizers, pesticides, and manure) into Pennsylvania streams is polluting the Chesapeake Bay.

MASSACHUSETTS: Held up licensing of New Hampshire's controversial Seabrook nuclear power plant by refusing to agree to an emergency evacuation plan.

MICHIGAN: Intense football rivalry between University of Michigan and Ohio State.

MINNESOTA: Knocks Iowa by saying that the state's license plate stands for "Idiot on Wheels Ahead."

MISSISSIPPI: Louisiana State University is arch-rival of Ole Miss.

MISSOURI: The Universities of Missouri and Kansas share a fiercely competitive sports rivalry dating back to the mid-nineteenth century.

MONTANA: Billboard that was near border with "criminally flat" neighbor said, "Welcome to North Dakota—Mountain Removal Project Completed."

NEBRASKA: Battling Colorado's proposed Twin Forks dam, which would decrease flow of South Platte River into the state.

NEVADA: Jokes that earthquake-prone California will fall into the Pacific Ocean and turn the state's desert into a beach.

NEW HAMPSHIRE: With no sales or income taxes, the state pokes fun at neighboring "Taxachusetts."

NEW JERSEY: Claims Hoboken, not Cooperstown, New York, was the site of the first baseball game. Has lived in giant New York's shadow for years, now starting to emerge.

NEW MEXICO: Miffed at people who don't realize that it is part of the United States; regularly asked if a visa is needed and if water is clean enough to drink.

NEW YORK: Won U.S. Supreme Court fight with New Jersey over ownership of Liberty and Ellis islands.

NORTH CAROLINA: Upset at Virginia Power Company's proposal to build a dam that would back water up into the New River Valley. Congress designated it a scenic river, preventing damming.

NORTH DAKOTA: Volleyed in billboard war with Montana: "Stay in North Dakota—Custer was healthy when he left."

OHIO: Bumper sticker barb: "How do you find Michigan? Drive north until you smell it and walk east until you step in it."

OKLAHOMA: Fighting Red River border war with Texas.

OREGON: Accused by neighbor of using discriminatory commuter tax on Washington state residents.

PENNSYLVANIA: Calls New Jersey "armpit of the nation" because of stench-spewing factories and New Jersey's geographical location.

RHODE ISLAND: Complains of summer homeowners from New York and New Jersey who act like "caged animals who've finally been let loose."

SOUTH CAROLINA: Rivalry with North Carolina over Andrew Jackson's birthplace.

SOUTH DAKOTA: The state, which has no income tax, has tried to lure businesses from neighboring Minnesota and Iowa.

TENNESSEE: Peeved at North Carolina over Pigeon River pollution from Champion International pulp and paper mill in Canton, North Carolina.

TEXAS: Upset at New Mexico for denying El Paso the right to drill for water in the fertile southern portion of New Mexico and import it.

UTAH: Haggles with Colorado over rights to Colorado River water.

VERMONT: Liberal, agricultural state looks down on conservative, industrialized New Hampshire.

VIRGINIA: Vying with North Carolina for the remains of the Union ironclad ship *Monitor,* mired at the bottom of the Atlantic.

WASHINGTON: "Caliphobic" about Californians moving into the state and sending traffic, home prices, and pollution soaring.

WEST VIRGINIA: Resents Virginians for looking down on them as uneducated and poor, and for referring to them as "hillbillies."

WISCONSIN: Complains of polluted air wafting over Lake Michigan from heavily industrialized Illinois and Indiana.

WYOMING: Derides Colorado "greenies"—named for their license plate color—who misuse state's natural resources.

Asking the Right Questions

Quality of life cannot be defined by a single factor. Or by two or three, for that matter. It is shaped by many forces. Each of us could come up with a list of the factors we believe to be important. This book, in order to be useful to as many people as possible, takes a particularly broad view, identifying 25 components. Some are deadly serious, such as public safety and health. Some might seem frivolous, such as recreation and the arts. But make no mistake. All have a direct impact on a state's quality of life.

We will refer to these 25 components as *sections.* Each is designed to answer a specific question about life in the United States:

1. *History*—Which state has had the richest past, both in terms of historic events and famous people?

2. *Terrain*—Which state has the most varied landscape, with everything from oceans and lakes to rangeland and mountains?

3. *Natural Resources*—Which state is blessed with the widest array of resources, ranging from good farmland to rich mineral deposits?

4. *Resource Conservation*—Which state uses energy and natural resources most wisely?

5. *Environment*—Which state has the cleanest air, water, and soil?

6. *Health*—Which state has the healthiest residents and the best health-care system?

7. *Children and Families*—Which state offers the best conditions in which to raise a family?

8. *Female Equality*—Which state gives women the best opportunity to succeed in government, the workplace, or their own businesses?

9. *Racial Equality*—Which state gives minorities the best chance to compete and coexist with whites?

10. *Housing*—Which state has the newest, largest, and most affordable homes?

11. *Education*—Which state does the best job of educating its young people?

12. *Applied Intelligence*—Which state makes the best use of its collective brain power?

13. *Arts*—Which state has the richest blend of artists of all types?

14. *Communications*—Which state has the best system for transmitting information, using both the spoken and printed word?

15. *Sports*—Which state is most strongly involved in athletics at the amateur and professional levels?

16. *Recreation*—Which state offers the best combination of leisure opportunities, ranging from parks and fitness centers to movie theaters and restaurants?

17. *Business*—Which state historically has had the best economic climate in which to operate a successful business in the manufacturing, retail, or service sectors?

18. *Personal Finances*—Which state provides the best opportunity for individual financial growth?

19. *Public Safety*—Which state has the safest streets and neighborhoods?

20. *Transportation*—Which state makes it easiest to get around, whether in a car, on public transit, or in a plane?

21. *Politics*—Which state has the political system that gives voters the best opportunity to participate in competitive elections, while exercising national clout?

22. *Government*—Which state has the most efficient government?

23. *National Relations*—Which state has the strongest connections with the rest of the country, whether in business, education, or everyday life?

24. *International Relations*—Which state has the strongest connections with the rest of the world?

25. *Future*—Which state faces the brightest future, in terms of demographics, economics, and politics?

This book will find the answers to all of these questions, and in the process will determine the answer to the biggest question of them all: Which of the 50 states offers the best quality of life?

We will collect a wide array of statistics during our search. What we need is a way to turn these numbers into fair, easy-to-understand rankings. That's where rates come in.

A Few Words on Rates

The simplest way to compare states is to use raw totals. Let's say you are from California and I am from Vermont. We're arguing—who knows why, but we are—about which of our states has the most medical specialists.

We go to the library and find a reference book. It says that California has 54,506 medical specialists; Vermont has only 1,081. California is the winner. Case closed.

But is it?

Raw totals obviously don't make for a fair contest. California has almost 30 million residents; tiny Vermont has fewer than 600,000. You would expect California to have more of *everything* than Vermont—more mountains, more farms, more hazardous waste sites, more shopping centers, more high school dropouts, more college graduates, more murderers, more *Fortune* 500 companies. And, of course, more medical specialists.

But what if there were a way to counterbalance California's huge population advantage? What if we were able to put the two states on an even footing? Then we could make a fair comparison that really would tell us something about the relative quality of life in California and Vermont.

Such a way exists, of course, and it's an easy one. All we need to do is convert our raw totals into rates.

Rates reduce the big picture to a human scale, making it possible for us to effectively compare states of varying sizes. Rates reveal the faulty thinking behind the American myth that says large automatically is better, small is inherently inferior. Several small states offer excellent quality of life, as we shall see, while a few giants don't live up to their inflated reputations.

How can we tell which states have earned superior grades and which deserve F's? Our first step is to eliminate the distortions that naturally result from comparisons based on raw totals.

Think of it in practical terms. It might sound impressive that California has 53,425 more medical specialists than Vermont. But what does it mean to you in everyday life? Nothing. It's not as if you will ever have the chance to consult with every medical expert from San Diego to the Oregon state line. If you visited one California specialist each day of your life, it would be 149 years before you dragged yourself out of the last waiting room.

The raw total of medical specialists, therefore, is of no value to us. What really matters is the *concentration* or *density* of those specialists. How many are there likely to be in any given part of the state? How easy would it be for you to find the specialist you need?

Rates provide the answer. They show us a cross-section of equal size from each state, allowing us to make quick and meaningful comparisons.

Simple division is all that is required. Rates often are expressed as ratios per 100,000 residents. So we divide the raw total of medical specialists by each state's population, then multiply by 100,000. You algebra fans will recognize the formula:

$$Rate = (Specialists / Population) \times 100{,}000$$

A few clicks on a pocket calculator will give us the rates, which in turn will give us a good idea of how medical specialists are distributed across California and Vermont. We now see a picture that is much different from what the raw totals showed us.

California has 183 specialists for every 100,000 residents. That's a respectable rate, well above the national average. But Vermont has 192 specialists per 100,000, one of the best rates in the nation. It obviously would be easier for you to find a medical specialist in Vermont than in California, so Vermont earns a higher score in this category.

Now the case is closed.

We use rates extensively in this book. They often follow the form above, taking cross-sections of 100,000 residents. Also common are percentages, which really are nothing more than rates per 100 people. You can say that 27 percent of Colorado adults have college degrees, or you can say there are 27 college graduates per 100 adults in Colorado. Same thing.

But many of our rates are expressed in unique terms. Consider the variety in this sample: acres of timberland per 1,000 square miles, registered historic places per 10,000 square miles, gallons of water used by each resident per day, annual deaths in motor vehicle accidents per 100,000 licensed drivers, housing costs per $1,000 of household income.

You even will find rates in this book that are based on units as large as 1 million residents. Vermont, you will learn, has 21.3 Olympic athletes per million. How can we come up with such a figure for a state with only 563,000 residents? It turns out that rates work both ways. They can reduce a state to a tiny cross-section, or they can expand it beyond its actual size. Either way accurately reflects the distribution of a specific element—medical specialists, Olympic athletes, whatever—within its borders.

Our use of rates will help you see America in a totally new way. You no longer will blindly assume that the state with the largest raw total is the best in a particular category. We will show you which states really are doing the most—or the least—with what they have. Some of the results will astound you.

New Jersey, one of our most urbanized states, has the nation's lowest hospital costs? Vermont, rural from end to end, is the best place in America to go shopping? Alaska has the most impressive record in high school athletics? Idaho uses the most water? North Carolina is the strongest manufacturing state?

These facts don't match our traditional understanding of America. But they are true, each and every one of them. We haven't noticed them before because we have been looking at our country in the wrong way. Rates give us the clear perspective we need.

Scoring

We now have a system that can be used to rank the states in any given category. It's a simple three-step procedure: (1) Get the raw totals for all 50 states. (2) Convert those raw totals to rates. (3) List the states from best to worst.

Easy enough. When we do the math, it tells us that Massachusetts has the nation's best rate when it comes to medical specialists. Vermont is no. 7, California is no. 10, and Idaho is in last place. That would be highly useful information if our only concern were the availability of specialists. But this book has a much broader scope. What we need is a formula to convert our data about specialists, as well as dozens of other statistical indicators, into a quality-of-life rating for each state.

We have such a formula, of course. This book, as we know, is divided into twenty-five sections, all of which are organized exactly the same way. Let's run through the scoring process step by step, using the Health section as an example.

Categories. A section is made up of five categories, each designed to illuminate a different aspect of the broad picture. All categories count equally toward the final score for the section; each, therefore, is worth 20 percent. The Health section consists of these categories: Life Expectancy, Major Causes of Death, Family Doctors, Specialists, and Hospital Costs.

Category scoring. A state's score in a category is a reflection of its relative standing among the fifty states. The score is expressed on a 100-point scale. The closer a state is to the top performance in the nation, the higher its total number of points.

Think of this scoring system as a rubber sheet stretching precisely from the two best states to the two worst states. Take the Family Doctors category, for example. Minnesota and South Dakota are at the top of the list—Minnesota with 42.7 family doctors per 100,000 residents and South Dakota with 42.5 per 100,000. At the bottom of the scale are Rhode Island with 16.0 family doctors per 100,000 and Massachusetts with 15.3 per 100,000.

Minnesota and South Dakota automatically earn 100 points in this category. We then pull the rubber sheet all the way down to Rhode Island and

Massachusetts, which both receive zero points. The scores of all other states are based on their relative positions between these extremes.

Here's how it works, using Wisconsin as an example. The first thing we do is measure the distance between the category's second-best state (South Dakota) and the second-worst state (Rhode Island). That range, which corresponds to the length of our rubber sheet, is 42.5 minus 16.0, equaling 26.5.

Then we determine Wisconsin's location by measuring the distance between it and Rhode Island. Wisconsin has 32.8 family doctors per 100,000 residents. That puts it 16.8 ahead of Rhode Island. Divide 16.8 into the total range (26.5), and you get 63 percent. So Wisconsin earns 63 points in this category.

That's all there is to it, except perhaps for one nagging question. Why, you ask, do we give identical scores to *two* states at the top and *two* at the bottom? The answer is that we're trying to maintain a level playing field. One state sometimes is far superior in a category. It could earn a substantial bulge in points that would carry it to victory in the entire section, even though it did poorly in the other four categories. Having two ultimate winners and two ultimate losers in each category prevents such distortion.

Take note of one more thing. You sometimes will see more than two states with either 100 or zero points. That's either because of ties, or because a state has a score (such as 99.6 or 0.4) that rounds off to the end of the scale.

Section scoring. The first step is easy. We add a state's category scores, then divide by five. Wisconsin received these scores in the Health section: 81, 28, 63, 29, and 76. That works out to a raw average of 55.4 points.

Now it's time to pull out the rubber sheet again. We first calculate the raw averages for every state, then stretch the sheet all the way from no. 1 to no. 50. Notice that for section scoring only, we run our scale between the best and worst states, not the second-best and second-worst. Only one state gets 100 points in a section, and only one gets a score of zero.

Minnesota leads the Health section with a raw average of 75.2, which earns it 100 points. Louisiana is at the bottom of the list with a raw average of 23.8, which converts to zero points for the section. Wisconsin, based on its relative location between top and bottom, ends up with a section score of 61.

Overall scoring. All that remains is to come up with a final score for each state. We essentially average the 25 section scores, but there is a slight twist. Ten sections are given extra weight because they are of critical daily importance to us all: Resource Conservation, Environment, Health, Children and Families, Housing, Education, Business, Personal Finances, Public Safety, and Future.

Overall scores are expressed on a 1,000-point scale. The ten weighted sections are worth 5 percent each in the final formula, meaning they collectively are responsible for half of the overall score. The other 15 sections are worth 3.33 percent each.

Letter grades. Section and overall scores are accompanied by letter grades, allowing you to assess a state's performance in a glance. (Grades are not given in categories.) The grading system is the same one you knew in school: A for excellence, down to F for failure. Here is the scale that is used throughout this book:

Score	Grade
100	A+
85–99	A
80–84	A–
75–79	B+
65–74	B
60–64	B–
55–59	C+
45–54	C
40–44	C–
35–39	D+
25–34	D
20–24	D–
0–19	F

So much for the technicalities; now it's time to get to work on the ratings. First come the 25 sections we have already talked so much about. Then we cap off the book with a chapter that includes detailed report cards for all 50 states.

The sections, as we've said, are all organized in the same manner. First there are the five categories, each with a chart that ranks the states from top to bottom. The categories are followed by a summary of the states' scores and grades for the section as a whole.

We will begin our statistical journey at a logical starting point, the History section. This is a trip that will be guided by Mencken's words: "Statistics, to be sure, are not always reliable, but we have nothing better, and we must make as much of them as we can."

Let us begin.

Glossary of Important Terms

Category. A single statistical measure that is used to assess a specific aspect of a state's quality of life. There are 125 categories in this book, five in each of the 25 sections.

East. One of the four major regions in the country. It includes Connecticut, Delaware, the District of Columbia, Maine, Maryland, Massachusetts, New Hampshire, New Jersey, New York, Pennsylvania, Rhode Island, Vermont, and West Virginia.

Large state. A state with more than 6 million residents. There are 13 large states.

Median. The middle number of a group in which the figures are arranged from biggest to smallest. Don't confuse *median* with *average*. Let's say that five states have 43, 27, 19, 15, and 11 electoral votes respectively. The median number is 19, while the average is 23.

Medium state. A state whose population is between 2 million and 6 million. There are 20 medium states.

Metropolitan area. A large city and its suburbs, or a combination of neighboring large cities and their suburbs, that are defined by the federal government as "socially and economically interrelated."

Midwest. One of the nation's four major regions. It includes Illinois, Indiana, Iowa, Kansas, Michigan, Minnesota, Missouri, Nebraska, North Dakota, Ohio, South Dakota, and Wisconsin.

Per capita. The average for each person living in an area. A per capita figure is calculated by taking any total number for the area and dividing it by the area's population. Let's say that a state has 1 million residents who earn a total of $18 billion a year. That works out to $18,000 per capita.

Rates. It usually is unfair to compare absolute totals from two states of different sizes. Projecting those totals to a common rate is a way of putting both states on an equal footing. Rates are commonly, though certainly not always, expressed as a number per 100,000 residents. Consider this example: State A has 1,060 police officers and a population of 2 million; State B has 7,400 officers and 5 million residents. State A's rate is 53 officers per 100,000 residents; State B has 148 officers per 100,000.

Section. A broad component of a state's quality of life, such as housing or education. This book identifies 25 sections.

Small state. A state with fewer than 2 million residents. There are 17 small states.

South. One of the nation's four major regions. It includes Alabama, Arkansas, Florida, Georgia, Kentucky, Louisiana, Mississippi, North Carolina, Oklahoma, South Carolina, Tennessee, Texas, and Virginia.

West. One of the nation's four major regions. It includes Alaska, Arizona, California, Colorado, Hawaii, Idaho, Montana, Nevada, New Mexico, Oregon, Utah, Washington, and Wyoming.

1

History

The Big Question

Which state has had the richest past, both in terms of historic events and famous people?

The Categories

1. European Settlement
2. Statehood
3. Historic Places
4. Historic Natives
5. Presidential Candidates

26 European Settlement

DOING THE MATH

We took the year of the first permanent European settlement within the current boundaries of each state. No credit for temporary villages that disappeared after the first harsh winter. We're talking permanent. (There is no denying that the Indians were here first, or that they built important civilizations. But face it: Our history is Eurocentric.)

BEST STATES

The Spanish put down roots in St. Augustine in 1565, making Florida the only state with a permanent European settlement in the sixteenth century. Virginia was the runner-up. Jamestown was settled in 1607.

WORST STATES

Oklahoma originally was known as Indian Territory, but the federal government eventually succumbed to pressure to allow white settlement. It opened the territory for the famous land rush in 1889. South Dakota's first white settlers had arrived 30 years before.

REGIONAL WINNERS

East—New York
South—Florida
Midwest—Michigan
West—New Mexico

BIGGEST SURPRISE

There was a permanent Spanish settlement at what is now Santa Fe, New Mexico, four years before the first Europeans decided to make New York their home.

THE BOTTOM LINE

European civilization arrived first on the Atlantic Seaboard. Twelve of the first 13 states on the list are strung along the Atlantic coast. The states of the Great Plains and Rocky Mountains generally were the last to be settled.

European Settlement

State	Year of First Permanent European Settlement	Points
1. Florida	1565	100
2. Virginia	1607	100
3. New Mexico	1610	99
4. New York	1614	97
5. Massachusetts	1620	95
6. New Hampshire	1623	94
7. Maine	1624	93
8. Connecticut	1634	89
Maryland	1634	89
10. Rhode Island	1636	88
11. Delaware	1638	88
12. North Carolina	1660	79
13. New Jersey	1664	77
14. Michigan	1668	76
15. South Carolina	1670	75
16. Pennsylvania	1682	70
Texas	1682	70
18. Arkansas	1686	69
19. Louisiana	1699	63
Mississippi	1699	63
21. Alabama	1702	62
22. Illinois	1720	55
23. Vermont	1724	54
24. Kansas	1727	52
West Virginia	1727	52
26. Georgia	1733	50
Indiana	1733	50
28. Missouri	1735	49
29. Wisconsin	1766	37
30. California	1769	36
Tennessee	1769	36
32. Kentucky	1774	34
33. Arizona	1776	33
34. Alaska	1784	30
35. Iowa	1788	28
Ohio	1788	28
37. Minnesota	1805	21
38. Montana	1809	20
39. Oregon	1811	19
Washington	1811	19
41. North Dakota	1812	19
42. Hawaii	1820	15
43. Nebraska	1823	14
44. Wyoming	1834	10
45. Idaho	1842	7
46. Utah	1847	5
47. Nevada	1849	4
48. Colorado	1858	0
49. South Dakota	1859	0
50. Oklahoma	1889	0

28 Statehood

DOING THE MATH

This category couldn't be simpler. We merely took the year that each state joined the Union. The original 13 states are listed in the order that they ratified the Constitution.

BEST STATES

Delaware was the first to sign on the dotted line, agreeing to the Constitution on December 7, 1787. It has called itself The First State ever since. New Jersey and Pennsylvania climbed aboard within days of Delaware.

WORST STATES

These states are worst in the sense that they have the shortest histories as part of the United States. Perhaps youngest is a better adjective. Alaska was admitted to the Union in January 1959. Hawaii became the 50th state just eight months later.

REGIONAL WINNERS

East—Delaware, New Jersey, Pennsylvania
South—Georgia, South Carolina, Virginia
Midwest—Ohio
West—California

BIGGEST SURPRISE

Gold was discovered in California in 1848, triggering the famous gold rush a year later. California's population grew so rapidly that it was admitted to the Union in 1850, well ahead of midwestern states such as Minnesota, Kansas, and Nebraska.

THE BOTTOM LINE

No surprise here. The United States was settled from Atlantic to Pacific, so eastern and southern states obviously entered the Union first. They hold the top 16 positions on the statehood list.

Statehood

State	Year Admitted to the Union	Points
1. Delaware	1787	100
New Jersey	1787	100
Pennsylvania	1787	100
4. Connecticut	1788	99
Georgia	1788	99
Maryland	1788	99
Massachusetts	1788	99
New Hampshire	1788	99
New York	1788	99
South Carolina	1788	99
Virginia	1788	99
12. North Carolina	1789	99
13. Rhode Island	1790	98
14. Vermont	1791	98
15. Kentucky	1792	97
16. Tennessee	1796	95
17. Ohio	1803	91
18. Louisiana	1812	85
19. Indiana	1816	83
20. Mississippi	1817	83
21. Illinois	1818	82
22. Alabama	1819	81
23. Maine	1820	81
24. Missouri	1821	80
25. Arkansas	1836	72
26. Michigan	1837	71
27. Florida	1845	66
Texas	1845	66
29. Iowa	1846	66
30. Wisconsin	1848	65
31. California	1850	63
32. Minnesota	1858	59
33. Oregon	1859	58
34. Kansas	1861	57
35. West Virginia	1863	56
36. Nevada	1864	55
37. Nebraska	1867	53
38. Colorado	1876	48
39. Montana	1889	41
North Dakota	1889	41
South Dakota	1889	41
Washington	1889	41
43. Idaho	1890	40
Wyoming	1890	40
45. Utah	1896	37
46. Oklahoma	1907	30
47. Arizona	1912	27
New Mexico	1912	27
49. Alaska	1959	0
Hawaii	1959	0

30 Historic Places

DOING THE MATH

The National Register of Historic Places, which was created in 1966, now has more than 52,000 listings. We took the number of historic places in each state and compared it to the state's land area. The result can be considered a measure of historical density, the number of registered sites per 10,000 square miles.

BEST STATES

Rhode Island is brimming with history. It has 561 registered historic places jammed into its 1,045 square miles. That expands to a ratio of 5,368 sites for every 10,000 square miles. Massachusetts is the only other state with a rate higher than 3,000.

WORST STATES

One can search in vain for historic sites on the tundra of Alaska. It has but five per 10,000 square miles. The rangeland of Nevada is only slightly better, with a rate of 20.

REGIONAL WINNERS

East—Rhode Island
South—Kentucky
Midwest—Ohio
West—Hawaii

BIGGEST SURPRISE

Ohio was the 17th state to join the Union, but it made up for lost time. It ranks seventh in the density of historic places.

THE BOTTOM LINE

The East has a virtual monopoly on historic sites. It holds the six top positions on this list, and 10 of the top 12.

Historic Places

State	Registered Historic Places Per 10,000 Square Miles	Points
1. Rhode Island	5,368	100
2. Massachusetts	3,205	100
3. Delaware	2,885	90
4. Connecticut	1,973	61
5. New Jersey	1,423	44
6. Maryland	1,056	33
7. Ohio	723	22
8. New Hampshire	637	19
9. Kentucky	557	17
10. New York	548	17
11. Pennsylvania	526	16
12. Vermont	466	14
13. Hawaii	394	12
14. South Carolina	340	10
15. Virginia	331	10
16. North Carolina	322	9
Maine	322	9
18. Tennessee	303	9
19. Indiana	250	7
20. Wisconsin	240	7
21. Georgia	225	6
22. West Virginia	215	6
23. Iowa	203	6
24. Michigan	196	6
25. Mississippi	189	5
26. Illinois	176	5
27. Louisiana	172	5
28. Arkansas	163	4
29. Minnesota	160	4
Alabama	160	4
31. Missouri	141	4
32. Washington	129	3
33. Florida	124	3
34. Utah	118	3
35. Oklahoma	113	3
36. California	102	3
37. Oregon	95	2
38. Idaho	94	2
39. Arizona	84	2
40. South Dakota	77	2
41. Texas	76	2
42. Colorado	71	2
43. Nebraska	67	1
44. Kansas	64	1
45. New Mexico	62	1
46. Montana	37	1
47. North Dakota	36	0
48. Wyoming	31	0
49. Nevada	20	0
50. Alaska	5	0

32 Historic Natives

DOING THE MATH

The *Dictionary of American Biography* is the definitive source for famous Americans from the past. Its 28 volumes contain the life stories of thousands of persons from colonial times to the 20th century, everyone from the Founding Fathers to baseball stars. We took the number of *DAB* subjects born in each state and computed it as a rate per 10,000 square miles.

BEST STATES

Massachusetts was the birthplace of 2,191 *DAB* subjects, which converts to 2,795 per 10,000 square miles, the highest rate in the country. The only other state above 2,000 is Rhode Island.

WORST STATES

The density of historic natives gets mighty thin in the mountainous states of the West. Alaska has not placed a single native son or daughter in the *DAB*. Arizona and Montana each have a couple of listings, but their rates also round off to zero.

REGIONAL WINNERS

East—Massachusetts
South—Virginia
Midwest—Ohio
West—Hawaii

BIGGEST SURPRISE

Virginia—home of Jamestown and Williamsburg, birthplace of presidents—does no better than 11th place on this list. It has had relatively few historic natives since the early 19th century.

THE BOTTOM LINE

It's a clean sweep for the East, which holds all top 10 positions in this category.

Historic Natives

State	Natives Profiled in the *Dictionary of American Biography* Per 10,000 Square Miles	Points
1. Massachusetts	2,795	100
2. Rhode Island	2,316	100
3. Connecticut	1,783	77
4. New Jersey	634	27
5. New York	531	23
6. Delaware	445	19
7. Maryland	433	19
8. New Hampshire	410	18
9. Pennsylvania	349	15
10. Vermont	327	14
11. Virginia	207	9
12. Ohio	176	8
13. Maine	132	6
14. South Carolina	111	5
15. Kentucky	88	4
16. Indiana	70	3
17. Illinois	68	3
18. North Carolina	59	3
19. Tennessee	53	2
20. Georgia	42	2
21. Michigan	32	1
22. Wisconsin	28	1
23. Missouri	27	1
24. West Virginia	24	1
Iowa	24	1
Louisiana	24	1
27. Hawaii	23	1
28. Alabama	20	1
29. Mississippi	16	1
30. Minnesota	10	0
31. California	9	0
32. Kansas	7	0
33. Nebraska	6	0
34. Arkansas	4	0
Florida	4	0
36. Washington	3	0
Texas	3	0
Oklahoma	3	0
Utah	3	0
40. Oregon	2	0
Colorado	2	0
42. South Dakota	1	0
New Mexico	1	0
Nevada	1	0
North Dakota	1	0
Wyoming	1	0
Idaho	1	0
48. Montana	0	0
Arizona	0	0
Alaska	0	0

34 Presidential Candidates

DOING THE MATH

The presidency is the highest honor that Americans can bestow on one of their own. We counted the number of electoral votes won by presidential candidates from each state in the 52 elections between 1789 and 1992. What mattered was where the candidate lived at the time of his election, not where he was born.

BEST STATES

New York dominated presidential elections between the Civil War and World War II, sometimes supplying both the Democratic and Republican nominees in the same year. Its residents have won 5,210 electoral votes. The runner-up is a relative newcomer to presidential politics, California, with 2,372.

WORST STATES

There is a very big tie for last place in this category. Fully 19 states have been shut out in national elections, never winning a single electoral vote.

REGIONAL WINNERS

East—New York
South—Virginia
Midwest—Ohio
West—California

BIGGEST SURPRISE

Included among the states with no electoral votes are one large state (Florida) and three of the original 13 states (Connecticut, Delaware, and Rhode Island).

THE BOTTOM LINE

Presidential elections are played for big stakes, which is why the big players do best. All seven states with more than 1,000 electoral votes currently have populations above 6 million.

Presidential Candidates

State	Electoral Votes Won By Home State Presidential Candidates, 1789-1992	Points
1. New York	5,210	100
2. California	2,372	100
3. Ohio	2,129	90
4. Virginia	1,194	50
5. Massachusetts	1,114	47
6. Texas	1,081	46
7. Illinois	1,067	45
8. Pennsylvania	786	33
9. New Jersey	754	32
10. Tennessee	731	31
11. Nebraska	493	21
12. Indiana	420	18
13. Georgia	389	16
14. Arkansas	370	16
15. Michigan	367	15
16. Missouri	321	14
17. Kentucky	263	11
18. New Hampshire	254	11
19. Minnesota	204	9
20. Maine	182	8
21. Louisiana	163	7
22. West Virginia	136	6
23. South Carolina	100	4
24. Arizona	52	2
25. Alabama	47	2
26. Iowa	22	1
27. South Dakota	17	1
28. Wisconsin	13	1
29. North Carolina	11	0
30. Kansas	8	0
31. Maryland	7	0
32. Alaska	0	0
Colorado	0	0
Connecticut	0	0
Delaware	0	0
Florida	0	0
Hawaii	0	0
Idaho	0	0
Mississippi	0	0
Montana	0	0
Nevada	0	0
New Mexico	0	0
North Dakota	0	0
Oklahoma	0	0
Oregon	0	0
Rhode Island	0	0
Utah	0	0
Vermont	0	0
Washington	0	0
Wyoming	0	0

36 History: Scores and Grades

BEST STATE

It is only fitting that the top honors in the History section go to Massachusetts, where the first shots of the American Revolution were fired. No other state has a higher ratio of historic natives; only Rhode Island has a larger density of registered historic places. Massachusetts also ranks fifth in the overall performance of home-state presidential candidates.

RUNNERS-UP

Rhode Island is the only state besides Massachusetts to score in the A range in this section. Its strength is its impressive proportion of historic sites. Third place goes to New York, which leads the nation in the number of electoral votes won by presidential contenders.

WORST STATES

There is an appropriate tie for last place in this section. Alaska and Hawaii are America's two youngest states. Neither has produced many historic figures, nor been able to boast of having its own candidate for the White House.

REGIONAL WINNERS

East—Massachusetts
South—Virginia
Midwest—Ohio
West—California

REGIONAL AVERAGES

East—60 (B–)
South—34 (D)
Midwest—24 (D–)
West—10 (F)

BIGGEST SURPRISE

Virginia is inordinately proud of its past, particularly the parts it played in the American Revolution and the Civil War. But it could do no better than a C+ in this section. It has surprisingly light densities of historic places and historic natives.

THE BOTTOM LINE

Head to the East if you are a history buff. The six states that earned A's or B's in this section are all in that region. The 17 states with F's, on the other hand, are all west of the Mississippi River.

38 History: Scores and Grades

State	Score	Points
1. Massachusetts	100	A+
2. Rhode Island	87	A
3. New York	75	B+
4. Connecticut	72	B
5. Delaware	65	B
6. New Jersey	61	B–
7. Virginia	58	C+
8. New Hampshire	52	C
9. Maryland	51	C
Ohio	51	C
11. Pennsylvania	50	C
12. California	42	C–
13. Maine	41	C–
14. South Carolina	40	C–
15. Illinois	39	D+
North Carolina	39	D+
17. Texas	38	D+
18. Vermont	37	D+
19. Georgia	35	D+
Tennessee	35	D+
21. Florida	34	D
Michigan	34	D
23. Kentucky	33	D
24. Arkansas	32	D
Indiana	32	D
Louisiana	32	D
27. Mississippi	30	D
Alabama	30	D
29. Missouri	29	D
30. New Mexico	24	D–
31. West Virginia	23	D–
32. Wisconsin	20	D–
Kansas	20	D–
34. Iowa	18	F
35. Minnesota	16	F
36. Nebraska	15	F
37. Oregon	12	F
38. Arizona	9	F
39. Washington	8	F
Montana	8	F
North Dakota	8	F
Nevada	8	F
43. Colorado	5	F
Wyoming	5	F
Idaho	5	F
46. Utah	4	F
South Dakota	4	F
48. Oklahoma	1	F
49. Alaska	0	F
Hawaii	0	F

2

Terrain

The Big Question

Which state has the most varied landscape, with everything from oceans and lakes to rangeland and mountains?

The Categories

1. Ocean Shoreline
2. Inland Water
3. Forests
4. Rangeland
5. Elevation Variation

40 Ocean Shoreline

DOING THE MATH

We wanted to gauge how important the ocean is to each state. So we added up its tidal shoreline, which includes its outer coast, offshore islands, sounds, and bays. Then we compared that figure to the state's total land area. The result is a ratio of tidal shoreline miles per 10,000 square miles of land. The higher the rate, the stronger the state's ties to the ocean.

BEST STATES

Rhode Island calls itself the Ocean State, and with good reason. It is America's smallest state (1,045 square miles), but it still has 384 miles of tidal shoreline. That works out to 3,675 miles of shore for every 10,000 square miles of land. The only other state with a rate above 3,000 is Maryland.

WORST STATES

A big tie here. Twenty-six states have no access to the ocean.

REGIONAL WINNERS

East—Rhode Island
South—Louisiana
Midwest—(none)
West—Hawaii

BIGGEST SURPRISE

New Jersey's reputation is that it has nothing but bedroom communities, factories, and landfills. But it actually has beautiful beaches, and lots of them. It holds third place in this category.

THE BOTTOM LINE

The ocean is most important to small states shoehorned along the coast. The five leaders in this category all have land areas below 10,000 square miles.

Ocean Shoreline

State	Miles of Tidal Shoreline Per 10,000 Square Miles of Land Area	Points
1. Rhode Island	3,675	100
2. Maryland	3,263	100
3. New Jersey	2,415	74
4. Delaware	1,949	60
5. Massachusetts	1,938	59
6. Louisiana	1,772	54
7. Hawaii	1,638	50
8. Florida	1,560	48
9. Connecticut	1,276	39
10. Maine	1,127	35
11. South Carolina	955	29
12. Virginia	837	26
13. North Carolina	693	21
14. Alaska	594	18
15. Washington	454	14
16. Georgia	405	12
17. New York	392	12
18. California	220	7
19. Oregon	147	5
20. New Hampshire	146	4
21. Texas	128	4
22. Alabama	120	4
23. Mississippi	77	2
24. Pennsylvania	20	1
25. Arizona	0	0
Arkansas	0	0
Colorado	0	0
Idaho	0	0
Illinois	0	0
Indiana	0	0
Iowa	0	0
Kansas	0	0
Kentucky	0	0
Michigan	0	0
Minnesota	0	0
Missouri	0	0
Montana	0	0
Nebraska	0	0
Nevada	0	0
New Mexico	0	0
North Dakota	0	0
Ohio	0	0
Oklahoma	0	0
South Dakota	0	0
Tennessee	0	0
Utah	0	0
Vermont	0	0
West Virginia	0	0
Wisconsin	0	0
Wyoming	0	0

42 Inland Water

DOING THE MATH

What if everyone in a state decided to go swimming or boating at the same time? An unlikely event, of course, but one that we simulated for this category. We wanted to see whose lakes were the least crowded, so we divided each state's population into its total area of inland water.

BEST STATES

America's most uncongested lakes are in Alaska, which has 86,051 square miles of inland water for its 550,000 residents. That works out to just six persons per square mile of lake. The best record in the continental United States belongs to Michigan, with a density of 232 people per square mile.

WORST STATES

It's easier finding mountains than lakes in West Virginia. Its inland water density is 12,366 persons per square mile. The other states above 10,000 are Indiana and Arizona.

REGIONAL WINNERS

East—Maine
South—Louisiana
Midwest—Michigan
West—Alaska

BIGGEST SURPRISE

Minnesota, the self-proclaimed Land of 10,000 Lakes, ranks just 10th in this category. Three of its neighbors—North Dakota, South Dakota, and Wisconsin—have lakes that are less crowded.

THE BOTTOM LINE

The Midwest is lake country. It places five states among the top 10 in this category, compared to three from the West and one each from the East and South.

Inland Water

State	Persons Per Square Mile of Inland Water	Points
1. Alaska	6	100
2. Michigan	232	100
3. Hawaii	246	100
4. Maine	272	100
5. North Dakota	374	99
6. Wisconsin	437	98
7. Louisiana	510	97
8. Montana	536	97
9. South Dakota	569	97
10. Minnesota	597	96
11. Utah	630	96
12. Wyoming	636	96
13. Washington	1,031	92
14. Florida	1,100	91
15. Oregon	1,193	90
16. Idaho	1,224	90
17. Delaware	1,245	90
18. North Carolina	1,299	89
19. Vermont	1,538	87
20. Nevada	1,580	86
21. Mississippi	1,693	85
22. Maryland	1,816	84
23. South Carolina	1,839	84
24. Virginia	1,951	83
25. Rhode Island	2,006	82
26. Arkansas	2,124	81
27. Massachusetts	2,214	80
28. Alabama	2,415	78
29. New York	2,481	77
30. Texas	2,540	77
31. Oklahoma	2,570	76
32. Ohio	2,799	74
33. New Hampshire	2,903	73
34. Nebraska	3,281	69
35. California	3,848	63
36. Georgia	4,256	59
37. Connecticut	4,709	55
38. Illinois	4,917	52
39. Tennessee	5,267	49
40. Kansas	5,399	48
41. Kentucky	5,427	47
42. New Jersey	5,932	42
43. Missouri	6,309	38
44. New Mexico	6,474	37
45. Iowa	6,925	32
46. Colorado	8,879	12
47. Pennsylvania	9,590	5
48. Arizona	10,069	0
49. Indiana	10,080	0
50. West Virginia	12,366	0

44 Forests

DOING THE MATH

The total land base of the United States is almost equally divided between forests (32 percent), rangeland (34 percent), and a third, rather imprecise heading called "other land" (34 percent), which includes everything from pastures to cities. We are concerned here with the first classification, the percentage of land covered by forests.

BEST STATES

Maine is the most thickly forested state, with 89.8 percent of its land area classified as wooded by the U.S. Forest Service. Neighboring New Hampshire is the only other entry above 80 percent. Another two Eastern states—West Virginia and Vermont—hold third and fourth place, respectively.

WORST STATES

Trees are a scarce commodity out on the Great Plains. Just ask the folks in North Dakota, where only 1 percent of the land is forested. Nebraska is only slightly better at 1.5 percent.

REGIONAL WINNERS

East—Maine
South—Alabama
Midwest—Michigan
West—Washington

BIGGEST SURPRISE

New York is an urban state that is paved from border to border, right? Not at all. Fully 62 percent of New York is forested, the ninth-best record in the nation.

THE BOTTOM LINE

Stay east of the Mississippi River if you want to see woods. The 15 states with the highest percentages of forested land are all in the East or the South.

Forests

State	Percentage of Land Area Covered by Forests	Points
1. Maine	89.8%	100
2. New Hampshire	88.1	100
3. West Virginia	77.5	88
4. Vermont	75.7	86
5. Alabama	66.9	76
6. Georgia	64.9	73
7. South Carolina	64.3	72
8. Virginia	63.2	71
9. New York	62.0	70
Massachusetts	62.0	70
11. North Carolina	61.0	69
12. Rhode Island	59.8	67
13. Pennsylvania	59.4	67
14. Connecticut	58.7	66
15. Mississippi	55.3	62
16. Washington	51.4	58
17. Arkansas	51.0	57
18. Tennessee	50.3	56
19. Michigan	50.1	56
20. Louisiana	48.7	55
21. Florida	48.4	54
Kentucky	48.4	54
23. Oregon	45.6	51
24. Wisconsin	44.1	49
25. New Jersey	42.7	48
26. Hawaii	42.5	47
27. Maryland	42.1	47
28. Idaho	41.4	46
29. California	39.5	44
30. Alaska	35.7	39
31. Delaware	33.0	36
32. Minnesota	32.7	36
33. Colorado	32.2	35
34. Utah	30.9	34
35. Missouri	28.4	31
36. Ohio	27.9	30
37. Arizona	26.7	29
38. New Mexico	23.9	26
39. Montana	23.6	26
40. Indiana	19.4	21
41. Oklahoma	16.6	17
42. Wyoming	16.1	17
43. Nevada	12.7	13
44. Illinois	12.0	12
45. Texas	8.1	8
46. Iowa	4.4	3
47. South Dakota	3.5	2
48. Kansas	2.6	1
49. Nebraska	1.5	0
50. North Dakota	1.0	0

46 Rangeland

DOING THE MATH

Everyone who did poorly in the Forests category gets a chance for revenge here, as we find out how much of each state's land is rangeland. It's a broader classification than you might expect. Rangeland includes any area where the vegetation is grass, grass-like plants, or shrubs, which covers everything from deserts and savannas to tundra and some types of coastal marshes.

BEST STATES

Nevada is a state of plateaus and deserts, most of which fit within this category. Fully 86 percent of the state is classified as rangeland, easily the highest figure in the nation. Second place goes to Wyoming, at 74.2 percent. Three other states, all in the West, are above 60 percent.

WORST STATES

Twenty-five states are totally without rangeland. Eleven are in the East, eight in the South, and six in the Midwest.

REGIONAL WINNERS

East—New York
South—Texas
Midwest—South Dakota
West—Nevada

BIGGEST SURPRISE

Most people picture the woods, lakes, and rushing streams of Yellowstone National Park when they think of Wyoming. But the park occupies only a small portion of the state's northwestern corner. Almost three-quarters of Wyoming actually is rangeland.

THE BOTTOM LINE

Go to the West for your home on the range. That's where you'll find 12 of the top 15 states in this category.

Rangeland

State	Percentage of Land Area Classified as Rangeland	Points
1. Nevada	86.0%	100
2. Wyoming	74.2	100
3. New Mexico	65.9	89
4. Arizona	65.1	88
5. Utah	61.1	82
6. Texas	57.5	78
7. Montana	53.0	71
8. South Dakota	50.3	68
9. Nebraska	48.7	66
10. Alaska	47.7	64
11. Colorado	42.1	57
12. Idaho	41.6	56
13. California	38.6	52
14. Oregon	35.8	48
15. Hawaii	34.1	46
16. Oklahoma	32.4	44
17. Kansas	31.9	43
18. North Dakota	28.6	39
19. Washington	17.7	24
20. Florida	12.7	17
21. Louisiana	1.6	2
22. Arkansas	0.7	1
23. Minnesota	0.6	1
24. Missouri	0.2	0
25. New York	0.1	0
26. Wisconsin	0.0	0
Iowa	0.0	0
Alabama	0.0	0
Connecticut	0.0	0
Delaware	0.0	0
Georgia	0.0	0
Illinois	0.0	0
Indiana	0.0	0
Kentucky	0.0	0
Maine	0.0	0
Maryland	0.0	0
Massachusetts	0.0	0
Michigan	0.0	0
Mississippi	0.0	0
New Hampshire	0.0	0
New Jersey	0.0	0
North Carolina	0.0	0
Ohio	0.0	0
Pennsylvania	0.0	0
Rhode Island	0.0	0
South Carolina	0.0	0
Tennessee	0.0	0
Vermont	0.0	0
Virginia	0.0	0
West Virginia	0.0	0

48 Elevation Variation

DOING THE MATH

This category requires nothing more than some simple subtraction. We wanted to find the state that offers the widest range of land forms—from soaring peaks to sheltered valleys. So we simply identified the lowest point in each state and subtracted its elevation from that of the highest point.

BEST STATES

No place in America stands above the 20,320-foot-high peak of Mount McKinley. Alaska's landscape plummets from this height all the way to sea level at the coasts of the Arctic and Pacific oceans. Second place belongs to California, with a difference of 14,776 feet between its highest and lowest points.

WORST STATES

Florida is America's flattest state, with an elevation range of only 345 feet. What else would you expect from a place whose highest point has the decidedly uninspiring name of Section 30, T6N, R20W? The hills are only slightly higher in Delaware, topping out at 442 feet.

REGIONAL WINNERS

East—New Hampshire
South—Texas
Midwest—South Dakota
West—Alaska

BIGGEST SURPRISE

The common perception is that Nevada is simply 109,806 square miles of desert. But it actually has rugged mountain ranges that tower as much as 12,670 feet above the desert floor.

THE BOTTOM LINE

The West scores a clean sweep in this category. The top 13 positions are held by the 13 western states.

Elevation Variation

State	Difference in Feet Between State's Highest and Lowest Points	Points
1. Alaska	20,320	100
2. California	14,776	100
3. Washington	14,410	97
4. Hawaii	13,796	93
5. Nevada	12,670	85
6. Arizona	12,563	85
7. Idaho	11,952	80
8. Utah	11,528	77
9. Oregon	11,239	75
10. Colorado	11,083	74
11. Montana	10,999	74
12. Wyoming	10,795	72
13. New Mexico	10,319	69
14. Texas	8,749	58
15. North Carolina	6,684	44
16. Tennessee	6,465	42
17. New Hampshire	6,288	41
18. South Dakota	6,276	41
19. Virginia	5,729	37
20. New York	5,344	34
21. Maine	5,267	34
22. Georgia	4,784	30
23. Oklahoma	4,684	30
24. West Virginia	4,621	29
25. Nebraska	4,586	29
26. Vermont	4,298	27
27. Kentucky	3,882	24
28. South Carolina	3,560	22
29. Massachusetts	3,487	21
30. Kansas	3,360	20
Maryland	3,360	20
32. Pennsylvania	3,213	19
33. North Dakota	2,756	16
34. Arkansas	2,698	16
35. Alabama	2,405	14
36. Connecticut	2,380	14
37. New Jersey	1,803	9
38. Minnesota	1,699	9
39. Missouri	1,542	8
40. Michigan	1,407	7
41. Wisconsin	1,370	6
42. Iowa	1,190	5
43. Ohio	1,094	5
44. Illinois	956	4
45. Indiana	937	3
46. Rhode Island	812	3
47. Mississippi	806	3
48. Louisiana	543	1
49. Delaware	442	0
50. Florida	345	0

50 Terrain: Scores and Grades

BEST STATE

Hawaii is one of America's smallest states. But its tiny space holds an unequaled diversity of terrain, earning the top score in this section. Its obvious strengths are its stunning volcanic peaks and miles upon miles of ocean beaches. But Hawaii also is 42.5 percent forested, and it ranks no. 3 in the availability of inland water.

RUNNERS-UP

Alaska calls itself the Last Frontier, an image reinforced by its stark, imposing terrain. No state has higher mountains or quieter lakes, which helped it finish no. 2 in this section. Utah earned the only other straight A.

WORST STATES

You won't find any mountains, ocean beaches, or rangeland in Indiana. And it has relatively few lakes or forests, which is why it ended up in last place. The story essentially is the same in Iowa, Illinois, and Missouri, the other three states with F's.

REGIONAL WINNERS

East—Maine
South—Texas, North Carolina
Midwest—South Dakota
West—Hawaii

REGIONAL AVERAGES

East—55 (C+)
South—51 (C)
Midwest—30 (D)
West—78 (B+)

BIGGEST SURPRISE

The West—blessed with mountains, rangeland, and ocean beaches—dominates this section. That's why it's so surprising to see Maine in seventh place. It's the only non-western state to crack the top 10.

THE BOTTOM LINE

The West is tops in terrain, as we've said. But how about the bottom of the scale? That belongs to the Midwest, the home of all four states with F's.

Terrain: Scores and Grades

State	Score	Grade
1. Hawaii	100	A+
2. Alaska	95	A
3. Utah	85	A
4. Washington	84	A–
Wyoming	84	A–
6. Nevada	83	A–
7. Idaho	79	B+
Maine	79	B+
Oregon	79	B+
10. Montana	78	B+
California	78	B+
12. Rhode Island	73	B
Maryland	73	B
14. Massachusetts	66	B
15. Texas	64	B–
North Carolina	64	B–
17. New Mexico	63	B–
18. New Hampshire	62	B–
Virginia	62	B–
20. Florida	60	B–
21. Louisiana	59	C+
South Dakota	59	C+
South Carolina	59	C+
24. Arizona	57	C+
25. Vermont	56	C+
26. New York	54	C
27. Delaware	52	C
28. Colorado	49	C
29. Connecticut	48	C
Georgia	48	C
New Jersey	48	C
32. Alabama	47	C
33. Oklahoma	46	C
34. Nebraska	45	C
Michigan	45	C
36. Arkansas	42	C–
North Dakota	42	C–
38. Wisconsin	41	C–
Mississippi	41	C–
40. Tennessee	39	D+
41. Minnesota	38	D+
42. Kentucky	32	D
43. West Virginia	30	D
44. Kansas	28	D
45. Ohio	27	D
46. Pennsylvania	22	D–
47. Missouri	17	F
48. Illinois	14	F
49. Iowa	5	F
50. Indiana	0	F

3

Natural Resources

The Big Question

Which states is blessed with the widest array of resources, ranging from good farmland to rich mineral deposits?

The Categories

1. Farm Marketings
2. Timberland
3. Nonfuel Mining
4. Crude Oil Reserves
5. Coal Reserves

54 Farm Marketings

DOING THE MATH

One way to measure industrial productivity is to total the value of manufactured goods. Why not use the same system for farming? We looked at each state's agricultural sales volume, commonly known as farm marketings. Then we divided that value by total land area, giving us a relative measure of agriculture's importance in each state.

BEST STATES

Tiny Delaware is an unheralded agricultural powerhouse, producing broilers, soybeans, corn, and greenhouse fruits and vegetables. Its annual farm marketings of $644 million translate to $329,412 per square mile. The runner-up is a well-known farm state, Iowa, with a rate of $184,680.

WORST STATES

The growing season is short in Alaska, and very little of its land can be tilled. That explains its agricultural yield of just $47 per square mile. Nevada, mostly mountainous or desert country, is next to last with farm marketings of $3,033 per square mile.

REGIONAL WINNERS

East—Delaware
South—Florida
Midwest—Iowa
West—California

BIGGEST SURPRISE

It's no contest. The biggest surprise has to be Delaware, no. 49 in total land area, but no. 1 in farm marketings per square mile.

THE BOTTOM LINE

The Midwest unsurprisingly is where you will find America's most productive farmland. The region holds six positions in the national top 10.

Farm Marketings

State	Value of Farm Marketings Per Square Mile	Points
1. Delaware	$329,412	100
2. Iowa	184,680	100
3. Illinois	142,788	77
4. Maryland	137,596	74
5. Indiana	137,469	74
6. California	120,912	65
7. Nebraska	115,052	62
8. Florida	105,710	57
9. Wisconsin	105,056	56
10. Ohio	101,873	54
11. North Carolina	99,901	53
12. Connecticut	92,054	49
13. Hawaii	91,546	49
14. Minnesota	88,059	47
15. New Jersey	87,209	46
16. Kansas	85,489	45
17. Pennsylvania	84,047	45
18. Arkansas	81,786	43
19. Kentucky	77,972	41
20. Rhode Island	67,943	36
21. Georgia	66,334	35
22. New York	63,654	33
23. Washington	57,313	30
24. Missouri	57,171	30
25. Michigan	56,030	29
26. Alabama	53,931	28
27. Virginia	53,538	28
28. Massachusetts	53,330	28
29. Mississippi	51,861	27
30. Oklahoma	51,748	27
31. Tennessee	49,466	26
32. Vermont	48,330	25
33. Texas	45,744	24
34. South Dakota	44,125	23
35. Louisiana	44,094	23
36. Colorado	40,615	21
37. South Carolina	39,055	20
38. North Dakota	36,771	19
39. Idaho	35,468	18
40. Oregon	24,083	12
41. Arizona	16,411	7
42. New Hampshire	14,940	7
43. Maine	14,904	7
44. West Virginia	14,032	6
45. New Mexico	12,598	5
46. Montana	11,034	4
47. Utah	9,188	3
48. Wyoming	7,899	3
49. Nevada	3,033	0
50. Alaska	47	0

56 Timberland

DOING THE MATH

This might appear to be the same as the Forests category in the Terrain section, but it isn't. Our inventory of forest land included everything from private property to local, state, and national parks. Timberland, on the other hand, is specifically defined as having trees that may legally be harvested. This category looks at each state's quantity of timberland per 1,000 square miles.

BEST STATES

Maine has timber reserves that cover 17.2 million acres. That works out to 556,423 acres of timberland per 1,000 square miles, the best rate in America. The only other state above 500,000 is New Hampshire.

WORST STATES

Tree farming is not a profitable business in Nevada, which has only 2,013 acres of timberland per 1,000 square miles. Reserves are only slightly better in North Dakota, with a rate of 4,899.

REGIONAL WINNERS

East—Maine
South—Alabama
Midwest—Michigan
West—Washington

BIGGEST SURPRISE

New England has the image of being an urban, industrial area that has played out most of its natural resources. But it actually has impressive timber reserves, placing all six of its states among the top 14 in America.

THE BOTTOM LINE

The nation's timberland remains concentrated in the East and South. The top 15 states in this category are all east of the Mississippi River.

Timberland

State	Acres of Timberland Per 1,000 Square Miles	Points
1. Maine	556,423	100
2. New Hampshire	535,511	100
3. West Virginia	489,849	91
4. Vermont	478,322	89
5. Alabama	426,778	80
6. South Carolina	404,470	75
7. Georgia	403,736	75
8. Virginia	389,792	73
9. Massachusetts	384,027	71
10. North Carolina	376,822	70
11. Connecticut	366,563	68
12. Pennsylvania	361,133	67
13. Mississippi	355,416	66
14. Rhode Island	352,153	65
15. New York	334,533	62
16. Arkansas	320,173	59
17. Louisiana	318,368	59
18. Tennessee	311,499	58
19. Michigan	305,656	57
20. Kentucky	299,733	56
21. Florida	282,201	52
22. Wisconsin	271,127	50
23. New Jersey	257,986	48
24. Washington	253,056	47
25. Maryland	251,867	47
26. Oregon	230,045	42
27. Delaware	198,465	36
28. Idaho	175,635	32
29. Ohio	174,371	32
30. Missouri	174,098	32
31. Minnesota	170,466	31
32. Indiana	119,766	22
33. Colorado	113,178	20
34. Hawaii	108,983	20
35. California	107,147	19
36. Montana	101,246	18
37. Illinois	72,491	13
38. Oklahoma	69,148	12
39. Texas	47,397	8
40. Wyoming	44,612	7
41. New Mexico	42,681	7
42. Utah	37,460	6
43. Arizona	33,342	5
44. Alaska	27,636	4
45. Iowa	26,130	4
46. South Dakota	19,065	3
47. Kansas	14,751	2
48. Nebraska	6,985	0
49. North Dakota	4,899	0
50. Nevada	2,013	0

58 Nonfuel Mining

DOING THE MATH

Mineral deposits far below the earth's surface are essential to the economies of many states. The mining industry extracts more than $32 billion of nonfuel minerals each year, covering the range from iron and copper ores to sand, gravel, and stone. This category translates each state's raw nonfuel mineral production into a rate per square mile.

BEST STATES

Maryland's annual nonfuel mineral production is worth roughly $323 million, a figure that is dwarfed by several states. But none can top Maryland's rate of $33,076 in mineral production per square mile. The runner-up is another surprise, New Jersey, at $28,799.

WORST STATES

The earth yields little in North Dakota, where nonfuel mineral production is only $257 per square mile. Alaska is next to last with a rate of $931.

REGIONAL WINNERS

East—Maryland
South—Georgia
Midwest—Michigan
West—Arizona

BIGGEST SURPRISE

The top 10 is full of surprises. Who thinks of Maryland, New Jersey, Georgia, Florida, Hawaii, Massachusetts, and Connecticut as efficient mining states? But they are.

THE BOTTOM LINE

The East, believe it or not, has the edge in this category, placing four states in the top 10. The West has three slots, the South two, and the Midwest one.

Nonfuel Mining

State	Value of Raw Nonfuel Mineral Production Per Square Mile	Points
1. Maryland	$33,076	100
2. New Jersey	28,799	100
3. Arizona	27,470	95
4. Georgia	26,598	92
5. Florida	26,383	91
6. Michigan	25,070	87
7. Hawaii	23,141	80
8. Nevada	22,141	76
9. Massachusetts	20,022	69
10. Connecticut	19,592	67
11. Pennsylvania	19,246	66
12. Minnesota	17,156	58
13. Ohio	16,601	56
14. Utah	16,361	55
15. California	15,814	53
16. New York	15,141	51
17. Tennessee	14,067	47
18. Rhode Island	13,877	46
19. Missouri	13,420	45
20. Indiana	12,969	43
21. Illinois	12,185	40
22. Alabama	11,895	39
23. North Carolina	11,762	39
24. South Carolina	11,533	38
25. Virginia	10,505	34
26. Kentucky	10,381	34
27. Wyoming	9,628	31
28. Delaware	8,338	27
29. Vermont	7,345	23
30. Washington	7,183	22
31. New Mexico	7,136	22
32. Iowa	6,938	22
33. Louisiana	6,249	19
34. Arkansas	5,510	16
35. Texas	5,269	16
36. West Virginia	5,137	15
37. New Hampshire	4,724	14
38. Kansas	4,508	13
39. Montana	4,145	12
40. Oklahoma	4,139	12
41. Idaho	4,092	11
42. Wisconsin	4,016	11
43. South Dakota	3,928	11
44. Colorado	3,745	10
45. Mississippi	2,333	5
46. Oregon	2,078	4
47. Maine	1,712	3
48. Nebraska	1,447	2
49. Alaska	931	0
50. North Dakota	257	0

60 Crude Oil Reserves

DOING THE MATH

Yes, the United States imports much of its oil, but it also has sizable domestic supplies. The U.S. Energy Department has inventoried what it calls "proved reserves," the known amount of oil still in the ground. We took that figure and divided it by land area, which tells us how many barrels of crude oil reserves each state has per square mile. A barrel, by the way, holds 42 gallons.

BEST STATES

California has oil reserves of 4.66 billion barrels, which equals 29,864 barrels per square mile. Texas finished a close second at 27,131 per square mile. The only other states above 10,000 were Louisiana, Alaska, and Oklahoma.

WORST STATES

Nineteen states have no proved reserves of oil. Nine are in the East, four are in the West, and three each are in the South and the Midwest.

REGIONAL WINNERS

East—West Virginia
South—Texas
Midwest—North Dakota
West—California

BIGGEST SURPRISE

Mississippi an oil state? It seems unlikely, but it's true. Mississippi has reserves totaling 227 million barrels, which works out to 4,839 barrels per square mile. Only seven states have greater densities of untapped oil.

THE BOTTOM LINE

The big oil states are right where you would expect them to be: along the Pacific and Gulf coasts.

Crude Oil Reserves

State	Barrels of Crude Oil Reserves Per Square Mile	Points
1. California	29,864	100
2. Texas	27,131	100
3. Louisiana	16,182	60
4. Alaska	11,438	42
5. Oklahoma	10,687	39
6. Wyoming	8,177	30
7. New Mexico	5,661	21
8. Mississippi	4,839	18
9. North Dakota	4,131	15
10. Kansas	3,923	14
11. Utah	3,030	11
12. Colorado	2,940	11
13. Illinois	2,356	9
14. Michigan	2,183	8
15. Ohio	1,587	6
16. Montana	1,518	6
17. West Virginia	1,287	5
18. Arkansas	1,152	4
19. Alabama	867	3
20. Kentucky	831	3
21. Florida	778	3
22. Pennsylvania	491	2
23. Nebraska	338	1
24. Indiana	335	1
25. Missouri*	87	0
New York*	87	0
Virginia*	87	0
Arizona*	87	0
Nevada*	87	0
South Dakota*	87	0
Tennessee*	87	0
32. Connecticut	0	0
Delaware	0	0
Georgia	0	0
Hawaii	0	0
Idaho	0	0
Iowa	0	0
Maine	0	0
Maryland	0	0
Massachusetts	0	0
Minnesota	0	0
New Hampshire	0	0
New Jersey	0	0
North Carolina	0	0
Oregon	0	0
Rhode Island	0	0

*The reserves in these states were combined under the heading of "miscellaneous" in the U.S. Energy Department report. The average per square mile is the overall figure for the seven states.

Crude Oil Reserves (continued)

State	Barrels of Crude Oil Reserves Per Square Mile	Points
South Carolina	0	0
Vermont	0	0
Washington	0	0
Wisconsin	0	0

Coal Reserves

DOING THE MATH

There are at least 472 billion short tons of coal still sitting underneath the United States, just waiting to be mined. So says an inventory conducted by the U.S. Energy Department. We took each state's demonstrated reserve base, as the department calls it, and calculated it as a rate per square mile.

BEST STATES

It seems that coal mining has forever been West Virginia's major industry, but there is much more coal left in its hills. Its demonstrated reserve base is 37.4 billion tons, which translates to 1,552,256 tons per square mile. Illinois is the only other state with coal reserves higher than 1 million tons a mile.

WORST STATES

The Energy Department lists 18 states that are without demonstrated reserves of coal. Included are nine eastern states, as well as three each in the South, Midwest, and West.

REGIONAL WINNERS

East—West Virginia
South—Kentucky
Midwest—Illinois
West—Montana

BIGGEST SURPRISE

The top four states in this category—West Virginia, Illinois, Montana, and Kentucky—are famous for their mining operations. But you can't say the same about no. 5 Wyoming, which has surprisingly strong coal reserves of 702,722 tons per square mile.

THE BOTTOM LINE

America's strongest coal belt roughly parallels the Ohio River from Pennsylvania to Illinois. Six of the category's top eight states border that river.

64 Coal Reserves

State	Short Tons of Coal Reserves Per Square Mile	Points
1. West Virginia	1,552,256	100
2. Illinois	1,409,014	100
3. Montana	824,518	59
4. Kentucky	746,074	53
5. Wyoming	702,722	50
6. Pennsylvania	652,271	46
7. Ohio	452,111	32
8. Indiana	284,338	20
9. Colorado	164,055	12
10. North Dakota	140,061	10
11. Alabama	95,720	7
12. Missouri	87,191	6
13. Maryland	77,995	6
14. Utah	75,185	5
15. Virginia	68,486	5
16. Texas	51,170	4
17. Iowa	39,213	3
18. New Mexico	36,973	3
19. Oklahoma	23,167	2
20. Washington	21,399	2
21. Tennessee	20,764	1
22. Kansas	11,956	1
23. Louisiana	11,284	1
24. Alaska	10,764	1
25. Arkansas	8,008	1
26. South Dakota	4,824	0
27. Arizona	2,346	0
28. Michigan	2,248	0
29. North Carolina	220	0
30. Oregon	182	0
31. Georgia	55	0
32. Idaho	53	0
33. California	0	0
Connecticut	0	0
Delaware	0	0
Florida	0	0
Hawaii	0	0
Maine	0	0
Massachusetts	0	0
Minnesota	0	0
Mississippi	0	0
Nebraska	0	0
Nevada	0	0
New Hampshire	0	0
New Jersey	0	0
New York	0	0
Rhode Island	0	0
South Carolina	0	0
Vermont	0	0
Wisconsin	0	0

Natural Resources: Scores and Grades

65

BEST STATE

The nation's most impressive array of natural resources belongs to Illinois, which finished no. 1 in this section. It did exceptionally well in the categories of Coal Reserves (where it placed second) and Farm Marketings (third). Illinois also is reasonably strong in mining for nonfuel minerals, and it has unexpected reserves of crude oil.

RUNNERS-UP

California finished in second place, just a whisker behind Illinois. Its strengths are its oil reserves and its rich farmland. The only other states to receive straight A's were three neighbors, Maryland, Pennsylvania, and West Virginia.

WORST STATES

The Dakota twins were seriously shortchanged when it came to natural resources. Both are below average in farm productivity, weak in nonfuel mining, and virtually without timber. The situation is somewhat worse in South Dakota, which is no. 50 in this section. North Dakota is no. 49.

REGIONAL WINNERS

East—Maryland, Pennsylvania
South—Florida, Georgia
Midwest—Illinois
West—California

REGIONAL AVERAGES

East—66 (B)
South—56 (C+)
Midwest—43 (C–)
West—30 (D)

BIGGEST SURPRISE

West Virginia, poor in so many ways, is rich in natural resources, ranking no. 5 in this section. It has the nation's most substantial coal reserves, and it is no. 3 in timberland.

66 THE BOTTOM LINE

The eastern half of America has a virtual monopoly on the nation's natural resources. California is the only one of the top 18 states in this section to be totally west of the Mississippi River.

Natural Resources: Scores and Grades

State	Score	Grade
1. Illinois	100	A+
2. California	99	A
3. Maryland	94	A
Pennsylvania	94	A
5. West Virginia	89	A
6. Florida	82	A–
Georgia	82	A–
8. New Jersey	78	B+
9. Kentucky	74	B
10. Connecticut	73	B
11. Michigan	71	B
Ohio	71	B
13. Massachusetts	65	B
14. Delaware	62	B–
Louisiana	62	B–
North Carolina	62	B–
17. Indiana	61	B–
18. Alabama	59	C+
19. Texas	57	C+
20. Hawaii	55	C+
21. Rhode Island	54	C
New York	54	C
23. Virginia	51	C
24. Vermont	50	C
25. Minnesota	49	C
26. South Carolina	48	C
27. Tennessee	47	C
28. Iowa	46	C
29. Arkansas	43	C–
30. New Hampshire	42	C–
Wyoming	42	C–
32. Wisconsin	40	C–
33. Mississippi	39	D+
34. Missouri	38	D+
35. Maine	36	D+
36. Arizona	35	D+
37. Washington	32	D
38. Montana	31	D
39. Oklahoma	27	D
40. Utah	21	D–
41. Nevada	19	F
Kansas	19	F
43. Colorado	18	F
44. Nebraska	14	F
45. Idaho	12	F
46. New Mexico	10	F
Oregon	10	F
48. Alaska	5	F
49. North Dakota	3	F
50. South Dakota	0	F

4

Resource Conservation

The Big Question

Which state uses energy and natural resources most wisely?

The Categories

1. Water Usage
2. Petroleum Consumption
3. Natural Gas Consumption
4. Electricity Consumption
5. Renewable Energy

Water Usage

DOING THE MATH

This category totals the amount of fresh water that each state withdraws for daily consumption. That includes drinking water, as well as water for other household purposes and industrial and agricultural uses. We then converted each state's total into a per capita figure.

BEST STATES

Rhode Island does a better job of conserving water than any other state. The average Rhode Island resident uses just 152 gallons daily. Two other states consume less than 250 gallons of water per person each day: Delaware and Vermont.

WORST STATES

It takes an enormous volume of water to sustain the crops that grow on the plains of south Idaho. Irrigation accounts for 92 percent of the state's daily water usage, which totals 22,200 gallons per person. The other states above 10,000 are Wyoming and Montana.

REGIONAL WINNERS

East—Rhode Island
South—Oklahoma
Midwest—Minnesota
West—Alaska

BIGGEST SURPRISE

Much of Oklahoma is arid, which may be the reason it has one of the nation's best water conservation records. It uses 386 gallons per person each day, which ranks no. 7 nationally.

THE BOTTOM LINE

The East, spared from the need for heavy irrigation, is the outstanding region in this category. It is the home of seven of the top 10 states.

70 Water Usage

State	Gallons of Fresh Water Withdrawn Daily Per Capita	Points
1. Rhode Island	152	100
2. Delaware	222	100
3. Vermont	235	100
4. New Jersey	307	99
5. Maryland	321	99
6. Connecticut	375	99
7. Oklahoma	386	99
8. New York	508	98
9. Florida	554	97
10. Minnesota	676	96
11. New Hampshire	688	96
12. Alaska	727	96
13. Maine	733	96
14. Virginia	853	95
15. Mississippi	885	94
16. Georgia	899	94
17. South Dakota	956	94
18. Iowa	960	94
19. Massachusetts	1,070	93
20. Hawaii	1,100	93
21. Kentucky	1,130	92
22. Ohio	1,180	92
23. Missouri	1,210	92
Pennsylvania	1,210	92
25. Texas	1,230	92
26. Illinois	1,250	91
27. North Carolina	1,260	91
28. Michigan	1,270	91
29. Wisconsin	1,400	90
30. California	1,420	90
31. Indiana	1,470	90
32. Washington	1,600	88
33. North Dakota	1,690	88
34. Tennessee	1,770	87
35. Arizona	1,960	85
36. South Carolina	2,040	85
37. Alabama	2,140	84
38. Louisiana	2,210	83
39. Kansas	2,310	83
40. New Mexico	2,320	82
41. Oregon	2,450	81
42. Arkansas	2,500	81
43. Utah	2,540	81
44. West Virginia	2,810	78
45. Nevada	3,860	70
46. Colorado	4,190	67
47. Nebraska	6,250	50
48. Montana	10,500	14
49. Wyoming	12,200	0
50. Idaho	22,200	0

Petroleum Consumption

DOING THE MATH

The U.S. Energy Department monitors the nation's consumption of petroleum products. Its annual report includes a total for each state, expressed in British thermal units (each BTU is the quantity of heat required to raise the temperature of one pound of water by one degree Fahrenheit). We divided each state's consumption total by its population, yielding a per capita rate.

BEST STATES

Arizona consumes 349.9 trillion BTUs of petroleum products a year, which is an intimidating, incomprehensible number. But it actually is an outstanding example of conservation. Arizona's record works out to 95.47 million BTUs per person, the lowest rate in America. Michigan is second at 96.05 million.

WORST STATES

Distances are great and winters are long in Alaska, so its energy needs are extraordinarily high. That explains its annual petroleum consumption of 422.55 million BTUs per person. Louisiana, with a per capita rate of 338.77 million, is next to last.

REGIONAL WINNERS

East—New York
South—North Carolina
Midwest—Michigan
West—Arizona

BIGGEST SURPRISE

Michigan has long had a reputation, deserved or not, for making big, gas-guzzling cars. But it nonetheless ranks no. 2 in the nation in efficiency of petroleum consumption.

THE BOTTOM LINE

The East and the Midwest are the regions that use petroleum products most wisely. Each placed four states in the top 10.

72 Petroleum Consumption

State	BTUs of Petroleum Consumed Per Capita	Points
1. Arizona	95,470,000	100
2. Michigan	96,051,000	100
3. Wisconsin	96,668,000	100
4. New York	98,538,000	99
5. Colorado	99,392,000	99
6. Rhode Island	100,199,000	98
7. Ohio	102,664,000	97
8. Maryland	104,852,000	96
9. Illinois	107,418,000	95
10. Pennsylvania	107,515,000	95
11. Iowa	109,758,000	94
12. North Carolina	110,227,000	94
13. Minnesota	113,142,000	93
14. Utah	113,290,000	93
15. South Carolina	115,887,000	92
16. Arkansas	118,077,000	91
17. California	119,015,000	91
18. Idaho	119,463,000	90
19. Tennessee	120,340,000	90
20. Missouri	120,539,000	90
21. Florida	121,595,000	89
22. Vermont	121,669,000	89
23. Virginia	121,706,000	89
24. Oregon	124,982,000	88
25. Georgia	127,678,000	87
26. Nebraska	129,087,000	86
27. Massachusetts	130,335,000	86
28. Connecticut	130,514,000	86
29. Alabama	130,809,000	86
30. Oklahoma	137,984,000	83
31. Kentucky	138,046,000	83
32. New Hampshire	138,412,000	83
33. Nevada	142,678,000	81
34. New Mexico	145,940,000	79
35. Indiana	151,136,000	77
36. South Dakota	151,724,000	77
37. Mississippi	153,089,000	77
38. New Jersey	155,420,000	76
39. Washington	162,029,000	73
40. West Virginia	163,078,000	72
41. Kansas	164,083,000	72
42. North Dakota	170,892,000	69
43. Montana	183,854,000	64
44. Maine	194,869,000	59
45. Delaware	198,798,000	58
46. Texas	262,353,000	31
47. Hawaii	265,703,000	30
48. Wyoming	277,533,000	25
49. Louisiana	338,767,000	0
50. Alaska	422,545,000	0

Natural Gas Consumption

DOING THE MATH

This category measures each state's consumption of natural gas. We calculated per capita figures from the raw totals that were collected by the U.S. Energy Department. The unit of measurement again is the British thermal unit. (See the previous category, Petroleum Consumption, for a definition of BTUs.)

BEST STATES

Natural gas is not a commonly used form of energy in Hawaii. The state annually consumes just 3 trillion BTUs, equaling 2.71 million BTUs per Hawaiian. Second place belongs to Maine, which uses 3.58 million BTUs of natural gas per resident.

WORST STATES

Natural gas is a favored fuel in Alaska, whose furnaces burn 326.8 trillion BTUs during the interminable winters. That works out to 594.18 million BTUs per capita. Louisiana, the nation's second-largest producer of natural gas, is also the second-largest consumer. It uses 387.89 million BTUs per resident.

REGIONAL WINNERS

East—Maine
South—North Carolina
Midwest—South Dakota
West—Hawaii

BIGGEST SURPRISE

New England's northern tier has long, frigid winters, but it doesn't rely much on natural gas for heat. Maine, Vermont, and New Hampshire hold second, third, and fourth places in this category, respectively.

THE BOTTOM LINE

Five of the 10 states that use natural gas most sparingly are in the East. Three are southern, and two are western.

74 Natural Gas Consumption

State	BTUs of Natural Gas Consumed Per Capita	Points
1. Hawaii	2,707,000	100
2. Maine	3,583,000	100
3. Vermont	11,900,000	98
4. New Hampshire	13,074,000	98
5. North Carolina	25,101,000	94
6. Florida	26,433,000	94
7. Virginia	30,499,000	93
8. Connecticut	30,696,000	93
9. Rhode Island	32,203,000	93
10. Washington	34,435,000	92
11. Arizona	35,143,000	92
12. South Dakota	36,637,000	91
13. Maryland	37,042,000	91
14. South Carolina	38,457,000	91
15. Oregon	39,303,000	91
16. Massachusetts	44,547,000	89
17. Idaho	46,474,000	89
18. Tennessee	46,647,000	89
19. Missouri	47,156,000	89
20. Georgia	49,305,000	88
21. New York	49,416,000	88
22. Kentucky	52,184,000	87
23. North Dakota	52,425,000	87
24. Montana	55,569,000	86
25. Nevada	55,657,000	86
26. New Jersey	56,791,000	86
27. Pennsylvania	57,271,000	86
28. Delaware	60,210,000	85
29. Alabama	62,113,000	85
30. Wisconsin	63,552,000	84
31. California	64,640,000	84
32. Minnesota	66,674,000	84
33. Nebraska	69,201,000	83
34. Ohio	71,660,000	82
35. West Virginia	71,946,000	82
36. Colorado	72,950,000	82
37. Utah	73,650,000	82
38. Iowa	79,114,000	80
39. Indiana	82,810,000	79
40. Illinois	83,990,000	79
41. Michigan	89,768,000	78
42. Arkansas	99,744,000	75
43. Mississippi	101,904,000	74
44. Kansas	142,292,000	64
45. New Mexico	165,940,000	58
46. Oklahoma	197,298,000	50
47. Texas	220,592,000	44
48. Wyoming	223,127,000	43
49. Louisiana	387,890,000	0
50. Alaska	594,181,000	0

Electricity Consumption

DOING THE MATH

How much electricity does each state use? The ever-vigilant U.S. Energy Department keeps those statistics, too. And we again converted its state-by-state totals into per capita averages. All figures are in British thermal units. (See the Petroleum Consumption category for an explanation of BTUs.)

BEST STATES

Residents of Rhode Island apparently take great care to conserve electricity; perhaps they wander their homes at night, turning off all unnecessary lights. Rhode Island uses 21.9 trillion BTUs of electricity a year, which translates to just 21.83 million per person, the nation's lowest rate. The runner-up is California, using 24.20 million BTUs per resident.

WORST STATES

Wyoming is the state that is most heavily dependent on electricity. It consumes 88.33 million BTUs per person. Washington, with per capita consumption of 63.82 million BTUs, is next to last.

REGIONAL WINNERS

East—Rhode Island
South—Florida
Midwest—Michigan
West—California

BIGGEST SURPRISE

California has the image of being a carefree, somewhat wasteful state. But that doesn't apply in this category. Only Rhode Island uses electricity more efficiently.

THE BOTTOM LINE

The East pays the closest attention to its electric bills. It placed seven states in this category's top 10. The West dominates the other end of the scale, with four of the bottom five states.

76 Electricity Consumption

State	BTUs of Electricity Consumed Per Capita	Points
1. Rhode Island	21,834,000	100
2. California	24,200,000	100
3. New York	24,524,000	99
4. Hawaii	25,541,000	97
5. Massachusetts	25,764,000	96
6. Alaska	26,363,000	95
7. New Hampshire	27,592,000	91
8. New Jersey	27,736,000	91
9. Connecticut	28,202,000	90
10. Vermont	28,419,000	89
11. Michigan	30,231,000	85
12. Utah	30,470,000	84
13. South Dakota	31,034,000	83
14. New Mexico	31,089,000	83
15. Colorado	31,876,000	81
16. Maine	32,003,000	80
17. Pennsylvania	32,948,000	78
18. Illinois	33,304,000	77
19. Wisconsin	34,300,000	75
20. Maryland	35,348,000	72
21. Missouri	35,939,000	70
22. Iowa	36,154,000	70
23. Minnesota	36,777,000	68
24. Kansas	37,368,000	67
25. North Dakota	37,402,000	67
26. Florida	37,849,000	66
27. Arizona	38,581,000	64
28. Nebraska	38,593,000	64
29. Arkansas	39,685,000	61
30. Virginia	40,084,000	60
31. Delaware	42,342,000	54
32. Georgia	42,358,000	54
33. Mississippi	42,596,000	54
34. West Virginia	44,004,000	50
35. Ohio	44,805,000	48
36. Indiana	45,526,000	46
37. Oklahoma	46,090,000	45
38. North Carolina	46,281,000	44
39. Nevada	46,339,000	44
40. Texas	47,683,000	41
41. Alabama	50,581,000	33
42. Oregon	51,583,000	31
43. Louisiana	51,587,000	31
44. Tennessee	53,967,000	25
45. South Carolina	54,430,000	24
46. Montana	55,944,000	20
47. Kentucky	56,553,000	18
48. Idaho	60,973,000	7
49. Washington	63,817,000	0
50. Wyoming	88,325,000	0

Renewable Energy

DOING THE MATH

The United States consumes 85 quadrillion BTUs of energy a year. Most of it—roughly 85 percent—is from one-shot sources such as petroleum, natural gas, and coal. Burn them, and they're gone. But there is a growing emphasis on developing renewable sources of energy, including hydro, wind, and solar energy. This category determines how much of each state's energy comes from renewable sources.

BEST STATES

Washington is the state that sets the pace in the field of renewable energy. Renewable sources, primarily hydropower, provide 53.5 percent of Washington's power. Two other states are above 40 percent: Oregon and Idaho.

WORST STATES

Petroleum, natural gas, and coal account for 99 percent of the energy consumed in Kansas. Only 0.3 percent comes from renewable sources, the worst record in the country. Texas, at 0.4 percent, is essentially just as bad.

REGIONAL WINNERS

East—Maine
South—Alabama
Midwest—South Dakota
West—Washington

BIGGEST SURPRISE

Cold-weather states tend to be the most advanced in developing renewable energy. But Alabama, Arkansas, Mississippi, and Georgia all have climbed into the national top 12.

THE BOTTOM LINE

The Northwest has harnessed its rivers for energy, setting an example for the rest of the nation. Four of the top five states in this category are from that corner of America.

78 Renewable Energy

State	Energy Consumed from Renewable Sources	Points
1. Washington	53.5%	100
2. Oregon	47.5	100
3. Idaho	46.5	98
4. South Dakota	29.4	62
5. Montana	29.0	61
6. Maine	27.0	56
7. Vermont	22.6	47
8. New Hampshire	20.2	42
9. Alabama	17.3	36
10. Arkansas	16.3	34
11. Mississippi	16.0	33
12. Georgia	15.9	33
13. California	13.4	28
14. North Carolina	12.6	26
Tennessee	12.6	26
16. South Carolina	11.7	24
17. New York	10.6	22
18. Nevada	9.8	20
19. Virginia	9.1	18
Minnesota	9.1	18
21. Connecticut	9.0	18
22. Arizona	8.9	18
23. Hawaii	8.0	16
24. Kentucky	6.5	13
25. Florida	5.8	11
26. Colorado	5.3	10
Louisiana	5.3	10
28. North Dakota	5.2	10
Massachusetts	5.2	10
30. Missouri	4.8	9
31. Wisconsin	4.6	9
Maryland	4.6	9
33. Michigan	4.3	8
34. Delaware	4.2	8
35. Rhode Island	4.1	8
36. Iowa	3.3	6
37. Utah	3.2	6
Oklahoma	3.2	6
39. Nebraska	3.1	6
Alaska	3.1	6
41. West Virginia	3.0	5
New Mexico	3.0	5
43. Pennsylvania	2.7	5
44. Wyoming	2.5	4
45. Ohio	2.4	4
46. Illinois	2.2	4
47. Indiana	2.1	3
48. New Jersey	1.0	1
49. Texas	0.4	0
50. Kansas	0.3	0

Resource Conservation: Scores and Grades

BEST STATE

Vermont has the reputation of being a "waste not, want not" type of state, so it's no surprise to see it holding first place in this section. Vermont has a consistently strong record of conserving energy and other natural resources. Only two states use less water or natural gas per person; only six get more of their energy from renewable sources.

RUNNERS-UP

Vermont's next-door neighbor, New Hampshire, is in second place, thanks to its efficient use of water, natural gas, and electricity. Eight other states—five from the East—earned straight A's in this section.

WORST STATES

Wyoming may be conservative politically, but it is wildly liberal when it comes to consuming energy and resources. No state uses more electricity per person; only Idaho uses more water per capita. Louisiana was the other state to receive an F in this section.

REGIONAL WINNERS

East—Vermont
South—Florida, Georgia, Virginia
Midwest—South Dakota
West—California, Oregon

REGIONAL AVERAGES

East—85 (A)
South—66 (B)
Midwest—75 (B+)
West—65 (B)

BIGGEST SURPRISE

Wyoming, Alaska, and Montana have been blessed with soaring mountains, rushing rivers, dense forests, and plenty of wide, open spaces. You might expect these natural wonders to have inspired strong traditions of conservation. But the evidence is to the contrary. All three are among this section's five worst states.

80 THE BOTTOM LINE

Most states are fairly efficient in their use of energy and natural resources. There were 21 A's (including pluses and minuses) and 25 B's.

Resource Conservation: Scores and Grades

State	Score	Grade
1. Vermont	100	A+
2. New Hampshire	96	A
3. South Dakota	95	A
New York	95	A
5. Rhode Island	93	A
6. California	91	A
Maine	91	A
Oregon	91	A
9. Connecticut	89	A
10. Massachusetts	86	A
11. Maryland	84	A–
12. Michigan	83	A–
13. Arizona	82	A–
Minnesota	82	A–
15. Wisconsin	81	A–
Florida	81	A–
Georgia	81	A–
Pennsylvania	81	A–
Virginia	81	A–
20. New Jersey	80	A–
Washington	80	A–
22. Missouri	79	B+
North Carolina	79	B+
24. Illinois	78	B+
Utah	78	B+
26. Iowa	77	B+
Arkansas	77	B+
28. Colorado	76	B+
29. Hawaii	75	B+
30. Mississippi	74	B
31. Alabama	72	B
Ohio	72	B
33. North Dakota	71	B
34. Tennessee	70	B
South Carolina	70	B
36. New Mexico	67	B
37. Delaware	66	B
38. Nevada	65	B
39. Indiana	64	B–
40. Kentucky	63	B–
41. Nebraska	62	B–
42. West Virginia	61	B–
Kansas	61	B–
44. Idaho	60	B–
Oklahoma	60	B–
46. Montana	49	C
47. Texas	39	D+
48. Alaska	36	D+
49. Louisiana	15	F
50. Wyoming	0	F

5

Environment

The Big Question

Which state has the cleanest air, water, and soil?

The Categories

1. Superfund Sites
2. Toxic Emissions
3. Drinking Water
4. Waste Generation
5. Environmental Spending

Superfund Sites

DOING THE MATH

The Comprehensive Environmental Response, Compensation, and Liability Act of 1980 established a federal program to clean up the nation's worst hazardous waste sites. The program, commonly known as Superfund, keeps a running list of locations in need of remedial action. We expressed the number of Superfund sites in each state as a rate per 10,000 square miles.

BEST STATES

Alaska has six Superfund sites, while Nevada has just one. But both are tied for first place with identical rates of 0.1 hazardous waste sites for every 10,000 square miles. Eight other states are below 1.0.

WORST STATES

New Jersey has the most sites on the Superfund list, 108. Combine that with its relatively small land area, and you get 145.6 sites per 10,000 square miles. Rhode Island and Delaware also have rates above 100.

REGIONAL WINNERS

East—West Virginia
South—Mississippi
Midwest—North Dakota
West—Nevada, Alaska

BIGGEST SURPRISE

The bottom of this category is dominated by densely settled states. That's why it's surprising to see tiny New Hampshire at no. 44, with 19.0 Superfund sites per 10,000 square miles.

THE BOTTOM LINE

The smaller the state, the less likely it is to have a serious hazardous waste problem. Texas and Georgia are the only states with populations above 4 million in the top 20.

84 Superfund Sites

State	Superfund Sites Per 10,000 Square Miles	Points
1. Nevada	0.1	100
Alaska	0.1	100
3. North Dakota	0.3	100
Wyoming	0.3	100
5. Mississippi	0.4	100
6. South Dakota	0.5	100
Montana	0.5	100
8. New Mexico	0.8	99
9. Arizona	0.9	99
Oregon	0.9	99
11. Nebraska	1.0	99
12. Idaho	1.1	99
Texas	1.1	99
14. Kansas	1.3	99
15. Oklahoma	1.5	99
16. Utah	1.6	99
Colorado	1.6	99
18. West Virginia	2.1	98
19. Georgia	2.2	98
20. Arkansas	2.3	98
21. Alabama	2.4	98
22. Louisiana	2.8	98
23. Maine	2.9	98
24. Hawaii	3.1	97
25. Missouri	3.3	97
26. Iowa	3.6	97
Tennessee	3.6	97
28. North Carolina	4.7	96
29. Kentucky	4.8	96
30. Minnesota	5.1	96
31. Virginia	5.6	95
32. California	6.1	95
33. Illinois	6.7	94
34. Washington	7.4	94
Wisconsin	7.4	94
36. South Carolina	8.0	93
37. Ohio	8.1	93
38. Vermont	8.6	93
39. Indiana	9.2	92
40. Florida	10.2	91
Maryland	10.2	91
42. Michigan	13.6	88
43. New York	17.8	85
44. New Hampshire	19.0	84
45. Pennsylvania	22.3	81
46. Connecticut	31.0	73
47. Massachusetts	33.2	71
48. Delaware	102.3	11
49. Rhode Island	114.8	0
50. New Jersey	145.6	0

Toxic Emissions

DOING THE MATH

The federal government requires each company with more than eight workers to report its air and water emissions of 313 toxic chemicals and chemical compounds each year. This information is compiled in the Environmental Protection Agency's Toxics Release Inventory. We compared each state's annual figure to its population, telling us the tons of toxic releases per 100,000 residents.

BEST STATES

About 400 tons of toxic chemicals are released in Hawaii each year. That works out to 36 tons per 100,000 residents, the most favorable rate in America. The runner-up is Vermont, with emissions of 89 tons per 100,000. No other state is below 100.

WORST STATES

The nation's worst toxic-emissions problem can be found in Louisiana, which has a release rate of 5,064 tons per 100,000 residents. Four other states are above 2,000: Utah, Montana, Tennessee, and Mississippi.

REGIONAL WINNERS

East—Vermont
South—Florida
Midwest—North Dakota
West—Hawaii

BIGGEST SURPRISE

California, the land of smog, is no. 5 in this category? That's right. Perhaps its tough emissions standards are having an impact. California has a surprisingly low rate of 163 tons of toxic releases per 100,000 residents.

THE BOTTOM LINE

The East has the edge in this category, placing five states in the top 10. The West is just a step behind with four entries.

86 Toxic Emissions

State	Tons of Toxic Releases Per 100,000 Residents	Points
1. Hawaii	36	100
2. Vermont	89	100
3. Colorado	112	99
4. Nevada	133	99
5. California	163	98
6. Maryland	167	98
7. New York	168	98
New Jersey	168	98
9. North Dakota	172	98
10. Massachusetts	173	98
11. South Dakota	216	96
12. Rhode Island	259	95
13. Connecticut	326	93
14. New Hampshire	370	92
15. Pennsylvania	376	92
16. Oregon	398	91
17. Florida	412	91
18. Washington	425	91
19. Wisconsin	460	90
20. Delaware	495	89
21. Illinois	521	88
22. Oklahoma	528	88
23. Nebraska	551	87
24. Kentucky	575	86
25. Idaho	576	86
26. Minnesota	594	86
27. Georgia	600	86
28. Maine	603	86
29. Virginia	643	84
30. Michigan	644	84
31. Missouri	670	84
32. Iowa	731	82
33. Ohio	776	81
34. North Carolina	935	76
35. South Carolina	964	75
36. Arizona	982	75
37. West Virginia	1,065	72
38. New Mexico	1,076	72
39. Arkansas	1,229	68
40. Texas	1,233	68
41. Wyoming	1,278	67
42. Alabama	1,393	63
43. Indiana	1,522	60
44. Kansas	1,812	51
45. Alaska	1,873	50
46. Mississippi	2,013	46
47. Tennessee	2,126	43
48. Montana	2,666	27
49. Utah	3,639	0
50. Louisiana	5,064	0

Drinking Water

DOING THE MATH

The Safe Drinking Water Act, as amended in 1986, sets the standards for almost all water destined for public use. It requires water suppliers to test for dozens of chemical and bacterial pollutants. This category calculates the percentage of each state's population that is served by water systems that, at some point, have been found in violation of the act.

BEST STATES

The quality of drinking water is consistently high in Maine, where only 1.2 percent of all residents have received water that failed to meet federal standards. Michigan and Nebraska also have confined their violations to less than 2 percent of their populations.

WORST STATES

New Jersey has serious problems in this category. All of its public water systems have failed to meet the Safe Drinking Water Act's standards at least once. Arizona is next to last, with 59.9 percent of its residents being served by systems that have violated the act.

REGIONAL WINNERS

East—Maine
South—Georgia
Midwest—Michigan
West—Colorado

BIGGEST SURPRISE

North Dakota, a national leader in controlling hazardous-waste dumping and toxic emissions, has not been as successful with its drinking water supply. It is no. 44 in this category.

THE BOTTOM LINE

The Midwest sets the pace in water quality. It landed four slots in the top 10, while the other three regions placed two states each.

88 Drinking Water

State	Residents Served by Water Systems with Violations of the Safe Drinking Water Act	Points
1. Maine	1.2%	100
2. Michigan	1.3	100
3. Nebraska	1.5	100
4. Indiana	2.2	98
5. Colorado	2.3	98
6. Georgia	3.7	96
7. Ohio	4.1	95
8. Maryland	4.3	95
9. California	4.6	94
Tennessee	4.6	94
11. Arkansas	5.8	92
12. Nevada	5.9	92
13. Missouri	6.0	92
14. New York	6.1	92
15. Delaware	6.2	92
16. Hawaii	6.3	91
West Virginia	6.3	91
18. South Carolina	6.8	91
19. Utah	7.2	90
20. Vermont	7.3	90
Virginia	7.3	90
22. New Mexico	7.5	89
23. Rhode Island	7.7	89
24. New Hampshire	8.0	89
25. Wisconsin	8.5	88
26. North Carolina	8.7	87
27. Illinois	8.9	87
28. Louisiana	9.1	87
29. Oregon	9.7	86
30. Texas	11.5	83
31. Kentucky	12.5	81
32. Kansas	12.7	81
33. Minnesota	13.1	80
34. Connecticut	14.5	77
35. Montana	16.0	75
36. Florida	16.2	75
Iowa	16.2	75
38. Oklahoma	16.5	74
39. Pennsylvania	16.6	74
40. Idaho	17.0	73
41. Alabama	17.5	72
42. Wyoming	18.7	70
43. South Dakota	20.2	68
44. Massachusetts	20.8	67
North Dakota	20.8	67
46. Mississippi	23.8	62
47. Washington	44.5	26
48. Alaska	48.0	20
49. Arizona	59.9	0
50. New Jersey	100.0	0

Waste Generation

DOING THE MATH

The Environmental Protection Agency estimates that the average American produces more than four pounds of garbage each day. That works out to three-quarters of a ton a year. Our interest, of course, was in how this figure varies across the country. We took the annual amount of commercial, residential, and institutional waste generated in each state, and converted it to a rate per 100,000 residents.

BEST STATES

The typical Mississippi resident produces slightly more than half a ton of garbage per year, which translates to 54,411 tons per 100,000 residents, the lowest rate in America. The runner-up is North Dakota, generating 62,598 tons per 100,000.

WORST STATES

Use it once and throw it away. Critics say that's the motto in California, which annually generates 151,210 tons of garbage per 100,000 persons. Also above 140,000 are Missouri, Virginia, Ohio, and Florida.

REGIONAL WINNERS

East—Vermont
South—Mississippi
Midwest—North Dakota
West—Utah

BIGGEST SURPRISE

Small states dominate this category. But Georgia, with a population of 6.5 million, ranks no. 3. It is the only state in the top 10 with more than 5 million residents.

THE BOTTOM LINE

The West has the best record of waste control, with four states among the national leaders. Each of the other three regions holds two slots in the top 10.

90 Waste Generation

State	Annual Tons of Solid Waste Generated Per 100,000 Residents	Points
1. Mississippi	54,411	100
2. North Dakota	62,598	100
3. Georgia	67,922	94
4. Vermont	69,272	92
5. Wisconsin	69,501	92
6. Utah	69,646	92
7. Wyoming	70,485	91
8. Colorado	72,860	88
9. Montana	75,094	85
10. Maine	77,362	82
11. Arizona	79,127	80
12. Pennsylvania	79,953	79
13. Nebraska	82,383	76
14. Iowa	82,823	76
15. Louisiana	82,938	76
16. Nevada	83,195	75
17. Idaho	84,409	74
18. Arkansas	85,070	73
19. Connecticut	88,226	69
20. North Carolina	90,511	67
21. Alaska	90,909	66
22. New Jersey	91,850	65
23. West Virginia	94,813	62
24. Kentucky	94,980	61
25. Oklahoma	95,359	61
26. Kansas	96,852	59
27. New Mexico	99,010	57
28. New Hampshire	99,188	56
29. Minnesota	100,571	55
30. Tennessee	102,522	52
31. Indiana	102,814	52
32. Washington	104,787	50
33. Texas	105,963	48
34. Maryland	106,672	48
35. Alabama	111,359	42
36. Delaware	112,613	40
37. Massachusetts	113,032	40
38. South Carolina	114,712	38
39. South Dakota	114,943	38
40. Oregon	116,115	36
41. Hawaii	117,329	35
42. Rhode Island	119,641	32
43. New York	122,290	29
44. Michigan	125,874	25
45. Illinois	127,723	22
46. Florida	144,535	2
47. Ohio	144,740	2
48. Virginia	145,466	1
49. Missouri	146,570	0
50. California	151,210	0

Environmental Spending

DOING THE MATH

The sure-fire way to measure a government's commitment to any cause is to check its budget. How much does it spend to control or solve a particular problem? We added up the amount spent by each state and its local governments on sewerage, conservation of natural resources, and solid waste management. We then reduced that total to a per capita average.

BEST STATES

Alaska is America's largest state in terms of land area. It also has the nation's highest cost of living. Those two factors explain why Alaska is no. 1 in this category, annually spending $546 per person on the environment. Second place goes to another state with wide, open spaces, Wyoming.

WORST STATES

Alabama each year allocates a paltry $94 per person for environmental matters. Oklahoma, with a per capita rate of $103, is next to last.

REGIONAL WINNERS

East—New Jersey
South—Florida
Midwest—Wisconsin
West—Alaska

BIGGEST SURPRISE

Rhode Island is among the 10 worst states in the Superfund Sites and Waste Generation categories, but it isn't spending much to solve its environmental problems. It ranks just 27th in this category.

THE BOTTOM LINE

Six of the 10 best states in this category are in the West. Six of the 10 worst states are in the South.

92 Environmental Spending

State	Per Capita Environmental Spending by State and Local Governments	Points
1. Alaska	$546	100
2. Wyoming	355	100
3. Hawaii	292	75
4. Washington	248	57
5. New Jersey	236	53
6. Arizona	218	46
7. California	211	43
8. New York	210	43
9. Delaware	202	39
10. Wisconsin	201	39
11. Florida	197	37
12. Connecticut	189	34
13. Idaho	188	34
14. Maryland	182	31
15. North Dakota	180	31
16. Minnesota	179	30
17. Vermont	176	29
Maine	176	29
19. Montana	174	28
20. Oregon	168	26
21. Massachusetts	167	25
22. Louisiana	165	24
23. New Hampshire	164	24
24. New Mexico	159	22
25. Virginia	156	21
26. Iowa	149	18
27. Rhode Island	146	17
28. Nebraska	143	16
29. Michigan	140	15
30. Pennsylvania	139	14
31. Utah	138	14
North Carolina	138	14
33. Nevada	134	12
34. Colorado	133	12
35. Georgia	131	11
36. Texas	129	10
37. Ohio	128	10
South Dakota	128	10
39. Kentucky	125	9
40. Illinois	123	8
41. Mississippi	120	7
42. South Carolina	119	6
43. Kansas	111	3
44. West Virginia	109	2
Indiana	109	2
46. Tennessee	108	2
47. Arkansas	104	1
Missouri	104	1
49. Oklahoma	103	0
50. Alabama	94	0

Environment: Scores and Grades

BEST STATE

Wyoming works hard to keep its air, water, and soil as clean as possible, earning the top score in this section. Only Alaska commits a larger share of its budget to environmental programs; just two states have fewer Superfund sites. Wyoming also generates proportionately less waste than all but six states.

RUNNERS-UP

Second place goes to Vermont, which has America's second-lowest rate of toxic emissions and which generates relatively little waste. Four other states received straight A's: Wisconsin, Hawaii, Colorado, and North Dakota.

WORST STATES

New Jersey is an industrial state wedged between two enormous metropolitan areas, a classic formula for environmental problems. It has the nation's highest concentration of Superfund sites and the largest proportion of water systems that have violated the Safe Drinking Water Act. The only other F belongs to Rhode Island.

REGIONAL WINNERS

East—Vermont
South—Georgia
Midwest—Wisconsin
West—Wyoming

REGIONAL AVERAGES

East—51 (C)
South—46 (C)
Midwest—53 (C)
West—63 (B–)

BIGGEST SURPRISE

The common perception is that large northern states have the most severe environmental problems. But the surprising truth is that three medium-sized southern states are among the eight worst in this section. Tennessee, Louisiana, and Alabama all received D's.

94 THE BOTTOM LINE

The West does the best job of protecting the environment. It is the home of four of the top 10 states in this section, and it easily has the best regional average.

Environment: Scores and Grades

State	Score	Grade
1. Wyoming	100	A+
2. Vermont	89	A
3. Wisconsin	88	A
4. Hawaii	86	A
5. Colorado	85	A
North Dakota	85	A
7. Maine	84	A–
8. Georgia	80	A–
9. Nebraska	76	B+
Nevada	76	B+
11. Idaho	71	B
12. Maryland	69	B
13. Iowa	62	B–
Minnesota	62	B–
New York	62	B–
16. Connecticut	61	B–
New Hampshire	61	B–
18. North Carolina	58	C+
Pennsylvania	58	C+
New Mexico	58	C+
Oregon	58	C+
22. Alaska	57	C+
23. Kentucky	55	C+
Arkansas	55	C+
25. California	54	C
26. West Virginia	51	C
27. Oklahoma	50	C
28. Washington	48	C
29. Mississippi	47	C
Montana	47	C
31. Michigan	45	C
South Dakota	45	C
33. Texas	43	C–
34. Indiana	42	C–
35. South Carolina	41	C–
36. Massachusetts	40	C–
Arizona	40	C–
38. Illinois	39	D+
39. Florida	38	D+
40. Utah	37	D+
41. Kansas	36	D+
42. Virginia	35	D+
43. Tennessee	34	D
44. Louisiana	33	D
45. Ohio	31	D
46. Alabama	28	D
47. Missouri	27	D
48. Delaware	26	D
49. Rhode Island	8	F
50. New Jersey	0	F

6

Health

The Big Question

Which state has the healthiest residents and the best health-care system?

The Categories

1. Life Expectancy
2. Major Causes of Death
3. Family Doctors
4. Specialists
5. Hospital Costs

Life Expectancy

DOING THE MATH

This category answers a straightforward question that's of interest to everyone: How long can the typical person expect to live? We found state-by-state life expectancy estimates that had been calculated by a branch of the U.S. Health and Human Services Department.

BEST STATES

The average resident of Hawaii can look forward to reaching the age of 77.02 years, the longest lifespan in the United States. Minnesota, with a life expectancy of 76.15 years, is in second place. An additional 11 states have figures above 75.

WORST STATES

Life is shortest in Louisiana, where the average resident dies after 71.74 years. Two other states—South Carolina and Mississippi—have life expectancies below 72.

REGIONAL WINNERS

East—Connecticut
South—Florida
Midwest—Minnesota
West—Hawaii

BIGGEST SURPRISE

Winters are long, dark, and frigid in the upper Midwest, conditions that you wouldn't think would be conducive to long lives. But the residents of Minnesota, Iowa, North Dakota, Nebraska, and Wisconsin are hardy. Those five states are among the top seven in this category.

THE BOTTOM LINE

The Sunbelt is the favorite haven for retirees, but it can't compete with colder areas when it comes to life expectancy. Hawaii and California are the only warm-weather states among the top 20.

98 Life Expectancy

State	Average Lifetime in Years	Points
1. Hawaii	77.02	100
2. Minnesota	76.15	100
3. Iowa	75.81	92
4. Utah	75.76	91
5. North Dakota	75.71	90
6. Nebraska	75.49	85
7. Wisconsin	75.35	81
8. Kansas	75.31	80
9. Colorado	75.30	80
10. Idaho	75.19	78
11. Washington	75.13	76
12. Connecticut	75.12	76
13. Massachusetts	75.01	73
14. Oregon	74.99	73
15. New Hampshire	74.98	73
16. South Dakota	74.97	73
17. Vermont	74.79	68
18. Rhode Island	74.76	68
19. Maine	74.59	64
20. California	74.57	63
21. Arizona	74.30	57
22. New Mexico	74.01	50
23. New Jersey	74.00	50
Florida	74.00	50
25. Montana	73.93	48
26. Wyoming	73.85	47
27. Indiana	73.84	46
Missouri	73.84	46
29. Arkansas	73.72	43
30. New York	73.70	43
31. Michigan	73.67	42
Oklahoma	73.67	42
33. Texas	73.64	42
34. Pennsylvania	73.58	40
35. Ohio	73.49	38
36. Virginia	73.43	37
37. Illinois	73.37	35
38. Maryland	73.32	34
39. Tennessee	73.30	34
40. Delaware	73.21	32
41. Kentucky	73.06	28
42. North Carolina	72.96	26
43. West Virginia	72.84	23
44. Nevada	72.64	18
45. Alabama	72.53	16
46. Alaska	72.24	9
47. Georgia	72.22	9
48. Mississippi	71.98	3
49. South Carolina	71.85	0
50. Louisiana	71.74	0

Major Causes of Death

DOING THE MATH

The three biggest killers in the United States are heart disease, cancer, and stroke, accounting for roughly 64 percent of all deaths each year. We totaled the deaths in those three classifications, then divided each state's figure by its population. The result is the annual number of deaths from major causes, expressed as a rate per 100,000 residents.

BEST STATES

Alaska has America's lowest death rate in each of the three classifications, so its combined figure obviously is the nation's best. There are 184.8 deaths from heart disease, cancer, and strokes per 100,000 Alaska residents. The runner-up is Utah, at 300.6 per 100,000.

WORST STATES

The major causes of death strike most heavily at two neighboring eastern states. West Virginia's death rate is 707.5 per 100,000 residents, while Pennsylvania's is 682.3.

REGIONAL WINNERS

East—New Hampshire
South—Texas
Midwest—Minnesota
West—Alaska

BIGGEST SURPRISE

Only two states have longer life expectancies than Iowa, so you might assume that it consequently has a low rate of deaths from major causes. Not so. Iowa is no. 44 in this category.

THE BOTTOM LINE

The West is the most successful region at avoiding modern life's leading killers. Nine of the 10 best states are western.

100 Major Causes of Death

State	Deaths from Heart Disease, Cancer, and Stroke Per 100,000 Residents	Points
1. Alaska	184.8	100
2. Utah	300.6	100
3. Colorado	376.5	80
4. Hawaii	383.7	78
5. New Mexico	384.3	78
6. Wyoming	422.0	68
7. California	443.6	63
8. Idaho	446.7	62
9. Texas	451.3	61
10. Nevada	468.0	56
11. Washington	471.9	55
12. Arizona	474.1	55
13. Georgia	481.5	53
14. New Hampshire	493.6	49
15. Virginia	493.7	49
16. Minnesota	496.7	49
17. Maryland	501.1	47
18. Vermont	508.8	45
19. Montana	512.3	45
20. South Carolina	532.0	39
21. Oregon	546.5	36
22. North Carolina	547.0	35
23. Michigan	550.7	34
24. Connecticut	551.0	34
25. Louisiana	557.2	33
26. Delaware	558.2	33
27. Massachusetts	573.5	29
28. Wisconsin	573.9	28
29. Illinois	581.3	26
30. North Dakota	581.4	26
31. Kansas	581.7	26
32. Indiana	583.1	26
33. Maine	587.1	25
34. New Jersey	589.5	24
35. Nebraska	596.3	23
36. Ohio	598.7	22
37. South Dakota	603.9	21
38. Alabama	605.1	20
39. Tennessee	606.5	20
40. New York	615.9	17
41. Kentucky	616.9	17
42. Oklahoma	627.3	14
43. Mississippi	635.8	12
44. Iowa	637.5	12
45. Rhode Island	639.9	11
46. Missouri	642.4	10
47. Arkansas	670.8	3
48. Florida	681.7	0
49. Pennsylvania	682.3	0
50. West Virginia	707.5	0

Family Doctors

DOING THE MATH

Family doctors are part of American folklore, the men and women who treated whatever malady might afflict you on your long journey from cradle to grave. Such general practitioners are less common in this age of specialization, but they do still exist. We took the number of doctors with general and family practices in each state, then translated that figure into a rate per 100,000 residents.

BEST STATES

The family doctor remains an everyday fixture in Minnesota, which has 1,866 general practitioners. That works out to 42.7 per 100,000 residents, the best rate in the United States. Neighboring South Dakota is just a step behind at 42.5.

WORST STATES

Most doctors have chosen to specialize in Massachusetts, which has just 15.3 general practitioners per 100,000. Rhode Island, with a rate of 16.0, is next to last.

REGIONAL WINNERS

East—Maine
South—Arkansas
Midwest—Minnesota
West—Wyoming

BIGGEST SURPRISE

The ranks of family doctors are thin in most large states, putting them near the bottom of this category. An exception is California, up at no. 23.

THE BOTTOM LINE

The Midwest is the remaining stronghold of the family doctor. It placed six states in this category's top 10. The five worst states, on the other hand, are all in the East.

102 Family Doctors

State	General/Family Practitioners Per 100,000 Residents	Points
1. Minnesota	42.7	100
2. South Dakota	42.5	100
3. Wyoming	41.0	94
4. North Dakota	40.7	93
5. Nebraska	39.4	88
6. Washington	38.2	84
7. Arkansas	37.8	82
8. Montana	35.9	75
9. Kansas	34.7	70
10. Indiana	34.2	69
11. Iowa	33.8	67
12. Maine	33.5	66
13. Vermont	33.4	66
14. Idaho	33.1	64
15. Wisconsin	32.8	63
16. Alaska	32.7	63
17. South Carolina	31.3	58
Colorado	31.3	58
19. West Virginia	31.1	57
20. Kentucky	30.2	54
21. Oregon	29.8	52
New Mexico	29.8	52
23. California	28.9	49
24. Pennsylvania	28.6	48
25. Mississippi	27.7	44
26. New Hampshire	27.5	43
27. Virginia	27.4	43
28. Oklahoma	27.3	43
29. Arizona	26.4	39
Illinois	26.4	39
31. Florida	26.3	39
32. North Carolina	25.9	37
33. Tennessee	25.4	36
34. Texas	25.0	34
35. Alabama	24.9	34
36. Delaware	24.8	33
Ohio	24.8	33
38. Hawaii	24.0	30
39. Utah	23.7	29
40. Louisiana	23.2	27
41. Nevada	21.1	19
42. Maryland	20.5	17
Georgia	20.5	17
44. Michigan	19.8	14
45. Missouri	18.7	10
46. New York	18.0	8
47. New Jersey	17.8	7
48. Connecticut	16.5	2
49. Rhode Island	16.0	0
50. Massachusetts	15.3	0

Specialists

DOING THE MATH

Many medical problems are too complicated or narrowly focused to be handled by a family doctor. That's when you call in a specialist, be it a cardiologist, dermatologist, neurosurgeon, ophthalmologist, urologist, or an expert in any of dozens of other fields. We totaled each state's medical and surgical specialists, then converted that figure to a rate per 100,000 residents.

BEST STATES

Massachusetts, entrenched in last place in the Family Doctors category, holds first place in this one. It has 15,955 medical and surgical specialists, which translates into a rate of 265 per 100,000 residents. Second place belongs to New York, with 257 specialists per 100,000.

WORST STATES

Idaho has only 875 specialists to serve its population of slightly more than 1 million. That's a rate of 87 per 100,000, the lowest in the country. Three other states are below 100: South Dakota, Alaska, and Wyoming.

REGIONAL WINNERS

East—Massachusetts
South—Florida, Virginia
Midwest—Illinois
West—Hawaii

BIGGEST SURPRISE

Tiny Vermont has 192 specialists per 100,000 residents, the seventh-best rate in America. It is the only state with a population below 1 million to be listed among the top 13.

THE BOTTOM LINE

Medical and surgical specialists are most numerous in the East, which holds the top eight positions in this category.

104 Specialists

State	Medical and Surgical Specialists Per 100,000 Residents	Points
1. Massachusetts	265	100
2. New York	257	100
3. Maryland	249	95
4. Connecticut	247	94
5. Rhode Island	208	70
6. New Jersey	204	68
7. Vermont	192	61
8. Pennsylvania	187	58
9. Hawaii	185	56
10. California	183	55
11. Illinois	170	47
12. Florida	160	41
Virginia	160	41
14. Missouri	159	41
Oregon	159	41
Colorado	159	41
Delaware	159	41
18. New Hampshire	158	40
19. Minnesota	157	40
Tennessee	157	40
21. Louisiana	156	39
Ohio	156	39
23. Arizona	150	35
24. Washington	148	34
Michigan	148	34
26. Utah	143	31
27. North Carolina	142	30
28. Wisconsin	140	29
29. Georgia	139	29
30. New Mexico	137	27
31. Texas	134	25
32. Maine	130	23
33. Kansas	129	22
34. West Virginia	128	22
Kentucky	128	22
36. Alabama	124	19
37. North Dakota	122	18
38. Nebraska	121	18
39. South Carolina	117	15
40. Montana	116	15
41. Nevada	115	14
42. Indiana	112	12
43. Oklahoma	111	12
44. Iowa	107	9
45. Arkansas	106	9
46. Mississippi	100	5
47. Wyoming	95	2
48. Alaska	92	0
South Dakota	92	0
50. Idaho	87	0

Hospital Costs

DOING THE MATH

Americans are concerned about the skyrocketing cost of health care. This category measures the daily cost for patients at community hospitals, including short-term general or special hospitals, but excluding psychiatric facilities and hospitals operated by the federal government. We have added an important twist, relating each state's figure to its per capita income.

BEST STATES

The average daily cost for a community-hospital patient is $613 in New Jersey, which has a per capita income of $25,666. That works out to the most affordable rate in the country, $239 per $10,000 of income. South Dakota is the runner-up at $243.

WORST STATES

Daily hospital costs are higher in Utah than anywhere else, $569 per $10,000 of income. Just three other states are above $500, and all are in the West: Arizona, Alaska, and New Mexico.

REGIONAL WINNERS

East—New Jersey
South—Virginia
Midwest—South Dakota
West—Montana

BIGGEST SURPRISE

Look right at the top of the list. Much of New Jersey is suburban territory that borders two expensive cities, New York City and Philadelphia. But, surprisingly, it has the nation's most cost-effective hospitals.

THE BOTTOM LINE

Hospital costs are most in tune with income levels in the Midwest, which holds six of the top 10 slots in this category. Rates are least affordable in the West, which has eight of the bottom 10 positions.

106 Hospital Costs

State	Average Daily Cost of a Community Hospital Patient Per $10,000 of Per Capita Income	Points
1. New Jersey	$239	100
2. South Dakota	243	100
3. Montana	258	95
4. Wyoming	273	89
5. North Dakota	274	89
6. Nebraska	277	88
7. Minnesota	280	87
8. New York	285	85
9. Iowa	286	85
10. Kansas	290	83
11. Hawaii	301	79
12. Maryland	306	78
13. New Hampshire	308	77
14. Wisconsin	309	76
15. Virginia	316	74
16. Connecticut	317	74
17. Maine	329	69
Mississippi	329	69
19. Vermont	332	68
20. Massachusetts	343	64
Pennsylvania	343	64
22. Rhode Island	345	64
23. Illinois	346	63
24. North Carolina	353	61
25. Idaho	357	59
26. Kentucky	360	58
27. Georgia	361	58
28. Arkansas	365	56
29. Delaware	370	55
30. Colorado	375	53
31. Missouri	379	52
Alabama	379	52
33. South Carolina	381	51
34. Michigan	384	50
Tennessee	384	50
36. Indiana	388	48
37. West Virginia	395	46
38. Florida	405	42
Ohio	405	42
40. Oklahoma	407	42
41. Washington	419	37
42. Nevada	432	33
43. Texas	436	31
44. California	450	26
45. Oregon	455	24
46. Louisiana	466	20
47. New Mexico	501	8
48. Alaska	508	5
49. Arizona	523	0
50. Utah	569	0

Health: Scores and Grades

BEST STATE

Minnesota clearly is the top state in this section, with a score 13 points higher than anyone else's. No state has a more favorable ratio of family doctors; only Hawaii has an average life expectancy that is longer. Hospital costs also are fairly reasonable in Minnesota, which finished seventh in that category.

RUNNERS-UP

Hawaii was the only state besides Minnesota to earn an A in this section. Its greatest strength is its life expectancy of 77.02 years, nearly a year ahead of the rest of the pack. Two states received grades of B+: North Dakota and Colorado.

WORST STATES

Expensive hospitals and the nation's shortest life expectancy can be found in Louisiana, which ranks no. 50. Neighboring Mississippi is next to last.

REGIONAL WINNERS

East—Vermont
South—Virginia
Midwest—Minnesota
West—Hawaii

REGIONAL AVERAGES

East—48 (C)
South—20 (D–)
Midwest—52 (C)
West—50 (C)

BIGGEST SURPRISE

More than 18 percent of Florida's residents are 65 or older, the highest concentration of elderly persons in America. You would expect such a state to be particularly sensitive to the need for good health care. But Florida ranks no. 39 in this section, earning a grade of D–.

108 THE BOTTOM LINE

The race for top honors is a dead heat between the Midwest and the West. Their average scores are virtually identical, and each placed four states among the 10 leaders. There is no doubt, on the other hand, that the South is the worst region in this section.

Health: Scores and Grades

State	Score	Grade
1. Minnesota	100	A+
2. Hawaii	87	A
3. North Dakota	77	B+
4. Colorado	75	B+
5. Vermont	74	B
6. Nebraska	71	B
7. Wyoming	70	B
8. South Dakota	68	B
9. Washington	65	B
10. New Hampshire	63	B–
Kansas	63	B–
Connecticut	63	B–
13. Montana	62	B–
14. Wisconsin	61	B–
15. Maryland	59	C+
16. Massachusetts	57	C+
Iowa	57	C+
18. Idaho	56	C+
19. California	53	C
20. New York	52	C
21. Utah	51	C
New Jersey	51	C
23. Maine	50	C
24. Virginia	49	C
25. Oregon	42	C–
26. New Mexico	37	D+
Rhode Island	37	D+
28. Illinois	35	D+
Pennsylvania	35	D+
30. Indiana	32	D
31. Arkansas	29	D
Delaware	29	D
Texas	29	D
34. North Carolina	27	D
35. Arizona	26	D
36. Tennessee	24	D–
37. Kentucky	23	D–
Alaska	23	D–
39. Michigan	21	D–
Ohio	21	D–
Florida	21	D–
42. Georgia	18	F
43. South Carolina	17	F
44. Missouri	16	F
45. Oklahoma	13	F
46. West Virginia	11	F
47. Alabama	8	F
Nevada	8	F
49. Mississippi	5	F
50. Louisiana	0	F

7

Children and Families

The Big Question

Which state offers the best conditions in which to raise a family?

The Categories

1. Birth Weight
2. Infant Mortality
3. Births to Single Teens
4. Children in Poverty
5. Marriage Stability

Birth Weight

DOING THE MATH

There is a strong correlation between birth weight and a baby's ability to survive. More than half of all infants who die during the first year of life weigh less than 5.5 pounds at birth. About 7 percent of all American newborns are classified as low-weight babies. This category determines the percentage in each state.

BEST STATES

Happy, healthy babies are the norm in Alaska, where just 4.8 percent of newborns weigh less than 5.5 pounds. New Hampshire is the only other state where fewer than 5 percent of births result in underweight babies.

WORST STATES

Poverty and malnutrition are contributing factors to Mississippi's serious birth-weight problem. Fully 9.5 percent of its babies are below the weight threshold. Low-weight births also occur more than 8.5 percent of the time in Louisiana, South Carolina, and Georgia.

REGIONAL WINNERS

East—New Hampshire
South—Oklahoma
Midwest—Minnesota, South Dakota
West—Alaska

BIGGEST SURPRISE

You might expect a direct connection between a state's level of prosperity and the health of its babies. But only two of the 10 best states in this category are among the 10 leaders in per capita income.

THE BOTTOM LINE

Four midwestern states are in the top 10 in this category, as are three each from the East and West. Eight of the 10 worst states are southern.

112 Birth Weight

State	Newborn Babies Weighing Less Than 5.5 Pounds	Points
1. Alaska	4.8%	100
2. New Hampshire	4.9	100
3. Oregon	5.0	98
4. Maine	5.1	95
Minnesota	5.1	95
South Dakota	5.1	95
7. Nebraska	5.3	91
Vermont	5.3	91
Washington	5.3	91
10. Iowa	5.4	88
11. North Dakota	5.5	86
12. Idaho	5.6	84
13. Utah	5.7	81
14. California	5.8	79
Massachusetts	5.8	79
16. Wisconsin	5.9	77
17. Rhode Island	6.1	72
18. Kansas	6.2	70
Montana	6.2	70
20. Arizona	6.3	67
21. Oklahoma	6.5	63
22. Connecticut	6.6	60
Indiana	6.6	60
24. New Jersey	6.9	53
Texas	6.9	53
26. Hawaii	7.1	49
Kentucky	7.1	49
Missouri	7.1	49
Ohio	7.1	49
Pennsylvania	7.1	49
West Virginia	7.1	49
32. Nevada	7.2	47
Virginia	7.2	47
34. Florida	7.4	42
New Mexico	7.4	42
Wyoming	7.4	42
37. Michigan	7.5	40
38. Delaware	7.6	37
Illinois	7.6	37
New York	7.6	37
41. Maryland	7.8	33
42. Colorado	8.0	28
North Carolina	8.0	28
44. Arkansas	8.2	23
Tennessee	8.2	23
46. Alabama	8.4	19
47. Georgia	8.7	12
South Carolina	8.7	12
49. Louisiana	9.2	0
50. Mississippi	9.5	0

Infant Mortality

DOING THE MATH

America's infant mortality rate has been cut in half since 1970, but the numbers are still striking. More than 20,000 babies die in the first month of life every year; an additional 15,000 die before reaching their first birthdays. The causes range from birth defects to sudden infant death syndrome. This category converts each state's annual total of infant deaths to a rate per 1,000 live births.

BEST STATES

Utah has the nation's lowest infant mortality rate. Just six of every 1,000 Utah babies die during the first year. Four New England states—Vermont, Maine, New Hampshire, and Massachusetts—have rates below seven, as does Hawaii.

WORST STATES

Infant deaths occur more frequently in Delaware than in any other state. Its rate is 12.7 per 1,000 births. Georgia is next to last at 12.4.

REGIONAL WINNERS

East—Vermont
South—Texas
Midwest—Minnesota
West—Utah

BIGGEST SURPRISE

Alaska has the nation's smallest percentage of low-weight births, giving its babies a key health advantage. But the state still does no better than 28th in this category.

THE BOTTOM LINE

The East and West have been equally successful in keeping infant mortality to a minimum; each has five states among the 12 best. The South, on the other hand, has seven of the 11 worst states.

114 Infant Mortality

State	Deaths Before Age 1 Per 1,000 Live Births	Points
1. Utah	6.0	100
2. Vermont	6.1	100
3. Maine	6.3	97
4. Hawaii	6.5	94
New Hampshire	6.5	94
6. Massachusetts	6.8	89
7. Nevada	7.1	84
8. Wyoming	7.2	83
9. Minnesota	7.3	81
10. Connecticut	7.4	79
Nebraska	7.4	79
Washington	7.4	79
13. Montana	7.6	76
Oregon	7.6	76
15. Iowa	7.7	75
Texas	7.7	75
17. California	7.8	73
Rhode Island	7.8	73
19. Maryland	8.1	68
Wisconsin	8.1	68
21. Kentucky	8.2	67
22. Colorado	8.3	65
23. New Mexico	8.5	62
24. New Jersey	8.6	60
25. Arizona	8.7	59
Idaho	8.7	59
27. Florida	8.9	56
28. Alaska	9.0	54
North Dakota	9.0	54
South Dakota	9.0	54
West Virginia	9.0	54
32. Indiana	9.4	48
Kansas	9.4	48
New York	9.4	48
Pennsylvania	9.4	48
36. Ohio	9.5	46
37. Louisiana	9.6	44
38. Tennessee	9.7	43
Virginia	9.7	43
40. Michigan	9.9	40
Oklahoma	9.9	40
42. Missouri	10.2	35
43. Illinois	10.3	33
44. Arkansas	10.4	32
45. South Carolina	10.7	27
46. North Carolina	11.0	22
47. Alabama	11.2	19
48. Mississippi	11.3	17
49. Georgia	12.4	0
50. Delaware	12.7	0

Births to Single Teens

DOING THE MATH

Morality is not the issue here; family stability is. It has been documented that single mothers are less likely than other teenagers to complete their high school educations. They are less likely than older women to get prenatal care. The unsurprising result is that single teens and their children suffer higher-than-normal rates of poverty and developmental disorders. This category determines how many of each state's births are to unmarried women in their teens.

BEST STATES

Single, teenaged mothers are rare in Utah, where they account for just 5 percent of all births. New Hampshire and Idaho are the only other states below 6 percent.

WORST STATES

Mississippi has by far the highest birth rate for single teens in America, 15.5 percent. Neighboring Louisiana is next to last in this category at 12.9 percent.

REGIONAL WINNERS

East—New Hampshire
South—Texas
Midwest—North Dakota
West—Utah

BIGGEST SURPRISE

Births to single teens occur most frequently in southern states and large states. Texas fits both of those classifications, yet it still has the nation's sixth-lowest rate.

THE BOTTOM LINE

Teenage pregnancy is least common in the East. It placed four states in the category's top 10, followed by three from the West. The problem is most serious in the South, with eight states in the bottom 10.

116 Births to Single Teens

State	Births to Unmarried Women Less Than 20 Years Old	Points
1. Utah	5.0%	100
2. New Hampshire	5.2	100
3. Idaho	5.9	91
4. North Dakota	6.0	90
Vermont	6.0	90
6. Alaska	6.3	86
Texas	6.3	86
8. Minnesota	6.4	84
9. Connecticut	6.6	82
Massachusetts	6.6	82
11. New Jersey	6.8	79
12. Iowa	7.2	74
Nebraska	7.2	74
Nevada	7.2	74
15. Washington	7.3	73
16. New York	7.4	71
17. Colorado	7.5	70
South Dakota	7.5	70
19. Hawaii	7.6	69
20. California	7.7	68
Wyoming	7.7	68
22. Kansas	7.8	66
23. Maine	7.9	65
Montana	7.9	65
25. Virginia	8.0	64
26. Oregon	8.1	62
27. Wisconsin	8.2	61
28. Maryland	8.3	60
29. Rhode Island	8.4	58
30. Pennsylvania	8.8	53
31. Kentucky	9.0	51
32. Michigan	9.1	49
Oklahoma	9.1	49
34. Delaware	9.3	47
35. West Virginia	9.7	42
36. Florida	9.9	39
Indiana	9.9	39
38. Missouri	10.1	36
39. Arizona	10.2	35
40. Ohio	10.3	34
41. Illinois	10.6	30
42. Tennessee	10.7	29
43. North Carolina	10.9	26
44. New Mexico	11.4	19
45. Alabama	11.5	18
Georgia	11.5	18
47. Arkansas	11.8	14
48. South Carolina	12.0	12
49. Louisiana	12.9	0
50. Mississippi	15.5	0

Children in Poverty

DOING THE MATH

Roughly 20 percent of America's children live in poverty, according to the latest figures from the U.S. Census Bureau. The numbers are even higher for minorities: 44 percent of black children are poor, as are 38 percent of Hispanic children. This category presents each state's poverty rate for all persons under the age of 18.

BEST STATES

New Hampshire has the nation's lowest poverty rate for all persons, so it's no surprise that it also is no. 1 in this specialized category. Just 7 percent of New Hampshire's children live in poverty, making it the lone state with a rate below 10 percent. Connecticut is in second place.

WORST STATES

One child of every three in Mississippi is poor; its poverty rate for children is a shocking 33.5 percent. Louisiana is next to last, the only other state with a rate above 30 percent.

REGIONAL WINNERS

East—New Hampshire
South—Virginia
Midwest—Minnesota
West—Alaska

BIGGEST SURPRISE

Utah ranks 48th in per capita income, topping just West Virginia and Mississippi. You would expect that to mean poverty is widespread in Utah, but that's not the case. Just 12.2 percent of Utah's children live in poverty, the ninth-best rate in America.

THE BOTTOM LINE

Six of the 10 best states are eastern; seven of the 10 worst states are southern.

118 Children in Poverty

State	Children Living Below the Poverty Level	Points
1. New Hampshire	7.0%	100
2. Connecticut	10.4	100
3. Alaska	10.9	98
Maryland	10.9	98
5. New Jersey	11.0	97
6. Hawaii	11.1	97
7. Vermont	11.5	95
8. Delaware	11.7	94
9. Utah	12.2	91
10. Minnesota	12.4	90
11. Nevada	12.8	88
12. Massachusetts	12.9	88
13. Virginia	13.0	88
14. Maine	13.2	87
15. Nebraska	13.5	85
Rhode Island	13.5	85
17. Indiana	13.9	83
Kansas	13.9	83
19. Iowa	14.0	83
Washington	14.0	83
21. Wyoming	14.1	82
22. Wisconsin	14.6	80
23. Colorado	15.0	78
24. Oregon	15.2	77
25. Pennsylvania	15.4	76
26. Idaho	15.8	74
27. Illinois	16.8	69
28. North Carolina	16.9	69
North Dakota	16.9	69
30. Missouri	17.4	66
31. Ohio	17.6	65
32. California	17.8	64
33. Michigan	18.2	63
34. Florida	18.3	62
35. New York	18.8	60
36. Georgia	19.8	55
37. Montana	19.9	54
38. South Dakota	20.1	53
39. Tennessee	20.7	50
40. South Carolina	20.8	50
41. Oklahoma	21.4	47
42. Arizona	21.7	46
43. Alabama	24.0	35
Texas	24.0	35
45. Kentucky	24.5	32
46. Arkansas	25.0	30
47. West Virginia	25.9	25
48. New Mexico	27.5	18
49. Louisiana	31.2	0
50. Mississippi	33.5	0

Marriage Stability

DOING THE MATH

Nearly 50 percent of all marriages end in divorce these days. Happy couples rejoice at 2.4 million weddings each year; unhappy ones file for 1.2 million divorces. We compared the annual number of weddings and dissolutions in each state, giving us the rate of divorces per 1,000 marriages.

BEST STATES

Nevada once specialized in dissolving marriages. But other states liberalized their divorce laws, forcing Nevada to switch to quickie weddings. A typical year sees more than 120,000 marriages in Nevada, compared to 14,000 divorces. The result is an artificially stable rate of just 113 divorces per 1,000 marriages. South Carolina is second at 259.

WORST STATES

Weddings don't seem to have lasting magic in Oklahoma, which has 752 divorces for every 1,000 marriages. Indiana and Oregon also have rates of 700 or higher.

REGIONAL WINNERS

East—Maryland
South—South Carolina
Midwest—South Dakota
West—Nevada

BIGGEST SURPRISE

Look right at the top of the list. Who would expect to find flashy Nevada leading this category? Its excellent score, of course, is inflated by out-of-staters coming in for no-frills weddings.

THE BOTTOM LINE

The East has a slight edge in this category, with four states in the top 10. The South has three slots, the West two, and the Midwest one.

120 Marriage Stability

State	Divorces Per 1,000 Marriages	Points
1. Nevada	113	100
2. South Carolina	259	100
3. Hawaii	267	98
4. Maryland	344	81
5. Massachusetts	347	81
6. Virginia	382	73
7. South Dakota	386	72
8. Vermont	410	67
9. Kentucky	422	64
10. New York	424	64
11. Minnesota	443	59
12. Pennsylvania	445	59
Connecticut	445	59
14. Louisiana	447	58
15. North Dakota	449	58
16. Wisconsin	450	58
New Jersey	450	58
18. New Hampshire	456	57
Iowa	456	57
20. Rhode Island	457	56
21. Maine	485	50
22. Illinois	491	49
23. Tennessee	494	48
24. Georgia	496	48
25. Arkansas	500	47
26. Texas	505	46
27. New Mexico	510	45
28. Mississippi	512	44
29. Ohio	514	44
30. Idaho	516	43
Missouri	516	43
32. Nebraska	528	41
33. Michigan	536	39
34. Utah	537	39
35. Delaware	543	37
36. Alabama	547	36
37. Kansas	550	36
38. California	576	30
39. Colorado	582	29
Florida	582	29
41. Washington	620	20
Alaska	620	20
43. North Carolina	626	19
44. Montana	629	18
45. Arizona	656	12
46. West Virginia	679	7
47. Wyoming	681	7
48. Oregon	700	3
49. Indiana	712	0
50. Oklahoma	752	0

Children and Families: Scores and Grades

BEST STATE

New Hampshire received top honors in this section, making it the best place in America to raise a family. It easily has the nation's smallest percentage of children living in poverty. Only Alaska has fewer low birth-weight babies; only Utah has fewer births to single teenagers. It also helps that a majority of New Hampshire couples stay together; the state ranks 18th in the Marriage Stability category.

RUNNERS-UP

Neighboring Vermont is in second place, just two points behind New Hampshire. It finished in the top 10 in all five categories. Six other states received straight A's: Massachusetts, Utah, Minnesota, Hawaii, Maine, and Nevada.

WORST STATES

Extreme poverty and poor health care combined to put Mississippi in last place in this section. It has the country's highest percentages of poor children, births to single teens, and low birth-weight babies. Also earning F's were three other southern states: Louisiana, Alabama, and Georgia.

REGIONAL WINNERS

East—New Hampshire
South—Virginia
Midwest—Minnesota
West—Utah

REGIONAL AVERAGES

East—71 (B)
South—32 (D)
Midwest—62 (B-)
West—66 (B)

BIGGEST SURPRISE

The South stresses family values, but it fails to back up its words. Conditions for children and families are almost universally discouraging across the region.

The exceptions are Virginia and Texas, the only southern states with above-average grades.

THE BOTTOM LINE

Exactly 10 states landed in the A range in this section: five from the East, three from the West, and two from the Midwest. The South can be found at the other end, with eight of the 10 worst scores.

Children and Families: Scores and Grades

State	Score	Grade
1. New Hampshire	100	A+
2. Vermont	98	A
3. Massachusetts	92	A
4. Utah	90	A
5. Minnesota	89	A
Hawaii	89	A
7. Maine	85	A
Nevada	85	A
9. Connecticut	82	A–
10. Iowa	81	A–
11. Nebraska	79	B+
12. Alaska	76	B+
North Dakota	76	B+
14. Idaho	74	B
15. New Jersey	73	B
Washington	73	B
Rhode Island	73	B
South Dakota	73	B
Wisconsin	73	B
20. Maryland	72	B
21. Oregon	65	B
Virginia	65	B
California	65	B
24. Kansas	62	B–
25. Texas	60	B–
26. Pennsylvania	57	C+
Montana	57	C+
Wyoming	57	C+
29. New York	56	C+
30. Colorado	54	C
31. Kentucky	52	C
32. Ohio	45	C
33. Michigan	44	C–
34. Indiana	43	C–
Missouri	43	C–
Florida	43	C–
37. Arizona	41	C–
38. Illinois	40	C–
39. Delaware	39	D+
40. South Carolina	36	D+
41. Oklahoma	35	D+
42. Tennessee	34	D
43. New Mexico	32	D
44. West Virginia	30	D
45. North Carolina	26	D
46. Arkansas	22	D–
47. Georgia	18	F
48. Alabama	17	F
49. Louisiana	11	F
50. Mississippi	0	F

8

Female Equality

The Big Question

Which state gives women the best opportunity to succeed in government, the workplace, or their own businesses?

The Categories

1. Women in Poverty
2. Employment Opportunities
3. Women in Bubiness
4. Women in Government
5. Violence Against Women

Women in Poverty

DOING THE MATH

Families headed by women are four times more likely than other American families to live in poverty. Approximately one-third of all women who are single parents are classified as poor. This category measures the poverty rate for female-headed households in each state.

BEST STATES

New Hampshire has the smallest proportion of women in poverty. Just 17.6 percent of its female-headed households are poor, which is roughly half of the national average. Hawaii is the only other state with a rate below 20 percent.

WORST STATES

Poverty is found throughout Mississippi, but it is a particularly serious problem for women trying to hold their families together by themselves. The state's poverty rate for female-headed households is an astounding 50.6 percent. Louisiana is next-to-last at 49.6 percent.

REGIONAL WINNERS

East—New Hampshire
South—Virginia
Midwest—Minnesota
West—Hawaii

BIGGEST SURPRISE

Nine of the 10 best states in this category also rank in the top 10 in per-capita income. The exception is Nevada, only 13th in income, but a strong no. 7 here.

THE BOTTOM LINE

Poverty is less of a problem for women who live on the two coasts. Six of the 10 leading states are eastern; the other four are western. Six of the 10 worst states, on the other hand, are southern.

126 Women in Poverty

State	Female-Headed Households Below the Poverty Level	Points
1. New Hampshire	17.6%	100
2. Hawaii	19.6	100
3. New Jersey	20.6	97
4. Maryland	20.9	96
5. Connecticut	21.7	93
6. Delaware	22.3	91
7. Nevada	23.2	88
8. Alaska	24.1	85
9. Massachusetts	24.7	83
10. California	26.2	78
11. Rhode Island	26.5	77
12. Virginia	26.7	76
13. Vermont	26.9	76
14. Pennsylvania	27.9	72
15. Florida	28.4	71
16. Minnesota	29.2	68
17. Indiana	29.6	67
Nebraska	29.6	67
19. Colorado	29.9	66
Maine	29.9	66
21. New York	30.1	65
Washington	30.1	65
23. Utah	30.3	64
24. Oregon	30.5	64
25. Illinois	30.7	63
26. Kansas	30.8	63
27. North Carolina	31.0	62
28. Wisconsin	31.2	61
29. Missouri	31.4	61
30. Arizona	31.6	60
31. Idaho	33.2	55
32. Iowa	33.5	54
33. Ohio	33.7	53
34. Georgia	34.3	51
Tennessee	34.3	51
36. Texas	35.4	47
37. Michigan	35.8	46
38. South Carolina	36.0	45
39. Wyoming	36.9	42
40. North Dakota	38.0	39
41. Oklahoma	38.3	38
42. South Dakota	38.7	36
43. Kentucky	39.6	33
44. Montana	39.7	33
45. West Virginia	39.8	33
46. Alabama	40.7	30
47. New Mexico	40.9	29
48. Arkansas	41.2	28
49. Louisiana	49.6	0
50. Mississippi	50.6	0

Employment Opportunities

DOING THE MATH

Do women get an equal break in the job market? That's what this category is designed to find out. We compared the annual average unemployment rates for men and women in each state, converting them to a single index. A score below 100 means women are more easily employed than men, while a figure above 100 indicates the employment balance is tipped toward the male side.

BEST STATES

Women definitely have an advantage in Vermont, which ranks no. 1 with an index of 61.0. The average jobless rate for Vermont women is 4.7 percent, compared to 7.7 percent for men. Second place in this category goes to Minnesota.

WORST STATES

The toughest job market for women is Louisiana, where the average unemployment rates are 7.8 percent for females and 6.6 percent for males, equaling an index of 118.2. Oregon is next to last.

REGIONAL WINNERS

East—Vermont
South—Oklahoma
Midwest—Minnesota
West—Alaska

BIGGEST SURPRISE

Oregon has a reputation for being a liberal, open-minded state, but it does poorly in this category, ranking 49th. Only Louisiana offers fewer job opportunities for women.

THE BOTTOM LINE

The East is the best region for women who are seeking employment. It placed six states in the top 10, along with three from the West and one from the Midwest.

Employment Opportunities

State	Women's Unemployment Index (Men=100)	Points
1. Vermont	61.0	100
2. Minnesota	65.6	100
3. Delaware	69.4	92
4. Alaska	69.7	92
5. Maine	73.3	85
6. Washington	76.1	79
7. Massachusetts	76.2	79
8. Nevada	77.0	77
9. West Virginia	79.1	73
10. New Jersey	79.5	73
11. Arizona	80.6	70
12. Pennsylvania	81.3	69
13. Wisconsin	81.4	69
14. Rhode Island	81.7	68
15. Iowa	82.0	68
16. New York	82.1	67
17. New Hampshire	83.3	65
18. Illinois	84.4	63
19. Ohio	85.3	61
20. Connecticut	86.1	59
21. Montana	86.5	59
22. Indiana	87.3	57
Oklahoma	87.3	57
24. Michigan	87.6	56
25. North Dakota	88.4	55
26. Nebraska	89.7	52
27. Missouri	89.9	52
California	89.9	52
29. New Mexico	90.3	51
30. Idaho	92.1	48
31. South Carolina	93.8	44
32. Colorado	94.1	44
33. Wyoming	96.2	39
34. North Carolina	98.3	35
35. Tennessee	98.5	35
36. Kentucky	98.6	35
37. Kansas	100.0	32
Maryland	100.0	32
39. Texas	103.1	26
40. Hawaii	103.7	25
41. Arkansas	104.2	24
Utah	104.2	24
43. Virginia	105.3	21
44. Florida	107.0	18
45. Mississippi	107.2	18
46. Georgia	108.3	15
47. South Dakota	109.1	14
48. Alabama	111.8	9
49. Oregon	116.1	0
50. Louisiana	118.2	0

Women in Business

DOING THE MATH

The business world still is male-oriented, but not as much as it once was. Women now own 30 percent of all private companies, generating almost 14 percent of the country's total sales volume. This category counts the number of women-owned businesses in each state, translating it to a rate per 10,000 women residents.

BEST STATES

Female entrepreneurs are taken seriously in Colorado, which boasts 89,400 businesses owned by women. That works out to 538 for every 10,000 female residents, the best rate in the nation. Alaska is just a step behind at 537. No other state has a rate above 500.

WORST STATES

Mississippi's business community is still dominated by men. There are only 29,000 women-owned businesses in the state, equal to 216 per 10,000 women residents. Neighboring Alabama does only slightly better with a rate of 228.

REGIONAL WINNERS

East—Vermont
South—Oklahoma
Midwest—Kansas
West—Colorado

BIGGEST SURPRISE

Wyoming commonly is portrayed as a rough-hewn, male-dominated state. But it actually ranks no. 4 in this category, offering an excellent business environment for women.

THE BOTTOM LINE

The frontier states of the West willingly accept women as equals in business, which is why six of the top 10 states are western. The South is just the opposite, with seven of the bottom 10 states.

130 Women in Business

State	Women-Owned Businesses Per 10,000 Women Residents	Points
1. Colorado	538	100
2. Alaska	537	100
3. Vermont	480	82
4. Wyoming	476	80
5. Montana	440	69
6. Kansas	424	63
7. Oregon	408	58
8. New Hampshire	401	56
9. Nebraska	399	55
Hawaii	399	55
11. North Dakota	396	54
12. Minnesota	395	54
13. Oklahoma	394	54
14. Maine	380	49
15. South Dakota	378	49
16. California	377	48
17. Idaho	375	48
18. Iowa	374	47
19. Washington	368	45
20. Connecticut	360	43
21. Massachusetts	356	41
22. Texas	346	38
23. Utah	344	37
24. Maryland	333	34
25. Florida	332	34
26. Missouri	330	33
New Mexico	330	33
28. Arizona	327	32
29. Nevada	319	30
30. Indiana	315	28
31. New York	304	25
32. Illinois	301	24
33. Virginia	299	23
34. New Jersey	294	21
35. Arkansas	291	20
36. Delaware	283	18
37. Kentucky	281	17
38. Michigan	280	17
39. Rhode Island	278	16
40. Wisconsin	277	16
41. Ohio	274	15
North Carolina	274	15
43. Pennsylvania	270	14
44. Tennessee	267	13
45. Georgia	264	12
46. Louisiana	255	9
47. West Virginia	242	5
48. South Carolina	237	3
49. Alabama	228	0
50. Mississippi	216	0

Women in Government

DOING THE MATH

Political commentators hailed 1992 as the "Year of the Woman" after several female candidates won high-profile U.S. Senate campaigns. But progress has been slow in the lower ranks, with women still holding no more than 20 percent of all state legislative seats. This category calculates the percentage of women in each state's legislature.

BEST STATES

Women are approaching parity in Washington's legislature, where they now hold 58 of 147 seats, equal to 39.5 percent. Arizona is in second place at 35.6 percent. Most of the female lawmakers are Democrats in Washington, while they're Republicans in Arizona.

WORST STATES

Politics is still a male sport in Kentucky, where women hold only six of the 138 legislative seats. That's 4.3 percent, the nation's worst figure. Alabama is next to last at 5.7 percent.

REGIONAL WINNERS

East—Vermont
South—North Carolina
Midwest—Kansas
West—Washington

BIGGEST SURPRISE

Only six states elected female governors before 1984. Kentucky and Alabama were in that select group, but have not extended the idea of sexual equality to their state legislatures. They are the two worst states in this category.

THE BOTTOM LINE

The West landed four states in the top 10, while the East and the Midwest have three each. The South is the clear loser, with eight of the 10 worst entries.

132 Women in Government

State	State Legislature Seats Held by Women	Points
1. Washington	39.5%	100
2. Arizona	35.6	100
3. Colorado	34.0	95
4. Vermont	33.9	94
5. New Hampshire	33.5	93
6. Maine	31.2	85
7. Idaho	30.5	83
8. Kansas	28.5	76
9. Minnesota	27.4	73
10. Wisconsin	27.3	72
11. Nevada	27.0	71
12. Oregon	26.7	70
13. Connecticut	25.1	65
14. Rhode Island	24.7	64
15. Wyoming	24.4	63
16. Hawaii	23.7	60
17. Maryland	23.4	59
18. California	23.3	59
19. Illinois	23.2	59
20. Massachusetts	23.0	58
21. Alaska	21.7	54
22. Ohio	21.2	52
23. Nebraska	20.4	49
24. South Dakota	20.0	48
25. Michigan	19.6	46
New Mexico	19.6	46
27. Indiana	19.3	45
Missouri	19.3	45
Montana	19.3	45
30. North Carolina	18.2	42
31. Florida	17.5	39
32. Georgia	17.4	39
33. West Virginia	16.4	36
34. North Dakota	16.3	35
35. New York	16.1	35
36. Texas	16.0	34
37. Iowa	14.7	30
38. Delaware	14.5	29
39. Utah	13.5	26
40. South Carolina	12.9	24
41. New Jersey	12.5	23
42. Tennessee	12.1	21
43. Virginia	11.4	19
44. Mississippi	10.9	17
45. Pennsylvania	9.9	14
46. Arkansas	9.6	13
47. Oklahoma	9.4	12
48. Louisiana	6.9	4
49. Alabama	5.7	0
50. Kentucky	4.3	0

Violence Against Women

DOING THE MATH

Violence against women has been increasing at a steady pace, as shown by Federal Bureau of Investigation statistics. The annual total of rapes grew 24 percent during the 1980s and kept climbing higher in the early 1990s. This category converts each state's number of reported rapes to an annual rate per 100,000 residents.

BEST STATES

Women are safest in North Dakota, where the annual rape rate is 18.3 per 100,000 residents. Montana, at 19.8, holds second place. Three other states have rape rates below 25: Iowa, Maine, and West Virginia.

WORST STATES

Violence against women has reached outrageous proportions in Alaska, which annually has 91.8 reported rapes per 100,000 residents. The second-worst state is Delaware, with a rate of 86.5 per 100,000.

REGIONAL WINNERS

East—Maine
South—Virginia
Midwest—North Dakota
West—Montana

BIGGEST SURPRISE

New York has America's second-worst violent crime rate, so you would naturally expect it to have a high frequency of violence against women. But it doesn't. Just eight states have lower rape rates than New York.

THE BOTTOM LINE

The East and Midwest tied for top honors in this category, each placing four states in the top 10. The West has five of the 10 states with the worst rape rates.

134 Violence Against Women

State	Reported Rapes Per 100,000 Residents	Points
1. North Dakota	18.3	100
2. Montana	19.8	100
3. Iowa	20.9	98
4. Maine	21.9	97
5. West Virginia	23.0	95
6. Wisconsin	25.4	92
7. Wyoming	25.9	91
8. Nebraska	28.1	88
9. New York	28.2	87
10. Pennsylvania	28.7	87
11. Idaho	28.9	86
12. New Jersey	29.1	86
13. Connecticut	29.2	86
14. New Hampshire	29.9	85
Virginia	29.9	85
16. Vermont	30.5	84
17. Rhode Island	30.9	83
18. Massachusetts	32.1	82
19. Hawaii	33.0	80
20. Missouri	34.0	79
21. North Carolina	34.6	78
22. Kentucky	35.4	77
23. Alabama	35.6	76
24. South Dakota	39.7	70
25. Minnesota	39.8	70
26. Illinois	40.0	70
27. Louisiana	40.9	68
28. Indiana	41.3	68
29. Georgia	42.3	66
30. Arizona	42.4	66
California	42.4	66
32. Arkansas	44.6	63
33. Kansas	44.8	63
34. Utah	45.6	61
35. Maryland	45.9	61
36. Mississippi	46.3	60
37. Tennessee	46.4	60
38. Colorado	47.0	59
39. Oklahoma	50.9	53
40. Florida	51.7	52
41. New Mexico	52.4	51
42. Ohio	52.5	51
43. Oregon	53.4	50
Texas	53.4	50
45. South Carolina	58.9	41
46. Nevada	66.0	31
47. Washington	70.3	24
48. Michigan	78.7	12
49. Delaware	86.5	0
50. Alaska	91.8	0

Female Equality: Scores and Grades

BEST STATE

It's fitting that the only female governor ever elected to three terms, Madeleine Kunin, is a Vermonter. Women have made greater strides toward equality in Vermont than anywhere else in America. No state has a better record of opening employment opportunities to women, while Colorado and Alaska are the only places with higher proportions of women-owned businesses. And don't forget politics: Vermont ranks no. 4 in the percentage of women in its legislature.

RUNNERS-UP

The two states directly east of Vermont earned the only straight A's in this section. New Hampshire has the lowest percentage of women living in poverty. Maine is among the six best states in the Employment Opportunities, Women in Government, and Violence Against Women categories.

WORST STATES

Women are in a decidedly inferior position in last-place Louisiana. No state offers fewer job opportunities to women; only Mississippi has a higher percentage of female-headed households in poverty. Besides Louisiana, only three states received F's: Mississippi, Alabama, and Arkansas.

REGIONAL WINNERS

East—Vermont
South—North Carolina
Midwest—Minnesota
West—Colorado

REGIONAL AVERAGES

East—67 (B)
South—25 (D)
Midwest—55 (C+)
West—61 (B–)

136 BIGGEST SURPRISE

The South has a strangehold on the bottom of this list, with nine of the 10 worst scores. The sole exception is no. 44 Michigan, one of just two midwestern states to receive below-average grades.

THE BOTTOM LINE

The East and the West both have regional averages in the B range—and both have five states among the section's top 11.

Female Equality: Scores and Grades

State	Score	Grade
1. Vermont	100	A+
2. New Hampshire	90	A
3. Maine	85	A
4. Minnesota	80	A–
Colorado	80	A–
6. Connecticut	75	B+
7. Massachusetts	74	B
8. Alaska	70	B
Arizona	70	B
10. Hawaii	67	B
Idaho	67	B
12. Wyoming	66	B
13. Washington	65	B
Nebraska	65	B
Wisconsin	65	B
16. Rhode Island	64	B–
17. Montana	63	B–
California	63	B–
19. New Jersey	62	B–
20. Iowa	61	B–
Kansas	61	B–
Nevada	61	B–
23. North Dakota	57	C+
Maryland	57	C+
25. Illinois	56	C+
New York	56	C+
27. Missouri	53	C
28. Indiana	52	C
29. Pennsylvania	49	C
30. Oregon	45	C
West Virginia	45	C
32. North Carolina	43	C–
Ohio	43	C–
34. Delaware	42	C–
35. Virginia	40	C–
36. South Dakota	38	D+
37. Florida	37	D+
Oklahoma	37	D+
Utah	37	D+
40. New Mexico	36	D+
41. Texas	32	D
42. Georgia	29	D
43. Tennessee	28	D
44. Michigan	27	D
45. Kentucky	23	D–
46. South Carolina	21	D–
47. Arkansas	19	F
48. Alabama	10	F
49. Mississippi	4	F
50. Louisiana	0	F

9

Racial Equality

The Big Question

Which state gives minorities the best chance to compete and coexist with whites?

The Categories

1. Minority Population
2. Income Disparity
3. Housing Disparity
4. Minority College Graduates
5. Minority Businesses

Minority Population

DOING THE MATH

There is strength in numbers. A racial minority will have more political power if it includes 30 percent of a state's voters, rather than 10 percent. A larger group also can better maintain a distinct culture. This category combines the minority groups recognized by the Census Bureau—blacks, Hispanics, American Indians, and Asian-Americans—and determines their collective percentage of each state's population.

BEST STATES

Asian-Americans really aren't minorities in Hawaii. They actually hold the majority, accounting for roughly two-thirds of the state's population. The other minority groups push the final figure to 72.1 percent. New Mexico is the only other state where at least half of all residents are minorities.

WORST STATES

Just 10,500 Vermont residents are classified as minorities. That's 1.9 percent of the state's population of 563,000. Two other states are below 4 percent: Maine and New Hampshire.

REGIONAL WINNERS

East—New York
South—Texas
Midwest—Illinois
West—Hawaii

BIGGEST SURPRISE

California's political establishment is dominated by whites, but minority groups are gaining strength. They now account for a surprisingly large 43.6 percent of California's residents.

THE BOTTOM LINE

The minority population is highest in the South, which placed five states in the top 10. The East and the Midwest, on the other hand, each hold four slots in the bottom 10.

140 Minority Population

State	Residents Classified As Minorities	Points
1. Hawaii	72.1%	100
2. New Mexico	50.0	100
3. California	43.6	87
4. Texas	39.7	79
5. Mississippi	37.0	73
6. Louisiana	34.4	68
7. New York	32.4	63
8. South Carolina	31.6	62
9. Maryland	30.7	60
10. Georgia	30.0	58
11. Arizona	28.9	56
12. Florida	27.2	53
13. Alabama	26.8	52
14. New Jersey	26.7	51
15. Alaska	26.5	51
16. Illinois	25.4	49
17. North Carolina	25.1	48
18. Virginia	24.2	46
19. Nevada	21.7	41
20. Delaware	20.9	39
21. Colorado	19.6	37
22. Oklahoma	19.3	36
23. Arkansas	17.8	33
Michigan	17.8	33
25. Tennessee	17.5	32
26. Connecticut	16.6	30
27. Washington	13.5	24
28. Missouri	13.1	23
29. Ohio	13.0	23
30. Pennsylvania	12.4	22
Massachusetts	12.4	22
32. Kansas	11.7	20
33. Rhode Island	10.7	18
34. Indiana	10.5	18
35. Oregon	9.4	15
36. Wyoming	9.2	15
37. South Dakota	8.9	14
Utah	8.9	14
39. Wisconsin	8.8	14
40. Kentucky	8.4	13
41. Montana	8.3	13
42. Idaho	7.9	12
43. Nebraska	7.6	12
44. Minnesota	6.3	9
45. North Dakota	5.9	8
46. West Virginia	4.2	5
47. Iowa	4.1	4
48. New Hampshire	2.7	1
49. Maine	2.0	0
50. Vermont	1.9	0

Income Disparity

DOING THE MATH

America preaches economic equality, but does not practice it. The median income for a white household is $31,400. But the typical Hispanic household earns just $24,150, and its black counterpart receives just $19,750. This category compares the median incomes for whites and each state's largest minority group. The result is a ratio of minority income per $1,000 of median white household income.

BEST STATES

The tables have been turned in Hawaii, where Asian-Americans have a median household income of $40,950, compared to white income of $37,406. That works out to $1,095 for minorities per $1,000 for whites. Maine, where Hispanics outearn whites, is the only other state above $1,000.

WORST STATES

All races are familiar with poverty in Louisiana, but whites still are much better off. The typical black family in Louisiana earns just $455 for every $1,000 in median white household income. Neighboring Mississippi is next to last.

REGIONAL WINNERS

East—Maine
South—Texas
Midwest—Missouri
West—Hawaii

BIGGEST SURPRISE

Wisconsin prides itself on being racially progressive, but its beliefs don't translate into economic reality. Just five states have greater income disparities between whites and minorities.

THE BOTTOM LINE

The West, with seven states in the top 10, offers minorities their best shot at economic equality. Six of the 10 worst states are southern.

142 Income Disparity

State	Median Minority Household Income Per $1,000 of Median White Household Income	Points
1. Hawaii	$1,095	100
2. Maine	1,035	100
3. Washington	992	92
4. Vermont	976	90
5. New Hampshire	960	87
6. Nevada	836	65
7. Wyoming	813	61
8. Oregon	780	55
9. Utah	766	53
10. Idaho	758	51
11. California	748	49
12. New Mexico	744	49
13. Maryland	733	47
14. Arizona	730	46
15. New Jersey	682	38
16. Colorado	679	37
17. Missouri	676	37
18. New York	673	36
19. Pennsylvania	667	35
Massachusetts	667	35
21. Delaware	662	35
22. Kansas	657	34
23. Texas	647	32
24. Indiana	646	32
25. Connecticut	645	32
Nebraska	645	32
27. Kentucky	641	31
28. Oklahoma	633	29
29. West Virginia	626	28
Tennessee	626	28
31. Florida	623	28
32. North Carolina	614	26
33. Illinois	611	25
34. Virginia	610	25
35. Rhode Island	606	25
Iowa	606	25
37. Minnesota	603	24
38. Montana	591	22
39. Ohio	590	22
40. Michigan	581	20
41. Georgia	576	19
42. South Carolina	550	15
43. Arkansas	538	13
44. Alaska	537	12
45. Wisconsin	536	12
46. Alabama	522	10
47. North Dakota	502	6
48. South Dakota	474	1
49. Mississippi	466	0
50. Louisiana	455	0

Housing Disparity

DOING THE MATH

The civil rights movement aimed to win the opportunity for blacks to live in previously all-white neighborhoods. That fight has not yet been won in much of America. This category looks at the housing gap in each state between whites and the largest minority group. The median value of minority-owned homes is expressed as a rate per $1,000 of median value for houses owned by whites.

BEST STATES

Washington's Asian-American residents own homes with a median value of $113,100, compared to $93,100 for white-owned houses. That works out to $1,215 in minority house value per $1,000 for whites. New York, Maine, Vermont, and New Hampshire also have rates above $1,000.

WORST STATES

Pennsylvania has an astonishingly wide housing gap. The typical black family in Pennsylvania lives in a $33,800 home, compared to a median house value of $72,200 for whites. The resulting rate is $468 per $1,000. Michigan is next to last.

REGIONAL WINNERS

East—New York
South—Oklahoma
Midwest—Minnesota
West—Washington

BIGGEST SURPRISE

The North is fond of lecturing the South about racial equality. But Pennsylvania, Michigan, and South Dakota have housing disparities much worse than those in the South.

THE BOTTOM LINE

Racial housing gaps generally are smallest in the East, with six of the 10 best states. Five of the 10 worst are southern.

144 Housing Disparity

State	Median Value of Minority-Owned Houses Per $1,000 of Median Value of White-Owned Houses	Points
1. Washington	$1,215	100
2. New York	1,111	100
3. Maine	1,051	90
4. Vermont	1,029	87
5. New Hampshire	1,015	85
6. Minnesota	935	72
7. Rhode Island	905	67
8. Massachusetts	877	63
9. Hawaii	861	60
10. Nevada	859	60
11. Wyoming	845	58
12. Oregon	842	57
13. Connecticut	817	53
14. Utah	814	53
15. Iowa	793	50
16. Oklahoma	781	48
17. New Mexico	761	45
18. North Dakota	758	44
19. California	752	43
20. Idaho	745	42
21. Colorado	742	42
22. Tennessee	736	40
23. Montana	735	40
24. Nebraska	726	39
25. Illinois	719	38
26. Kansas	715	37
27. West Virginia	707	36
28. Maryland	698	34
29. Missouri	695	34
30. Arizona	689	33
31. Mississippi	685	32
32. Ohio	682	32
33. Indiana	680	32
34. North Carolina	676	31
35. Kentucky	675	31
36. Wisconsin	666	29
37. Louisiana	664	29
38. Florida	662	29
39. Georgia	652	27
40. Alaska	649	27
41. Alabama	647	26
42. South Carolina	642	26
43. Arkansas	640	25
44. New Jersey	638	25
45. Delaware	626	23
46. Virginia	617	22
47. Texas	606	20
48. South Dakota	527	8
49. Michigan	480	0
50. Pennsylvania	468	0

Minority College Graduates

DOING THE MATH

"A mind is a terrible thing to waste." That famous commercial tag-line for the United Negro College Fund reinforces the point that education gives minorities the best chance of attaining full social and economic equality. This category calculates the percentage of adults (age 25 or older) in all minority groups who have earned bachelor's degrees.

BEST STATES

The minority population in New Hampshire is small, but it also is well-educated. Fully 3,875 of the state's 11,570 minority adults are college graduates. That's 33.5 percent. Neighboring Vermont is the only other state above 30 percent.

WORST STATES

There is a vast difference in the minority populations of South Carolina and Wyoming, but the math is the same. Just 48,400 of South Carolina's 586,290 minority adults have college degrees; the corresponding figures in Wyoming are 1,090 and 13,200. Both work out to 8.3 percent.

REGIONAL WINNERS

East—New Hampshire
South—Virginia
Midwest—Iowa
West—Hawaii, Washington

BIGGEST SURPRISE

West Virginia has the lowest percentage of college graduates of all races, just 12.3 percent. But its minorities do substantially better, 16.2 percent, good for 13th place in this category.

THE BOTTOM LINE

Minority college graduates are most numerous in the East, which has six of the 10 leading states. The West placed five states in the bottom 10.

146 Minority College Graduates

State	Minority Persons Age 25 or Older Who Are College Graduates	Points
1. New Hampshire	33.5%	100
2. Vermont	32.5	100
3. Massachusetts	21.7	56
4. Iowa	21.1	53
5. New Jersey	20.5	50
6. Minnesota	19.7	47
7. Maryland	19.6	47
8. Hawaii	19.1	45
Washington	19.1	45
10. Maine	18.5	42
11. Oregon	17.8	39
12. California	17.7	39
13. West Virginia	16.2	33
Connecticut	16.2	33
15. New York	15.7	31
16. Utah	15.5	30
17. Illinois	15.2	29
18. Colorado	14.9	27
Nebraska	14.9	27
20. Virginia	14.7	27
21. Kansas	14.1	24
22. Delaware	13.8	23
23. Rhode Island	13.7	22
24. Missouri	13.5	22
25. Pennsylvania	13.1	20
26. Michigan	12.8	18
27. North Dakota	12.6	18
28. Oklahoma	12.5	17
29. Indiana	12.4	17
30. Georgia	12.2	16
Ohio	12.2	16
32. Wisconsin	12.0	15
33. Texas	11.8	14
Florida	11.8	14
35. Tennessee	11.5	13
36. Nevada	11.0	11
37. North Carolina	10.4	8
38. Montana	10.2	8
39. Alabama	10.1	7
40. Kentucky	10.0	7
41. Louisiana	9.8	6
Idaho	9.8	6
43. South Dakota	9.6	5
44. Arizona	9.5	5
45. Mississippi	9.2	4
46. New Mexico	8.9	3
Arkansas	8.9	3
Alaska	8.9	3
49. South Carolina	8.3	0
Wyoming	8.3	0

Minority Businesses

DOING THE MATH

Racial minorities own 1.2 million companies, generating annual receipts of $78 billion. The dominant groups are blacks and Hispanics, each owning roughly 420,000 businesses. Asian-Americans have 350,000 companies, American Indians 20,000. This category expresses each state's number of minority-owned businesses as a rate per 10,000 minority residents.

BEST STATES

America's youngest states easily offer the best environments for minority entrepreneurs. Alaska has 6,011 minority-owned businesses, which translates to 413 per 10,000 minority residents. Hawaii is close behind with a rate of 409. Vermont is the only other state with a rate above 300.

WORST STATES

South Dakota's 62,200 minority group members own just 539 businesses, equal to 87 companies per 10,000 minority residents. Alabama is next to last, with a rate of 106.

REGIONAL WINNERS

East—Vermont
South—Florida
Midwest—Kansas
West—Alaska

BIGGEST SURPRISE

California would seem an ideal place for minority businesses. It ranks no. 1 in minority population (nearly 13 million) and no. 3 in percentage of minority residents (43.6 percent). But it does no better than no. 6 in this category, behind such unlikely places as Vermont and New Hampshire.

THE BOTTOM LINE

The West, with five states in the top 10, is the best region for minority entrepreneurs. The South has five of the 11 worst states, while the Midwest has four.

148 Minority Businesses

State	Minority-Owned Businesses Per 10,000 Minority Residents	Points
1. Alaska	413	100
2. Hawaii	409	100
3. Vermont	310	67
4. Florida	278	57
5. New Hampshire	267	53
6. California	250	48
7. Colorado	244	46
8. Texas	226	40
9. New Mexico	224	39
10. Maryland	221	38
11. Oregon	215	36
12. Wyoming	213	35
13. Washington	204	32
14. Maine	202	32
15. Virginia	197	30
16. Idaho	194	29
West Virginia	194	29
18. New Jersey	189	27
19. Kansas	178	24
20. Utah	177	23
21. New York	170	21
22. Missouri	167	20
23. Kentucky	161	18
Nebraska	161	18
25. Nevada	158	17
26. Iowa	157	17
27. Indiana	156	16
Ohio	156	16
29. Minnesota	151	15
Connecticut	151	15
31. Massachusetts	150	15
32. Illinois	149	14
Montana	149	14
34. Tennessee	148	14
35. Delaware	146	13
Pennsylvania	146	13
37. North Carolina	145	13
38. Louisiana	143	12
Oklahoma	143	12
40. Arizona	141	12
Georgia	141	12
42. South Carolina	129	7
43. Arkansas	128	7
44. Michigan	127	7
45. Rhode Island	126	7
North Dakota	126	7
47. Mississippi	117	4
48. Wisconsin	109	1
49. Alabama	106	0
50. South Dakota	87	0

Racial Equality: Scores and Grades

BEST STATE

Hawaii, no. 1 in this section, offers a clear, but tough-to-duplicate formula for racial parity. It is the only state where minorities are in the majority, freeing them to compete with whites on an equal footing. Hawaii, as a result, is one of just two states where the median income for minority households is larger than that for whites. Only Alaska has a higher rate of minority-owned businesses.

RUNNERS-UP

Vermont—yes, Vermont—is the only other state in the A range. Its minority population is tiny (just 1.9 percent), but it finished among the top five states in the other four categories. Four states received B's: New Hampshire, Washington, California, and Maine.

WORST STATES

There is an enormous gap between whites and other residents of South Dakota, where American Indians are the dominant minority. No state has a lower rate of minority-owned businesses; just two have wider income and housing disparities between races. Eight other states earned F's.

REGIONAL WINNERS

East—Vermont
South—Texas
Midwest—Minnesota
West—Hawaii

REGIONAL AVERAGES

East—47 (C)
South—26 (D)
Midwest—22 (D–)
West—48 (C)

BIGGEST SURPRISE

Who would ever guess that Vermont and New Hampshire would be among the states coming closest to the ideal of racial equality? They may have small minority populations, but they earned second and third places, respectively.

150 THE BOTTOM LINE

The West and East have virtually identical regional averages; each also has five states in the top 10. The Midwest, with five of the bottom 10 states, is the worst region for minorities.

Racial Equality: Scores and Grades

State	Score	Grade
1. Hawaii	100	A+
2. Vermont	84	A–
3. New Hampshire	79	B+
4. Washington	70	B
5. California	63	B–
Maine	63	B–
7. New York	59	C+
8. New Mexico	55	C+
9. Maryland	53	C
10. Oregon	46	C
11. Nevada	44	C–
Alaska	44	C–
13. Massachusetts	43	C–
New Jersey	43	C–
Colorado	43	C–
16. Texas	42	C–
17. Florida	41	C–
18. Utah	38	D+
19. Wyoming	37	D+
Minnesota	37	D+
21. Connecticut	36	D+
22. Illinois	34	D
23. Arizona	33	D
24. Virginia	32	D
Iowa	32	D
26. Oklahoma	30	D
Idaho	30	D
28. Kansas	29	D
Rhode Island	29	D
Missouri	29	D
31. Delaware	28	D
32. Georgia	27	D
West Virginia	27	D
34. Nebraska	26	D
Tennessee	26	D
North Carolina	26	D
37. Indiana	23	D–
Louisiana	23	D–
Mississippi	23	D–
40. South Carolina	22	D–
41. Ohio	21	D–
42. Kentucky	19	F
43. Montana	18	F
Alabama	18	F
45. Pennsylvania	16	F
46. North Dakota	14	F
Arkansas	14	F
48. Michigan	13	F
49. Wisconsin	11	F
50. South Dakota	0	F

10

Housing

The Big Question

Which state has the newest, largest, and most affordable homes?

The Categories

1. Housing Costs
2. Rent
3. Housing Age
4. Housing Size
5. Property Taxes

Housing Costs

DOING THE MATH

Our mission in this category was to find the place with the most affordable housing. We took the median value of all owner-occupied homes in each state, then divided that figure by the state's median household income. The result is a ratio of housing costs per $1,000 of income.

BEST STATES

Nowhere is housing more affordable than in Iowa. The median value of Iowa homes is $45,900, while the state's median household income is $26,229. That works out to $1,750 in housing costs per $1,000 of income, the best ratio in America. Indiana is the runner-up at $1,872.

WORST STATES

Most Hawaii residents can dream about owning a home, but they can't actually afford to do it. The median value of Hawaii houses is $245,300, which converts to $6,317 per $1,000 of household income. California, with a rate of $5,461, isn't much better.

REGIONAL WINNERS

East—West Virginia
South—Oklahoma
Midwest—Iowa
West—Wyoming

BIGGEST SURPRISE

Small and medium-sized states hold nine of the top 10 places in this category. The exception is one of America's largest states, Michigan, which ranks no. 5 in housing affordability.

THE BOTTOM LINE

The Midwest has a monopoly on affordable housing. Eight of the 10 best states in this category are midwestern.

154 Housing Costs

State	Housing Costs Per $1,000 of Household Income	Points
1. Iowa	$1,750	100
2. Indiana	1,872	100
3. Kansas	1,913	99
4. Nebraska	1,937	98
5. Michigan	1,954	98
6. South Dakota	2,009	96
7. Oklahoma	2,040	95
8. Wisconsin	2,123	93
9. North Dakota	2,188	91
10. Arkansas	2,189	91
11. Texas	2,206	91
12. Ohio	2,212	91
13. Kentucky	2,241	90
14. Mississippi	2,265	89
15. Missouri	2,268	89
16. Wyoming	2,273	89
17. Alabama	2,276	89
18. Alaska	2,280	89
19. West Virginia	2,303	88
20. Idaho	2,304	88
21. South Carolina	2,327	87
22. Utah	2,338	87
23. Tennessee	2,354	87
24. Minnesota	2,394	85
25. Pennsylvania	2,398	85
26. Georgia	2,457	84
27. Montana	2,462	84
Oregon	2,462	84
29. North Carolina	2,469	83
30. Illinois	2,508	82
31. Louisiana	2,665	78
32. Virginia	2,730	76
33. Colorado	2,744	76
34. Florida	2,805	74
35. Delaware	2,870	72
36. Arizona	2,908	71
37. New Mexico	2,910	71
38. Maryland	2,958	70
39. Washington	2,995	69
40. Nevada	3,086	66
41. Maine	3,138	65
42. Vermont	3,206	63
43. New Hampshire	3,562	53
44. New Jersey	3,966	42
45. New York	3,992	41
46. Rhode Island	4,148	37
47. Connecticut	4,262	33
48. Massachusetts	4,406	29
49. California	5,461	0
50. Hawaii	6,317	0

Rent

DOING THE MATH

Not everyone owns a home. Millions of Americans rent because they move too often, like the convenience when it comes to property maintenance, or just can't afford a mortgage. This category compares the median annual rent and median household income in each state. The answer is expressed as the rate of annual rent per $10,000 of income.

BEST STATES

Alabama is a renter's paradise. Median annual rent is only $2,748, while the state's median household income is $23,597. That equals $1,165 of rent for every $10,000 of income. Second place in renting affordability belongs to Iowa, with a rate of $1,194.

WORST STATES

The typical California renter shells out $6,732 a year to the landlord, the equivalent of $1,881 per $10,000 of median household income. Hawaii is next to last in this category. Its rate is $1,851 per $10,000.

REGIONAL WINNERS

East—West Virginia
South—Alabama
Midwest—Iowa
West—Wyoming

BIGGEST SURPRISE

Rents are exorbitant in large states such as California, Florida, Massachusetts, and New York. But Ohio (population 10.8 million) breaks the mold. It has the nation's sixth-most-affordable stock of rental units.

THE BOTTOM LINE

The Midwest is the home of four of this category's 10 best states. The West holds three slots, the South two, and the East one.

156 Rent

State	Annual Rent Per $10,000 of Household Income	Points
1. Alabama	$1,165	100
2. Iowa	1,194	100
3. Wyoming	1,196	100
4. Indiana	1,213	97
5. Utah	1,222	96
6. Ohio	1,237	93
7. Idaho	1,240	93
8. Kansas	1,253	91
9. South Carolina	1,261	90
10. West Virginia	1,275	88
11. North Carolina	1,279	87
12. Mississippi	1,281	87
13. Missouri	1,284	86
14. South Dakota	1,290	85
15. Nebraska	1,301	84
16. Arkansas	1,305	83
17. Montana	1,310	82
18. Oklahoma	1,318	81
19. Tennessee	1,321	81
20. Michigan	1,327	80
21. Pennsylvania	1,329	79
22. Kentucky	1,331	79
23. Wisconsin	1,349	76
24. Illinois	1,373	73
25. North Dakota	1,375	72
26. Louisiana	1,421	65
27. Georgia	1,422	65
28. Maryland	1,441	62
Colorado	1,441	62
30. Texas	1,457	60
31. Alaska	1,458	60
32. Delaware	1,462	59
33. Connecticut	1,467	58
34. Washington	1,474	57
35. Virginia	1,480	56
36. Minnesota	1,491	55
37. Oregon	1,515	51
38. Vermont	1,523	50
39. New Jersey	1,528	49
40. Maine	1,542	47
41. Rhode Island	1,551	46
42. New Mexico	1,554	45
43. New York	1,558	45
44. New Hampshire	1,582	41
45. Arizona	1,612	36
46. Massachusetts	1,643	32
47. Nevada	1,722	20
48. Florida	1,755	15
49. Hawaii	1,851	0
50. California	1,881	0

Housing Age

DOING THE MATH

Old houses can make wonderful homes. They can be exhilaratingly challenging to renovate. But they also can deteriorate beyond repair, becoming a major headache for the surrounding community. We decided to check the age of America's housing stock, looking for the state with the smallest proportion of homes built before 1940.

BEST STATES

The desert has bloomed in Nevada since the attack on Pearl Harbor. Casinos, resorts, and hotels have sprung up in what was wilderness just 50 years ago. And don't forget houses: Only 2.9 percent of Nevada's housing stock predates 1940. Three other states are below 4 percent: Alaska, Arizona, and Florida.

WORST STATES

The housing stock in Massachusetts is getting creaky. Fully 38.9 percent of its units were built before 1940, easily the highest percentage in the nation. Vermont is next to last at 36.5 percent.

REGIONAL WINNERS

East—Delaware
South—Florida
Midwest—Missouri
West—Nevada

BIGGEST SURPRISE

The East is America's oldest region, so you would expect it to have the oldest houses. That's why eastern states are confined to the bottom 20 of this category, with two exceptions. Delaware and Maryland are in 21st and 22nd places, respectively.

THE BOTTOM LINE

If you want a modern house, go to the West. Or to the South. It really doesn't matter, since each region has five states among the 10 leaders.

158 Housing Age

State	Homes Built Before 1940	Points
1. Nevada	2.9%	100
2. Alaska	3.0	100
3. Arizona	3.2	99
4. Florida	3.7	98
5. Hawaii	6.7	89
6. Texas	7.1	88
7. Georgia	8.1	85
New Mexico	8.1	85
9. South Carolina	8.5	84
10. Mississippi	8.6	83
11. Alabama	9.3	81
12. Arkansas	9.4	81
13. North Carolina	9.9	79
14. Tennessee	10.2	79
15. Louisiana	10.6	77
16. California	10.7	77
17. Virginia	11.0	76
18. Oklahoma	12.4	72
19. Colorado	13.0	70
20. Utah	13.5	69
21. Delaware	14.3	66
22. Maryland	15.5	63
23. Wyoming	15.6	62
24. Washington	15.7	62
25. Idaho	15.9	61
Kentucky	15.9	61
27. Oregon	16.8	59
28. Missouri	20.4	48
29. Michigan	20.8	47
30. Montana	21.8	44
31. West Virginia	23.7	38
32. Indiana	24.2	37
33. Kansas	24.5	36
Minnesota	24.5	36
35. New Jersey	24.6	36
36. North Dakota	24.7	35
37. Connecticut	25.5	33
38. Ohio	25.8	32
39. Illinois	27.1	28
New Hampshire	27.1	28
41. Wisconsin	28.5	24
42. South Dakota	30.4	18
43. Nebraska	30.7	17
44. Rhode Island	34.0	7
45. Maine	34.9	5
46. Iowa	35.0	4
47. Pennsylvania	35.1	4
48. New York	35.7	2
49. Vermont	36.5	0
50. Massachusetts	38.9	0

Housing Size

DOING THE MATH

Americans always seem to want more space. The early settlers trudged westward in search of cheap, plentiful land. Getting some additional elbow room, fortunately for us, is not nearly as difficult these days. Large homes can be found almost anywhere. This category measures each state's percentage of houses with four or more bedrooms.

BEST STATES

Large families are common in Utah; it's the only state with an average of more than three persons per housing unit. So it comes as no surprise that Utah has the nation's biggest inventory of large homes, 29.1 percent. The runner-up is Maryland, 21.4 percent.

WORST STATES

Small houses are the rule in Arkansas, where only 8.4 percent of all units have four or more bedrooms. Two other states are below 10 percent: Florida and Oklahoma.

REGIONAL WINNERS

East—Maryland
South—Virginia
Midwest—North Dakota
West—Utah

BIGGEST SURPRISE

Arkansas ranks 20th in the average number of persons per housing unit, so you would expect to find it in the middle of the pack in this category. But it's all the way down in last place.

THE BOTTOM LINE

The Midwest and West each placed four states among the top 12, while the East has three. The South, on the other hand, includes eight of the 10 worst states on this list.

160 Housing Size

State	Houses with 4 or More Bedrooms	Points
1. Utah	29.1%	100
2. Maryland	21.4	100
3. North Dakota	21.3	99
4. New Jersey	21.0	97
5. Colorado	20.7	94
Virginia	20.7	94
7. Vermont	20.5	93
8. Idaho	20.1	90
South Dakota	20.1	90
10. Minnesota	19.7	87
Nebraska	19.7	87
Wyoming	19.7	87
13. Delaware	19.6	86
14. Iowa	19.3	83
15. Montana	19.0	81
16. Connecticut	18.9	80
17. Pennsylvania	18.0	73
18. Massachusetts	17.6	70
19. Washington	17.4	69
20. Ohio	17.2	67
21. Maine	17.1	66
Wisconsin	17.1	66
23. Kansas	17.0	65
New Hampshire	17.0	65
25. New York	16.7	63
26. Michigan	15.5	54
27. Illinois	15.3	52
28. Indiana	14.8	48
29. Kentucky	14.2	43
30. Georgia	14.1	43
31. Oregon	14.0	42
32. West Virginia	13.8	40
33. California	13.7	39
Rhode Island	13.7	39
35. Missouri	13.6	39
36. Alaska	13.4	37
Hawaii	13.4	37
38. Tennessee	13.2	35
39. Alabama	12.5	30
Nevada	12.5	30
41. North Carolina	12.0	26
South Carolina	12.0	26
43. Mississippi	11.9	25
44. Arizona	11.7	24
45. Louisiana	11.2	20
46. Texas	10.9	17
47. New Mexico	10.8	17
48. Oklahoma	9.0	2
49. Florida	8.7	0
50. Arkansas	8.4	0

Property Taxes

DOING THE MATH

Every homeowner is well aware that the mortgage is not his or her only financial concern. There also is the little—sometimes not so little—matter of the property tax bill. We checked each state's property tax load, computing it as a per capita rate.

BEST STATES

Alabama fully deserves to be called a tax haven. Its property taxes work out to $163 per person, easily the lowest rate in America. New Mexico ranks no. 2 at $218. Five other states have property tax averages that fall below $300 per resident.

WORST STATES

The general cost of living in Alaska is expensive, so why would you expect taxes to be any different? Property taxes are a steep $1,246 per person. Next to last is New Hampshire, where property taxes equal $1,151 per resident. Three other states are above $1,000.

REGIONAL WINNERS

East—West Virginia
South—Alabama
Midwest—Missouri
West—New Mexico

BIGGEST SURPRISE

New Hampshire brags about not having a sales tax or an individual income tax. But why doesn't it ever mention property taxes? Because they're outlandishly high, topped only by Alaska.

THE BOTTOM LINE

The South traditionally believes in limiting governmental powers, including the power to tax. Eight of the 12 best states in this category are southern. Five of the 10 worst are eastern.

162 Property Taxes

State	Property Taxes Per Capita	Points
1. Alabama	$163	100
2. New Mexico	218	100
3. Arkansas	228	99
4. Kentucky	252	96
5. West Virginia	256	96
6. Louisiana	269	95
7. Oklahoma	277	94
8. Delaware	304	91
9. Tennessee	321	89
10. Mississippi	341	87
Missouri	341	87
12. North Carolina	353	86
13. Hawaii	384	82
14. South Carolina	401	80
15. Idaho	414	79
16. Nevada	425	78
17. Utah	432	77
18. Indiana	472	73
19. North Dakota	476	72
20. Georgia	494	70
21. Ohio	516	68
Pennsylvania	516	68
23. South Dakota	583	61
24. Washington	584	61
25. Maryland	590	60
26. Virginia	598	59
27. California	602	59
28. Florida	612	58
29. Arizona	636	55
30. Texas	651	54
31. Kansas	658	53
32. Iowa	660	53
33. Colorado	684	50
34. Minnesota	709	47
35. Maine	722	46
36. Wisconsin	738	44
37. Illinois	754	43
38. Nebraska	762	42
39. Massachusetts	778	40
40. Rhode Island	806	37
41. Michigan	820	35
42. Vermont	822	35
43. Montana	828	35
44. Oregon	854	32
45. Wyoming	901	27
46. New York	1,023	14
47. Connecticut	1,056	10
48. New Jersey	1,149	0
49. New Hampshire	1,151	0
50. Alaska	1,246	0

Housing: Scores and Grades

BEST STATE

Utah offers a wide selection of reasonably priced houses, earning this section's no. 1 ranking. No state has a higher percentage of homes with four or more bedrooms, and only four states have lower rents. Mortgages and property taxes in Utah are less expensive than the national average. And only 13.5 percent of the state's houses predate World War II.

RUNNERS-UP

Rental units are very reasonable, and the supply of large houses is plentiful. Those are the two main reasons that Idaho took second place in this section. The only other state to receive an A was Alabama, which has America's lowest rents and lightest property taxes.

WORST STATES

New York and Rhode Island are locked in a tie for last place. Both have the same problems: old housing stocks, steep mortgages, and high property taxes. Five other states also received F's.

REGIONAL WINNERS

East—Delaware
South—Alabama
Midwest—North Dakota
West—Utah

REGIONAL AVERAGES

East—32 (D)
South—70 (B)
Midwest—63 (B-)
West—55 (C+)

BIGGEST SURPRISE

Most eastern states did poorly in this section, but not no. 4 Delaware. It earned a B+, thanks to its low property taxes and its impressive inventory of large houses.

164 THE BOTTOM LINE

The South is the clear winner. It has the highest regional average in this section, and it can boast of five states in the top 10. Housing is worst in the East, which includes eight of the 10 bottom states.

Housing: Scores and Grades

State	Score	Grade
1. Utah	100	A+
2. Idaho	93	A
3. Alabama	89	A
4. Delaware	79	B+
5. Mississippi	78	B+
Tennessee	78	B+
7. Kentucky	77	B+
North Dakota	77	B+
South Carolina	77	B+
10. Wyoming	76	B+
11. North Carolina	74	B
Virginia	74	B
13. Indiana	72	B
Maryland	72	B
Arkansas	72	B
16. Colorado	71	B
17. Ohio	70	B
South Dakota	70	B
West Virginia	70	B
Missouri	70	B
21. Georgia	69	B
22. Kansas	68	B
Oklahoma	68	B
24. Iowa	66	B
25. Louisiana	64	B–
26. Nebraska	62	B–
27. Montana	61	B–
28. New Mexico	58	C+
Washington	58	C+
30. Michigan	56	C+
31. Minnesota	55	C+
Texas	55	C+
Pennsylvania	55	C+
34. Wisconsin	52	C
35. Nevada	49	C
36. Alaska	46	C
37. Arizona	45	C
38. Illinois	43	C–
39. Oregon	39	D+
40. Florida	30	D
41. Vermont	29	D
42. Maine	24	D–
43. New Jersey	22	D–
44. Connecticut	19	F
45. Hawaii	16	F
46. New Hampshire	8	F
47. California	4	F
48. Massachusetts	2	F
49. Rhode Island	0	F
New York	0	F

11

Education

The Big Question

Which state does the best job of educating its young people?

The Categories

1. High School Dropouts
2. High School Graduates
3. Standardized Tests
4. College Students
5. Education Spending

High School Dropouts

DOING THE MATH

It takes a simple three-step process to determine each state's high school dropout rate. Step no. 1: We count all of the 16-to-19-year-olds in a state. Step no. 2: We find out how many of them are neither high school graduates nor currently enrolled in school. Step no. 3: We divide the number of dropouts into the total number of teenagers age 16 and older.

BEST STATES

North Dakota has the nation's lowest dropout rate. Only about 1,700 of its 36,900 16-to-19-year-olds are not graduates or students. That's just 4.6 percent. The runner-up is next-door Minnesota, 6.4 percent.

WORST STATES

About 9,000 of Nevada's 59,900 16-to-19-year-olds are classified as dropouts. That equals a rate of 15.2 percent, the highest in America. Four other states are above 14 percent: Arizona, Florida, California, and Georgia.

REGIONAL WINNERS

East—Vermont
South—Virginia
Midwest—North Dakota
West—Wyoming

BIGGEST SURPRISE

California has a reputation for being an innovator in education, setting a pace that other states follow. But no one wants to emulate its severe dropout problem. Just three states have rates higher than California's 14.2 percent.

THE BOTTOM LINE

The Midwest places the greatest emphasis on keeping kids in school. That's the region where you will find six of the 10 states with the lowest dropout rates.

168 High School Dropouts

State	Persons Ages 16 to 19 Who Are Not in School and Are Not High School Graduates	Points
1. North Dakota	4.6%	100
2. Minnesota	6.4	100
3. Iowa	6.6	97
4. Wyoming	6.9	93
5. Nebraska	7.0	93
6. Wisconsin	7.1	91
7. Hawaii	7.5	86
8. South Dakota	7.7	83
9. Vermont	8.0	80
10. Montana	8.1	79
11. Maine	8.3	76
12. Massachusetts	8.5	74
13. Kansas	8.7	71
Utah	8.7	71
15. Ohio	8.9	69
16. Connecticut	9.0	67
17. Pennsylvania	9.1	66
18. New Hampshire	9.4	62
19. New Jersey	9.6	60
20. Colorado	9.8	58
21. New York	9.9	56
22. Michigan	10.0	55
Virginia	10.0	55
24. Delaware	10.4	50
Idaho	10.4	50
Oklahoma	10.4	50
27. Washington	10.6	48
Illinois	10.6	48
29. West Virginia	10.9	44
Alaska	10.9	44
Maryland	10.9	44
32. Rhode Island	11.1	42
33. Missouri	11.4	38
Indiana	11.4	38
Arkansas	11.4	38
36. South Carolina	11.7	34
New Mexico	11.7	34
38. Oregon	11.8	33
Mississippi	11.8	33
40. North Carolina	12.5	24
Louisiana	12.5	24
42. Alabama	12.6	23
43. Texas	12.9	19
44. Kentucky	13.3	14
45. Tennessee	13.4	13
46. Georgia	14.1	4
47. California	14.2	2
48. Florida	14.3	1
49. Arizona	14.4	0
50. Nevada	15.2	0

High School Graduates

DOING THE MATH

It stands to reason that an adult who has earned a high school diploma will be more likely to support local schools and to insist that his or her children hit the books. Our logical conclusion is that states with high graduation rates probably have the best systems of public education. This category seeks to identify those states by figuring out the percentage of persons age 25 and older who have high school diplomas.

BEST STATES

Alaska places the highest value on a high school education. Fully 86.6 percent of its adults have earned their diplomas. Second place belongs to Utah at 85.1 percent.

WORST STATES

Education is far from universal in Mississippi, where only 64.3 percent of all adults ever graduated from high school. That's the lowest rate in the country, topped only slightly by next-to-last Kentucky's 64.6 percent.

REGIONAL WINNERS

East—New Hampshire
South—Virginia
Midwest—Minnesota
West—Alaska

BIGGEST SURPRISE

The biggest surprise comes right at the top. Alaska has the image of being a raw, uncivilized wilderness. It actually has the nation's highest proportion of high school graduates.

THE BOTTOM LINE

The West clearly is the dominant region in this category. It sweeps the first five positions and holds seven of the top 11.

170 High School Graduates

State	Persons Age 25 or Older Who Are High School Graduates	Points
1. Alaska	86.6%	100
2. Utah	85.1	100
3. Colorado	84.4	97
4. Washington	83.8	94
5. Wyoming	83.0	90
6. Minnesota	82.4	87
7. New Hampshire	82.2	86
8. Nebraska	81.8	84
9. Oregon	81.5	82
10. Kansas	81.3	81
11. Montana	81.0	80
12. Vermont	80.8	79
13. Hawaii	80.1	76
Iowa	80.1	76
15. Massachusetts	80.0	75
16. Idaho	79.7	74
17. Connecticut	79.2	71
18. Maine	78.8	69
Nevada	78.8	69
20. Arizona	78.7	69
21. Wisconsin	78.6	68
22. Maryland	78.4	67
23. Delaware	77.5	63
24. South Dakota	77.1	61
25. Michigan	76.8	60
26. New Jersey	76.7	59
North Dakota	76.7	59
28. California	76.2	57
Illinois	76.2	57
30. Ohio	75.7	54
31. Indiana	75.6	54
32. Virginia	75.2	52
33. New Mexico	75.1	51
34. New York	74.8	50
35. Pennsylvania	74.7	49
36. Oklahoma	74.6	49
37. Florida	74.4	48
38. Missouri	73.9	45
39. Texas	72.1	37
40. Rhode Island	72.0	36
41. Georgia	70.9	31
42. North Carolina	70.0	26
43. Louisiana	68.3	18
South Carolina	68.3	18
45. Tennessee	67.1	12
46. Alabama	66.9	11
47. Arkansas	66.3	8
48. West Virginia	66.0	7
49. Kentucky	64.6	0
50. Mississippi	64.3	0

Standardized Tests

DOING THE MATH

College-bound high school seniors generally take one of two standardized admissions tests. The American College Test (ACT), the exam of choice in 28 states, is scored from one to 36 points. The Scholastic Assessment Test (SAT), formerly called the Scholastic Aptitude Test, which is favored in 22 states, is graded from 400 to 1,600 points. The scoring scales used by ACT and SAT are so different that it is impossible directly to compare their results. This category converts each state's average score on its dominant test to a 100-point scale, allowing direct comparisons.

BEST STATES

Iowa and Wisconsin lead the way on the ACT, with mean scores of 20.1. Washington has the best SAT performance, averaging 939. All three states earn 100 points on our index. Just slightly behind is New Hampshire.

WORST STATES

Mississippi is no. 50 with an average ACT score of 15.9, which translates to 78.01 on our index. North Carolina is next to last.

REGIONAL WINNERS

East—New Hampshire
South—Virginia
Midwest—Iowa, Wisconsin
West—Washington

BIGGEST SURPRISE

Students in most midwestern states do well on standardized tests. Indiana, which ranks 43rd, is the glaring exception.

THE BOTTOM LINE

The Midwest and West ran a dead heat in this category, each with five states among the 11 leaders. The South dominates the bottom end, with eight of the 11 worst states.

172 Standardized Tests

State	Standardized Test Index	Points
1. Iowa	100.00	100
Washington	100.00	100
Wisconsin	100.00	100
4. New Hampshire	98.70	93
5. Montana	98.43	92
6. Minnesota	97.91	89
7. Oregon	97.77	88
8. Colorado	97.38	86
Nebraska	97.38	86
10. South Dakota	96.34	81
Wyoming	96.34	81
12. Maryland	95.36	76
13. Idaho	94.76	73
Kansas	94.76	73
Ohio	94.76	73
16. Connecticut	94.25	70
17. Arizona	94.24	70
Missouri	94.24	70
Nevada	94.24	70
20. California	93.88	68
21. Utah	93.72	67
22. Massachusetts	93.69	67
Vermont	93.69	67
24. Delaware	93.32	65
25. Illinois	93.19	64
26. Virginia	93.14	64
27. North Dakota	92.67	62
28. Maine	92.21	59
29. Michigan	92.15	59
30. Rhode Island	91.84	57
31. New Jersey	91.65	56
32. New York	90.91	52
33. Hawaii	90.54	50
34. Florida	90.35	50
35. Pennsylvania	90.17	49
36. Texas	88.50	40
37. Alabama	88.48	40
Alaska	88.48	40
Tennessee	88.48	40
40. Kentucky	87.96	37
New Mexico	87.96	37
42. Oklahoma	87.43	34
43. Indiana	87.38	34
44. Arkansas	86.91	32
45. West Virginia	85.86	26
46. Louisiana	84.29	18
47. Georgia	82.93	11
48. South Carolina	81.26	2
49. North Carolina	80.89	0
50. Mississippi	78.01	0

College Students

DOING THE MATH

We wanted to see how much emphasis each state places on higher education. An easy (and obvious) way to get the answer is to compare college enrollment figures. We took the total number of students in all colleges—two-year and four-year, public and private—and converted it to a rate per 100,000 residents.

BEST STATES

Massachusetts includes roughly 536,000 college students in its population of 6 million. That means it has 8,919 students among every 100,000 residents, the highest rate in the nation. Rhode Island is close behind with 8,904 per 100,000.

WORST STATES

America's weakest rate of university enrollment is found in Arkansas, which has just 5,203 college students for every 100,000 residents. West Virginia is next to last at 5,426.

REGIONAL WINNERS

East—Massachusetts
South—Virginia
Midwest—Michigan
West—California

BIGGEST SURPRISE

Maine does reasonably well at the high school level; it is among the 20 states with the fewest dropouts and the highest graduation rates. But college is a different story: Maine does no better than 44th in this category.

THE BOTTOM LINE

It's a narrow victory for the East, with five states in the top 10. The West holds four of the remaining slots, the Midwest one. The South, on the other hand, has six of the 10 worst states.

174 College Students

State	College Students Per 100,000 Residents	Points
1. Massachusetts	8,919	100
2. Rhode Island	8,904	100
3. California	8,710	94
4. Utah	8,537	89
5. Colorado	8,118	77
6. Arizona	8,091	77
7. New York	8,000	74
8. Michigan	7,738	66
9. Maryland	7,680	65
10. Delaware	7,674	65
11. Kansas	7,552	61
12. North Dakota	7,522	60
13. Nebraska	7,480	59
14. Hawaii	7,459	58
15. Minnesota	7,452	58
16. Illinois	7,425	57
17. Wyoming	7,409	57
18. Connecticut	7,390	56
19. New Mexico	7,268	53
20. Vermont	7,262	53
21. Iowa	7,125	49
22. Virginia	7,123	49
23. Wisconsin	7,106	48
24. Texas	7,059	47
25. Oregon	7,030	46
26. Alaska	7,001	45
27. Oklahoma	6,975	45
28. New Hampshire	6,954	44
29. Washington	6,927	43
30. New Jersey	6,706	37
31. North Carolina	6,634	35
32. Idaho	6,633	35
33. Ohio	6,625	34
34. Missouri	6,589	33
35. Indiana	6,570	33
36. Pennsylvania	6,480	30
37. Alabama	6,401	28
38. Florida	6,301	25
39. Montana	6,286	25
40. Louisiana	6,238	23
41. South Carolina	6,164	21
42. Nevada	6,148	21
43. Mississippi	6,138	20
44. Maine	6,008	17
45. South Dakota	5,970	16
46. Georgia	5,839	12
47. Kentucky	5,750	9
48. Tennessee	5,731	9
49. West Virginia	5,426	0
50. Arkansas	5,203	0

Education Spending

DOING THE MATH

A presidential commission warned in 1983 that the entire nation had been placed at risk because of the poor quality of America's schools. One of the panel's recommendations was that education funding should be strengthened. Did anyone take the hint? We looked at the amount annually spent on public schools by each state and all of its localities. That combined total is expressed as a per capita rate.

BEST STATES

It is costly to maintain a public school system across an area as vast as Alaska, which leads the nation with education spending of $2,265 per resident. Second place goes to Wyoming, with per capita school funding of $1,726.

WORST STATES

Public schools in Tennessee must get by on just $884 per capita, the stingiest education allowance in the country. Neighboring Kentucky parcels out only $917 per resident.

REGIONAL WINNERS

East—Vermont
South—Virginia
Midwest—North Dakota
West—Alaska

BIGGEST SURPRISE

North Dakota is far from being a rich state, ranking 40th in per capita income. But it still believes in providing for its public schools. Just five states have higher rates of education spending.

THE BOTTOM LINE

Three regions are roughly equal in this category. The East has four states among the top 10, while the Midwest and West have three apiece.

176 Education Spending

State	Per Capita Education Spending by State and Local Governments	Points
1. Alaska	$2,265	100
2. Wyoming	1,726	100
3. Vermont	1,511	73
4. Delaware	1,434	64
5. New York	1,413	61
6. North Dakota	1,329	51
7. Minnesota	1,319	50
8. Wisconsin	1,317	49
9. Oregon	1,298	47
10. New Jersey	1,297	47
11. Washington	1,275	44
12. Michigan	1,274	44
13. Nebraska	1,243	40
14. Connecticut	1,238	40
15. Iowa	1,236	39
16. New Mexico	1,233	39
17. Virginia	1,222	38
18. Colorado	1,220	37
19. Arizona	1,216	37
20. Rhode Island	1,192	34
21. Kansas	1,191	34
Maine	1,191	34
Utah	1,191	34
24. California	1,189	34
25. Maryland	1,186	33
26. Montana	1,182	33
27. Texas	1,142	28
28. North Carolina	1,137	27
29. South Carolina	1,133	27
30. Indiana	1,130	26
31. Pennsylvania	1,111	24
32. New Hampshire	1,099	22
33. Ohio	1,095	22
34. Georgia	1,080	20
35. Illinois	1,036	15
36. Florida	1,035	15
37. Alabama	1,024	13
38. Massachusetts	1,021	13
39. Nevada	1,018	12
40. Oklahoma	1,015	12
41. Hawaii	1,005	11
42. South Dakota	996	10
43. Idaho	990	9
44. West Virginia	980	8
45. Louisiana	979	8
Mississippi	979	8
47. Missouri	969	6
48. Arkansas	921	0
49. Kentucky	917	0
50. Tennessee	884	0

Education: Scores and Grades

BEST STATE

Wyoming places a high priority on public education, and the result is the no. 1 ranking in this section. Only Alaska spends proportionately more on its schools. Wyoming is among the five states with the fewest dropouts (just 6.9 percent) and the best high school graduation rates (83.0 percent). And it ranks a respectable 10th in standardized test scores.

RUNNERS-UP

Minnesota is the only state with a straight A in this section. It has America's second-lowest dropout rate, and its students do well on standardized tests. Six states, including three in the Midwest, received grades of A–.

WORST STATES

Mississippi and Kentucky have different weaknesses but the same outcomes. They are tied for last place in this section. Mississippi has the nation's worst high school graduation rate and its lowest standardized test scores. Kentucky is next to last in the High School Graduates and Education Spending categories. Eight other states also earned F's.

REGIONAL WINNERS

East—Vermont
South—Virginia
Midwest—Minnesota
West—Wyoming

REGIONAL AVERAGES

East—59 (C+)
South—16 (F)
Midwest—65 (B)
West—65 (B)

BIGGEST SURPRISE

The biggest surprise in this section has to be the first-place finish by Wyoming. It outperformed several midwestern states known for their strong school systems.

178 THE BOTTOM LINE

It's another draw between the Midwest and West, each with five states among the 12 best. The bottom of the list belongs almost entirely to the South, home of nine of the 10 states that received F's.

Education: Scores and Grades

State	Score	Grade
1. Wyoming	100	A+
2. Minnesota	90	A
3. Nebraska	84	A–
4. Iowa	83	A–
Utah	83	A–
6. Wisconsin	82	A–
Colorado	82	A–
8. Vermont	81	A–
9. North Dakota	75	B+
Alaska	75	B+
Massachusetts	75	B+
Washington	75	B+
13. Kansas	72	B
14. Montana	69	B
15. Delaware	68	B
New Hampshire	68	B
Connecticut	68	B
18. Oregon	65	B
New York	65	B
20. Maryland	62	B–
Michigan	62	B–
22. Hawaii	61	B–
23. Rhode Island	58	C+
24. New Jersey	55	C+
Virginia	55	C+
26. California	54	C
Maine	54	C
28. Arizona	53	C
Ohio	53	C
South Dakota	53	C
31. Idaho	50	C
Illinois	50	C
33. Pennsylvania	44	C–
34. New Mexico	43	C–
35. Missouri	37	D+
36. Oklahoma	36	D+
37. Indiana	35	D+
38. Nevada	31	D
Texas	31	D
40. Florida	22	D–
41. Alabama	15	F
42. North Carolina	14	F
43. South Carolina	12	F
44. Louisiana	9	F
45. West Virginia	7	F
46. Georgia	5	F
Arkansas	5	F
48. Tennessee	4	F
49. Mississippi	0	F
Kentucky	0	F

12

Applied Intelligence

The Big Question

Which state makes the best use of its collective brain power?

The Categories

1. College Graduates
2. Doctoral Degrees
3. Patents
4. Research and Development
5. MacArthur Fellows

College Graduates

DOING THE MATH

The future belongs to areas with highly educated work forces. That's what the experts tell us. So we decided to see which states are best positioned in that regard. This category looks at each state's percentage of adults (age 25 or older) who have bachelor's degrees.

BEST STATES

First place is held jointly by two neighbors, Connecticut and Massachusetts. Exactly 27.2 percent of the adults in both states are college graduates. Next in line is Colorado at 27 percent even.

WORST STATES

West Virginia has a dearth of college-educated workers. Only 12.3 percent of its adults have met all the requirements for bachelor's degrees. Three other states are below 15 percent: Arkansas, Kentucky, and Mississippi.

REGIONAL WINNERS

East—Connecticut, Massachusetts
South—Virginia
Midwest—Minnesota
West—Colorado

BIGGEST SURPRISE

Iowa earned an A– in the Education section, but that impressive grade doesn't translate to success in *higher* education. Only 16.9 percent of its adults have college degrees, putting Iowa in 40th place in this category.

THE BOTTOM LINE

The East places the greatest emphasis on college education. It holds seven of the top 10 slots on this list. The South, on the other hand, includes seven of the 10 worst states.

182 College Graduates

State	Persons Age 25 or Older Who Are College Graduates	Points
1. Connecticut	27.2%	100
Massachusetts	27.2	100
3. Colorado	27.0	99
4. Maryland	26.5	95
5. New Jersey	24.9	83
6. Virginia	24.5	81
7. New Hampshire	24.4	80
8. Vermont	24.3	79
9. California	23.4	73
10. New York	23.1	71
11. Alaska	23.0	70
12. Hawaii	22.9	69
Washington	22.9	69
14. Utah	22.3	65
15. Minnesota	21.8	61
16. Delaware	21.4	58
17. Rhode Island	21.3	58
18. Kansas	21.1	56
19. Illinois	21.0	55
20. Oregon	20.6	53
21. New Mexico	20.4	51
22. Arizona	20.3	50
Texas	20.3	50
24. Montana	19.8	47
25. Georgia	19.3	43
26. Nebraska	18.9	40
27. Maine	18.8	40
Wyoming	18.8	40
29. Florida	18.3	36
30. North Dakota	18.1	35
31. Pennsylvania	17.9	33
32. Missouri	17.8	32
Oklahoma	17.8	32
34. Idaho	17.7	32
Wisconsin	17.7	32
36. Michigan	17.4	29
North Carolina	17.4	29
38. South Dakota	17.2	28
39. Ohio	17.0	27
40. Iowa	16.9	26
41. South Carolina	16.6	24
42. Louisiana	16.1	20
43. Tennessee	16.0	19
44. Alabama	15.7	17
45. Indiana	15.6	17
46. Nevada	15.3	14
47. Mississippi	14.7	10
48. Kentucky	13.6	2
49. Arkansas	13.3	0
50. West Virginia	12.3	0

Doctoral Degrees

DOING THE MATH

Advanced scientific research is conducted almost exclusively by persons who already hold or are completing work toward their doctorates. We counted the number of doctoral degrees awarded annually in each state in the physical and life sciences as well as engineering. These fields cover the spectrum from mathematics and computer sciences to chemistry and earth sciences. State totals were converted to rates per 1 million residents.

BEST STATES

Massachusetts Institute of Technology and Harvard University are just two of the colleges that guarantee Massachusetts a steady supply of doctoral candidates. The state's annual output is 176 doctoral degrees per million residents. Rhode Island is the runner-up, with 122 per million.

WORST STATES

Alaska annually awards just 15 doctoral degrees per million residents. Nevada and Maine are the only other states that have rates below 20.

REGIONAL WINNERS

East—Massachusetts
South—North Carolina
Midwest—Iowa
West—Utah

BIGGEST SURPRISE

Only five states have proportionately fewer adults with bachelor's degrees than Indiana. That's why it's so surprising to see Indiana rank no. 8 here, with an impressive annual rate of 92 doctoral degrees per million residents.

THE BOTTOM LINE

The East has five states in this category's top 10. The other five slots are split between the Midwest (three) and the West (two).

184 Doctoral Degrees

State	Doctoral Degrees Awarded in Physical/Life Sciences and Engineering Per Million Residents	Points
1. Massachusetts	176	100
2. Rhode Island	122	100
3. Iowa	112	90
4. Utah	109	88
5. Colorado	108	86
6. Delaware	104	82
7. Maryland	96	75
8. Indiana	92	71
9. New York	91	70
10. Illinois	88	67
11. Wisconsin	87	67
12. Connecticut	83	63
13. Minnesota	80	60
14. New Mexico	79	59
North Carolina	79	59
Arizona	79	59
17. Wyoming	77	57
18. Oregon	75	55
19. Kansas	71	52
20. California	70	51
21. Pennsylvania	69	50
Michigan	69	50
23. Washington	67	48
Texas	67	48
25. Ohio	64	45
26. Virginia	63	44
27. Nebraska	61	42
North Dakota	61	42
29. Missouri	56	37
Idaho	56	37
31. Oklahoma	54	35
Louisiana	54	35
33. New Jersey	50	31
34. Montana	49	30
35. New Hampshire	45	27
36. Vermont	44	26
Georgia	44	26
38. Hawaii	42	24
Alabama	42	24
40. Tennessee	41	23
41. South Carolina	40	22
42. Mississippi	36	18
43. Florida	32	14
44. Arkansas	28	11
45. Kentucky	27	9
46. West Virginia	23	6
47. South Dakota	20	3
48. Maine	19	2
49. Nevada	17	0
50. Alaska	15	0

Patents

DOING THE MATH

America's creative minds never stop working. Just ask the U.S. Patent and Trademark Office, which issues patents for more than 52,000 inventions and original designs annually. That's about 1,000 every week. We broke down this national total, counting the number of patents granted to persons in each state. Those figures are expressed as rates per 100,000 residents.

BEST STATES

DuPont Co., the petrochemical giant, is based in Delaware. That goes a long way toward explaining the state's leading role in the research and development of new industrial processes. Delaware annually receives 65.2 patents per 100,000 residents. Connecticut takes second place in this category, with a rate of 46.0 per 100,000.

WORST STATES

Mississippi's 2.5 million residents come up with fewer than 130 patented inventions in a typical year. The resulting rate of 5.0 patents per 100,000 is the nation's lowest. South Dakota is next to last at 5.9.

REGIONAL WINNERS

East—Delaware
South—Oklahoma
Midwest—Minnesota
West—California

BIGGEST SURPRISE

Look right at the top of the list. Tiny Delaware outpaces all of the major industrial states in terms of inventive genius.

THE BOTTOM LINE

The East is the region that most vigorously pursues patents. Six of its states are in this category's top 10. The Midwest holds three slots, the West one.

186 Patents

State	Patents Granted Per 100,000 Residents	Points
1. Delaware	65.2	100
2. Connecticut	46.0	100
3. New Jersey	40.0	85
4. Massachusetts	35.1	73
5. Minnesota	33.7	69
6. New Hampshire	29.6	59
7. Michigan	29.1	58
8. California	26.6	52
9. Vermont	25.8	50
10. Illinois	25.7	49
11. Colorado	25.2	48
12. New York	25.1	48
Ohio	25.1	48
14. Wisconsin	24.9	47
15. Pennsylvania	23.7	44
16. Oregon	22.5	41
17. Utah	21.4	39
18. Arizona	20.1	35
Oklahoma	20.1	35
20. Washington	19.5	34
21. Indiana	18.9	32
Idaho	18.9	32
23. Texas	18.7	32
24. Maryland	18.6	32
25. Rhode Island	18.0	30
26. Florida	14.7	22
27. Iowa	14.0	20
28. Missouri	13.7	19
29. Virginia	13.3	18
30. Kansas	13.2	18
31. New Mexico	13.1	18
32. North Carolina	12.8	17
33. Louisiana	12.0	15
34. South Carolina	11.7	14
35. Tennessee	11.5	14
36. Georgia	11.2	13
37. Nevada	10.6	12
38. Nebraska	9.3	9
West Virginia	9.3	9
40. Maine	9.2	8
41. Montana	9.0	8
42. Alabama	8.8	7
43. Kentucky	8.4	6
44. Wyoming	7.9	5
45. North Dakota	7.8	5
46. Hawaii	7.6	4
47. Arkansas	6.3	1
48. Alaska	6.2	1
49. South Dakota	5.9	0
50. Mississippi	5.0	0

DOING THE MATH

Much of the scientific research and development work in this country is funded by the federal government. We looked at where that money is channeled, measuring annual federal R&D obligations to government agencies, universities, and private laboratories in each state. Obligations are defined as the value of research orders placed, contracts awarded, and services received by the government. State totals were converted to per capita rates.

BEST STATES

The atomic bomb was developed half a century ago in New Mexico, whose laboratories still attract more than $2 billion a year in federal R&D obligations. That works out to $1,466 per resident, the most favorable rate in the nation. The only other state above $1,000 is Maryland.

WORST STATES

Research and development subsidies are a minuscule $73 million in Kentucky, equal to $20 per person. South Dakota is next to last with a rate of $22.

REGIONAL WINNERS

East—Maryland
South—Virginia
Midwest—Missouri
West—New Mexico

BIGGEST SURPRISE

New Mexico's dominance in this category is surprising to those who are unfamiliar with the work done at places like Los Alamos and White Sands.

THE BOTTOM LINE

The West is the most effective region at attracting federal research and development funds. Five of its states are in the national top 10. The East holds three slots among the leaders, the South two.

188 Research and Development

State	Federal Obligations for Research and Development Per Capita	Points
1. New Mexico	$1,466	100
2. Maryland	1,014	100
3. California	535	52
4. Colorado	491	47
5. Massachusetts	479	46
6. Virginia	449	43
7. Alabama	408	39
8. Washington	363	34
9. Nevada	356	34
10. Rhode Island	313	29
11. Utah	301	28
12. Missouri	243	22
13. Idaho	195	17
14. Texas	188	17
15. Connecticut	182	16
16. Ohio	179	16
17. Florida	175	15
18. New Jersey	171	15
19. Pennsylvania	165	14
20. New York	161	14
21. Arizona	137	12
Minnesota	137	12
23. Alaska	130	11
24. Tennessee	118	10
25. Vermont	107	9
26. New Hampshire	88	7
Hawaii	88	7
28. North Carolina	85	6
Wyoming	85	6
30. Illinois	80	6
31. Mississippi	77	6
32. Michigan	74	5
33. Indiana	71	5
34. Iowa	69	5
35. South Carolina	64	4
36. Georgia	61	4
37. Oregon	59	4
38. West Virginia	58	4
39. Maine	55	3
40. Wisconsin	54	3
41. North Dakota	52	3
Kansas	52	3
43. Delaware	48	3
44. Montana	45	2
45. Louisiana	43	2
46. Oklahoma	37	2
47. Nebraska	32	1
48. Arkansas	24	0
49. South Dakota	22	0
50. Kentucky	20	0

MacArthur Fellows

DOING THE MATH

Several unsuspecting Americans are informed each year that they have won large financial awards from the John D. and Catherine T. MacArthur Foundation. These five-year, six-figure stipends are commonly called "genius grants" because they are given in recognition of outstanding academic and creative accomplishments. This category counts how many MacArthur fellows were chosen from each state during the program's first 15 years, expressed as a rate per 1 million residents.

BEST STATES

Fifty-one residents of Massachusetts were named MacArthur fellows in the period of 1978–1992, which works out to 8.48 per million residents. That more than doubles the rate of the no. 2 state, New York, which has 4.06 winners per million.

WORST STATES

Ten states still are waiting for their first MacArthur fellowships. The largest concentration of these shutouts, five states, can be found in the West.

REGIONAL WINNERS

East—Massachusetts
South—North Carolina
Midwest—South Dakota
West—New Mexico

BIGGEST SURPRISE

Sparsely populated South Dakota is the top non-eastern state in this category, ranking sixth overall. It has had two MacArthur fellows, which equals 2.87 per million residents.

THE BOTTOM LINE

The MacArthur Foundation is in Chicago, but it leans toward the East. Seven of the 10 leading states in this category are eastern.

190 MacArthur Fellows

State	MacArthur Fellows (1978–1992) Per Million Residents	Points
1. Massachusetts	8.48	100
2. New York	4.06	100
3. Rhode Island	3.99	98
4. Vermont	3.55	87
5. Connecticut	3.35	82
6. South Dakota	2.87	71
7. New Jersey	2.85	70
8. New Hampshire	2.71	67
9. New Mexico	2.64	65
10. California	2.22	55
11. Illinois	1.92	47
12. Arizona	1.91	47
13. Delaware	1.50	37
14. Maryland	1.46	36
15. Montana	1.25	31
16. Utah	1.16	29
17. Iowa	1.08	27
18. North Carolina	1.06	26
19. Michigan	0.97	24
20. Mississippi	0.78	19
21. Indiana	0.72	18
22. Virginia	0.65	16
23. Washington	0.62	15
24. Colorado	0.61	15
25. Pennsylvania	0.59	15
Missouri	0.59	15
27. Texas	0.53	13
28. Louisiana	0.47	12
29. Georgia	0.46	11
Minnesota	0.46	11
31. Arkansas	0.43	10
32. Tennessee	0.41	10
33. Kansas	0.40	10
34. Oregon	0.35	9
35. Oklahoma	0.32	8
36. Kentucky	0.27	7
37. Alabama	0.25	6
38. Florida	0.23	6
39. Wisconsin	0.20	5
40. Ohio	0.18	5
41. Alaska	0.00	0
Hawaii	0.00	0
Idaho	0.00	0
Maine	0.00	0
Nebraska	0.00	0
Nevada	0.00	0
North Dakota	0.00	0
South Carolina	0.00	0
West Virginia	0.00	0
Wyoming	0.00	0

Applied Intelligence: Scores and Grades

BEST STATE

The brain power in Massachusetts is unmatched by any other state, as clearly demonstrated by its overwhelming victory in this section. Massachusetts won three of the five categories; no state has higher proportions of college graduates, doctoral candidates, or MacArthur fellows. It also ranks no. 4 in getting patents and no. 5 in federal research and development funding.

RUNNERS-UP

Second-ranked Connecticut has its own reasons to brag. It is tied with Massachusetts for the highest percentage of college graduates, and only Delaware tops it in qualifying for patents. One other state received a grade in the A range, Maryland.

WORST STATES

No. 50 West Virginia has America's smallest rate of college graduates, and it never has won a MacArthur fellowship. Kentucky and Arkansas are tied for next-to-last place.

REGIONAL WINNERS

East—Massachusetts
South—Virginia
Midwest—Illinois
West—Colorado, New Mexico

REGIONAL AVERAGES

East—58 (C+)
South—19 (F)
Midwest—32 (D)
West—39 (D+)

BIGGEST SURPRISE

New Mexico is the national leader in obtaining research and development funding, and it also has won a respectable share of MacArthur fellowships. The result? Sixth place overall.

THE BOTTOM LINE

America's brains are concentrated at its regional extremes. The East includes seven of the 10 states that received A's or B's in this section, while the West has the other three. The bottom of the list is dominated by the South, home of eight states with F's.

Applied Intelligence: Scores and Grades

State	Score	Grade
1. Massachusetts	100	A+
2. Connecticut	86	A
3. Maryland	80	A–
4. Rhode Island	74	B
5. New York	71	B
6. Colorado	69	B
New Mexico	69	B
8. New Jersey	66	B
California	66	B
10. Delaware	65	B
11. Vermont	58	C+
Utah	58	C+
13. New Hampshire	55	C+
14. Illinois	51	C
15. Minnesota	49	C
16. Arizona	46	C
Virginia	46	C
18. Washington	45	C
19. Iowa	37	D+
Michigan	37	D+
21. Oregon	36	D+
22. Texas	35	D+
23. Pennsylvania	34	D
Wisconsin	34	D
25. Indiana	31	D
Ohio	31	D
27. Kansas	30	D
North Carolina	30	D
29. Missouri	26	D
30. Idaho	25	D
Montana	25	D
32. Oklahoma	23	D–
33. Wyoming	22	D–
34. Hawaii	21	D–
South Dakota	21	D–
36. Georgia	20	D–
37. Florida	19	F
38. Alabama	18	F
Nebraska	18	F
40. North Dakota	17	F
41. Louisiana	16	F
Alaska	16	F
43. Tennessee	14	F
44. South Carolina	11	F
45. Nevada	10	F
46. Maine	9	F
Mississippi	9	F
48. Kentucky	1	F
Arkansas	1	F
50. West Virginia	0	F

13

Arts

The Big Question

Which state has the richest blend of artists of all types?

The Categories

1. Arts Funding
2. Theater
3. Dance
4. Entertainers
5. Museums and Galleries

Arts Funding

DOING THE MATH

Few of the arts are self-sustaining. It usually takes public money to keep philharmonic orchestras playing, community theaters functioning, and art museums open. We looked at each state's annual appropriation to arts agencies, converting it to a rate per 100,000 residents.

BEST STATES

The Hawaii legislature's annual arts allocation is more than $12 million, which translates to an impressive $1,088,899 per 100,000 residents. No other state even comes close to this high level of commitment. New York holds second place with a rate of $283,385 per 100,000.

WORST STATES

Arts agencies know better than to expect much from the Texas legislature, which appropriates a paltry $19,933 per 100,000 residents. Mississippi is the only other state to fall below $20,000.

REGIONAL WINNERS

East—New York
South—Florida
Midwest—Ohio
West—Hawaii

BIGGEST SURPRISE

West Virginia, which ranks 49th in per capita income, has little money to spare. But it digs deep for the arts. Just nine states make proportionately larger appropriations.

THE BOTTOM LINE

The East is the region that believes most strongly in public support for the arts. Six of the top 10 states are eastern. Five of the bottom 10 states, on the other hand, are from the South.

196 Arts Funding

State	State Appropriations for State Arts Agencies Per 100,000 Residents	Points
1. Hawaii	$1,088,899	100
2. New York	283,385	100
3. Alaska	260,364	91
4. Utah	248,636	87
5. Massachusetts	209,840	72
6. Delaware	197,147	67
7. Florida	180,754	61
8. Maryland	155,658	52
9. New Jersey	151,397	50
10. West Virginia	132,962	43
11. Ohio	111,828	35
12. South Carolina	104,187	32
13. Oklahoma	101,558	31
14. Rhode Island	100,698	31
15. Pennsylvania	98,502	30
16. Michigan	98,462	30
17. Montana	97,622	29
18. Minnesota	96,297	29
19. Illinois	90,526	27
20. Kentucky	89,607	26
21. Tennessee	88,148	26
22. Missouri	87,551	26
23. Vermont	85,080	25
24. North Carolina	81,883	24
25. Wyoming	77,313	22
26. New Mexico	73,861	20
27. Connecticut	66,839	18
28. Nebraska	66,413	18
29. Idaho	66,038	17
30. Virginia	64,910	17
31. Maine	61,482	16
32. South Dakota	58,190	15
33. California	56,983	14
34. Arizona	56,426	14
35. Oregon	54,082	13
36. Georgia	51,528	12
37. Indiana	50,722	12
38. Wisconsin	49,509	11
39. Washington	49,230	11
40. New Hampshire	46,799	10
41. Colorado	46,630	10
42. Iowa	44,977	9
43. Kansas	43,261	9
44. North Dakota	42,879	9
45. Arkansas	41,387	8
46. Alabama	39,074	7
47. Nevada	29,867	4
48. Louisiana	22,180	1
49. Mississippi	19,977	0
50. Texas	19,933	0

Theater

DOING THE MATH

Any mention of live theater causes most people to think of Broadway or the active theater districts in Chicago and Los Angeles. Those are the pinnacles of the acting profession, to be sure, but they are not the extent of it. The Census Bureau counts 4,435 theatrical organizations throughout the United States. We translated each state's total into a rate per 1 million residents.

BEST STATES

It's no surprise to find New York in first place. It has 1,006 theatrical producers and services, almost one-quarter of the nation's total. That works out to a rate of 55.9 per 1 million residents. The elaborate stage shows in Las Vegas are largely responsible for Nevada's no. 2 ranking.

WORST STATES

You have to search far and wide to find live theater in Mississippi. The state has only nine theatrical producers and services, equal to 3.5 per million. Louisiana is next to last at 4.3.

REGIONAL WINNERS

East—New York
South—Tennessee
Midwest—Minnesota
West—Nevada

BIGGEST SURPRISE

Only four states have more than 30 theatrical organizations per 1 million residents. You would expect to find New York, Nevada, and California in that group. But the fourth member is a surprise: Vermont.

THE BOTTOM LINE

Live theater is a matter of bicoastal interest. Five of the top 10 states are eastern, while four are western.

198 Theater

State	Theatrical Producers and Services Per Million Residents	Points
1. New York	55.9	100
2. Nevada	39.1	100
3. California	32.0	80
4. Vermont	30.2	74
5. Hawaii	28.0	68
6. Alaska	25.5	61
7. New Hampshire	24.3	58
8. Tennessee	22.1	51
9. Connecticut	21.3	49
10. Delaware	21.0	48
11. Rhode Island	19.9	45
Minnesota	19.9	45
13. Oregon	18.3	40
14. New Jersey	18.0	39
15. Nebraska	17.7	39
16. Montana	17.5	38
Washington	17.5	38
18. Maine	17.1	37
19. Massachusetts	17.0	36
20. Illinois	16.4	35
21. Colorado	15.5	32
22. Wyoming	15.4	32
23. Florida	13.9	28
24. Missouri	13.5	26
25. Wisconsin	12.1	22
26. Georgia	11.7	21
27. Maryland	11.3	20
28. New Mexico	11.2	20
29. Pennsylvania	10.7	18
30. Utah	10.4	18
Arizona	10.4	18
Texas	10.4	18
33. Virginia	10.3	17
34. South Dakota	10.1	17
35. Michigan	9.5	15
36. North Dakota	9.4	15
37. Ohio	9.0	14
38. Oklahoma	7.9	10
39. Indiana	7.8	10
40. North Carolina	7.7	10
41. Iowa	7.2	8
42. Kentucky	7.1	8
43. Kansas	6.9	7
44. Arkansas	6.8	7
45. Idaho	6.0	5
46. South Carolina	5.2	2
47. West Virginia	5.0	2
48. Alabama	4.9	2
49. Louisiana	4.3	0
50. Mississippi	3.5	0

Dance

DOING THE MATH

The Census Bureau, which knows about such things, says there are exactly 4,018 dance studios, schools, and halls across the country. They teach everything from the most demanding ballet to the most unstructured modern dance. This category expresses each state's number of dance centers as a rate per 1 million residents.

BEST STATES

Footloose Rhode Island is the dancing capital of the United States. Its residents have their choice of 26 dance studios, schools, and halls, equal to 25.9 per million residents. New Jersey is the only other state with a rate above 25.

WORST STATES

Dancing has not captured the fancy of people in North Dakota. Their state has just two dance centers. That's 3.1 per million, easily the lowest figure in the nation. Mississippi is next to last, with a rate of 7.0.

REGIONAL WINNERS

East—Rhode Island
South—Alabama
Midwest—Iowa
West—Utah

BIGGEST SURPRISE

Utah has the reputation of being a strait-laced, conventional state, but its residents actually love to dance. Utah has 24.4 dance studios, schools, and halls per million residents, good for third place nationally.

THE BOTTOM LINE

The East is in a dancing mood, with five of this category's 10 leaders. Four of the 10 worst states are in the West; three are in the South.

200 Dance

State	Dance Studios, Schools, and Halls Per Million Residents	Points
1. Rhode Island	25.9	100
2. New Jersey	25.1	100
3. Utah	24.4	96
4. Connecticut	23.1	89
Vermont	23.1	89
6. Iowa	21.6	81
7. Alabama	21.5	80
8. South Carolina	21.2	79
9. Delaware	21.0	77
10. Kansas	20.2	73
11. Alaska	20.0	72
12. New Hampshire	19.8	71
13. New York	19.7	70
14. Nebraska	19.6	70
15. Massachusetts	19.3	68
16. Virginia	19.2	68
17. Minnesota	19.0	66
18. Florida	18.4	63
19. North Carolina	18.3	62
20. Missouri	18.0	61
21. Texas	17.6	59
22. Kentucky	16.8	54
23. Georgia	16.7	53
24. New Mexico	16.5	52
25. Indiana	15.5	47
Maryland	15.5	47
27. Ohio	15.0	44
Washington	15.0	44
29. Pennsylvania	14.9	44
30. Wisconsin	14.7	43
31. Colorado	14.0	38
32. Arizona	13.9	38
33. Oklahoma	13.4	35
34. Wyoming	13.2	34
35. Louisiana	13.0	33
36. Idaho	12.9	33
37. California	12.8	32
38. Illinois	12.4	30
Michigan	12.4	30
40. Maine	12.2	29
41. Arkansas	11.9	27
42. Oregon	11.6	25
43. Tennessee	11.5	25
44. Montana	10.0	17
Nevada	10.0	17
46. Hawaii	9.9	16
47. West Virginia	9.5	14
48. South Dakota	7.2	1
49. Mississippi	7.0	0
50. North Dakota	3.1	0

Entertainers

DOING THE MATH

Entertainer is a vague word; it can be used to describe just about anyone who gets on stage with the hope of receiving applause or laughter. The Census Bureau keeps count of professional entertainers and entertainment groups, ranging from full orchestras to small comedy troupes. This category takes each state's total and converts it to a rate per 1 million residents.

BEST STATES

Nevada, with its large resorts and casinos, has a steady need for entertainers. Most of the big-name performers fly in from New York or Los Angeles. But Nevada also has an excellent supply of in-state talent, 66.6 entertainers and entertainment groups per million, the nation's best rate. Second place belongs to California.

WORST STATES

West Virginia is not an entertaining state. Not with just 2.8 entertainment groups per million. Mississippi is next to last at 4.3.

REGIONAL WINNERS

East—New York
South—Tennessee
Midwest—Wisconsin
West—Nevada

BIGGEST SURPRISE

Wisconsin is not heralded as one of America's entertainment centers, but it's among just seven states that have rates above 20. The rest of the Midwest, including much larger Illinois, Ohio, and Michigan, is behind.

THE BOTTOM LINE

It's a three-way tie. The East, Midwest, and West each have three states in the top 10. The South has the fewest entertainers, placing four states in the bottom 10.

202 Entertainers

State	Entertainers and Entertainment Groups Per Million Residents	Points
1. Nevada	66.6	100
2. California	58.4	100
3. New York	42.3	70
4. Tennessee	36.3	59
5. Hawaii	28.0	44
6. Rhode Island	20.9	31
7. Wisconsin	20.4	30
8. Missouri	19.9	29
9. Nebraska	19.6	28
10. Connecticut	18.9	27
11. New Jersey	18.5	26
12. Illinois	16.3	22
13. Minnesota	16.2	22
14. Colorado	15.2	20
15. Oregon	14.8	19
16. Vermont	14.2	18
Washington	14.2	18
18. South Dakota	12.9	16
19. Alaska	12.7	16
20. New Hampshire	12.6	15
Iowa	12.6	15
Arizona	12.6	15
23. Massachusetts	12.0	14
24. New Mexico	11.9	14
25. Pennsylvania	11.5	13
Virginia	11.5	13
27. Montana	11.3	13
28. Florida	11.2	13
29. Utah	9.9	10
30. Maine	9.8	10
31. Maryland	9.6	10
Indiana	9.6	10
33. Louisiana	9.5	10
Texas	9.5	10
35. Michigan	9.1	9
36. Kentucky	9.0	9
37. North Carolina	8.9	9
Oklahoma	8.9	9
39. Ohio	8.3	7
40. Arkansas	8.1	7
41. Kansas	7.7	6
42. Delaware	7.5	6
43. Georgia	7.1	5
44. Idaho	7.0	5
45. Alabama	6.7	4
46. South Carolina	4.9	1
47. North Dakota	4.7	1
48. Wyoming	4.4	0
49. Mississippi	4.3	0
50. West Virginia	2.8	0

Museums and Galleries

DOING THE MATH

America's heritage, both historical and artistic, can be found in the nation's 2,800 museums and art galleries. This category includes metropolitan museums that display priceless masterworks, as well as small galleries devoted to contemporary regional artists. Each state's number of museums and galleries is expressed as a rate per 1 million residents.

BEST STATES

No state has done more to showcase its history and culture than South Dakota, which has 25 museums and art galleries. That's the equivalent of 35.9 per million. Two other states have rates above 30: Vermont and Maine.

WORST STATES

Museums and galleries are few and far between in Mississippi, which has only 10. Its rate is a scant 3.9 per million. West Virginia is next to last at 5.0.

REGIONAL WINNERS

East—Vermont
South—Tennessee
Midwest—South Dakota
West—Montana

BIGGEST SURPRISE

The biggest surprise in this category is the way it is dominated by small states, led by South Dakota. We don't find a state with more than 4 million residents until no. 11 Massachusetts.

THE BOTTOM LINE

The East has a longer history than the other three regions, so it follows that the East is more interested in preserving its heritage. It has six states in the top 10. The Midwest and West have two each.

204 Museums and Galleries

State	Museums and Art Galleries Per Million Residents	Points
1. South Dakota	35.9	100
2. Vermont	33.7	100
3. Maine	30.9	90
4. Montana	27.5	79
5. Rhode Island	23.9	66
6. Hawaii	23.5	64
7. Connecticut	22.8	62
8. New Hampshire	22.5	61
Delaware	22.5	61
10. North Dakota	21.9	59
11. Massachusetts	20.3	53
12. Alaska	20.0	52
13. Wyoming	19.8	52
14. New York	18.2	46
Kansas	18.2	46
16. Colorado	17.0	42
17. Minnesota	14.6	34
18. Oregon	14.4	33
Iowa	14.4	33
20. Nebraska	13.9	31
21. Idaho	12.9	28
22. Ohio	12.8	27
23. New Mexico	12.5	26
24. Wisconsin	12.3	25
25. Tennessee	11.9	24
26. Arizona	11.5	23
27. Virginia	11.3	22
28. North Carolina	11.2	21
29. Louisiana	11.1	21
30. Indiana	10.6	20
Pennsylvania	10.6	20
32. Maryland	10.5	19
33. Texas	9.5	16
34. Missouri	9.4	15
Arkansas	9.4	15
36. Washington	9.2	15
South Carolina	9.2	15
38. California	8.6	13
39. Illinois	8.4	12
40. Kentucky	7.9	10
41. Oklahoma	7.6	9
42. Nevada	7.5	9
43. Florida	7.3	8
44. Georgia	6.9	7
Michigan	6.9	7
46. New Jersey	6.5	5
47. Utah	5.2	1
Alabama	5.2	1
49. West Virginia	5.0	0
50. Mississippi	3.9	0

Arts: Scores and Grades

BEST STATE

The arts are alive in New York, which not only holds first place in this section, but also earned the only A. New York offers the most exciting variety of live theater in America and ranks no. 2 in state support for the arts and no. 3 in quantity of entertainers. Even its worst category rankings are the envy of most states: 13th in Dance and 14th in Museums and Galleries.

RUNNERS-UP

An impressive array of museums and art galleries is the primary reason for Vermont's second-place finish in this section. It is also among the top five states in theater and dance. There is a third-place tie between Alaska and Hawaii. Both fund their arts agencies generously.

WORST STATES

Who else but Mississippi would be last in this section? It's the natural choice, having finished last or next to last in all five categories. Three other states received F's: West Virginia, Arkansas, and Louisiana.

REGIONAL WINNERS

East—New York
South—Tennessee
Midwest—Minnesota
West—Alaska, Hawaii

REGIONAL AVERAGES

East—57 (C+)
South—27 (D)
Midwest—36 (D+)
West—46 (C)

BIGGEST SURPRISE

California, which fancies itself to be the world's creative center, does no better than ninth in this section. It is weak in the areas of dance and museums, and it gives relatively little financial support to the arts.

206 THE BOTTOM LINE

The arts are most popular on the two coasts. Six of this section's top 10 states are eastern; the other four are western. The South dominates the bottom 10 with six entries.

Arts: Scores and Grades

State	Score	Grade
1. New York	100	A+
2. Vermont	79	B+
3. Alaska	76	B+
Hawaii	76	B+
5. Rhode Island	71	B
6. Delaware	67	B
7. Connecticut	63	B–
Massachusetts	63	B–
9. California	62	B–
10. Nevada	59	C+
11. New Jersey	57	C+
12. New Hampshire	56	C+
13. Utah	55	C+
14. Minnesota	51	C
15. Nebraska	48	C
Tennessee	48	C
17. Maine	47	C
18. Montana	46	C
19. Florida	45	C
20. Missouri	41	C–
21. South Dakota	39	D+
22. Maryland	38	D+
Iowa	38	D+
24. Colorado	37	D+
Kansas	37	D+
26. Wyoming	36	D+
27. Virginia	35	D+
28. New Mexico	34	D
Wisconsin	34	D
Oregon	34	D
31. South Carolina	33	D
Ohio	33	D
Illinois	33	D
North Carolina	33	D
Washington	33	D
36. Pennsylvania	32	D
37. Arizona	28	D
Kentucky	28	D
39. Texas	26	D
Indiana	26	D
41. Georgia	25	D
42. Alabama	24	D–
Oklahoma	24	D–
Michigan	24	D–
45. Idaho	23	D–
46. North Dakota	22	D–
47. Louisiana	17	F
Arkansas	17	F
49. West Virginia	15	F
50. Mississippi	0	F

14

Communications

The Big Question

Which state has the best system for transmitting information, using both the spoken and printed word?

The Categories

1. Telephone Service
2. Cable Television
3. Broadcasting Stations
4. Newspaper Circulation
5. Library Spending

Telephone Service

DOING THE MATH

The telephone is the closest thing we have to a universal, two-way communications device. But its wires don't extend to everybody. Some people can't afford a phone; a few don't want one. This category looks at the reach of each state's telephone network, computing the percentage of homes without phone service.

BEST STATES

The nation's most comprehensive telephone system can be found in Massachusetts, where only 2.1 percent of all households lack phones. Five other states have rates below 3 percent: Minnesota, Connecticut, Hawaii, Pennsylvania, and Wisconsin.

WORST STATES

Poverty is so extensive in Mississippi that thousands of people are unable to pay monthly phone bills. That's the major reason why 12.6 percent of Mississippi households are without telephones, the worst rate in the nation. New Mexico is the only other state above 11 percent.

REGIONAL WINNERS

East—Massachusetts
South—Florida
Midwest—Minnesota
West—Hawaii

BIGGEST SURPRISE

Money does not guarantee universal telephone service. New York and Alaska both have high per capita incomes, but they do poorly in this category. New York is 16th, Alaska 38th.

THE BOTTOM LINE

Telephone systems are most extensive in the East, which placed six states among the top 10. The biggest service gaps can be found in the South, with seven of the 10 worst states.

210 Telephone Service

State	Dwelling Units Without Telephones	Points
1. Massachusetts	2.1%	100
2. Minnesota	2.4	100
3. Connecticut	2.6	98
Hawaii	2.6	98
Pennsylvania	2.6	98
6. Wisconsin	2.8	96
7. California	3.0	94
8. Delaware	3.1	93
New Jersey	3.1	93
Rhode Island	3.1	93
11. Maryland	3.2	92
12. Iowa	3.4	90
New Hampshire	3.4	90
14. North Dakota	3.5	89
Washington	3.5	89
16. Nebraska	3.6	88
17. Maine	3.7	87
18. Utah	4.0	84
19. Michigan	4.1	83
20. Colorado	4.2	82
21. Kansas	4.4	80
22. Oregon	4.5	79
Vermont	4.5	79
24. Illinois	4.6	78
25. Ohio	4.7	77
26. New York	5.0	74
27. Missouri	5.2	72
28. Florida	5.3	71
29. Nevada	5.4	70
Virginia	5.4	70
31. Wyoming	5.6	68
32. Idaho	5.8	66
33. Indiana	5.9	65
34. South Dakota	6.0	64
35. Montana	6.9	55
36. North Carolina	7.1	53
Tennessee	7.1	53
38. Alaska	8.3	41
Georgia	8.3	41
Louisiana	8.3	41
41. Arizona	8.5	39
42. Texas	8.6	38
43. Alabama	8.7	37
44. Oklahoma	8.8	36
45. South Carolina	9.1	33
46. Kentucky	10.2	22
47. West Virginia	10.3	21
48. Arkansas	10.9	15
49. New Mexico	12.4	0
50. Mississippi	12.6	0

Cable Television

DOING THE MATH

Cable television offers Americans an unprecedented variety of quality news and entertainment programs. It also, of course, has greatly expanded the number of mindless sitcoms available with a click of the remote control. Some cable operations now carry 100 channels; futurists predict that a 500-channel system is not too far away. This category measures cable TV's power by figuring each state's rate of basic cable subscribers per 100,000 residents.

BEST STATES

Cable television is ubiquitous in Delaware, which counts 266,400 subscribers among its population of 666,000. That translates to 39,998 subscribers per 100,000 residents. Hawaii is second at 30,840.

WORST STATES

Cable has not met wide acceptance in Utah, which actually has fewer subscribers than Delaware (236,900) despite having nearly triple the population. Its rate is 13,753 per 100,000. Alaska is next to last.

REGIONAL WINNERS

East—Delaware
South—Florida
Midwest—Nebraska
West—Hawaii

BIGGEST SURPRISE

Residents of Illinois, Wisconsin, and Minnesota have the money, but they apparently lack the desire for cable television. These three adjoining states can be found in 44th through 46th places.

THE BOTTOM LINE

It's not surprising that seven of the top 10 states are in the urban East, where it is most cost-effective to extend cable service. The less densely populated Midwest and West each have four states among the bottom 10.

212 Cable Television

State	Basic Cable Subscribers Per 100,000 Residents	Points
1. Delaware	39,998	100
2. Hawaii	30,840	100
3. New Hampshire	29,108	88
4. Connecticut	28,827	86
5. Rhode Island	27,028	73
6. Pennsylvania	26,407	68
7. Wyoming	26,247	67
8. Florida	25,447	61
9. New Jersey	25,446	61
10. Massachusetts	25,329	60
11. Nevada	25,179	59
12. West Virginia	24,956	58
13. Nebraska	23,803	49
14. Washington	23,214	45
15. Maine	22,703	41
16. Ohio	22,410	39
17. Virginia	22,285	38
18. North Dakota	21,990	36
19. Kentucky	21,822	35
20. Kansas	21,677	34
21. Colorado	21,647	34
22. Oregon	21,586	33
23. Michigan	21,501	33
24. Louisiana	21,037	29
25. Arkansas	20,901	29
26. Iowa	20,884	28
27. Georgia	20,880	28
28. Tennessee	20,846	28
29. Oklahoma	20,637	27
30. North Carolina	20,615	26
31. Maryland	20,450	25
32. California	20,421	25
33. Montana	20,413	25
34. Alabama	20,404	25
35. South Dakota	20,010	22
36. Indiana	19,864	21
37. South Carolina	19,796	21
38. New Mexico	19,776	20
39. New York	19,649	20
40. Vermont	19,630	19
41. Idaho	19,565	19
42. Missouri	19,158	16
43. Arizona	18,628	12
44. Illinois	18,421	11
45. Wisconsin	17,892	7
46. Minnesota	17,438	4
47. Mississippi	17,304	3
48. Texas	17,064	1
49. Alaska	16,937	0
50. Utah	13,753	0

Broadcasting Stations

DOING THE MATH

Surveys show that more Americans get their news from television than from any other medium. Radio also is flexing its muscles these days, as controversial talk shows reach audiences of record proportions. We counted the TV and radio stations in each state, converting the number of outlets into a rate per 100,000 residents.

BEST STATES

Wyoming has 68 radio and 12 television stations, an impressive total for a state whose population is only 454,000. Its rate of 17.6 broadcasting outlets per 100,000 residents is the best in America. Just a shade behind is second-place Alaska at 17.5.

WORST STATES

New Jersey, sandwiched between the massive New York City and Philadelphia media markets, never developed much of a broadcasting industry. It has only 1.5 television and radio stations for every 100,000 residents. California is next to last with a rate of 2.4.

REGIONAL WINNERS

East—Vermont
South—Arkansas
Midwest—South Dakota
West—Wyoming

BIGGEST SURPRISE

New York and California, the homes of the national networks, are America's media giants. But they have surprisingly few radio and television stations for states of their size. Both are among the three worst entries in this category.

THE BOTTOM LINE

The wide, open West has the nation's most impressive array of broadcasting stations relative to population. Five western states are in the top 10.

214 Broadcasting Stations

State	Radio and Television Stations Per 100,000 Residents	Points
1. Wyoming	17.6	100
2. Alaska	17.5	100
3. Montana	15.5	87
South Dakota	15.5	87
5. North Dakota	13.8	76
6. Vermont	11.2	58
7. Idaho	10.7	55
8. Arkansas	10.5	54
9. New Mexico	10.2	52
10. Mississippi	9.9	50
11. Maine	9.4	47
12. Nebraska	9.3	45
13. West Virginia	9.0	44
14. Iowa	8.5	40
Kentucky	8.5	40
16. Alabama	7.7	35
17. Tennessee	7.4	33
18. Kansas	7.3	32
19. Oregon	7.1	31
20. South Carolina	6.9	29
21. Hawaii	6.8	29
22. Nevada	6.7	28
23. Colorado	6.5	27
24. New Hampshire	6.4	26
25. Oklahoma	6.2	25
North Carolina	6.2	25
27. Georgia	6.1	25
Wisconsin	6.1	25
Minnesota	6.1	25
30. Missouri	6.0	24
31. Utah	5.7	22
Louisiana	5.7	22
33. Indiana	5.1	18
34. Washington	4.9	17
Virginia	4.9	17
36. Texas	4.7	15
37. Arizona	4.4	13
38. Michigan	4.1	11
39. Pennsylvania	3.9	10
40. Florida	3.8	9
41. Ohio	3.7	9
42. Delaware	3.6	8
43. Illinois	3.5	7
44. Rhode Island	3.4	6
45. Massachusetts	3.2	5
Connecticut	3.2	5
47. Maryland	2.7	2
48. New York	2.6	1
49. California	2.4	0
50. New Jersey	1.5	0

Newspaper Circulation

DOING THE MATH

So much is said about the ascendancy of television that you would assume no one reads anymore. Not true. More than 59 million newspapers are sold from coast to coast every day. This category adds up the weekday circulations of all daily papers printed in each state, then converts that figure to a rate per 1,000 residents.

BEST STATES

Newspapers are still influential in Colorado, where 1.02 million copies are sold each day. That works out to daily circulation of 310 papers per 1,000 residents, the best showing in America. Massachusetts is at virtually the same level with a rate of 309.

WORST STATES

Much of Maryland depends on the two dailies from Washington, D.C., which cut into the sales of in-state papers. The result is the nation's worst circulation rate, 148 per 1,000. Mississippi is next to last at 156.

REGIONAL WINNERS

East—Massachusetts
South—Florida
Midwest—Nebraska
West—Colorado

BIGGEST SURPRISE

Utah is one of the nation's most literate states; only Alaska has a higher percentage of high school graduates. But newspaper sales lag in Utah, putting it 48th in this category.

THE BOTTOM LINE

America's most avid readers are in the East and Midwest, each with four states in the top 10. Newspaper sales are weakest in the South, with eight of the bottom 10 states.

216 Newspaper Circulation

State	Daily Newspaper Circulation Per 1,000 Residents	Points
1. Colorado	310	100
2. Massachusetts	309	100
3. Nebraska	297	92
4. North Dakota	291	88
5. New York	289	87
6. Rhode Island	285	84
7. Indiana	270	74
8. Pennsylvania	268	73
9. Alaska	264	70
10. Iowa	256	66
11. Connecticut	255	65
12. Ohio	251	62
13. Idaho	247	60
14. Washington	244	57
Florida	244	57
16. Michigan	243	57
17. South Dakota	242	56
18. Oregon	238	54
19. West Virginia	237	53
Montana	237	53
21. Oklahoma	236	53
22. Illinois	229	48
Vermont	229	48
24. Wisconsin	228	47
25. Minnesota	218	41
26. Hawaii	217	40
Maine	217	40
28. Nevada	216	39
Delaware	216	39
California	216	39
31. North Carolina	214	38
32. Kansas	212	37
33. New Jersey	211	36
34. New Hampshire	209	35
35. Wyoming	207	34
36. New Mexico	206	33
37. Missouri	203	31
38. Arizona	200	29
39. Texas	192	23
40. Alabama	185	19
41. South Carolina	183	18
Tennessee	183	18
43. Georgia	181	17
Virginia	181	17
45. Kentucky	179	15
Arkansas	179	15
47. Louisiana	174	12
48. Utah	168	8
49. Mississippi	156	0
50. Maryland	148	0

Library Spending

DOING THE MATH

Public libraries offer a wide selection of books to everyone, whether young or old, high school dropout or college graduate, inner city dweller or small town resident. This category measures each state's commitment to such an ideal. It adds the spending on libraries by the state and all its local governments, with the combined total expressed as a per capita rate.

BEST STATES

Alaska is far and away the most generous state with its libraries, allocating almost $20 million a year for a rate of $36.18 per resident. Connecticut has the best record in the lower 48, with library spending of $28.10 per capita.

WORST STATES

Mississippi has five times the population of Alaska, but its library allocation is smaller ($14.7 million a year). That's just $5.73 per resident. The other states with rates below $8 are Arkansas and West Virginia.

REGIONAL WINNERS

East—Connecticut
South—Virginia
Midwest—Indiana
West—Alaska

BIGGEST SURPRISE

Nevada, the land of roulette wheels and slot machines, also has a bookish side. It ranks no. 4 in library spending, with an impressive per capita rate of $23.99.

THE BOTTOM LINE

Library spending is highest in the East and West. Both regions hold four positions among this category's 10 leaders. Eight of the 10 worst states are in the South.

218 Library Spending

State	Annual State and Local Government Library Expenditures Per Capita	Points
1. Alaska	$36.18	100
2. Connecticut	28.10	100
3. Washington	25.46	87
4. Nevada	23.99	80
5. Maryland	23.84	80
6. Massachusetts	23.71	79
7. New York	23.53	78
8. Wyoming	23.30	77
9. Indiana	22.43	73
10. Illinois	22.15	71
11. Wisconsin	21.53	68
12. Arizona	21.20	67
13. Virginia	21.06	66
14. New Jersey	21.01	66
15. Hawaii	19.82	60
16. Colorado	18.87	56
17. California	18.75	55
18. Iowa	18.55	54
19. Minnesota	18.42	54
20. Oregon	17.01	47
21. New Hampshire	16.47	44
22. Ohio	16.01	42
23. Utah	15.86	41
24. Rhode Island	15.65	40
25. South Dakota	14.81	36
26. North Carolina	14.11	33
27. Michigan	14.03	33
28. Florida	13.88	32
29. New Mexico	12.89	27
30. Missouri	12.59	26
Nebraska	12.59	26
32. Louisiana	12.56	25
33. Kansas	12.42	25
34. Idaho	12.33	24
35. Maine	12.20	24
36. Vermont	12.05	23
37. Montana	11.71	21
38. South Carolina	10.14	14
39. Delaware	10.02	13
40. North Dakota	9.98	13
41. Kentucky	9.69	12
42. Oklahoma	9.56	11
43. Texas	9.11	9
44. Pennsylvania	8.39	5
45. Alabama	8.23	5
46. Georgia	8.13	4
47. Tennessee	8.01	4
48. West Virginia	7.26	0
49. Arkansas	7.25	0
50. Mississippi	5.73	0

Communications: Scores and Grades

BEST STATE

News and ideas are transmitted most easily in Connecticut, which has America's best communications system. Only Alaska spends more on its libraries; just two states have telephone networks that reach a higher percentage of homes. Connecticut also is strong in the telecast and print forms of mass communications. It ranks no. 4 in cable television penetration and no. 11 in newspaper circulation.

RUNNERS-UP

Wyoming and Massachusetts, tied for second place, reached that position in different ways. Wyoming's strength is broadcasting; it has the nation's best proportion of television and radio stations. Massachusetts has the most extensive telephone system and is no. 2 in daily newspaper readership.

WORST STATES

Mississippi is buried in last place in this section. No state spends less on its libraries or has a higher percentage of homes without telephones. And only Maryland has lower newspaper circulation than Mississippi. Texas is the other state that earned an F.

REGIONAL WINNERS

East—Connecticut
South—Florida
Midwest—North Dakota
West—Wyoming

REGIONAL AVERAGES

East—69 (B)
South—27 (D)
Midwest—63 (B–)
West—65 (B)

BIGGEST SURPRISE

Many residents of Wyoming and Alaska live in isolation. Those two states have the lowest population densities in America. But they have compensated by developing excellent communications systems, both earning A's.

220 THE BOTTOM LINE

Ten states scored in the A range in this section; five are western. The South nearly recorded a clean sweep at the bottom end of this list. It has nine of the 10 worst states.

Communications: Scores and Grades

State	Score	Grade
1. Connecticut	100	A+
2. Wyoming	97	A
Massachusetts	97	A
4. Hawaii	91	A
5. Alaska	86	A
6. North Dakota	83	A–
7. Nebraska	82	A–
Colorado	82	A–
9. Rhode Island	81	A–
10. Washington	80	A–
11. New Hampshire	76	B+
12. Iowa	75	B+
13. Nevada	74	B
14. South Dakota	70	B
15. New York	69	B
16. New Jersey	67	B
Pennsylvania	67	B
18. Delaware	66	B
Indiana	66	B
20. Oregon	63	B–
Wisconsin	63	B–
22. Montana	62	B–
Maine	62	B–
24. Florida	59	C+
25. Ohio	58	C+
Vermont	58	C+
27. Idaho	57	C+
28. Minnesota	56	C+
29. Michigan	54	C
Illinois	54	C
31. California	53	C
32. Kansas	51	C
Virginia	51	C
34. Maryland	49	C
35. West Virginia	41	C–
North Carolina	41	C–
37. Missouri	39	D+
38. Arizona	36	D+
39. Utah	34	D
40. Oklahoma	33	D
41. Tennessee	27	D
42. New Mexico	26	D
43. Louisiana	25	D
44. Kentucky	24	D–
45. Alabama	23	D–
46. Georgia	21	D–
South Carolina	21	D–
48. Arkansas	20	D–
49. Texas	11	F
50. Mississippi	0	F

15

Sports

The Big Question

Which state is most strongly involved in athletics at the amateur and professional levels?

The Categories

1. High School Athletes
2. College Champions
3. Olympic Athletes
4. Professional Champions
5. Spectator Seats

High School Athletes

DOING THE MATH

More than 5.4 million American high school students defend their schools' honor through sports. Football, with 912,000 athletes, is the most popular game with boys, followed by basketball (518,000). Girls are most likely to compete at basketball (392,000) or track and field (359,000). This category counts the number of high school athletes in each state, expressing it as a rate per 100,000 residents.

BEST STATES

Basketball, track and field, and volleyball are the favorite sports in Alaska, where 29,448 students participate in interscholastic athletics. That works out to 5,354 high school athletes among every 100,000 residents, the best rate in the nation. Iowa is the only other state with a rate above 5,000.

WORST STATES

High school sports receive little emphasis in Florida, which has just 1,163 participants per 100,000 residents. Next to last is Kentucky at 1,416.

REGIONAL WINNERS

East—Vermont
South—Texas
Midwest—Iowa
West—Alaska

BIGGEST SURPRISE

Florida is noted for the quality of its high school football, but its other sports programs are surprisingly low-profile. No other state has a smaller ratio of high school athletes to residents, partly the result of Florida's large elderly population.

THE BOTTOM LINE

The Midwest is the heartland of high school athletics, with five states in the top 10. The South dominates the bottom of this list, placing six in the bottom 10.

224 High School Athletes

State	High School Sports Participants Per 100,000 Residents	Points
1. Alaska	5,354	100
2. Iowa	5,031	100
3. Nebraska	4,468	84
4. South Dakota	4,199	77
5. North Dakota	4,048	73
6. Montana	3,908	69
7. Vermont	3,817	66
8. Wyoming	3,777	65
9. Maine	3,625	61
10. Kansas	3,602	60
11. Idaho	3,578	60
12. Washington	3,138	48
13. Oregon	3,050	45
14. Wisconsin	3,048	45
15. Delaware	2,867	40
16. Texas	2,824	39
Michigan	2,824	39
18. New Hampshire	2,747	37
19. Minnesota	2,740	37
20. Arkansas	2,697	35
21. Colorado	2,653	34
22. Missouri	2,595	33
23. Ohio	2,528	31
24. Indiana	2,470	29
25. Utah	2,322	25
26. New Jersey	2,291	24
27. Massachusetts	2,256	23
28. Connecticut	2,247	23
29. Illinois	2,212	22
30. Nevada	2,156	20
31. New Mexico	2,111	19
32. Oklahoma	2,079	18
33. Rhode Island	1,950	15
34. Tennessee	1,927	14
35. Hawaii	1,861	12
Louisiana	1,861	12
37. Arizona	1,845	12
38. Pennsylvania	1,777	10
39. Alabama	1,734	9
40. South Carolina	1,731	9
41. Virginia	1,726	9
42. West Virginia	1,710	8
43. New York	1,621	6
44. North Carolina	1,581	5
45. Georgia	1,580	5
46. Mississippi	1,571	4
47. California	1,552	4
48. Maryland	1,515	3
49. Kentucky	1,416	0
50. Florida	1,163	0

College Champions

DOING THE MATH

We wanted to know which state has had the most success in college sports, so we consulted the records of the National Collegiate Athletic Association. We counted every NCAA champion in 21 sports, ranging from football to field hockey, over a 10-year period (1983–1992). Both men's and women's sports were included. Each state's results were translated into a rate of national championships per 100 colleges.

BEST STATES

Utah, which has only 15 colleges, nonetheless took 12 national championships during the study period, including five titles alone in skiing. Its resulting rate is 80 championships per 100 colleges. Second place goes to Arkansas, a powerhouse in track and field.

WORST STATES

Five states did not win a single national college sports title during the decade: Alaska, Idaho, New Mexico, Rhode Island, and South Dakota.

REGIONAL WINNERS

East—West Virginia
South—Arkansas
Midwest—North Dakota
West—Utah

BIGGEST SURPRISE

California's colleges easily led the country with 85 national championships during the decade; Texas was the runner-up with 27. But it was a different story when the raw totals were converted to rates, as California was outpaced by six much smaller states.

THE BOTTOM LINE

The South, with four states in the top 10, has a slight edge in college sports. The West has three states among the leaders, the Midwest two, and the East one.

226 College Champions

State	National Sports Champions Per 100 Colleges, 1983–1992	Points
1. Utah	80.0	100
2. Arkansas	48.6	100
3. Louisiana	38.9	80
4. North Dakota	35.0	72
5. West Virginia	32.1	66
6. Wisconsin	31.1	64
7. California	27.4	56
8. Oklahoma	18.8	39
9. Arizona	18.4	38
10. Virginia	18.1	37
11. Florida	16.8	35
12. Texas	15.7	32
13. Iowa	15.5	32
14. North Carolina	15.2	31
15. Nebraska	14.7	30
16. Alabama	13.8	28
17. Vermont	13.6	28
18. Hawaii	13.3	27
19. Massachusetts	11.2	23
20. Nevada	11.1	23
Wyoming	11.1	23
22. Mississippi	10.9	22
23. Maryland	10.5	22
Washington	10.5	22
25. Delaware	10.0	21
26. Kentucky	9.7	20
27. Georgia	9.5	19
28. Oregon	8.7	18
29. Connecticut	8.5	18
New Jersey	8.5	18
31. Michigan	8.2	17
32. Pennsylvania	6.8	14
33. Kansas	5.7	12
34. Illinois	5.3	11
Montana	5.3	11
36. Ohio	5.2	11
37. Minnesota	5.1	11
38. Indiana	5.0	10
39. New York	4.9	10
40. South Carolina	4.7	10
41. Tennessee	4.6	9
42. New Hampshire	3.6	7
43. Colorado	3.5	7
44. Maine	3.2	7
45. Missouri	2.2	4
46. Alaska	0.0	0
Idaho	0.0	0
New Mexico	0.0	0
Rhode Island	0.0	0
South Dakota	0.0	0

Olympic Athletes

DOING THE MATH

There is perhaps no higher honor for a U.S. athlete than to stand on the victory platform at the Olympics, clutching a gold medal as the "Star Spangled Banner" is played and the American flag is raised. This category checks each state's involvement in the 1992 summer and winter games, expressed as a rate of Olympic athletes per 1 million residents.

BEST STATES

Vermont sent 12 athletes to the Olympics in 1992: 10 in the winter and two in the summer. That's impressive for a state with only 563,000 residents; it works out to a rate of 21.3 Olympic athletes per million. Colorado and Alaska are the only other states with rates above 10.

WORST STATES

Nebraska was the only state that failed to place an athlete on the 1992 Olympic team. Mississippi had a single representative, good for a rate of 0.4 per million.

REGIONAL WINNERS

East—Vermont
South—Florida
Midwest—Minnesota
West—Colorado

BIGGEST SURPRISE

Texas is a breeding ground for athletes, with above-average performances in the High School Athletes and College Champions categories. But it has scant success in the Olympics, ranking just 27th here.

THE BOTTOM LINE

Most Olympic athletes can be found at one end of the country or the other. The East and the West each have four states among the 10 leaders.

228 Olympic Athletes

State	1992 Olympic Athletes Per Million Residents	Points
1. Vermont	21.3	100
2. Colorado	11.2	100
3. Alaska	10.9	97
4. Rhode Island	8.0	70
5. Utah	7.0	61
6. Massachusetts	6.6	58
Minnesota	6.6	58
8. New Hampshire	6.3	55
9. Oregon	6.0	52
10. Wisconsin	5.7	49
11. California	5.5	47
12. Montana	5.0	43
13. New Mexico	4.6	39
14. Washington	4.5	38
Hawaii	4.5	38
16. Wyoming	4.4	37
17. Nevada	4.2	35
18. Arizona	4.1	34
19. Idaho	4.0	33
Connecticut	4.0	33
21. Maine	3.3	26
22. Maryland	3.1	25
23. Delaware	3.0	24
24. Florida	2.9	23
25. New Jersey	2.8	23
26. New York	2.7	21
27. Texas	2.5	20
28. Illinois	2.4	19
Virginia	2.4	19
30. Iowa	2.2	16
31. Kansas	2.0	15
32. South Carolina	1.7	12
Arkansas	1.7	12
Georgia	1.7	12
West Virginia	1.7	12
Louisiana	1.7	12
37. Michigan	1.6	11
Oklahoma	1.6	11
North Dakota	1.6	11
40. Ohio	1.5	10
41. Indiana	1.4	10
South Dakota	1.4	10
Pennsylvania	1.4	10
44. North Carolina	1.2	7
45. Tennessee	1.0	6
Missouri	1.0	6
47. Kentucky	0.8	4
48. Alabama	0.7	3
49. Mississippi	0.4	0
50. Nebraska	0.0	0

Professional Champions

DOING THE MATH

Professional sports have captured America's fancy in the 1990s like never before, with new attendance records seemingly being set annually. The most popular teams, of course, are those that win. This category counts each state's professional champions and runners-up in baseball, football, basketball, and hockey from 1968 through 1992. That total is expressed as a rate per 10 million residents.

BEST STATES

Fans in Massachusetts don't always have it easy. Baseball's Boston Red Sox and football's New England Patriots break hearts almost every year. But Boston's basketball (Celtics) and hockey (Bruins) franchises have winning traditions, accounting for most of the 19 Massachusetts teams that qualified for their leagues' championship games or series during the last quarter century. That's equal to 31.6 appearances per 10 million residents. Maryland is second with a rate of 23 per 10 million.

WORST STATES

Fully 27 states did not have any professional champions or runners-up from 1968 through 1992.

REGIONAL WINNERS

East—Massachusetts
South—Kentucky
Midwest—Missouri
West—Colorado

BIGGEST SURPRISE

Big-league baseball is new to Colorado; hockey failed there. But football's Denver Broncos qualified for four Super Bowls to singlehandedly earn sixth place in this category for Colorado.

THE BOTTOM LINE

The East and the West both have four states in the top 10; the other two are from the Midwest.

230 Professional Champions

State	Teams in Championship Games or Series Per 10 Million Residents, 1968–1992	Points
1. Massachusetts	31.6	100
2. Maryland	23.0	100
3. Missouri	19.5	85
4. Pennsylvania	18.5	81
5. Minnesota	18.3	80
6. Colorado	15.2	66
7. New York	13.9	60
8. California	12.8	56
9. Utah	11.6	50
10. Oregon	10.6	46
11. Indiana	9.0	39
12. Kentucky	8.1	35
13. Ohio	6.5	28
14. Wisconsin	6.1	27
15. Michigan	5.4	23
16. Illinois	5.2	23
17. Texas	4.7	20
18. Washington	4.1	18
19. Florida	3.9	17
20. Georgia	3.1	13
21. Arizona	2.7	12
22. New Jersey	2.6	11
23. Louisiana	2.4	10
24. Alabama	0.0	0
Alaska	0.0	0
Arkansas	0.0	0
Connecticut	0.0	0
Delaware	0.0	0
Hawaii	0.0	0
Idaho	0.0	0
Iowa	0.0	0
Kansas	0.0	0
Maine	0.0	0
Mississippi	0.0	0
Montana	0.0	0
Nebraska	0.0	0
Nevada	0.0	0
New Hampshire	0.0	0
New Mexico	0.0	0
North Carolina	0.0	0
North Dakota	0.0	0
Oklahoma	0.0	0
Rhode Island	0.0	0
South Carolina	0.0	0
South Dakota	0.0	0
Tennessee	0.0	0
Vermont	0.0	0
Virginia	0.0	0
West Virginia	0.0	0
Wyoming	0.0	0

Spectator Seats

DOING THE MATH

Demand for professional sports tickets often exceeds supply. It is close to impossible to get into games in many places. We wanted to know which state offers the best access for the sports fan, so we multiplied stadium capacity by the number of home games for all teams in baseball, football, basketball, and hockey. We then divided each state's total into its population, yielding the annual rate of spectator seats per 1,000 residents.

BEST STATES

Colorado is the sports fan's paradise, with 2,268 seats per 1,000 residents. That's because baseball's Colorado Rockies and football's Denver Broncos play in cavernous Mile High Stadium (capacity: 76,273). Missouri, with teams in both St. Louis and Kansas City, is second in this category.

WORST STATES

A total of 26 states currently are without big-league teams in any of the four major sports.

REGIONAL WINNERS

East—Maryland
South—Georgia
Midwest—Missouri
West—Colorado

BIGGEST SURPRISE

Wisconsin's major-league teams have kept a low profile in recent years, a nice way of saying they haven't been winning. But their fans are doing all right, with 1,132 seats per 1,000 residents, America's fifth-best rate.

THE BOTTOM LINE

Fans get the biggest break in the Midwest, home of four states in this category's top 10. The West is just behind with three.

232 Spectator Seats

State	Seats at Professional Games Per 1,000 Residents	Points
1. Colorado	2,268	100
2. Missouri	1,789	100
3. Minnesota	1,468	82
4. Washington	1,242	69
5. Wisconsin	1,132	63
6. Ohio	1,131	63
7. Maryland	1,121	63
8. Pennsylvania	1,085	61
9. California	993	55
10. Georgia	843	47
11. Illinois	761	43
12. Massachusetts	730	41
13. Michigan	704	39
14. New York	703	39
15. Texas	649	36
16. Florida	519	29
17. Utah	474	26
18. Arizona	373	21
19. New Jersey	364	20
20. Indiana	209	12
21. Connecticut	204	11
22. Oregon	186	10
23. North Carolina	147	8
24. Louisiana	131	7
25. Alabama	0	0
Alaska	0	0
Arkansas	0	0
Delaware	0	0
Hawaii	0	0
Idaho	0	0
Iowa	0	0
Kansas	0	0
Kentucky	0	0
Maine	0	0
Mississippi	0	0
Montana	0	0
Nebraska	0	0
Nevada	0	0
New Hampshire	0	0
New Mexico	0	0
North Dakota	0	0
Oklahoma	0	0
Rhode Island	0	0
South Carolina	0	0
South Dakota	0	0
Tennessee	0	0
Vermont	0	0
Virginia	0	0
West Virginia	0	0
Wyoming	0	0

Sports: Scores and Grades

BEST STATE

Colorado is the most well-rounded state in American sports, earning first place in this section. It is an outstanding producer of athletes; only Vermont had a higher participation rate in the 1992 Olympics. It also is a dream for spectators; no state even comes close to Colorado's proportion of available seats at professional games. And those spectators have good reason to cheer. Colorado ranks sixth in the Professional Champions category.

RUNNERS-UP

Minnesota is the only state to receive a straight A in this section. Its strength is professional sports, where it ranks no. 5 in championships and no. 3 in available spectator seats. Third place belongs to Utah, largely because of its prowess in amateur athletics.

WORST STATES

Mississippi is not athletically inclined. It has no major-league teams, and only one of its athletes qualified for the 1992 Olympics. Tennessee is next to last.

REGIONAL WINNERS

East—Massachusetts
South—Arkansas, Texas
Midwest—Minnesota
West—Colorado

REGIONAL AVERAGES

East—38 (D+)
South—18 (F)
Midwest—45 (C)
West—46 (C)

BIGGEST SURPRISE

Utah does not leap to mind as a sports giant, but it ranks a strong no. 3 in this section. No state has a higher proportion of college champions than Utah; just four states do a better job of turning out Olympic athletes.

234 THE BOTTOM LINE

The West, placing five states in the top 11, is the best region for the sports aficionado. The South clearly is the worst, with eight states among the bottom 10.

Sports: Scores and Grades

State	Score	Grade
1. Colorado	100	A+
2. Minnesota	86	A
3. Utah	84	A–
4. Wisconsin	79	B+
5. Massachusetts	78	B+
6. Missouri	72	B
7. California	68	B
8. Maryland	67	B
9. Alaska	61	B–
10. Washington	60	B–
Vermont	60	B–
12. Pennsylvania	53	C
13. Oregon	52	C
14. North Dakota	46	C
15. Iowa	43	C–
Arkansas	43	C–
Texas	43	C–
18. Ohio	42	C–
19. New York	39	D+
20. Michigan	37	D+
21. Wyoming	35	D+
Montana	35	D+
23. Louisiana	34	D
24. Illinois	33	D
25. Arizona	32	D
26. Nebraska	31	D
27. Florida	28	D
28. Indiana	26	D
New Hampshire	26	D
30. Georgia	25	D
New Jersey	25	D
32. Maine	24	D–
Idaho	24	D–
34. Kansas	22	D–
South Dakota	22	D–
36. West Virginia	21	D–
Connecticut	21	D–
Delaware	21	D–
Rhode Island	21	D–
40. Nevada	19	F
41. Hawaii	18	F
42. Oklahoma	15	F
43. Virginia	14	F
44. Kentucky	12	F
45. New Mexico	11	F
46. North Carolina	9	F
47. Alabama	5	F
48. South Carolina	2	F
49. Tennessee	1	F
50. Mississippi	0	F

16

Recreation

The Big Question

Which state offers the best combination of leisure opportunities, ranging from parks and fitness centers to movie theaters and restaurants?

The Categories

1. Park Visitors
2. Fitness Centers
3. Movies and Videos
4. Shopping
5. Restaurants and Bars

Park Visitors

DOING THE MATH

Americans love the great outdoors. Why else would we pay 1.2 *billion* visits each year to national and state recreation areas? This category measures the popularity of the state parks, national parks, and national forests in each state, adding up their visitor counts over the course of a year. The grand total is expressed as a rate per 1,000 residents.

BEST STATES

The mountains and geysers of Yellowstone National Park have made Wyoming world-famous. Yellowstone is the principal reason for Wyoming's astounding annual park attendance of 13.5 million, which works out to 29,724 park visitors per 1,000 residents. Alaska is second at 22,732.

WORST STATES

The state and national parks in Louisiana have little drawing power. Their total annual attendance is roughly 2.5 million, equal to 608 visitors per 1,000 residents. Texas is next to last, with a rate of 1,638.

REGIONAL WINNERS

East—Maine
South—Kentucky
Midwest—South Dakota
West—Wyoming

BIGGEST SURPRISE

Texas seems to have the ingredients for an outstanding parks system. It has all types of terrain and a large population base to draw from. But only Louisiana has a lower rate of park usage than Texas.

THE BOTTOM LINE

The West has a virtual monopoly on popular parks, with nine states in the top 10. Five of the 10 worst states are southern.

238 Park Visitors

State	Visitors to National and State Parks and Forests Per 1,000 Residents	Points
1. Wyoming	29,724	100
2. Alaska	22,732	100
3. Oregon	21,844	96
4. Hawaii	21,696	95
5. Montana	17,996	78
6. South Dakota	17,854	77
7. Utah	15,165	64
8. Idaho	14,587	61
9. Washington	14,244	60
10. Colorado	11,883	49
11. Nevada	10,400	42
12. New Mexico	9,424	37
13. Kentucky	8,846	34
14. Arizona	8,820	34
15. Tennessee	7,411	27
16. Maine	6,260	22
17. Ohio	6,054	21
18. West Virginia	5,991	21
19. Nebraska	5,942	20
20. Oklahoma	5,912	20
21. California	5,841	20
22. Rhode Island	5,325	17
23. New Hampshire	4,933	16
24. Arkansas	4,902	15
25. North Carolina	4,746	15
26. Virginia	4,630	14
27. Iowa	4,394	13
28. Mississippi	4,288	13
29. Delaware	4,126	12
30. Pennsylvania	4,116	12
31. Vermont	4,058	11
32. New York	4,037	11
33. Missouri	4,031	11
34. Massachusetts	3,784	10
35. Georgia	3,566	9
36. Illinois	3,372	8
37. Minnesota	3,154	7
38. Michigan	3,150	7
39. Wisconsin	2,857	6
40. North Dakota	2,592	5
41. South Carolina	2,499	4
42. Maryland	2,384	4
43. Connecticut	2,230	3
44. Indiana	2,213	3
45. Florida	1,925	1
46. Alabama	1,833	1
47. New Jersey	1,821	1
48. Kansas	1,683	0
49. Texas	1,638	0
50. Louisiana	608	0

Fitness Centers

DOING THE MATH

America supposedly is in the midst of a physical fitness revolution. Sales of workout videos and exercise equipment have never been higher. But, ironically, surveys also show that more Americans are out of shape than ever before. This category gauges the opportunities for year-round exercise in each state, converting its total number of fitness centers to a rate per 1 million residents.

BEST STATES

Vermont's 563,000 residents have their choice of 34 "physical fitness facilities," as the Census Bureau calls them. That equals 60.4 fitness centers per 1 million persons, the highest rate in the nation. Two other states are above 50: North Dakota and New Hampshire.

WORST STATES

Mississippi has only 36 fitness centers for its nearly 2.6 million residents. The resulting rate of 14.0 per million is America's lowest. Kentucky is next to last at 19.3.

REGIONAL WINNERS

East—Vermont
South—Virginia
Midwest—North Dakota
West—Washington

BIGGEST SURPRISE

The fitness revolution apparently has not hit with full force in the states that usually set America's trends. New York does no better than 26th in this category, while California is 27th.

THE BOTTOM LINE

Easterners, with six of the top 10 states, have the best opportunity to stay fit all year long. The region with the fewest fitness centers is the South, which placed seven states in the bottom 10.

240 Fitness Centers

State	Physical Fitness Facilities Per Million Residents	Points
1. Vermont	60.4	100
2. North Dakota	53.2	100
3. New Hampshire	51.4	95
4. Connecticut	46.2	79
5. Massachusetts	43.7	72
6. Nebraska	42.5	68
7. Washington	42.3	68
8. Rhode Island	41.9	67
9. Montana	41.3	65
10. Maine	40.7	63
11. Delaware	40.5	63
12. Colorado	38.3	56
13. Alaska	38.2	56
14. Kansas	37.1	53
15. Utah	36.6	51
16. Virginia	36.0	49
17. Wyoming	35.2	47
18. New Jersey	34.8	46
19. Idaho	33.8	43
20. Pennsylvania	33.7	43
21. Maryland	32.6	39
22. Oregon	32.4	39
23. Missouri	32.2	38
24. Oklahoma	32.1	38
25. Ohio	31.1	35
26. New York	31.0	35
27. California	30.4	33
Florida	30.4	33
New Mexico	30.4	33
30. Illinois	30.1	32
31. Nevada	30.0	31
32. Minnesota	29.7	31
33. West Virginia	29.0	29
34. Indiana	28.9	28
35. Iowa	28.8	28
36. South Dakota	28.7	28
37. Texas	28.6	27
38. North Carolina	28.1	26
39. Wisconsin	27.4	24
40. Tennessee	27.1	23
41. Georgia	26.9	22
42. Louisiana	26.8	22
43. Michigan	26.5	21
44. Arkansas	25.1	17
45. Hawaii	24.4	15
46. Arizona	24.3	15
47. South Carolina	22.4	9
48. Alabama	21.5	7
49. Kentucky	19.3	0
50. Mississippi	14.0	0

Movies and Videos

DOING THE MATH

The advent of the video cassette recorder in the 1980s elevated movies to unprecedented popularity. Americans still can see first-run films in the nation's 6,940 theaters, almost all with multiple screens, but they now can also choose movies at any of 16,407 video rental stores. This category adds up the theaters and video stores in each state, expressing the total as a rate per 1 million residents.

BEST STATES

Movie stars rarely make live appearances in Wyoming, but they're seen nightly on big and small screens. Wyoming's 454,000 residents have access to 37 movie theaters and 39 video rental stores, for a combined rate of 167.4 per million. Alaska is just a step behind at 167.3.

WORST STATES

New Jersey's raw numbers seem impressive: 166 theaters, 408 video stores. But its rate of 74.3 per million is America's lowest. Pennsylvania is next to last at 76.5.

REGIONAL WINNERS

East—Vermont
South—South Carolina
Midwest—South Dakota
West—Wyoming

BIGGEST SURPRISE

California, the center of the film industry, ranks just 29th in this category. It's behind such unlikely leaders as Wyoming, Alaska, and Montana.

THE BOTTOM LINE

Movies are most easily available in the West, which has five of the 10 best states. The bottom is a draw, as the East and South each have four states among the 10 worst.

Movies and Videos

State	Movie Theaters and Video Rental Stores Per Million Residents	Points
1. Wyoming	167.4	100
2. Alaska	167.3	100
3. Montana	166.5	99
4. Vermont	154.5	86
5. New Hampshire	152.4	84
6. Idaho	137.0	67
7. Oregon	129.8	59
8. South Dakota	122.1	50
9. Minnesota	120.5	48
10. Delaware	120.1	48
11. New Mexico	117.5	45
12. Missouri	116.1	44
13. Washington	114.2	42
14. Indiana	113.3	41
15. South Carolina	113.0	40
16. Maine	112.4	40
17. Arkansas	110.2	37
18. West Virginia	107.6	34
19. Connecticut	107.4	34
20. Nevada	106.5	33
21. Tennessee	104.4	31
22. Maryland	104.2	30
23. Kansas	102.9	29
24. Iowa	102.6	29
25. North Carolina	102.1	28
26. Colorado	102.0	28
27. Utah	99.8	26
28. Hawaii	97.5	23
29. California	97.1	23
30. Massachusetts	95.7	21
31. Mississippi	93.7	19
32. Oklahoma	93.1	18
33. Illinois	92.6	18
34. Kentucky	92.3	17
35. Georgia	92.2	17
36. Virginia	91.0	16
37. North Dakota	90.8	16
38. Arizona	90.6	16
39. Ohio	87.7	12
40. Nebraska	86.8	11
41. Michigan	86.2	11
42. Wisconsin	83.6	8
43. New York	82.2	6
44. Alabama	81.9	6
45. Florida	79.8	4
Rhode Island	79.8	4
47. Louisiana	79.4	3
48. Texas	79.2	3
49. Pennsylvania	76.5	0
50. New Jersey	74.3	0

Shopping

DOING THE MATH

The shopping mall is modern America's courthouse square. It's where people gather to pass the time, meet friends, tell stories—and shop. There is no shortage of outlets for the latter activity. This country has more than 1.5 million retail establishments; roughly 470,000 are classified as large stores, those with 10 or more employees. This category counts the large stores in each state, converting the total to a rate per 100,000 residents.

BEST STATES

Vermont offers the strongest concentration of large retail establishments in America. It has 1,476 stores with 10 or more employees, which works out to 262 per 100,000 residents. Second place belongs to Hawaii, with a rate of 257.

WORST STATES

The retail pickings are slim in Mississippi, with only 151 large stores per 100,000 residents, the nation's lowest rate. Also below 160 are New York and Louisiana.

REGIONAL WINNERS

East—Vermont
South—Virginia
Midwest—Minnesota
West—Hawaii

BIGGEST SURPRISE

New York supposedly is a shopper's paradise—Bloomingdale's, Macy's, Fifth Avenue. But it actually has only 154 large stores per 100,000 residents, putting it in 49th place.

THE BOTTOM LINE

America's most dedicated shoppers can be found in the East, which has half of the 12 leading states. The South, with six states in the bottom 10, generally has the fewest stores.

244 Shopping

State	Retail Establishments with 10 or More Employees Per 100,000 Residents	Points
1. Vermont	262	100
2. Hawaii	257	100
3. New Hampshire	239	82
4. Delaware	236	80
5. Minnesota	219	63
6. Oregon	217	61
7. Maine	216	60
8. Maryland	213	58
Wyoming	213	58
10. Massachusetts	212	57
Iowa	212	57
Montana	212	57
13. Wisconsin	210	54
14. Indiana	208	53
Nebraska	208	53
16. Nevada	206	50
17. South Dakota	205	50
Connecticut	205	50
19. Virginia	204	49
20. North Carolina	203	47
Washington	203	47
22. Kansas	202	47
Colorado	202	47
24. North Dakota	201	46
25. Florida	198	43
Georgia	198	43
27. Ohio	197	42
Missouri	197	42
29. Rhode Island	196	41
Idaho	196	41
31. Arizona	192	37
32. Michigan	191	36
33. Illinois	189	34
34. Kentucky	186	31
Tennessee	186	31
New Mexico	186	31
37. South Carolina	184	29
38. Pennsylvania	182	27
39. California	180	26
40. Utah	178	23
41. New Jersey	177	23
42. Texas	176	22
Oklahoma	176	22
44. Alaska	167	13
45. Alabama	166	12
46. West Virginia	165	11
47. Arkansas	163	9
48. Louisiana	159	5
49. New York	154	0
50. Mississippi	151	0

Restaurants and Bars

DOING THE MATH

Americans are quick to defend the traditional home-cooked family meal, but most enjoy the chance to leave food preparation to the professionals. That's why there are more than 400,000 restaurants and bars in the United States, doing enough business to support a total annual payroll of $49 billion. This category measures the popularity of the eating and drinking establishments in each state, translating their combined annual payroll into a rate per 1,000 residents.

BEST STATES

Hawaii has 2,350 restaurants and bars, which pay their employees $482 million a year. That equals a payroll of $435,410 per 1,000 residents, easily the highest rate in the nation. Alaska holds second place at $296,782.

WORST STATES

Relatively few Mississippi residents eat out, which is why the state's restaurants and bars support a total payroll of just $107,017 per 1,000 residents. Arkansas is next to last.

REGIONAL WINNERS

East—Massachusetts
South—Florida
Midwest—Minnesota
West—Hawaii

BIGGEST SURPRISE

Alaska does not pop to mind as one of America's gastronomic centers. But its 1,026 restaurants and bars do a heavy volume of business, earning Alaska second place.

THE BOTTOM LINE

Dining out is most popular in the West, home of six of the nation's top 10 states. Restaurants do poorly in the South, which has five states in the bottom 10.

246 Restaurants and Bars

State	Restaurant and Bar Annual Payroll Per 1,000 Residents	Points
1. Hawaii	$435,410	100
2. Alaska	296,782	100
3. Massachusetts	261,038	79
4. Nevada	240,599	68
5. Florida	236,215	65
6. Colorado	232,952	63
7. California	229,945	61
8. Washington	229,344	61
9. Delaware	228,099	60
10. New Hampshire	226,936	60
11. Vermont	226,917	60
12. Connecticut	217,218	54
13. Rhode Island	215,894	53
14. Maryland	211,164	51
15. Georgia	208,909	49
16. Oregon	205,821	47
17. New York	199,808	44
18. Arizona	198,689	43
19. Virginia	196,502	42
20. Minnesota	195,955	42
21. Illinois	195,650	42
22. New Jersey	195,300	41
23. Maine	193,857	41
24. Missouri	193,522	40
25. Indiana	192,767	40
26. Texas	191,920	39
27. Ohio	190,393	39
28. Michigan	190,063	38
29. North Carolina	186,259	36
30. Tennessee	185,772	36
31. Wisconsin	185,571	36
32. Wyoming	183,575	35
33. South Carolina	182,431	34
34. New Mexico	181,269	33
35. Kansas	178,987	32
36. Montana	178,857	32
37. Nebraska	177,895	31
38. Pennsylvania	169,115	26
39. Kentucky	166,993	25
40. Iowa	164,400	24
41. Oklahoma	160,152	21
42. North Dakota	158,055	20
43. South Dakota	156,154	19
44. Louisiana	155,702	19
45. Utah	148,197	14
46. Idaho	145,546	13
47. Alabama	138,449	9
48. West Virginia	124,372	0
49. Arkansas	123,628	0
50. Mississippi	107,017	0

Recreation: Scores and Grades

BEST STATE

Alaska is America's fun state, offering the finest variety of recreational opportunities in the nation. The state's strength is its vast expanse of wilderness. More than 12.5 million people enjoy its national and state parks each year. But Alaska also offers a wide array of indoor activities, a necessity when the thermometer drops to 40 below. Only Wyoming has a higher availability rate for movie theaters and video rental stores; only Hawaii has busier restaurants and bars.

RUNNERS-UP

Vermont, no. 2 in this section, leads the nation in two disparate recreational activities. No other state has higher proportions of fitness centers or large stores. Also earning A's are Wyoming, New Hampshire, Hawaii, Montana, and Oregon.

WORST STATES

Mississippi is not such a fun place. It suffers from a paucity of recreational opportunities, having the fewest fitness centers, large stores, and restaurants of any of the 50 states. Alabama is next to last in this section. Five other states were also hit with F's.

REGIONAL WINNERS

East—Vermont
South—Virginia
Midwest—South Dakota
West—Alaska

REGIONAL AVERAGES

East—50 (C)
South—22 (D–)
Midwest—39 (D+)
West—66 (B)

BIGGEST SURPRISE

New York seems to have everything that's needed for a good time, whether it's the urban pleasures of New York City or the wild beauty of the Adirondack Mountains. But the state ranks 44th in this section, earning an F.

THE BOTTOM LINE

The West has seven of the 10 states that offer the best recreational opportunities, while the South includes six of the 10 worst.

Recreation: Scores and Grades

State	Score	Grade
1. Alaska	100	A+
2. Vermont	96	A
3. Wyoming	91	A
New Hampshire	91	A
5. Hawaii	89	A
6. Montana	88	A
7. Oregon	80	A–
8. Washington	73	B
9. Delaware	69	B
10. Colorado	63	B–
11. Massachusetts	61	B–
12. Maine	58	C+
13. Idaho	57	C+
Nevada	57	C+
South Dakota	57	C+
16. Connecticut	55	C+
17. Minnesota	47	C
18. North Dakota	46	C
19. Nebraska	45	C
Maryland	45	C
Rhode Island	45	C
22. New Mexico	44	C–
23. Utah	43	C–
24. Missouri	42	C–
25. Virginia	41	C–
26. Indiana	39	D+
California	39	D+
28. Kansas	38	D+
29. North Carolina	36	D+
30. Iowa	35	D+
Ohio	35	D+
32. Tennessee	34	D
Florida	34	D
Arizona	34	D
35. Georgia	32	D
36. Illinois	30	D
37. Wisconsin	28	D
38. Oklahoma	26	D
39. South Carolina	25	D
40. Michigan	24	D–
41. New Jersey	23	D–
Pennsylvania	23	D–
43. Kentucky	22	D–
44. New York	19	F
West Virginia	19	F
46. Texas	18	F
47. Arkansas	14	F
48. Louisiana	5	F
49. Alabama	1	F
50. Mississippi	0	F

17

Business

The Big Question

Which state historically has had the best economic climate in which to operate a successful business in the manufacturing, retail, or service sectors?

The Categories

1. Gross State Product
2. Economic Growth
3. Manufacturing Productivity
4. Retail Trade
5. Service Sector Strength

Gross State Product

DOING THE MATH

We have all heard of the gross national product, which is featured in monthly newspaper stories and is discussed knowingly by economists in television interviews. GNP is the total market value of all goods and services produced in the United States in a given year—in short, the nation's economic output. The federal government, using the same formula, also tracks gross *state* products. This category takes each state's GSP and expresses it as a per capita rate.

BEST STATES

Add up the annual value of goods and services produced in Alaska and your calculator will take you to the vicinity of $20 billion. The per capita average is $35,604, easily the highest rate in America. Connecticut has the top GSP on the mainland, $27,035 per person.

WORST STATES

Mississippi's gross state product sounds impressive in its raw form: $38 billion. But it is uninspiring as a per capita rate: $14,821, lowest in the nation. West Virginia is next to last.

REGIONAL WINNERS

East—Connecticut
South—Virginia
Midwest—Illinois
West—Alaska

BIGGEST SURPRISE

Most large states also are big in an economic sense. The exception is Florida, no. 4 in population, but no. 39 in this category.

THE BOTTOM LINE

The East and West each include five states in the top 10. The South and West, on the other hand, each have four among the 10 worst.

252 Gross State Product

State	Gross State Product Per Capita	Points
1. Alaska	$35,604	100
2. Connecticut	27,035	100
3. New Jersey	26,310	94
4. New York	24,517	78
5. Wyoming	24,482	78
6. Massachusetts	24,068	74
7. California	23,434	69
8. Nevada	23,261	67
9. Hawaii	23,245	67
10. Delaware	23,150	66
11. Illinois	22,437	60
12. New Hampshire	22,096	57
13. Virginia	22,062	57
14. Minnesota	21,385	51
15. Maryland	20,722	45
16. Vermont	20,430	42
17. Colorado	20,091	39
18. Georgia	20,033	39
19. Texas	20,019	39
20. Washington	19,773	37
21. Nebraska	19,718	36
22. Kansas	19,705	36
23. North Carolina	19,624	35
24. Michigan	19,562	35
25. Missouri	19,559	35
26. Ohio	19,503	34
27. Wisconsin	19,211	32
28. Pennsylvania	19,180	31
29. Maine	19,116	31
30. Indiana	18,996	30
31. Iowa	18,932	29
32. Tennessee	18,919	29
33. Louisiana	18,753	28
34. Rhode Island	18,751	28
35. Oregon	18,338	24
36. Kentucky	17,872	20
37. Arizona	17,819	20
38. North Dakota	17,576	17
39. Florida	17,542	17
40. South Carolina	17,250	15
41. Alabama	16,799	11
42. New Mexico	16,775	10
43. Oklahoma	16,638	9
44. Montana	16,401	7
45. Utah	16,329	7
46. Idaho	16,225	6
47. South Dakota	15,999	4
48. Arkansas	15,810	2
49. West Virginia	15,573	0
50. Mississippi	14,821	0

Economic Growth

DOING THE MATH

Much can happen during a decade. Political administrations that were wildly popular at the beginning can fall into disfavor by the end; tastes in fashion and music can change markedly. And the economy can undergo serious adjustments, either for better or worse. This category measures each state's economic growth during the 1980s, calculating the rate of change in its gross state product between 1980 and 1989.

BEST STATES

New Hampshire was a remarkable growth story in the 1980s. Its gross state product of $9.3 billion in 1980 shot up to $24.5 billion by decade's end. No state could match this increase of 162.5 percent. Second place belongs to Florida.

WORST STATES

Don't blame Wyoming residents for noticing little change during the 1980s; their state's GSP grew just 1.9 percent. Louisiana was the only other state below 30 percent.

REGIONAL WINNERS

East—New Hampshire
South—Florida
Midwest—Minnesota
West—Nevada

BIGGEST SURPRISE

The press wrote much about the Sunbelt's growth in the 1980s, giving the impression that the entire South was booming. But Oklahoma and Louisiana missed the trend; both had GSP growth below 40 percent.

THE BOTTOM LINE

Economic growth in the 1980s was concentrated in the East, with six states in the top 10. The West placed four states in the bottom 10.

254 Economic Growth

State	Change in Gross State Product, 1980–1989	Points
1. New Hampshire	162.5%	100
2. Florida	137.1	100
3. Nevada	135.6	99
4. Virginia	133.7	97
5. Vermont	133.5	97
6. Georgia	133.3	97
7. New Jersey	129.6	93
8. Maine	127.1	91
9. Maryland	123.4	88
10. Connecticut	122.6	87
11. Massachusetts	120.9	86
12. South Carolina	120.1	85
North Carolina	120.1	85
Arizona	120.1	85
15. Delaware	119.0	84
16. California	118.4	84
17. New York	104.9	72
Tennessee	104.9	72
19. Hawaii	104.1	71
20. Rhode Island	102.6	70
21. Alabama	93.0	61
22. Minnesota	91.0	60
23. Washington	88.0	57
24. Missouri	87.7	57
25. Utah	87.2	56
26. Arkansas	82.8	52
27. Pennsylvania	80.5	50
28. Illinois	78.7	49
29. Colorado	78.1	48
30. Wisconsin	77.1	47
31. Kentucky	76.9	47
32. Indiana	76.6	47
33. Mississippi	76.5	47
34. Michigan	74.9	45
35. Ohio	74.0	45
36. Kansas	72.6	43
37. Oregon	72.5	43
38. Nebraska	69.8	41
39. Idaho	69.0	40
40. Texas	66.1	38
41. South Dakota	58.1	31
42. New Mexico	52.5	26
43. Iowa	50.1	24
44. West Virginia	43.7	18
45. Alaska	40.3	15
46. Montana	38.4	13
Oklahoma	38.4	13
48. North Dakota	34.8	10
49. Louisiana	23.1	0
50. Wyoming	1.9	0

Manufacturing Productivity

DOING THE MATH

America built its economy by making things—cars, appliances, and millions of other products. Manufacturing is still essential for the nation's economic vitality, regardless of talk about the preeminence of the service sector. This category measures the health of each state's manufacturing base. It begins with a statistic known as "value added by manufacture," which is the price of a finished item minus all the costs (labor, materials, electricity, etc.) to produce it. Each state's total is expressed as a rate per 1,000 residents.

BEST STATES

North Carolina workers annually manufacture goods with $57.7 billion of total value added. That works out to a nation-leading $8,700,256 per 1,000 residents. Indiana is the only other state with a rate above $8 million.

WORST STATES

Nevada adds just $1.5 billion in value to manufactured goods each year, equal to $1,222,629 per 1,000 residents. Hawaii is next to last.

REGIONAL WINNERS

East—Connecticut
South—North Carolina
Midwest—Indiana
West—Washington

BIGGEST SURPRISE

Most people think the nation's manufacturing leader is from the Midwest, maybe Michigan or Ohio. The actual no. 1 is North Carolina, stereotyped as a tobacco state.

THE BOTTOM LINE

The Midwest, with five of the 10 best states, leads the nation in manufacturing productivity. The West dominates the bottom 10 with seven states.

256 Manufacturing Productivity

State	Value Added by Manufacture Per 1,000 Residents	Points
1. North Carolina	$8,700,256	100
2. Indiana	8,103,229	100
3. Wisconsin	7,581,848	92
4. Ohio	7,410,104	90
5. Connecticut	7,248,616	87
6. Iowa	7,023,190	84
7. Michigan	6,971,329	83
8. Delaware	6,774,174	80
9. Kentucky	6,412,157	75
10. Tennessee	6,201,558	72
11. Illinois	6,192,240	71
12. South Carolina	6,027,846	69
13. Missouri	5,912,644	67
14. Minnesota	5,898,149	67
15. New Jersey	5,844,618	66
16. Massachusetts	5,834,791	66
17. Vermont	5,742,629	65
18. Georgia	5,584,903	62
19. Pennsylvania	5,391,761	60
20. Louisiana	5,359,408	59
21. Arkansas	5,303,275	58
22. Alabama	5,286,315	58
23. Virginia	5,254,760	57
24. Kansas	5,245,319	57
25. Rhode Island	5,133,200	56
26. Washington	5,110,027	55
27. California	5,026,132	54
28. New Hampshire	5,021,190	54
29. Mississippi	4,971,901	53
30. Texas	4,923,188	53
31. Maine	4,793,485	51
32. New York	4,754,441	50
33. Nebraska	4,721,229	50
34. Oregon	4,649,331	48
35. Colorado	4,195,052	42
36. Idaho	3,900,298	37
37. Oklahoma	3,779,148	35
38. Utah	3,546,895	32
39. West Virginia	3,536,921	32
40. Maryland	3,288,789	28
41. Arizona	3,251,269	28
42. Alaska	2,527,091	17
43. South Dakota	2,341,810	14
44. Florida	2,302,728	13
45. Wyoming	1,859,031	7
46. North Dakota	1,737,559	5
47. Montana	1,488,736	1
48. New Mexico	1,486,535	1
49. Hawaii	1,405,686	0
50. Nevada	1,222,629	0

Retail Trade

DOING THE MATH

Shopping is more than just a diverting activity; it's big business. Nearly 20 million Americans are in retail trade, working everywhere from the regional shopping mall to the corner grocery. Consumers spend more than $1.8 trillion at these stores each year. This category determines the strength of each state's retail sector, computing total annual sales per household.

BEST STATES

Stores in Hawaii do the briskest business in America. The typical Hawaiian household spends $31,121 a year on retail goods. Three other states have rates above $24,000: New Hampshire, Alaska, and Delaware.

WORST STATES

Residents of West Virginia have little disposable income, and the stores feel the pinch. The average household in West Virginia annually spends just $14,718 on retail items. Mississippi is next to last at $15,131.

REGIONAL WINNERS

East—New Hampshire
South—Virginia
Midwest—Minnesota
West—Hawaii

BIGGEST SURPRISE

New York has the reputation of being one of America's retail centers, but its sales don't live up to the image. The typical New York household spends $18,667 on retail goods, putting it in 29th place.

THE BOTTOM LINE

The retail sector is strongest in the East, which has seven of the 10 leading states in this category. Sales are slowest in the South, home of five of the 10 worst states.

258 Retail Trade

State	Annual Retail Sales Per Household	Points
1. Hawaii	$31,121	100
2. New Hampshire	28,373	100
3. Alaska	24,533	71
4. Delaware	24,145	68
5. New Jersey	22,579	56
6. Massachusetts	22,488	56
7. Connecticut	22,435	55
8. Maine	22,149	53
9. California	21,245	46
10. Vermont	21,223	46
11. Maryland	20,790	43
12. Virginia	20,459	40
13. Oregon	20,159	38
14. Florida	20,056	37
15. Minnesota	20,050	37
16. Nevada	19,938	36
17. Illinois	19,840	36
18. Michigan	19,765	35
19. Wisconsin	19,691	34
20. Texas	19,631	34
21. Utah	19,501	33
22. Georgia	19,417	32
23. Washington	19,370	32
24. Rhode Island	19,276	31
25. Louisiana	19,260	31
26. Colorado	18,864	28
27. Arizona	18,703	27
28. South Carolina	18,685	27
29. New York	18,667	27
30. North Dakota	18,630	26
31. Pennsylvania	18,413	25
32. Missouri	18,281	24
33. Indiana	18,153	23
34. North Carolina	17,995	22
35. South Dakota	17,921	21
36. Ohio	17,880	21
37. Iowa	17,724	20
38. Kansas	17,540	18
39. Montana	17,478	18
40. Alabama	17,435	17
41. Tennessee	17,384	17
42. Kentucky	17,283	16
43. Arkansas	17,205	16
44. Nebraska	17,113	15
45. New Mexico	17,044	14
46. Oklahoma	16,780	12
47. Idaho	16,591	11
48. Wyoming	16,314	9
49. Mississippi	15,131	0
50. West Virginia	14,718	0

Service Sector Strength

DOING THE MATH

No segment of the U.S. economy is growing faster than the service sector, which added jobs at an annual rate of 4 percent in the early 1990s. More than 30 million Americans now work for service employers, ranging from advertising agencies to auto repair shops, from dance studios to dental clinics. This category counts these service sector establishments in each state, expressing the total as a rate per 100,000 residents.

BEST STATES

Vermont, with 6,096 employers in this classification, has the healthiest service sector in America. Its rate is 1,083 service businesses per 100,000 residents. The only other state above a rate of 1,000 is Colorado.

WORST STATES

The service sector in Mississippi is weak, with just 606 employers per 100,000 residents. Four other states are below 700: Alabama, West Virginia, Utah, and Kentucky.

REGIONAL WINNERS

East—Vermont
South—Florida
Midwest—Nebraska
West—Colorado

BIGGEST SURPRISE

You would expect a large, expanding state such as California to have a robust service sector. But it does no better than 15th place in this category.

THE BOTTOM LINE

Five of the top 10 states are from the East; four are from the West. The South wins a clear decision at the bottom of the list, with six of the 10 lowest entries.

260 Service Sector Strength

State	Service Sector Establishments Per 100,000 Residents	Points
1. Vermont	1,083	100
2. Colorado	1,052	100
3. Connecticut	974	80
4. New Hampshire	967	78
5. Wyoming	959	76
Alaska	959	76
7. Florida	955	75
8. Montana	931	69
9. Massachusetts	922	66
New Jersey	922	66
11. Rhode Island	912	64
12. Oregon	908	63
13. Delaware	899	60
14. Maine	890	58
15. California	885	57
16. Washington	876	54
17. Nebraska	875	54
18. North Dakota	872	53
19. New York	868	52
20. Nevada	867	52
21. South Dakota	858	50
22. Hawaii	851	48
23. Minnesota	844	46
24. Kansas	843	46
25. Maryland	838	45
26. Missouri	836	44
27. Iowa	826	41
28. Arizona	824	41
29. Virginia	821	40
30. Pennsylvania	805	36
31. Idaho	796	34
32. Illinois	795	34
33. New Mexico	792	33
34. Oklahoma	781	30
35. Texas	780	30
Georgia	780	30
37. Wisconsin	775	28
38. Ohio	767	26
39. Tennessee	764	26
40. North Carolina	741	20
41. Indiana	739	19
42. Michigan	726	16
43. Louisiana	716	13
44. South Carolina	713	12
45. Arkansas	712	12
46. Kentucky	690	6
47. Utah	689	6
48. West Virginia	684	5
49. Alabama	666	0
50. Mississippi	606	0

Business: Scores and Grades

BEST STATE

Connecticut went through some rocky times in the early 1990s, but this section takes a long-range view. The underlying, historical strength of its business climate is what earned first place for Connecticut. Only Alaska has a larger GSP on a per capita basis; only Vermont and Colorado have greater concentrations of service businesses. Connecticut's manufacturing and retail sectors are also impressive. It is no. 5 in value added by manufacture and no. 7 in retail sales per household.

RUNNERS-UP

New Hampshire, no. 2 in this section, set the pace for economic growth in the 1980s with a 162.5 percent increase in GSP. New Hampshire also has America's second-strongest retail sector. Four other states earned A's: New Jersey, Delaware, Vermont, and Massachusetts.

WORST STATES

The business climate in West Virginia is decidedly unpromising. No state has lower retail sales per household; only Mississippi has a weaker GSP. Six other states were hit with F's: New Mexico, Oklahoma, Mississippi, Montana, and both Dakotas.

REGIONAL WINNERS

East—Connecticut
South—Virginia
Midwest—Minnesota
West—California

REGIONAL AVERAGES

East—68 (B)
South—38 (D+)
Midwest—42 (C–)
West—42 (C–)

262 BIGGEST SURPRISE

States don't need to be big to be economically strong. Among the top 10 are several unexpected entries, including New Hampshire, Delaware, Vermont, Hawaii, and Maine.

THE BOTTOM LINE

America's soundest long-range business climate is in the East, which earned eight of this section's 12 A's and B's. The West, on the other hand, has four of the 10 worst states, while the South has three.

Business: Scores and Grades

State	Score	Grade
1. Connecticut	100	A+
2. New Hampshire	94	A
3. New Jersey	90	A
4. Delaware	86	A
5. Vermont	83	A–
Massachusetts	83	A–
7. California	72	B
8. Virginia	67	B
9. Hawaii	65	B
Maine	65	B
11. Alaska	63	B–
New York	63	B–
13. North Carolina	58	C+
Minnesota	58	C+
Georgia	58	C+
16. Colorado	57	C+
17. Nevada	56	C+
18. Illinois	55	C+
Maryland	55	C+
Rhode Island	55	C+
21. Florida	53	C
22. Washington	51	C
23. Wisconsin	50	C
24. Missouri	49	C
25. Indiana	46	C
26. Ohio	45	C
Oregon	45	C
Tennessee	45	C
Michigan	45	C
30. South Carolina	43	C–
31. Pennsylvania	42	C–
32. Arizona	41	C–
Kansas	41	C–
34. Iowa	40	C–
Nebraska	40	C–
36. Texas	39	D+
37. Wyoming	32	D
38. Kentucky	31	D
39. Alabama	26	D
40. Arkansas	24	D–
41. Utah	22	D–
42. Louisiana	21	D–
Idaho	21	D–
44. South Dakota	18	F
45. North Dakota	16	F
46. Montana	15	F
47. Mississippi	13	F
48. Oklahoma	12	F
49. New Mexico	8	F
50. West Virginia	0	F

18

Personal Finances

The Big Question

Which state provides the best opportunity for individual financial growth?

The Categories

1. Per Capita Income
2. Income Growth
3. Unemployment
4. Poverty
5. Upper Incomes

Per Capita Income

DOING THE MATH

The Founding Fathers intended everyone to share equally in the blessings of life, liberty, and the pursuit of happiness. But they didn't say anything about the blessings of money. Wide financial disparities have always existed between states. This category looks at each state's per capita income, which is determined by totaling the money received annually by all residents (including children) and dividing it into the state's population.

BEST STATES

America's highest standard of living can be found in Connecticut, which has a per capita income of $26,022. New Jersey is second at $25,666. Ten other states have income levels above $20,000.

WORST STATES

Poverty is widespread in Mississippi, depressing the state's per capita income to $13,328, the lowest figure in the nation. West Virginia is next to last at $14,301. Also below $15,000 are Utah, Arkansas, and New Mexico.

REGIONAL WINNERS

East—Connecticut
South—Virginia
Midwest—Illinois
West—Hawaii

BIGGEST SURPRISE

Several small states are giants in terms of per capita income. The top 10 includes New Hampshire, Hawaii, Alaska, and Delaware—each with fewer than 1.2 million residents.

THE BOTTOM LINE

America's highest income levels are found in the East, which placed seven states in this category's top 10. Six of the bottom states, on the other hand, are from the South.

266 Per Capita Income

State	Per Capita Income	Points
1. Connecticut	$26,022	100
2. New Jersey	25,666	100
3. Massachusetts	23,003	77
4. New York	22,471	72
5. Maryland	22,189	69
6. New Hampshire	21,760	66
7. Hawaii	21,190	61
8. Alaska	21,067	60
9. California	20,847	58
10. Delaware	20,816	57
11. Illinois	20,731	57
12. Virginia	20,082	51
13. Nevada	19,783	48
14. Washington	19,484	46
15. Colorado	19,358	44
16. Pennsylvania	19,306	44
17. Rhode Island	19,207	43
18. Minnesota	19,125	42
19. Florida	18,992	41
20. Michigan	18,655	38
21. Kansas	18,322	35
22. Vermont	17,997	33
23. Wisconsin	17,939	32
24. Missouri	17,928	32
25. Ohio	17,770	31
26. Nebraska	17,718	30
27. Oregon	17,575	29
28. Maine	17,454	28
29. Georgia	17,436	28
30. Iowa	17,296	26
31. Texas	17,230	26
32. Indiana	17,179	25
33. Wyoming	16,937	23
34. North Carolina	16,853	22
35. Arizona	16,579	20
36. Tennessee	16,486	19
37. South Dakota	16,071	16
38. Montana	15,675	12
39. Kentucky	15,626	12
40. North Dakota	15,605	11
41. Oklahoma	15,541	11
42. Alabama	15,518	11
43. South Carolina	15,467	10
44. Idaho	15,333	9
45. Louisiana	15,046	7
46. New Mexico	14,644	3
47. Arkansas	14,629	3
48. Utah	14,625	3
49. West Virginia	14,301	0
50. Mississippi	13,328	0

Income Growth

DOING THE MATH

It's one thing for a state to be a national leader in per capita income; it's quite another for it to maintain that level. Average incomes are constantly on the rise because of inflation and local economic conditions. This category measures the growth rate for each state's per capita income between 1986 and 1991.

BEST STATES

No state could match Hawaii's rapid income growth during this half decade. Its per capita income expanded from $15,305 in 1986 to $21,190 in 1991, an increase of 38.5 percent. Mississippi is second at 35.7 percent.

WORST STATES

Alaska residents fought a losing battle with inflation between 1986 and 1991. Their state's per capita income inched up only 15.4 percent from $18,256 to $21,067. Arizona is the only other state below 20 percent.

REGIONAL WINNERS

East—New Jersey
South—Mississippi
Midwest—South Dakota
West—Hawaii

BIGGEST SURPRISE

Who would expect to see Mississippi as a leader in any income category? It's a surprising no. 2 here, still with a low per capita income ($13,328), but at least a little closer to the rest of America.

THE BOTTOM LINE

Income levels are rising most rapidly in the South, which includes six of the top 12 states. Six of the 10 worst states are in the West.

268 Income Growth

State	Change in Per Capita Income, 1986–1991	Points
1. Hawaii	38.5%	100
2. Mississippi	35.7	100
3. Kentucky	35.3	98
4. South Dakota	35.2	97
5. New Jersey	34.2	91
6. Alabama	34.1	90
7. South Carolina	33.4	86
8. Connecticut	33.0	84
9. Idaho	32.3	79
10. Tennessee	32.2	79
North Carolina	32.2	79
Maine	32.2	79
13. Vermont	32.1	78
14. New York	31.5	74
15. West Virginia	31.3	73
16. Pennsylvania	31.2	73
17. Delaware	31.0	72
18. Arkansas	30.5	68
Nebraska	30.5	68
20. Massachusetts	30.2	67
21. Oregon	30.0	66
22. Illinois	29.9	65
23. Maryland	29.3	61
24. Montana	29.2	61
Rhode Island	29.2	61
26. Louisiana	29.1	60
27. Iowa	28.9	59
28. Washington	28.6	57
29. Virginia	28.4	56
30. Indiana	28.1	54
31. Utah	27.9	53
32. Florida	27.5	51
New Hampshire	27.5	51
34. Wisconsin	27.3	50
35. Wyoming	27.2	49
Georgia	27.2	49
37. Minnesota	26.5	45
38. Kansas	26.3	44
39. Ohio	26.2	43
40. North Dakota	26.0	42
41. Nevada	25.9	41
42. Missouri	25.6	39
43. New Mexico	25.2	37
44. Colorado	24.2	31
45. Texas	24.1	30
46. Oklahoma	23.9	29
47. Michigan	23.5	27
48. California	21.9	17
49. Arizona	19.1	0
50. Alaska	15.4	0

Unemployment

DOING THE MATH

Most economic statistics go in one ear and out the other. Who, after all, can relate to a 0.3 percent increase in the gross domestic product? But all of us understand one economic figure—the unemployment rate. The higher it goes, the greater the odds that we'll be out of work. This category averages each state's annual unemployment rates for the decade of 1982–1991.

BEST STATES

High unemployment is unknown in Nebraska. Its *worst* jobless rate during the decade was 6.1 percent in 1982. Eight states didn't have a single year that good. Nebraska's 10-year average of 4.3 percent is America's best. Hawaii and South Dakota are tied for second at 4.4 percent.

WORST STATES

West Virginia's average unemployment rate from 1982 to 1991 was 12.0 percent; its worst year, 1983, saw unemployment at 18.0 percent. Louisiana is the only other state with a 10-year rate above 10 percent.

REGIONAL WINNERS

East—New Hampshire
South—Virginia
Midwest—Nebraska
West—Hawaii

BIGGEST SURPRISE

The myth is that farm states have declining economies and seriously high unemployment. The reality is that Nebraska, Kansas, and both Dakotas are among the eight states with the lowest jobless rates.

THE BOTTOM LINE

Five of this category's 11 leading states are eastern; four are midwestern. The South has five of the 10 states at the bottom.

270 Unemployment

State	Average Annual Unemployment Rate, 1982–1991	Points
1. Nebraska	4.3%	100
2. Hawaii	4.4	100
South Dakota	4.4	100
4. New Hampshire	4.5	99
5. Connecticut	4.8	94
6. Vermont	5.0	90
7. Kansas	5.1	89
North Dakota	5.1	89
9. Virginia	5.2	87
10. Maryland	5.3	85
Massachusetts	5.3	85
12. Delaware	5.4	84
13. North Carolina	5.7	78
Minnesota	5.7	78
New Jersey	5.7	78
16. Rhode Island	5.9	74
Maine	5.9	74
18. Utah	6.1	71
Georgia	6.1	71
20. Iowa	6.2	69
21. Colorado	6.3	67
22. New York	6.4	66
Florida	6.4	66
24. Arizona	6.6	62
25. South Carolina	6.7	61
Wisconsin	6.7	61
27. Wyoming	6.8	58
28. Nevada	6.9	57
Missouri	6.9	57
Oklahoma	6.9	57
31. California	7.1	54
32. Texas	7.2	51
33. Montana	7.3	49
34. Indiana	7.4	48
Idaho	7.4	48
Pennsylvania	7.4	48
37. Tennessee	7.7	42
38. Oregon	7.8	40
39. Washington	8.0	36
40. New Mexico	8.1	34
41. Ohio	8.2	34
Illinois	8.2	34
43. Arkansas	8.3	31
44. Kentucky	8.7	25
45. Alaska	9.3	14
46. Alabama	9.4	12
47. Mississippi	9.9	3
Michigan	9.9	3
49. Louisiana	10.1	0
50. West Virginia	12.0	0

Poverty

DOING THE MATH

Life is a day-to-day struggle for the 7 million families that are living below the poverty level. That means 10.7 percent of all American families are officially classified as poor. The problem is particularly severe for minorities, with poverty rates of 29.3 percent for blacks and 25.0 percent for Hispanics. This category looks at each state's overall poverty rate for families of all races.

BEST STATES

No state has managed to wipe out poverty, but New Hampshire has come closest. Just 4.4 percent of its families are classified as poor. Also below 6 percent are Connecticut and New Jersey.

WORST STATES

No racial or ethnic group is immune from poverty in Mississippi, where 20.2 percent of all families are poor. Louisiana is next to last, with a rate of 19.4 percent. Three other states are at 16 percent or higher.

REGIONAL WINNERS

East—New Hampshire
South—Virginia
Midwest—Minnesota
West—Hawaii

BIGGEST SURPRISE

Poverty is severe throughout the South. At least 9 percent of the families are poor in every southern state—except Virginia, which ranks a respectable fourteenth on the national scale, with a poverty rate of 7.7 percent.

THE BOTTOM LINE

Eight of the 10 states with the lowest poverty rates are in the East; eight of the 10 worst rates are found in the South.

272 Poverty

State	Families Below Poverty Level	Points
1. New Hampshire	4.4%	100
2. Connecticut	5.0	100
3. New Jersey	5.6	96
4. Hawaii	6.0	93
Maryland	6.0	93
6. Delaware	6.1	92
7. Massachusetts	6.7	88
8. Alaska	6.8	88
Rhode Island	6.8	88
10. Vermont	6.9	87
11. Minnesota	7.3	84
Nevada	7.3	84
13. Wisconsin	7.6	82
14. Virginia	7.7	81
15. Washington	7.8	81
16. Indiana	7.9	80
17. Maine	8.0	79
Nebraska	8.0	79
19. Pennsylvania	8.2	78
20. Kansas	8.3	77
21. Iowa	8.4	76
22. Colorado	8.6	75
Utah	8.6	75
24. Oregon	8.7	74
25. Florida	9.0	72
Illinois	9.0	72
27. California	9.3	70
Wyoming	9.3	70
29. Idaho	9.7	67
Ohio	9.7	67
31. North Carolina	9.9	66
32. New York	10.0	65
33. Missouri	10.1	65
34. Michigan	10.2	64
35. North Dakota	10.9	59
36. Arizona	11.4	56
37. Georgia	11.5	55
38. South Dakota	11.6	54
39. South Carolina	11.9	52
40. Montana	12.0	51
41. Tennessee	12.4	49
42. Oklahoma	13.0	44
43. Texas	14.1	37
44. Alabama	14.3	35
45. Arkansas	14.8	32
46. Kentucky	16.0	24
West Virginia	16.0	24
48. New Mexico	16.5	20
49. Louisiana	19.4	0
50. Mississippi	20.2	0

Upper Incomes

DOING THE MATH

Who is in a better position than the Internal Revenue Service to know how much money Americans really earn? The IRS receives 115 million individual tax returns every year. Of particular interest on each form is the adjusted gross income, the figure that determines the resulting tax bill. The IRS says that 840,000 returns list adjusted gross incomes higher than $200,000. This category expresses each state's number of such upper-income households as a rate per 100,000 tax returns.

BEST STATES

Fully 22,750 of Connecticut's 1.66 million tax returns report adjusted gross incomes of more than $200,000. That translates to 1,372 upper-income households per 100,000 returns. New Jersey and New York also are above 1,000.

WORST STATES

Few residents of Montana are wealthy. It has just 331 upper-income households per 100,000 returns. Mississippi is next-to-last at 347.

REGIONAL WINNERS

East—Connecticut
South—Florida
Midwest—Illinois
West—California

BIGGEST SURPRISE

A small group of people holds a large proportion of Florida's wealth. That's why the state ranks seventh in this category, even though it's just 19th in per capita income.

THE BOTTOM LINE

Five of the top 10 states are eastern; three are western. There's a three-way tie at the bottom. The East, South, and Midwest each have three states among the 11 worst.

274 Upper Incomes

State	Tax Returns With Adjusted Gross Income Above $200,000 Per 100,000 Returns	Points
1. Connecticut	1,372	100
2. New Jersey	1,155	100
3. New York	1,098	93
4. California	983	79
5. Massachusetts	880	66
6. Illinois	876	65
7. Florida	857	63
Nevada	857	63
9. Maryland	843	61
10. Hawaii	809	57
11. Texas	698	43
12. Washington	683	42
13. Delaware	666	39
14. Rhode Island	657	38
15. Pennsylvania	650	37
16. Virginia	645	37
17. Minnesota	638	36
18. Georgia	634	36
19. Colorado	622	34
20. Michigan	599	31
21. New Hampshire	594	31
22. Arizona	578	29
23. Kansas	569	28
24. Oregon	561	26
25. Missouri	539	24
26. Tennessee	536	23
27. Ohio	535	23
28. Louisiana	524	22
29. Wisconsin	513	21
30. Alaska	512	20
31. Indiana	491	18
32. Oklahoma	487	17
33. North Carolina	481	17
34. Kentucky	480	17
35. Nebraska	472	15
36. Wyoming	467	15
37. Utah	466	15
38. Alabama	460	14
39. Idaho	440	11
40. Vermont	415	8
South Carolina	415	8
42. Maine	413	8
43. South Dakota	412	8
44. Iowa	402	7
45. Arkansas	381	4
46. West Virginia	356	1
47. North Dakota	352	1
48. New Mexico	349	0
49. Mississippi	347	0
50. Montana	331	0

Personal Finances: Scores and Grades

BEST STATE

Connecticut is no. 1 in this section, meaning it offers America's best environment for individual financial growth. No other state has a higher per capita income or a larger proportion of upper-income households. Only New Hampshire has fewer families living below the poverty level. Nor has unemployment historically been much of a problem. Connecticut had an average jobless rate of just 4.8 percent from 1982 through 1991, fifth-best in the nation.

RUNNERS-UP

New Jersey is second to Connecticut in the Per Capita Income and Upper Incomes categories. It holds the same postion in the section as a whole. The only other state in the A range is Hawaii, thanks to its strong income growth and low unemployment.

WORST STATES

It's difficult to make ends meet in Louisiana, the last-place state. Its rates are severely high for poverty (19.4 percent of families) and unemployment (10.1 percent in 1982–1991). F's also went to seven other states, including four from the South.

REGIONAL WINNERS

East—Connecticut
South—Virginia
Midwest—Nebraska, Illinois
West—Hawaii

REGIONAL AVERAGES

East—63 (B–)
South—27 (D)
Midwest—39 (D+)
West—36 (D+)

276 BIGGEST SURPRISE

The West bills itself as the land of opportunity, but only one of its 13 states earned an above-average grade in this section. Hawaii is a strong no. 3, making it the only western state in the top 10.

THE BOTTOM LINE

The East, with eight of the top 10 scores, is the best region for personal financial growth. The South holds six of the 11 worst slots.

Personal Finances: Scores and Grades

State	Score	Grade
1. Connecticut	100	A+
2. New Jersey	96	A
3. Hawaii	83	A–
4. Massachusetts	76	B+
5. New York	72	B
Maryland	72	B
7. New Hampshire	66	B
Delaware	66	B
9. Virginia	57	C+
10. Rhode Island	55	C+
11. Vermont	53	C
12. Nevada	52	C
Nebraska	52	C
Florida	52	C
Illinois	52	C
16. Minnesota	50	C
17. Pennsylvania	49	C
California	49	C
19. South Dakota	48	C
20. Kansas	47	C
21. Maine	46	C
22. North Carolina	44	C–
Washington	44	C–
24. Colorado	42	C–
25. Wisconsin	40	C–
26. Georgia	39	D+
27. Iowa	38	D+
Oregon	38	D+
29. Indiana	35	D+
30. Utah	33	D
South Carolina	33	D
Missouri	33	D
33. Wyoming	32	D
Idaho	32	D
Tennessee	32	D
36. North Dakota	29	D
37. Ohio	28	D
38. Texas	25	D
39. Alaska	24	D–
40. Kentucky	22	D–
Montana	22	D–
42. Arizona	20	D–
43. Michigan	19	F
Alabama	19	F
45. Oklahoma	17	F
46. Arkansas	13	F
47. Mississippi	4	F
48. West Virginia	2	F
49. New Mexico	1	F
50. Louisiana	0	F

19

Public Safety

The Big Question

Which state has the safest streets and neighborhoods?

The Categories

1. All Crimes
2. Violent Crimes
3. Police Presence
4. Public Saftey Spending
5. Prison Population

All Crimes

DOING THE MATH

America's crime statistics are shocking—and depressing. Police in this country investigate 14.5 million crimes each year, including 3 million burglaries, 1 million assaults, 100,000 rapes, and 23,000 murders. This category adds up the annual number of all reported crimes, regardless of severity. Each state's total is then converted to a rate per 100,000 residents.

BEST STATES

West Virginia has America's lowest overall crime rate. It annually has just 2,663 reported crimes per 100,000 residents. The only other state with a figure below 3,000 is North Dakota.

WORST STATES

Miami and Tampa have exceptionally high crime rates; Jacksonville is also well above the national average. So it comes as no surprise that Florida holds last place in this category, with 8,547 reported crimes per 100,000. Texas and Arizona also have rates above 7,000.

REGIONAL WINNERS

East—West Virginia
South—Kentucky
Midwest—North Dakota
West—Montana

BIGGEST SURPRISE

Thirteen of the 14 states with the lowest crime rates have fewer than 4 million residents. The exception is Pennsylvania, which ranks no. 6 despite its population of 11.9 million.

THE BOTTOM LINE

The East has five of the 10 best states, followed by the Midwest with three. The West, on the other hand, placed five states in the bottom 10.

280 All Crimes

State	Reported Crimes Per 100,000 Residents	Points
1. West Virginia	2,663	100
2. North Dakota	2,794	100
3. South Dakota	3,079	94
4. Kentucky	3,358	89
5. New Hampshire	3,448	87
6. Pennsylvania	3,559	85
7. Montana	3,648	83
8. Maine	3,768	81
9. Vermont	3,955	77
10. Iowa	4,134	73
11. Idaho	4,196	72
12. Mississippi	4,221	72
13. Nebraska	4,354	69
14. Wyoming	4,389	68
15. Wisconsin	4,466	67
16. Minnesota	4,496	66
17. Virginia	4,607	64
18. Indiana	4,818	60
19. Ohio	5,033	55
20. Rhode Island	5,039	55
21. Arkansas	5,175	53
22. Massachusetts	5,322	50
23. Connecticut	5,364	49
24. Alabama	5,366	49
25. Tennessee	5,367	49
26. Missouri	5,416	48
27. New Jersey	5,431	48
28. Kansas	5,534	45
29. Utah	5,608	44
30. Oklahoma	5,669	43
31. Alaska	5,702	42
32. Oregon	5,755	41
33. Delaware	5,869	39
34. North Carolina	5,889	38
35. Hawaii	5,970	37
36. Colorado	6,074	35
37. Illinois	6,132	34
38. Michigan	6,138	33
39. South Carolina	6,179	33
40. Maryland	6,209	32
41. New York	6,245	31
42. Nevada	6,299	30
43. Washington	6,304	30
44. Louisiana	6,425	28
45. Georgia	6,493	26
46. New Mexico	6,679	23
47. California	6,773	21
48. Arizona	7,406	8
49. Texas	7,819	0
50. Florida	8,547	0

Violent Crimes

DOING THE MATH

The Federal Bureau of Investigation divides all crimes into two classifications. Property crimes include larceny, burglary, and motor vehicle theft. Violent crimes are murder, rape, robbery, and assault. We are concerned here with the latter group. We came up with each state's annual total of violent crimes, expressing it as a rate per 100,000 residents.

BEST STATES

People who live in North Dakota are not hot-tempered souls. Only 415 violent crimes are reported in the entire state each year, equal to 65 per 100,000 residents. Four other states have rates below 150: Vermont, New Hampshire, Maine, and Montana.

WORST STATES

Florida police are kept busy with a yearly caseload of 1,250 murders, 6,800 rapes, 53,000 robberies, and 96,000 assaults. The state's violent crime rate is 1,184 per 100,000. Also above 1,000 are New York, California, and Illinois.

REGIONAL WINNERS

East—Vermont
South—Virginia
Midwest—North Dakota
West—Montana

BIGGEST SURPRISE

It's no surprise that the four states with the worst violent crime rates are large; each has a population of at least 11 million. But the entry just ahead of them, no. 46 South Carolina, is a relatively small 3.5 million.

THE BOTTOM LINE

Four of the top 10 states are eastern; three each are midwestern and western. Five of the bottom 10 are southern.

282 Violent Crimes

State	Reported Violent Crimes Per 100,000 Residents	Points
1. North Dakota	65	100
2. Vermont	117	100
3. New Hampshire	119	100
4. Maine	132	99
5. Montana	140	98
6. South Dakota	182	94
7. West Virginia	191	93
8. Hawaii	242	88
9. Wisconsin	277	85
10. Utah	287	84
11. Idaho	290	83
12. Iowa	303	82
13. Wyoming	310	82
14. Minnesota	316	81
15. Nebraska	335	79
16. Virginia	373	76
17. Mississippi	389	74
18. Kentucky	438	69
19. Pennsylvania	450	68
20. Rhode Island	462	67
21. Kansas	500	63
22. Indiana	505	63
23. Oregon	506	63
24. Washington	523	61
25. Connecticut	540	60
26. Colorado	559	58
27. Ohio	562	57
28. Oklahoma	584	55
29. Arkansas	593	55
30. Alaska	614	53
31. New Jersey	635	51
32. North Carolina	658	48
33. Arizona	671	47
34. Nevada	677	47
35. Delaware	714	43
36. Tennessee	726	42
37. Massachusetts	736	41
38. Georgia	738	41
39. Missouri	763	38
40. Michigan	803	34
41. New Mexico	835	31
42. Texas	840	31
43. Alabama	844	31
44. Louisiana	951	20
45. Maryland	956	20
46. South Carolina	973	18
47. Illinois	1,039	12
48. California	1,090	7
49. New York	1,164	0
50. Florida	1,184	0

Police Presence

DOING THE MATH

Studies conducted at the University of Maryland have shown there is a direct link between a community's crime rate and the size of its police force. This category measures the adequacy of police staffing in each state, expressing the number of law enforcement employees as a rate per 10,000 reported crimes. The higher the number, the more police officers there are to handle each case.

BEST STATES

Wyoming is among America's safest states. One reason is its superior level of police staffing. There are 1,876 law enforcement employees in Wyoming handling an annual load of 20,189 reported crimes. That works out to 929 employees per 10,000 crimes. New Jersey ranks second, with a rate of 792.

WORST STATES

The police in Washington are woefully understaffed, with just 351 employees per 10,000 crimes. The situation is virtually the same in neighboring Oregon, next to last with a rate of 363.

REGIONAL WINNERS

East—New Jersey
South—Kentucky
Midwest—North Dakota
West—Wyoming

BIGGEST SURPRISE

Large states often are strapped by budgetary problems, which is why they understaff their police departments. New Jersey, no. 2 in this category, is an exception.

THE BOTTOM LINE

The East, with four of the 10 best states, has the strongest police presence. Staffing is worst in the West, which has five states in the bottom 10.

Police Presence

State	Law Enforcement Employees Per 10,000 Reported Crimes	Points
1. Wyoming	929	100
2. New Jersey	792	100
3. West Virginia	769	95
4. North Dakota	745	89
5. Montana	674	72
6. South Dakota	647	66
7. New Hampshire	639	64
8. Wisconsin	626	61
9. Pennsylvania	624	61
10. Kentucky	608	57
11. Idaho	606	57
12. Virginia	575	49
13. Nebraska	568	48
14. Illinois	552	44
Rhode Island	552	44
16. Maryland	551	44
17. Alabama	539	41
18. Oklahoma	534	40
19. Tennessee	533	40
20. New York	532	39
21. Kansas	531	39
22. Georgia	528	38
23. Maine	527	38
24. Vermont	520	37
25. Colorado	517	36
26. Iowa	515	35
27. Massachusetts	495	31
28. Nevada	493	30
29. Connecticut	488	29
30. Hawaii	484	28
31. Delaware	483	28
32. Alaska	479	27
33. Missouri	475	26
34. New Mexico	472	25
North Carolina	472	25
36. Indiana	471	25
37. Ohio	470	25
Mississippi	470	25
39. Minnesota	466	24
40. Florida	458	22
41. Arizona	457	22
42. Louisiana	453	21
43. Arkansas	452	21
44. Michigan	433	16
45. California	432	16
46. Texas	421	14
47. South Carolina	416	12
48. Utah	387	6
49. Oregon	363	0
50. Washington	351	0

Public Safety Spending

DOING THE MATH

Keeping the peace is an expensive task. The typical state annually spends $98 per resident on public safety: $22 for police services and $76 for prisons. Multiply $98 by a few million residents, and you'll see the large amounts of money involved. This category measures each state's financial commitment to public safety, totaling its per capita expenditures on police and corrections.

BEST STATES

No state allocates more money to its police than Alaska's $75 per person. Nor does anyone spend more on prisons than Alaska's per capita average of $228. Those two figures add up to $303 per resident, tops in the nation. Delaware is in second place at $175.

WORST STATES

Crime is not a serious problem in North Dakota, so public safety gets a fairly low financial priority. No state spends less on police and corrections than North Dakota's $35 per person, though West Virginia comes close at $36.

REGIONAL WINNERS

East—Delaware
South—Virginia
Midwest—Michigan
West—Alaska

BIGGEST SURPRISE

Most of this category's leaders also have high income levels. Not Arizona. It's only 35th in per capita income, but it's no. 9 in public safety spending.

THE BOTTOM LINE

The East spends the most on public safety, placing six states in the top 10. The Midwest spends the least, with five states in the bottom 10.

286 Public Safety Spending

State	Annual Per Capita Spending on Police and Corrections	Points
1. Alaska	$303	100
2. Delaware	175	100
3. Connecticut	170	96
4. Maryland	160	89
5. New York	140	75
6. Massachusetts	138	74
7. Virginia	134	70
8. California	126	64
9. Arizona	123	63
10. Rhode Island	119	59
11. Nevada	116	58
12. New Jersey	112	55
South Carolina	112	55
Georgia	112	55
15. New Mexico	110	53
16. Michigan	107	51
17. Oregon	103	48
18. North Carolina	99	46
19. Kansas	96	43
20. Washington	94	42
Vermont	94	42
22. Tennessee	92	40
23. Florida	89	38
24. Hawaii	88	37
Colorado	88	37
Louisiana	88	37
27. Wyoming	86	36
28. Kentucky	84	35
29. Montana	83	34
30. Maine	79	31
31. Illinois	78	30
32. Oklahoma	77	29
33. Idaho	75	28
34. Texas	73	27
35. Ohio	72	26
36. Wisconsin	71	25
Iowa	71	25
38. Pennsylvania	70	25
39. Indiana	69	24
Utah	69	24
41. Nebraska	62	19
Alabama	62	19
43. New Hampshire	61	18
44. South Dakota	60	17
45. Minnesota	58	16
Arkansas	58	16
47. Missouri	57	15
48. Mississippi	48	8
49. West Virginia	36	0
50. North Dakota	35	0

Prison Population

DOING THE MATH

Fully 739,000 Americans have unenviable, 24-hour-a-day jobs. They are prisoners, serving sentences of more than one year in the nation's correctional facilities. Roughly 688,000 are in state prisons, while 51,000 are held by the federal government. This category counts the number of state and federal prisoners within each state, expressing the result as a rate per 100,000 residents.

BEST STATES

North Dakota has few hardened criminals. Its prisons hold just 435 inmates with sentences longer than one year, which works out to 68 prisoners per 100,000 residents. Two other states are below 100: Minnesota and West Virginia.

WORST STATES

The prisons in South Carolina are jammed with 16,208 inmates. That's equal to 465 per 100,000 residents, the worst rate in the country. Also above 400 are Nevada and Louisiana.

REGIONAL WINNERS

East—West Virginia
South—Tennessee
Midwest—North Dakota
West—Utah

BIGGEST SURPRISE

Most large states have prison populations to match. The sole exception is Massachusetts, which has only 131 inmates per 100,000 residents, America's seventh-best rate.

THE BOTTOM LINE

Five eastern and four midwestern states are among the 10 with the fewest prisoners. At the other end of the list is the South, with five of the 10 worst states.

288 Prison Population

State	State and Federal Prisoners (Sentenced to More Than 1 Year) Per 100,000 Residents	Points
1. North Dakota	68	100
2. Minnesota	73	100
3. West Virginia	87	96
4. Maine	121	87
Vermont	121	87
New Hampshire	121	87
7. Massachusetts	131	84
8. Iowa	143	81
9. Utah	144	81
10. Nebraska	145	81
11. Wisconsin	150	79
12. Hawaii	154	78
13. Rhode Island	158	77
14. Washington	164	75
15. Montana	178	72
16. Pennsylvania	188	69
17. South Dakota	193	68
18. Idaho	195	67
19. New Mexico	202	65
20. Tennessee	213	62
Colorado	213	62
22. Indiana	228	58
Oregon	228	58
24. Kansas	233	57
25. Connecticut	236	56
26. Illinois	241	55
27. Wyoming	244	54
28. Kentucky	245	54
29. North Carolina	268	47
30. New Jersey	273	46
31. Virginia	282	44
32. Arkansas	286	42
33. Missouri	292	41
34. Ohio	293	40
35. Texas	295	40
36. New York	305	37
37. Mississippi	314	35
38. California	316	34
39. Georgia	334	30
40. Delaware	336	29
41. Alaska	337	29
42. Florida	343	27
43. Maryland	350	25
44. Michigan	369	20
45. Arizona	376	18
46. Alabama	380	17
47. Oklahoma	390	14
48. Louisiana	441	1
49. Nevada	443	0
50. South Carolina	465	0

Public Safety: Scores and Grades

BEST STATE

North Dakota is America's safest state. It has the lowest violent crime rate, just 65 per 100,000 persons; no other state is below 117. It also has the smallest share of prisoners per 100,000 residents. And only West Virginia has a total crime rate lower than North Dakota. A key factor is the state's high level of police staffing. North Dakota is no. 4 in the Police Presence category.

RUNNERS-UP

West Virginia, as already mentioned, has America's lowest total crime rate. It is also among the three states with the smallest prison populations and highest police staffing levels. The result is second place in this section. Three other states earned straight A's: Montana, New Hampshire, and Vermont.

WORST STATES

Public safety is a relative term in last-place Florida. It has the nation's highest rates of violent crimes and all crimes. Also receiving F's were Louisiana, Texas, South Carolina, and California.

REGIONAL WINNERS

East—West Virginia
South—Kentucky, Virginia
Midwest—North Dakota
West—Montana

REGIONAL AVERAGES

East—69 (B)
South—32 (D)
Midwest—57 (C+)
West—49 (C)

BIGGEST SURPRISE

Small states dominate this section. No surprise there. The eight states with A's have a *combined* population of 7.3 million. What is shocking is that Pennsylvania (population: 11.9 million) bucked this trend also to make the top 10.

290 THE BOTTOM LINE

America's safest region is the East, which has five of the 11 leading states. The South clearly is the most dangerous region, placing five states in the bottom 10.

Public Safety: Scores and Grades

State	Score	Grade
1. North Dakota	100	A+
2. West Virginia	98	A
3. Montana	90	A
4. New Hampshire	89	A
5. Vermont	85	A
6. Wyoming	84	A–
7. South Dakota	83	A–
8. Maine	82	A–
9. Wisconsin	76	B+
10. Pennsylvania	73	B
Idaho	73	B
12. Kentucky	72	B
Virginia	72	B
14. Rhode Island	71	B
New Jersey	71	B
16. Iowa	69	B
Nebraska	69	B
18. Connecticut	67	B
19. Minnesota	66	B
20. Massachusetts	64	B–
21. Hawaii	60	B–
22. Alaska	54	C
23. Kansas	53	C
24. Delaware	50	C
Utah	50	C
26. Tennessee	48	C
27. Indiana	47	C
Colorado	47	C
29. Mississippi	42	C–
30. Maryland	41	C–
Oregon	41	C–
32. Washington	40	C–
33. North Carolina	39	D+
34. Ohio	38	D+
35. New Mexico	36	D+
36. Georgia	34	D
37. Arkansas	33	D
38. New York	31	D
Oklahoma	31	D
40. Illinois	29	D
41. Missouri	27	D
42. Nevada	26	D
43. Arizona	24	D–
44. Alabama	23	D–
45. Michigan	22	D–
46. California	18	F
47. South Carolina	10	F
48. Texas	8	F
49. Louisiana	7	F
50. Florida	0	F

20

Transportation

The Big Question

Which state makes it easiest to get around, whether in a car, on public transit, or in a plane?

The Categories

1. Road Mileage
2. Motor Vehicle Deaths
3. Pavement Condition
4. Public Transit Usage
5. Airline Service

Road Mileage

DOING THE MATH

The recipe for traffic congestion requires two ingredients: too many cars and too few roads. This category looks for the states that have avoided such problems. We added up the length of all roads—from city streets to interstate highways—and multiplied this distance by the number of available lanes. (A four-lane highway, after all, has twice as much space as a two-lane road.) The resulting total of lane-miles is expressed as a rate per 100,000 residents.

BEST STATES

North Dakotans have no worries about traffic jams. The state has 175,133 lane-miles of roads, which works out to a spacious 27,407 lane-miles for every 100,000 persons. Neighboring South Dakota is the only other state above 20,000.

WORST STATES

Hawaii's 1.1 million residents jostle for position on just 8,802 lane-miles. That's only 794 lane-miles per 100,000 persons. New Jersey is next to last, with a rate of 954.

REGIONAL WINNERS

East—Vermont
South—Oklahoma
Midwest—North Dakota
West—Montana

BIGGEST SURPRISE

Small states generally have the fewest traffic problems. But tiny Delaware and Rhode Island, both in the bottom 10, are exceptions.

THE BOTTOM LINE

Traffic runs smooth and free in the Midwest and West. Each has five states in the top 10. Congestion is a serious problem in the East, with seven of the 10 worst states.

294 Road Mileage

State	Lane-Miles Per 100,000 Residents	Points
1. North Dakota	27,407	100
2. South Dakota	21,775	100
3. Montana	18,171	83
4. Wyoming	17,743	81
5. Idaho	12,579	56
6. Nebraska	11,836	52
7. Kansas	10,933	48
8. Iowa	8,274	35
9. Nevada	7,769	33
10. New Mexico	7,510	31
11. Oklahoma	7,292	30
12. Oregon	6,811	28
13. Arkansas	6,594	27
14. Minnesota	6,056	25
15. Mississippi	5,791	23
16. Utah	5,215	20
17. Vermont	5,159	20
18. Alaska	4,902	19
19. Colorado	4,864	19
20. Missouri	4,843	19
21. Alabama	4,642	18
22. Wisconsin	4,601	18
23. West Virginia	3,968	14
24. Kentucky	3,919	14
25. South Carolina	3,834	14
26. Texas	3,793	14
27. Maine	3,725	13
28. Tennessee	3,600	13
29. Georgia	3,526	12
30. Washington	3,458	12
31. Indiana	3,457	12
32. Arizona	2,995	10
33. North Carolina	2,973	10
34. Louisiana	2,910	9
35. New Hampshire	2,751	9
36. Michigan	2,650	8
37. Illinois	2,497	7
38. Virginia	2,340	7
39. Ohio	2,209	6
40. Pennsylvania	2,047	5
41. Florida	1,790	4
42. Delaware	1,747	4
43. Maryland	1,316	2
44. New York	1,305	2
45. Rhode Island	1,302	2
46. Connecticut	1,295	2
47. California	1,220	1
48. Massachusetts	1,193	1
49. New Jersey	954	0
50. Hawaii	794	0

Motor Vehicle Deaths

DOING THE MATH

The American road can be a dangerous place. More than 11 million motor vehicle accidents are reported in the United States each year, involving 14 million cars, 4.5 million trucks, and 180,000 motorcycles. Nearly 50,000 people die as a result. This category checks each state's road safety record, converting its number of deaths in motor vehicle accidents to a rate per 100,000 licensed drivers.

BEST STATES

America's safest roads are in Rhode Island, which annually has 12.5 motor vehicle deaths per 100,000 drivers. Four other states have death rates below 20: Massachusetts, New Jersey, Connecticut, and New Hampshire.

WORST STATES

About 500 of New Mexico's 1.07 million drivers die each year in motor vehicle accidents. That works out to 46.5 per 100,000, the nation's worst rate. South Carolina is next to last.

REGIONAL WINNERS

East—Rhode Island
South—Virginia
Midwest—Ohio
West—Washington

BIGGEST SURPRISE

Rhode Island, Massachusetts, New Jersey, and Connecticut have serious traffic congestion problems. You would also expect each to have accordingly large numbers of motor vehicle accidents. But they actually have the nation's four lowest death rates.

THE BOTTOM LINE

America's safest drivers are in the East, which holds nine of the top 10 slots. The most dangerous can be found in the South, with five states in the bottom 10.

296 Motor Vehicle Deaths

State	Motor Vehicle Deaths Per 100,000 Licensed Drivers	Points
1. Rhode Island	12.5	100
2. Massachusetts	14.4	100
3. New Jersey	15.9	95
4. Connecticut	17.1	90
5. New Hampshire	18.7	84
6. Pennsylvania	20.8	76
7. Ohio	20.9	76
8. New York	21.3	74
9. Maryland	21.6	73
Vermont	21.6	73
11. Illinois	21.8	73
12. Minnesota	22.5	70
13. Wisconsin	22.9	68
14. Maine	23.9	65
15. Nebraska	24.1	64
16. Michigan	24.3	63
17. Washington	24.4	63
Virginia	24.4	63
19. Iowa	24.5	63
20. Kansas	25.8	58
Hawaii	25.8	58
Utah	25.8	58
23. California	26.1	57
Oregon	26.1	57
25. North Dakota	26.4	56
26. Colorado	26.6	55
27. Oklahoma	28.4	48
28. Indiana	29.0	46
29. Texas	29.1	45
30. Delaware	29.5	44
31. Missouri	29.7	43
32. Alaska	30.3	41
33. North Carolina	30.4	41
34. South Dakota	31.1	38
35. Florida	32.0	35
36. Idaho	34.5	25
37. Georgia	34.9	24
38. Arkansas	35.1	23
Montana	35.1	23
40. Tennessee	35.2	23
41. Kentucky	35.4	22
Louisiana	35.4	22
43. Arizona	36.1	20
44. Wyoming	37.4	15
45. West Virginia	37.5	15
46. Alabama	39.8	6
Mississippi	39.8	6
48. Nevada	40.5	3
49. South Carolina	41.4	0
50. New Mexico	46.5	0

Pavement Condition

DOING THE MATH

The federal government quantifies everything, even the condition of the nation's roads. The Federal Highway Administration uses a five-point scale known as the Present Serviceability Rating. A PSR of 5.0 means a highway is in perfect condition; a 0.1 road is beyond hope. This category calculates the percentage of each state's principal highways with PSRs in the top range between 3.5 and 5.0.

BEST STATES

Wyoming drivers have come to expect a smooth ride. Fully 1,814 of Wyoming's 2,106 miles of principal highways are graded at 3.5 or better; that's 86.1 percent. Two other states are above 80 percent: Wisconsin and North Carolina.

WORST STATES

New Hampshire's road system has deteriorated to an alarming degree. Just 11.4 percent of the principal highways in New Hampshire receive PSRs between 3.5 and 5.0. North Dakota is next to last.

REGIONAL WINNERS

East—Maryland
South—North Carolina
Midwest—Wisconsin
West—Wyoming

BIGGEST SURPRISE

Ice and snow take their toll on northern roads, which is why most northern states get low PSRs. The key exceptions are the two leaders, Wyoming and Wisconsin.

THE BOTTOM LINE

The South, with five states in the top 10, has America's smoothest roads. Highways are in the worst condition in the Midwest, which has four of the nation's bottom 10 states.

298 Pavement Condition

State	Principal Highway Miles with Present Serviceability Ratings of 3.5 or Higher	Points
1. Wyoming	86.1%	100
2. Wisconsin	82.1	100
3. North Carolina	81.9	100
4. Florida	78.5	95
5. Maryland	78.0	94
6. Alabama	76.1	91
7. Mississippi	71.1	84
8. South Dakota	70.6	84
9. Georgia	68.3	80
10. Washington	66.9	78
11. Indiana	66.6	78
12. South Carolina	62.8	72
13. Virginia	62.6	72
14. Connecticut	62.3	72
15. Delaware	58.7	67
16. Oklahoma	58.1	66
17. New York	57.0	64
18. Utah	56.5	63
19. Illinois	55.7	62
20. Colorado	54.0	60
Nebraska	54.0	60
22. Tennessee	52.9	58
23. Maine	52.1	57
24. Kansas	51.9	57
25. Louisiana	50.5	55
26. Montana	50.4	55
27. Arizona	49.3	53
28. Texas	48.2	52
29. New Jersey	48.0	51
Rhode Island	48.0	51
Idaho	48.0	51
32. California	47.1	50
33. Arkansas	45.1	47
34. Oregon	42.5	43
35. Massachusetts	41.6	42
36. Kentucky	40.3	40
37. West Virginia	40.1	40
38. Ohio	39.9	40
39. Iowa	39.8	40
40. Nevada	39.7	39
41. Hawaii	39.4	39
42. New Mexico	38.9	38
43. Michigan	37.0	36
44. Minnesota	35.4	33
45. Alaska	33.7	31
46. Missouri	32.8	30
47. Pennsylvania	32.5	29
48. Vermont	12.8	1
49. North Dakota	12.1	0
50. New Hampshire	11.4	0

Public Transit Usage

DOING THE MATH

Public transit is a necessary component of a well-rounded transportation system. Buses, subways, and elevated trains carry thousands who otherwise would have no way to get around or would be forced to edge their cars onto already-jammed expressways. This category counts the number of public transit users per 1,000 commuters.

BEST STATES

Nowhere is public transit more popular than in New York, where 24.8 percent of all workers get to their jobs by bus or train. That's a rate of 248 transit users per 1,000 commuters. The only other state with a rate above 100 is Illinois.

WORST STATES

Public transit is virtually nonexistent in South Dakota, where just three of every 1,000 commuters take the bus to work. Arkansas, at five per 1,000, is next to last. Nine other states have rates below 10.

REGIONAL WINNERS

East—New York
South—Virginia
Midwest—Illinois
West—Hawaii

BIGGEST SURPRISE

It's no surprise that public transit is well developed in most large states. But there are two notable exceptions. Michigan and North Carolina both have fewer than 17 transit users per 1,000 commuters.

THE BOTTOM LINE

The East, with five states in this category's top 10, has America's most advanced public transit systems. Southern commuters still rely on their cars. Four of the 10 worst states are in the South.

300 Public Transit Usage

State	Public Transit Users Per 1,000 Commuters	Points
1. New York	248	100
2. Illinois	101	100
3. New Jersey	88	86
4. Massachusetts	83	81
5. Maryland	81	79
6. Hawaii	74	72
7. Pennsylvania	64	61
8. California	49	46
9. Washington	45	42
10. Virginia	40	36
11. Connecticut	39	35
12. Minnesota	36	32
13. Oregon	34	30
14. Louisiana	30	26
15. Colorado	29	25
16. Georgia	28	24
17. Nevada	27	23
18. Ohio	25	21
Rhode Island	25	21
Wisconsin	25	21
21. Alaska	24	20
Delaware	24	20
23. Utah	23	19
24. Texas	22	18
25. Arizona	21	17
26. Florida	20	16
Missouri	20	16
28. Idaho	19	15
29. Kentucky	16	11
Michigan	16	11
31. Wyoming	14	9
32. Indiana	13	8
Tennessee	13	8
34. Iowa	12	7
Nebraska	12	7
36. South Carolina	11	6
West Virginia	11	6
38. New Mexico	10	5
North Carolina	10	5
40. Maine	9	4
41. Alabama	8	3
Mississippi	8	3
43. New Hampshire	7	2
Vermont	7	2
45. Kansas	6	1
Montana	6	1
North Dakota	6	1
Oklahoma	6	1
49. Arkansas	5	0
50. South Dakota	3	0

Airline Service

DOING THE MATH

Travelers who decide not to drive have three choices of common carriers: plane, bus, and train. Fully 92 percent decide to fly, with 438 million Americans annually taking 6.6 million flights. This category counts the number of passengers boarding commercial flights in each state, translating the total into a rate per 100,000 residents.

BEST STATES

The only convenient way for Hawaiians to get to the American mainland is to fly. The demand for air service is further inflated by the state's strong tourist trade. These two factors account for Hawaii's annual total of 14.25 million air passengers, equal to 1,286,322 per 100,000 residents. Nevada, also dependent on tourism, is no. 2.

WORST STATES

Delaware has no commercial air service, relying on nearby airports in Baltimore, Philadelphia, and Washington, D.C. West Virginia is next to last, with a rate of 13,051 passengers per 100,000 residents.

REGIONAL WINNERS

East—Massachusetts
South—Georgia
Midwest—Illinois
West—Hawaii

BIGGEST SURPRISE

This category is dominated by major tourist attractions (Hawaii, Nevada) or hubs for large airlines (Colorado, Georgia). Utah is neither, but still is an impressive no. 7.

THE BOTTOM LINE

Commercial air service is most important to the West; it has six states in the top 10. The South, with four in the bottom 10, has the fewest flights.

302 Airline Service

State	Enplaned Passengers Per 100,000 Residents	Points
1. Hawaii	1,286,322	100
2. Nevada	760,386	100
3. Alaska	417,839	54
4. Colorado	391,523	51
5. Georgia	361,004	47
6. Arizona	329,546	42
7. Utah	312,721	40
8. Texas	273,360	35
9. Florida	263,420	34
10. Illinois	258,891	33
11. Missouri	249,677	32
12. Minnesota	207,793	26
13. North Carolina	193,371	24
14. California	179,962	22
15. Washington	173,767	22
16. Tennessee	166,671	21
17. Massachusetts	160,476	20
18. New Mexico	157,572	19
19. New York	145,987	18
20. Pennsylvania	134,324	16
21. New Jersey	129,106	16
22. Michigan	124,315	15
23. Oregon	121,346	14
24. Ohio	108,041	13
25. Rhode Island	105,755	12
26. Louisiana	98,688	11
27. Oklahoma	95,462	11
28. Maryland	92,461	11
29. Montana	92,189	11
30. Nebraska	75,636	8
31. North Dakota	75,563	8
32. Idaho	70,792	8
33. Connecticut	70,352	8
34. Indiana	57,010	6
35. Wisconsin	56,807	6
36. Vermont	54,439	6
37. South Carolina	53,126	5
38. Maine	49,205	5
39. South Dakota	47,453	5
40. Alabama	46,326	4
41. Virginia	40,534	4
42. Arkansas	40,503	4
43. Iowa	38,901	3
44. Kentucky	33,388	3
45. Wyoming	32,243	3
46. New Hampshire	24,163	1
47. Kansas	22,688	1
48. Mississippi	17,581	1
49. West Virginia	13,051	0
50. Delaware	0	0

Transportation: Scores and Grades

BEST STATE

Illinois has the best transportation system in America. Fully 10.1 percent of its commuters get to work by bus or elevated train; only New York makes more extensive use of public transit. Illinois is also among the 10 best states in terms of airline service. And its roads are safe (Illinois has the nation's eleventh lowest death rate) and reasonably well-maintained (19th in pavement condition).

RUNNERS-UP

Excellent airline service is the major reason that Hawaii holds second place in this section. No state comes close to its annual rate of commercial air traffic. Hawaii is also no. 6 in public transit usage. Four other states earned A's: Maryland, New York, New Jersey, and Massachusetts.

WORST STATES

It isn't easy to get around in mountainous West Virginia, the last-place state in this section. Only Delaware gets weaker service from commercial airlines; just five states have higher death rates from motor vehicle accidents. Six other states also received F's.

REGIONAL WINNERS

East—Maryland, New York
South—Georgia
Midwest—Illinois
West—Hawaii

REGIONAL AVERAGES

East—52 (C)
South—33 (D)
Midwest—52 (C)
West—54 (C)

304 BIGGEST SURPRISE

South Dakota is not an airline hub or an innovator in public transit. But it nonetheless earns a B+ in this section, thanks to its well-maintained, uncongested highway system.

THE BOTTOM LINE

Four of the 10 best states are eastern; three each are midwestern and western. The South, on the other hand, includes seven of the 11 states with the worst transportation systems.

Transportation: Scores and Grades

State	Score	Grade
1. Illinois	100	A+
2. Hawaii	97	A
3. Maryland	92	A
New York	92	A
5. New Jersey	87	A
6. Massachusetts	85	A
7. South Dakota	76	B+
8. Washington	71	B
9. Wisconsin	69	B
10. Colorado	68	B
11. Wyoming	67	B
12. Connecticut	66	B
13. Utah	63	B–
14. Nevada	62	B–
15. Nebraska	58	C+
16. Georgia	56	C+
Pennsylvania	56	C+
Minnesota	56	C+
Rhode Island	56	C+
20. Florida	55	C+
21. Virginia	54	C
22. North Carolina	53	C
23. California	51	C
24. Montana	49	C
Oregon	49	C
26. Alaska	45	C
Kansas	45	C
North Dakota	45	C
Texas	45	C
30. Ohio	41	C–
Oklahoma	41	C–
32. Idaho	40	C–
33. Indiana	38	D+
34. Iowa	37	D+
35. Maine	35	D+
36. Arizona	34	D
37. Missouri	33	D
38. Delaware	30	D
39. Michigan	29	D
40. Louisiana	24	D–
Tennessee	24	D–
Alabama	24	D–
43. Mississippi	21	D–
44. Vermont	14	F
45. Arkansas	13	F
46. South Carolina	11	F
New Hampshire	11	F
48. New Mexico	9	F
49. Kentucky	8	F
50. West Virginia	0	F

21

Politics

The Big Question

Which state has the political system that gives voters the best opportunity to participate in competitive elections, while exercising national clout?

The Categories

1. Voter Turnout
2. Electoral Votes
3. Presidential Election Trends
4. Political Party Competition
5. State Legislature Turnover

Voter Turnout

DOING THE MATH

Democracy, if it is to be effective, requires strong involvement by the people. The word itself, democracy, stems from the Greek *demos,* meaning common people. This category measures the willingness of adults to take part in democracy's simplest ritual, voting. We ranked the states according to the average percentage of adults who went to the polls in the four presidential elections from 1980 through 1992.

BEST STATES

Voting is taken seriously in Minnesota, which has an average voter turnout of 68.8 percent in national elections. Take 1992 for example: Roughly 2.35 million Minnesota adults voted that year; just 930,000 stayed home. Maine and Montana are tied for second place at 65.6 percent.

WORST STATES

Only 41.1 percent of South Carolina's adults care enough to vote in presidential elections. Its 1992 turnout was 1.18 million voters, compared to 1.49 million stay-at-homes. Georgia is next to last at 42.4 percent.

REGIONAL WINNERS

East—Maine
South—Louisiana
Midwest—Minnesota
West—Montana

BIGGEST SURPRISE

America's two biggest states, the ones with the most at stake in national elections, are surprisingly casual about voting. New York is 40th in this category, California 41st.

THE BOTTOM LINE

The Midwest places the most emphasis on voting, with five states in the top 10. Six of the 10 worst states are southern.

308 Voter Turnout

State	Average Turnout in Presidential Elections, 1980–1992	Points
1. Minnesota	68.8%	100
2. Maine	65.6	100
Montana	65.6	100
4. Wisconsin	65.2	98
5. South Dakota	64.2	94
6. North Dakota	64.0	93
7. Utah	63.0	89
8. Idaho	62.7	88
9. Iowa	62.0	84
10. Oregon	61.5	82
11. Connecticut	61.0	80
12. Vermont	60.8	79
13. Alaska	59.5	74
14. Massachusetts	58.6	70
15. Michigan	58.4	69
16. Missouri	57.8	66
Nebraska	57.8	66
18. Kansas	57.6	66
19. Colorado	57.5	65
20. Washington	57.3	64
21. New Hampshire	57.1	63
22. Ohio	56.9	62
23. Illinois	56.6	61
24. Rhode Island	56.4	60
25. Indiana	55.4	56
26. Wyoming	55.2	55
27. New Jersey	55.1	55
28. Louisiana	54.9	54
29. Delaware	53.9	50
30. Oklahoma	53.4	47
31. Pennsylvania	52.4	43
32. Mississippi	51.8	41
33. Arkansas	51.1	38
34. Maryland	50.9	37
35. New Mexico	50.7	36
36. Kentucky	50.6	35
37. West Virginia	50.4	34
38. Alabama	50.0	33
39. Virginia	49.8	32
40. New York	49.5	31
41. California	48.7	27
Tennessee	48.7	27
43. Florida	47.9	24
44. Arizona	47.7	23
45. Texas	46.7	19
46. North Carolina	46.1	16
47. Nevada	44.0	7
48. Hawaii	43.6	5
49. Georgia	42.4	0
50. South Carolina	41.1	0

Electoral Votes

DOING THE MATH

Politics, at its most basic level, is all about numbers. Presidential politics is about one number in particular—270. That's how many votes it takes in the Electoral College for a candidate to become president. The Constitution says that each state's total of electoral votes must correspond to its number of senators and congressmen. This category measures each state's voting strength in the Electoral College, and hence its power in national politics.

BEST STATES

By far the biggest prize in presidential elections is California, which has 54 electoral votes. That total, by itself, is exactly 20 percent of the 270 votes needed to win the presidency. Two other states are above 30: New York (33) and Texas (32).

WORST STATES

The Constitution guarantees each state a minimum of three electoral votes. Seven states currently are at that level.

REGIONAL WINNERS

East—New York
South—Texas
Midwest—Illinois
West—California

BIGGEST SURPRISE

North Carolina is not often mentioned as a major player in national politics. But it now is no. 10 in population, meaning it also is no. 10 in this category, with an impressive 14 electoral votes.

THE BOTTOM LINE

There is a strong regional balance in the Electoral College. The East, South, and Midwest each placed three states in the top 10. California was the only state to make it from the West.

310 Electoral Votes

State	Electoral Votes	Points
1. California	54	100
2. New York	33	100
3. Texas	32	97
4. Florida	25	73
5. Pennsylvania	23	67
6. Illinois	22	63
7. Ohio	21	60
8. Michigan	18	50
9. New Jersey	15	40
10. North Carolina	14	37
11. Georgia	13	33
Virginia	13	33
13. Indiana	12	30
Massachusetts	12	30
15. Missouri	11	27
Tennessee	11	27
Washington	11	27
Wisconsin	11	27
19. Maryland	10	23
Minnesota	10	23
21. Alabama	9	20
Louisiana	9	20
23. Arizona	8	17
Colorado	8	17
Connecticut	8	17
Kentucky	8	17
Oklahoma	8	17
South Carolina	8	17
29. Iowa	7	13
Mississippi	7	13
Oregon	7	13
32. Arkansas	6	10
Kansas	6	10
34. Nebraska	5	7
New Mexico	5	7
Utah	5	7
West Virginia	5	7
38. Hawaii	4	3
Idaho	4	3
Maine	4	3
Nevada	4	3
New Hampshire	4	3
Rhode Island	4	3
44. Alaska	3	0
Delaware	3	0
Montana	3	0
North Dakota	3	0
South Dakota	3	0
Vermont	3	0
Wyoming	3	0

Presidential Election Trends

DOING THE MATH

Central to the American political system is the idea of consensus, of encouraging disparate regions to rally around a common idea or candidate. This category evaluates a state's willingness to join such a consensus. We calculated the percentage of presidential elections in which each state has given its electoral votes to the winner.

BEST STATES

New Mexico, with its strong Hispanic heritage and low population density, seems an unlikely barometer of national political trends. But it has voted for the national winner in 20 of 21 presidential elections since becoming a state, a record of 95.2 percent. Illinois is second at 86.4 percent.

WORST STATES

Alabama commonly is at odds with the national political mood. It has matched the national results in just 22 of 43 elections, which works out to 51.2 percent. Mississippi is only slightly better at 52.4 percent.

REGIONAL WINNERS

East—New York
South—Oklahoma
Midwest—Illinois
West—New Mexico

BIGGEST SURPRISE

Politicians once claimed, "As goes Maine, so goes the nation." It is a worthless rule. Maine is in 32nd place, matching national results just 68.2 percent of the time.

THE BOTTOM LINE

The West, with six states in the top 10, is most in tune with national political trends. The South, with eight in the bottom 10, is most out of touch.

312 Presidential Election Trends

State	Frequency of State Winner Matching National Winner in Presidential Elections	Points
1. New Mexico	95.2%	100
2. Illinois	86.4	100
3. California	86.1	99
4. New York	84.3	94
5. Pennsylvania	82.7	89
6. Ohio	81.3	85
7. Arizona	81.0	84
8. Montana	80.8	83
9. Utah	80.0	81
10. Nevada	78.8	78
11. Wisconsin	78.4	76
12. Oklahoma	77.3	73
13. Idaho	76.9	72
Wyoming	76.9	72
15. Minnesota	76.5	71
Oregon	76.5	71
17. West Virginia	75.8	69
18. Indiana	75.6	68
19. Michigan	75.0	66
Missouri	75.0	66
New Hampshire	75.0	66
North Dakota	75.0	66
23. New Jersey	73.1	61
Washington	73.1	61
25. Iowa	73.0	61
26. Kansas	72.7	60
27. Rhode Island	72.5	59
28. Colorado	70.0	52
29. Florida	69.4	50
30. Connecticut	69.2	50
31. Nebraska	68.8	48
32. Maine	68.2	46
33. North Carolina	68.0	46
34. Tennessee	67.3	44
Massachusetts	67.3	44
36. Alaska	66.7	42
Hawaii	66.7	42
38. Maryland	66.3	41
39. Virginia	66.0	40
40. Vermont	64.7	36
41. Louisiana	63.6	33
42. Delaware	63.5	33
43. Kentucky	62.7	30
44. South Dakota	61.5	27
45. Texas	60.0	22
46. Georgia	58.8	19
South Carolina	58.8	19
48. Arkansas	57.9	16
49. Mississippi	52.4	0
50. Alabama	51.2	0

Political Party Competition

DOING THE MATH

Democracy, needless to say, works best when voters are offered a choice between two (or more) qualified candidates for any public office. This category seeks to determine whether the Democratic and Republican parties stage competitive campaigns in each state. We studied all races for governor from 1946 through 1992, counting the number of close elections, those in which the winner received less than 55 percent of the vote.

BEST STATES

Voters in Alaska and New Mexico are accustomed to making tough decisions. Those two states have the nation's most competitive political systems, with 88.9 percent of their gubernatorial elections classified as close. Wisconsin is third at 77.8 percent.

WORST STATES

Elections rarely generate much suspense in Florida. Only one of its 13 gubernatorial elections (7.7 percent) between 1946 and 1992 could be considered close. The only other state below 10 percent is Alabama.

REGIONAL WINNERS

East—New York
South—Virginia
Midwest—Wisconsin
West—Alaska, New Mexico

BIGGEST SURPRISE

The common perception is that New York is a Democratic stronghold, where Republicans have virtually no hope of victory. New York actually has a strong two-party system, ranking fourth in this category.

THE BOTTOM LINE

Political parties are most competitive in the West, which has five states in the top 12. Eight of the nine worst states are southern.

314 Political Party Competition

State	Percent of Gubernatorial Elections, 1946–1992, in Which Winner Gained Less than 55% of the Vote	Points
1. Alaska	88.9%	100
New Mexico	88.9	100
3. Wisconsin	77.8	86
4. New York	75.0	83
Washington	75.0	83
6. Maine	68.8	75
7. Kansas	68.4	75
8. Hawaii	66.7	72
Idaho	66.7	72
Illinois	66.7	72
Pennsylvania	66.7	72
West Virginia	66.7	72
13. Michigan	64.7	70
14. Connecticut	61.5	66
15. Massachusetts	58.8	63
16. Delaware	58.3	62
Montana	58.3	62
Wyoming	58.3	62
19. Minnesota	56.3	59
20. Arizona	55.6	59
21. Nebraska	52.9	55
22. Iowa	52.6	55
23. Virginia	50.0	52
24. Colorado	46.7	48
Ohio	46.7	48
26. New Hampshire	45.8	47
27. Oregon	42.9	43
28. California	41.7	41
Indiana	41.7	41
Kentucky	41.7	41
New Jersey	41.7	41
North Carolina	41.7	41
Oklahoma	41.7	41
Rhode Island	41.7	41
Utah	41.7	41
36. North Dakota	41.2	41
37. South Dakota	36.8	35
Texas	36.8	35
39. Missouri	33.3	31
Nevada	33.3	31
Vermont	33.3	31
42. Maryland	25.0	21
Mississippi	25.0	21
South Carolina	25.0	21
45. Tennessee	21.4	16
46. Arkansas	18.2	12
47. Louisiana	16.7	10
48. Georgia	15.4	9
49. Alabama	8.3	0
50. Florida	7.7	0

State Legislature Turnover

DOING THE MATH

The Founding Fathers felt it would be best if government were run by "citizen-legislators," officeholders who would serve for a few short years before returning to their everyday occupations. It seems a quaint ideal in this era of professional politicians who cling to public office. We measured the turnover in state legislatures between 1979 and 1989, checking to see how many citizen-legislators are still around.

BEST STATES

Steady infusions of new blood keep the state governments fresh in Washington and West Virginia. Fully 90 percent of the members of both states' legislatures in 1979 had left office by 1989. Colorado is just a step behind with a turnover rate of 89 percent.

WORST STATES

The legislative wheels spin slowly in Arkansas and Illinois. Both states have turnover rates of 49 percent, meaning that more than half of 1979's lawmakers were still hanging around a decade later. New York is next to last at 55 percent.

REGIONAL WINNERS

East—West Virginia
South—Mississippi
Midwest—Kansas, South Dakota
West—Washington

BIGGEST SURPRISE

You would expect scant legislative turnover in Florida, whose political system is generally uncompetitive. But a rate of 83 percent earns Florida 12th place.

THE BOTTOM LINE

Citizen-legislators still can be found in the West, which includes six of the top 11 states. The Midwest and the South each have four of the 10 worst states.

316 State Legislature Turnover

State	Turnover in State Legislature, 1979-1989	Points
1. Washington	90%	100
West Virginia	90	100
3. Colorado	89	98
4. Alaska	88	95
5. Maine	87	93
Montana	87	93
Utah	87	93
8. Mississippi	86	90
New Hampshire	86	90
10. Nevada	85	88
Oklahoma	85	88
12. Florida	83	83
Oregon	83	83
Vermont	83	83
15. Connecticut	82	80
Hawaii	82	80
17. Idaho	81	78
Kansas	81	78
South Dakota	81	78
Texas	81	78
21. New Jersey	80	76
North Carolina	80	76
Rhode Island	80	76
24. Wisconsin	79	73
Wyoming	79	73
26. Nebraska	78	71
27. Iowa	76	66
New Mexico	76	66
29. Arizona	75	63
30. Missouri	74	61
31. Minnesota	72	56
North Dakota	72	56
South Carolina	72	56
34. Louisiana	71	54
35. California	70	51
36. Massachusetts	69	49
37. Alabama	68	46
Delaware	68	46
Pennsylvania	68	46
40. Georgia	67	44
41. Maryland	65	39
Michigan	65	39
Ohio	65	39
44. Tennessee	62	32
Virginia	62	32
46. Kentucky	61	29
47. Indiana	60	27
48. New York	55	15
49. Arkansas	49	0
Illinois	49	0

Politics: Scores and Grades

BEST STATE

The political system in Wisconsin is strongly responsive to its voters, earning the no. 1 ranking in this section. Only in Alaska and New Mexico do close elections occur more frequently; just three states have better rates of voter participation. Wisconsin is also in tune with national political trends, matching the presidential election results in four of every five campaigns.

RUNNERS-UP

Montana holds second place, thanks to an impressive voter-turnout record that is topped only by Minnesota. Montana also ranks no. 5 in terms of legislative turnover. Five other states earned straight A's: Washington, New York, California, Maine, and Pennsylvania.

WORST STATES

The political process in Arkansas is truly uninspiring. Elections are rarely close; no state retains more of its legislative incumbents. It's no wonder that only 51 percent of Arkansas voters even bother to go to the polls. Also receiving F's are Alabama, Georgia, and South Carolina.

REGIONAL WINNERS

East—New York
South—Oklahoma
Midwest—Wisconsin
West—Montana

REGIONAL AVERAGES

East—66 (B)
South—32 (D)
Midwest—71 (B)
West—74 (B)

BIGGEST SURPRISE

Bill Clinton's political savvy must be innate; it certainly can't be attributed to the experience he gained in Arkansas. No state has a political system that is less responsive to voters or to national trends.

318 THE BOTTOM LINE

The political process works best in the West, which has six of the 10 leading states in this section. The South includes eight of the nine states that earned D's or F's.

Politics: Scores and Grades

State	Score	Grade
1. Wisconsin	100	A+
2. Montana	92	A
3. Washington	91	A
4. New York	87	A
5. California	85	A
Maine	85	A
Pennsylvania	85	A
8. Idaho	83	A–
Alaska	83	A–
Utah	83	A–
11. Minnesota	82	A–
New Mexico	82	A–
13. Illinois	77	B+
Michigan	77	B+
Ohio	77	B+
16. Connecticut	76	B+
Oregon	76	B+
18. Kansas	75	B+
19. West Virginia	73	B
20. Colorado	72	B
21. Iowa	71	B
22. New Jersey	69	B
23. New Hampshire	68	B
24. Oklahoma	67	B
25. Wyoming	65	B
26. Massachusetts	63	B–
North Dakota	63	B–
28. Missouri	62	B–
Texas	62	B–
30. Nebraska	60	B–
Arizona	60	B–
32. Rhode Island	57	C+
33. South Dakota	56	C+
34. Florida	54	C
Vermont	54	C
36. Indiana	51	C
37. North Carolina	49	C
38. Nevada	46	C
39. Hawaii	44	C–
40. Delaware	40	C–
Virginia	40	C–
42. Louisiana	33	D
43. Mississippi	31	D
44. Maryland	30	D
45. Kentucky	27	D
46. Tennessee	25	D
47. South Carolina	13	F
48. Georgia	10	F
49. Alabama	8	F
50. Arkansas	0	F

22

Government

The Big Question

Which state has the most efficient government?

The Categories

1. State Taxes
2. State Debt
3. Government Employees
4. Government Units
5. State Constitution Length

State Taxes

DOING THE MATH

George Bush will forever regret breaking a six-word promise: "Read my lips. No new taxes." The voter rebellion against Bush's "revenue enhancement" plan was a key factor in his 1992 defeat. This category looks at this unpopular topic, taking the total of all state taxes—individual and corporate income, sales, tobacco, alcohol, death, gift, etc.—and converting it to a per capita rate. Local property taxes are not included.

BEST STATES

New Hampshire has no sales tax or individual income tax. Its state government annually takes just $565 per person, the nation's lowest state tax load. Second place belongs to South Dakota, with a rate of $751.

WORST STATES

Alaska has America's highest cost of living—and its highest taxes. The state tax load works out to an astounding $3,169 per person. The other non-mainland state, Hawaii, is next to last at $2,325.

REGIONAL WINNERS

East—New Hampshire
South—Tennessee
Midwest—South Dakota
West—Colorado

BIGGEST SURPRISE

Eastern states have no qualms about hitting their taxpayers where it hurts. The East has only one representative in the top 16. The surprise is that it's the first-place state, New Hampshire.

THE BOTTOM LINE

Taxes are lowest in the South, which has five states in this category's top 10. The East has five of the 10 worst states, while the West has four.

322 State Taxes

State	State Taxes Per Capita	Points
1. New Hampshire	$ 565	100
2. South Dakota	751	100
3. Tennessee	870	92
4. Texas	923	89
5. Mississippi	949	87
6. Colorado	952	87
7. Alabama	964	86
8. Missouri	969	86
9. Arkansas	998	84
10. Montana	1,012	83
11. Louisiana	1,014	83
12. Florida	1,037	82
Oregon	1,037	82
14. Utah	1,051	81
15. Ohio	1,056	81
16. Georgia	1,080	79
17. Pennsylvania	1,089	79
18. Virginia	1,090	78
19. Indiana	1,102	78
20. Nebraska	1,103	78
21. South Carolina	1,105	78
22. Kansas	1,121	76
23. Illinois	1,151	75
24. Idaho	1,159	74
25. North Carolina	1,165	74
26. Michigan	1,185	72
27. North Dakota	1,189	72
28. Vermont	1,207	71
29. Oklahoma	1,216	70
30. Iowa	1,233	69
31. Rhode Island	1,252	68
32. Arizona	1,256	68
33. Maine	1,262	68
34. West Virginia	1,293	66
35. Nevada	1,310	64
36. Maryland	1,317	64
37. New Mexico	1,347	62
38. Kentucky	1,358	61
39. Wyoming	1,386	60
40. Wisconsin	1,416	58
41. California	1,477	54
42. New Jersey	1,501	52
43. Connecticut	1,514	52
44. New York	1,567	48
45. Minnesota	1,591	47
46. Washington	1,592	47
47. Massachusetts	1,615	45
48. Delaware	1,714	39
49. Hawaii	2,325	0
50. Alaska	3,169	0

State Debt

DOING THE MATH

We all know about the federal debt. Commentators warn that it is spiraling out of control, that it could plunge the nation into another recession. What is not often discussed is that the states also carry various degrees of long-term debt. This category looks at each state's total indebtedness, translating it into a per capita rate.

BEST STATES

Kansas' total debt is $337 million, which sounds terrible until expressed as a rate. It works out to $135 per resident, easily the lightest debt load carried by any of the 50 state governments. Texas ranks no. 2 with a rate of $443 million.

WORST STATES

Alaska's 550,000 residents are struggling under a state debt of $5.29 billion, which is $9,282 per person. That's nearly twice the load of the next-to-last state, Delaware.

REGIONAL WINNERS

East—Pennsylvania
South—Texas
Midwest—Kansas
West—Arizona

BIGGEST SURPRISE

New Hampshire takes such a conservative approach toward taxes that you also would expect it to do well in this category. It doesn't. New Hampshire carries a debt of $3,735 per person. Only four states are worse.

THE BOTTOM LINE

The South, with six states in the top 10, is the region that is most successful at keeping government debt low. Debt loads are highest in the East, which includes seven of the bottom 10 states.

324 State Debt

State	State Debt Per Capita	Points
1. Kansas	$ 135	100
2. Texas	443	100
3. North Carolina	518	98
4. Mississippi	545	98
5. Georgia	551	97
6. Tennessee	563	97
7. Iowa	580	97
8. Arizona	677	95
9. Arkansas	744	93
10. Colorado	788	92
11. Indiana	824	91
12. Florida	835	91
13. Minnesota	889	90
14. Pennsylvania	973	88
15. Nebraska	996	87
16. Alabama	1,031	86
17. Virginia	1,034	86
18. Ohio	1,039	86
19. California	1,052	86
20. Michigan	1,079	85
21. Idaho	1,080	85
Utah	1,080	85
23. Missouri	1,120	84
24. New Mexico	1,131	84
25. Oklahoma	1,175	83
26. South Carolina	1,177	83
27. Washington	1,299	80
28. Nevada	1,330	79
29. Wisconsin	1,337	79
30. North Dakota	1,518	75
31. West Virginia	1,538	74
32. Maryland	1,549	74
33. Illinois	1,580	73
34. Kentucky	1,623	72
35. Montana	1,994	64
36. Wyoming	2,004	64
37. Maine	2,093	61
38. Oregon	2,208	59
39. New Jersey	2,453	53
40. South Dakota	2,495	52
41. Louisiana	2,523	51
42. Vermont	2,621	49
43. New York	2,869	43
44. Massachusetts	3,519	28
45. Hawaii	3,702	24
46. New Hampshire	3,735	23
47. Connecticut	3,952	18
48. Rhode Island	4,375	8
49. Delaware	4,728	0
50. Alaska	9,282	0

Government Employees

DOING THE MATH

Doing more with less. That's a phrase often heard in the private sector, where companies are slashing their work forces and exhorting their remaining workers to increase productivity. Government is not yet under the same pressure, but it is increasingly coming under scrutiny. We totaled the number of state and local government employees, expressing each state's result as a rate per 100,000 residents.

BEST STATES

Nowhere is government leaner than in Pennsylvania, which has just 4,061 state and local government employees per 100,000 residents. The no. 2 entry in this category, New Hampshire, has a rate of 4,620.

WORST STATES

Residents of Wyoming have firsthand experience with bureaucracy. Their state has 7,778 government workers per 100,000 residents, the highest rate in America. Alaska, at 7,715, is the only other state above 6,500.

REGIONAL WINNERS

East—Pennsylvania
South—Florida
Midwest—Missouri
West—California

BIGGEST SURPRISE

The West has the reputation of being a fiercely independent region that disdains big government. How then can it be explained that the four worst states in this category are western?

THE BOTTOM LINE

The level of government employment generally is lowest in the East, which has five states in the top 10. The bottom 10, on the other hand, is dominated by the West (four entries) and the Midwest (three).

326 Government Employees

State	State and Local Government Employees Per 100,000 Residents	Points
1. Pennsylvania	4,061	100
2. New Hampshire	4,620	100
3. Rhode Island	4,648	99
4. Massachusetts	4,650	99
5. California	4,704	97
6. Connecticut	4,732	96
7. Missouri	4,778	95
8. Ohio	4,846	93
9. Nevada	4,882	92
10. Illinois	4,896	91
11. Florida	4,952	89
12. Tennessee	5,045	86
13. Arizona	5,052	86
14. Maryland	5,061	86
15. West Virginia	5,071	85
16. Utah	5,126	84
17. Michigan	5,128	84
18. Indiana	5,148	83
19. Wisconsin	5,167	82
20. Arkansas	5,191	82
21. Maine	5,229	80
22. Kentucky	5,267	79
23. Minnesota	5,304	78
24. Washington	5,307	78
25. Vermont	5,333	77
26. North Carolina	5,356	76
27. New Jersey	5,385	75
Virginia	5,385	75
29. Oregon	5,395	75
30. South Dakota	5,413	74
31. Delaware	5,441	73
32. Texas	5,484	72
33. Idaho	5,502	72
34. Colorado	5,505	71
35. North Dakota	5,603	68
36. South Carolina	5,625	68
37. Hawaii	5,673	66
38. Alabama	5,684	66
39. Louisiana	5,740	64
40. Georgia	5,787	62
41. Oklahoma	5,830	61
42. Mississippi	5,863	60
43. Iowa	5,869	60
44. Nebraska	6,166	50
45. Kansas	6,202	49
46. New York	6,219	48
47. Montana	6,436	41
48. New Mexico	6,499	39
49. Alaska	7,715	0
50. Wyoming	7,778	0

Government Units

DOING THE MATH

There are 86,743 government units in the United States, ranging from the gigantic federal administration to tiny rural townships. Since 1972, this governmental web has become tangled with the addition of nearly 10,000 special districts that provide such services as waste disposal, fire protection, and water supply. This category counts the number of government units in each state, converting it to a rate per 100,000 residents.

BEST STATES

Hawaii has just 21 governments—the state, three counties, Honolulu, and 16 special districts. That works out to an efficient 1.9 units per 100,000 residents. Just three other states have rates below 10: Virginia, Florida, and Maryland.

WORST STATES

The more fragmentation, the better. That seems to be the rule in North Dakota, which is administered by 2,795 governments. That's a rate of 437.4 units per 100,000 persons. Neighboring South Dakota is next to last.

REGIONAL WINNERS

East—Maryland
South—Virginia
Midwest—Michigan
West—Hawaii

BIGGEST SURPRISE

Massachusetts government is inefficient in many ways; its taxes and debt are among the worst in America. But it sets a fine example in this category, ranking no. 7.

THE BOTTOM LINE

Four of the top 10 states are from the South, three each from the East and West. The Midwest, with six of the 10 worst states, is the home of fragmented government.

328 Government Units

State	Government Units Per 100,000 Residents	Points
1. Hawaii	1.9	100
2. Virginia	7.5	100
3. Florida	8.0	100
4. Maryland	8.7	100
5. Louisiana	10.9	99
6. Rhode Island	12.8	98
7. Massachusetts	14.1	97
8. North Carolina	14.4	97
9. California	15.1	97
10. Arizona	16.3	96
11. Connecticut	17.5	96
12. Nevada	17.6	96
13. New York	18.4	96
14. Tennessee	19.7	95
15. South Carolina	20.2	95
16. Georgia	20.4	95
17. New Jersey	21.0	95
18. Alabama	28.1	92
19. Texas	29.0	91
20. Michigan	29.3	91
21. Alaska	32.0	90
22. Ohio	32.6	90
New Mexico	32.6	90
24. Mississippi	34.9	89
25. Kentucky	36.5	88
26. Utah	36.9	88
Washington	36.9	88
28. West Virginia	39.5	87
29. Delaware	42.2	86
30. Pennsylvania	45.4	85
31. New Hampshire	47.9	84
32. Oregon	52.3	82
33. Indiana	53.7	82
34. Colorado	55.4	81
35. Wisconsin	56.3	81
36. Oklahoma	57.9	80
37. Illinois	59.6	79
38. Arkansas	62.7	78
39. Maine	65.1	77
40. Missouri	65.8	77
41. Iowa	68.6	76
42. Minnesota	82.7	70
43. Idaho	109.7	59
44. Vermont	122.6	54
45. Wyoming	126.9	53
46. Kansas	158.1	40
47. Montana	163.3	38
48. Nebraska	189.9	27
49. South Dakota	259.1	0
50. North Dakota	437.4	0

State Constitution Length

DOING THE MATH

America's Founding Fathers were noted for their eloquence. The Declaration of Independence and Constitution emphatically and concisely stated the new nation's hopes and aims. The 50 states had their own founding fathers (and, in a few cases, mothers). Were they able to establish similarly clear frameworks for government? We used a simple test to find the answer, totaling the number of words in each state's constitution.

BEST STATES

It is fitting that Vermont, home of the stereotypically taciturn Yankee, is no. 1 in this category. Its constitution uses just 6,600 words to set 75 concise rules for operation of the state's government. Second place belongs to neighboring New Hampshire, at 9,200 words.

WORST STATES

No state has a more muddled and confused constitution than Alabama's 174,000-word document, which includes amendments on the disposal of dead farm animals and the marketing of catfish products. New York is next to last at 80,000 words.

REGIONAL WINNERS

East—Vermont
South—North Carolina
Midwest—Indiana
West—Utah

BIGGEST SURPRISE

Alabama is sparing with its tax dollars, but not with its words. Its larger-than-life constitution includes 287 sections and more than 500 amendments.

THE BOTTOM LINE

State constitutions are most concise in the East, which placed four states in the top 10. Verbiage flows unchecked in the South, which has five of the 10 worst states.

330 State Constitution Length

State	Number of Words in State Constitution	Points
1. Vermont	6,600	100
2. New Hampshire	9,200	100
3. Indiana	9,377	100
4. Minnesota	9,500	100
5. Connecticut	9,564	99
6. North Carolina	11,000	97
Utah	11,000	97
8. Rhode Island	11,399	97
9. Kansas	11,865	96
10. Montana	11,866	96
11. Iowa	12,500	95
12. Alaska	13,000	95
13. Illinois	13,200	94
14. Maine	13,500	94
Wisconsin	13,500	94
16. Tennessee	15,300	91
17. New Jersey	17,086	89
18. Hawaii	17,453	88
19. Virginia	18,500	87
20. Delaware	19,000	86
21. Michigan	20,000	85
22. Nebraska	20,048	85
23. North Dakota	20,564	84
24. Nevada	20,770	84
25. Idaho	21,500	83
26. Pennsylvania	21,675	82
27. South Carolina	22,500	81
28. South Dakota	23,300	80
29. Kentucky	23,500	80
30. Mississippi	24,000	79
31. Massachusetts	24,122	79
32. Georgia	25,000	78
33. Florida	25,100	78
34. West Virginia	25,600	77
35. Oregon	26,090	76
36. New Mexico	27,200	75
37. Arizona	28,876	72
38. Washington	29,400	71
39. Wyoming	31,800	68
40. California	33,350	66
41. Ohio	36,900	61
42. Arkansas	40,720	55
43. Maryland	41,349	55
44. Missouri	42,000	54
45. Colorado	45,679	48
46. Louisiana	51,448	40
47. Texas	62,000	25
48. Oklahoma	68,800	16
49. New York	80,000	0
50. Alabama	174,000	0

Government: Scores and Grades

BEST STATE

America's most efficient state government can be found in Tennessee. New Hampshire and South Dakota are the only states with lower taxes; just five states carry lighter debt loads. Tennessee also earns praise for having a relatively small public work force, with just 5,045 state and local government employees per 100,000 residents, twelfth best in the nation.

RUNNERS-UP

North Carolina, which holds second place in this section, has kept its debt down to $518 per resident. Only two states have done better. North Carolina also is no. 6 in the State Constitution Length category and no. 8 in Government Units. Five other states earned straight A's: Florida, Utah, Indiana, Pennsylvania, and Virginia.

WORST STATES

It seems that everything is expensive in Alaska, and the government does nothing to help the situation. No state has higher taxes or carries a heavier debt load; only Wyoming has a higher proportion of government workers. One other state was hit with an F, New York.

REGIONAL WINNERS

East—Pennsylvania
South—Tennessee
Midwest—Indiana
West—Utah

REGIONAL AVERAGES

East—63 (B-)
South—76 (B+)
Midwest—70 (B)
West—59 (C+)

BIGGEST SURPRISE

Michigan's government was buried in debt and blasted by critics for inefficiency in the 1980s. Its turnaround has been dramatic. Michigan is tied for eighth place in this section, earning an A–.

THE BOTTOM LINE

The South, with five states in the top 11, leads the nation in government efficiency. The West holds four slots in the bottom 10, while the Midwest has three.

Government: Scores and Grades

State	Score	Grade
1. Tennessee	100	A+
2. North Carolina	93	A
3. Florida	92	A
4. Utah	91	A
5. Indiana	90	A
Pennsylvania	90	A
7. Virginia	87	A
8. Arizona	84	A–
Michigan	84	A–
10. Nevada	83	A–
Mississippi	83	A–
12. Illinois	82	A–
Georgia	82	A–
Ohio	82	A–
15. New Hampshire	80	A–
South Carolina	80	A–
17. California	78	B+
18. Iowa	77	B+
19. Missouri	76	B+
Wisconsin	76	B+
21. Arkansas	75	B+
22. West Virginia	74	B
23. Minnesota	72	B
24. Kentucky	71	B
Maine	71	B
26. Colorado	70	B
Maryland	70	B
Texas	70	B
29. Oregon	68	B
Idaho	68	B
31. Rhode Island	67	B
32. New Jersey	65	B
Washington	65	B
34. Connecticut	64	B–
Kansas	64	B–
36. Vermont	60	B–
New Mexico	60	B–
38. Massachusetts	59	C+
39. Louisiana	55	C+
40. Alabama	53	C
41. Nebraska	51	C
42. Montana	50	C
43. Oklahoma	45	C
44. South Dakota	44	C–
45. North Dakota	41	C–
46. Delaware	36	D+
47. Hawaii	34	D
48. Wyoming	22	D–
49. New York	18	F
50. Alaska	0	F

23

National Relations

The Big Question

Which state has the strongest connections with the rest of the country, whether in business, education, or everyday life?

The Categories

1. Federal Spending
2. Population Influx
3. Domestic Travel
4. *Fortune* 500 Companies
5. Student Migration

Federal Spending

DOING THE MATH

You might expect the federal government to provide equal levels of assistance to all 50 states, but it doesn't. It spends more on some than on others. This category adds up all federal expenditures in each state, including grants to state and local governments, wages of federal workers, Social Security and Medicare payments, federal retirement benefits, student grants, and procurement contracts. The result is expressed as a per capita rate.

BEST STATES

The federal government annually spends more than $4 billion in sparsely populated Alaska. That works out to $6,873 per resident, the top figure in the nation. Second place belongs to Maryland, with a rate of $6,589.

WORST STATES

Government largess is a foreign concept in Indiana, where federal spending is a paltry $3,529 per person. Wisconsin is next to last at $3,563.

REGIONAL WINNERS

East—Maryland
South—Virginia
Midwest—North Dakota
West—Alaska

BIGGEST SURPRISE

Outsiders who dismiss New Mexico as desert wilderness will be shocked to learn that no other state receives a higher per capita share of federal procurement contracts. That helps New Mexico gain a strong no. 3 ranking in overall federal spending.

THE BOTTOM LINE

The East includes four of the 10 states that draw the most federal money, while the West has three. The region that gets shortchanged is the Midwest, with five states in the bottom 10.

336 Federal Spending

State	Federal Expenditures Per Capita	Points
1. Alaska	$6,873	100
2. Maryland	6,589	100
3. New Mexico	6,572	99
4. Virginia	6,416	94
5. Hawaii	5,600	67
6. Massachusetts	5,474	63
7. North Dakota	5,452	62
8. Maine	5,290	57
9. Mississippi	5,107	51
10. Rhode Island	5,041	49
11. Missouri	5,025	48
12. Montana	4,967	46
13. Colorado	4,952	46
14. Alabama	4,920	45
15. Connecticut	4,846	42
16. South Dakota	4,684	37
17. Washington	4,678	37
18. Florida	4,648	36
19. Pennsylvania	4,640	36
20. New York	4,632	35
21. California	4,526	32
22. Wyoming	4,506	31
23. Tennessee	4,485	30
West Virginia	4,485	30
25. Oklahoma	4,450	29
26. Kansas	4,442	29
27. Idaho	4,425	28
28. South Carolina	4,415	28
29. New Jersey	4,405	28
30. Louisiana	4,340	26
31. Arizona	4,309	25
32. Nebraska	4,280	24
33. Georgia	4,191	21
34. Arkansas	4,151	19
35. Kentucky	4,139	19
36. Iowa	4,053	16
37. Nevada	4,052	16
38. Texas	3,956	13
39. Ohio	3,950	13
40. Oregon	3,934	12
41. Utah	3,925	12
42. Delaware	3,897	11
43. New Hampshire	3,853	10
44. Illinois	3,818	8
45. Vermont	3,801	8
46. Michigan	3,788	7
47. North Carolina	3,761	7
48. Minnesota	3,751	6
49. Wisconsin	3,563	0
50. Indiana	3,529	0

Population Influx

DOING THE MATH

Some states are microcosms of America, blessed with a wide mixture of people who have lived in different parts of the country. Other states stick to themselves, with few residents who ever have dared to venture beyond their hometowns. We measured each state's exposure to outside influences and experiences, calculating the percentage of its American-born residents who are natives of other states.

BEST STATES

It sometimes seems as if everyone in Nevada is originally from somewhere else. Fully 76.1 percent of the state's American-born residents are natives of other states. Also above 60 percent are Florida, Alaska, and Arizona.

WORST STATES

Pennsylvania is the most insular of the 50 states. Just 17.2 percent of its current residents who are U.S. natives were born in other states. Also below 20 percent are Louisiana and New York.

REGIONAL WINNERS

East—New Hampshire
South—Florida
Midwest—Kansas
West—Nevada

BIGGEST SURPRISE

New York is commonly thought to be a population magnet, drawing the best and brightest from throughout the country. It actually tends to stick with its own kind, ranking 48th in this category.

THE BOTTOM LINE

It's no surprise that America's youngest region attracts the most outsiders. Seven of this category's top 10 states are western. The South has the largest number of stay-at-homes, with four states in the bottom 10.

338 Population Influx

State	Percentage of American-Born Residents Who Are Natives of Other States	Points
1. Nevada	76.1%	100
2. Florida	65.1	100
3. Alaska	64.4	98
4. Arizona	63.0	95
5. Wyoming	56.6	81
6. Colorado	54.7	77
7. New Hampshire	54.2	76
8. Oregon	51.0	69
9. Washington	48.4	63
10. Delaware	48.1	63
11. Idaho	47.9	62
12. Maryland	46.7	60
13. New Mexico	45.4	57
14. Virginia	42.9	51
15. Vermont	41.0	47
16. California	40.8	47
17. Montana	40.0	45
18. Connecticut	37.7	40
19. New Jersey	37.4	39
20. Kansas	37.1	39
21. Oklahoma	35.2	35
22. Hawaii	34.2	32
23. Georgia	33.7	31
24. Arkansas	32.2	28
25. South Carolina	30.6	25
26. Utah	30.4	24
27. Rhode Island	30.0	23
Tennessee	30.0	23
29. Maine	29.4	22
30. Missouri	29.2	21
31. South Dakota	29.0	21
32. Texas	28.9	21
33. Nebraska	28.6	20
34. North Carolina	28.3	19
35. Indiana	27.7	18
36. North Dakota	25.7	14
37. Illinois	24.6	11
38. Minnesota	24.4	11
39. Ohio	24.1	10
40. Massachusetts	24.0	10
41. Alabama	23.3	9
42. Michigan	22.2	6
43. Mississippi	22.1	6
44. West Virginia	22.0	6
45. Kentucky	21.9	5
46. Wisconsin	21.6	5
47. Iowa	21.2	4
48. New York	19.8	1
49. Louisiana	19.4	0
50. Pennsylvania	17.2	0

Domestic Travel

DOING THE MATH

Most of us receive our broadest exposure to other states as tourists. Americans annually spend more than $290 billion on domestic travel, covering everything from weekend getaways to cross-country tours. This category determines how much of that money is spent in each state, then translates that figure into a per capita rate.

BEST STATES

The bright lights of Las Vegas and Reno attract tourists who spend almost $11 billion a year in Nevada. That equals $9,135 per Nevada resident, almost double the performance of any other state. Second place belongs to Hawaii, with a rate of $5,168.

WORST STATES

Relatively few Americans make a point of seeing Rhode Island; its domestic travel spending works out to just $667 per resident. Also below $700 are West Virginia and Indiana.

REGIONAL WINNERS

East—Vermont
South—Florida
Midwest—North Dakota
West—Nevada

BIGGEST SURPRISE

Pennsylvania, the birthplace of American independence, has two of the nation's largest cities, and is noted for its aggressive tourism advertising campaigns. But it ranks no better than 44th in attracting domestic travel spending.

THE BOTTOM LINE

American tourists are enchanted by the West. Eight of the top 10 states are in that region. The Midwest, on the other hand, has four states in the bottom 10.

340 Domestic Travel

State	Domestic Travel Spending Per Capita	Points
1. Nevada	$9,135	100
2. Hawaii	5,168	100
3. Wyoming	2,203	34
4. Florida	2,017	30
5. Alaska	1,908	27
6. Vermont	1,633	21
7. Colorado	1,628	21
8. Montana	1,626	21
9. New Mexico	1,452	17
10. California	1,361	15
11. Arizona	1,309	14
12. Virginia	1,307	14
13. Utah	1,293	14
14. Idaho	1,290	14
South Carolina	1,290	14
16. New Jersey	1,263	13
17. Georgia	1,200	12
18. Tennessee	1,185	11
19. Oregon	1,169	11
20. Delaware	1,163	11
21. North Dakota	1,162	11
22. Maine	1,141	10
23. New Hampshire	1,110	10
24. Missouri	1,092	9
25. Massachusetts	1,084	9
26. New York	1,073	9
27. South Dakota	1,052	8
28. Louisiana	1,029	8
29. Illinois	1,018	8
30. Nebraska	1,011	7
31. North Carolina	1,010	7
32. Texas	991	7
33. Washington	984	7
34. Connecticut	976	7
35. Maryland	933	6
36. Arkansas	928	6
37. Iowa	920	5
38. Kansas	908	5
39. Minnesota	880	4
40. Kentucky	839	4
41. Alabama	836	3
42. Wisconsin	812	3
43. Oklahoma	789	2
44. Pennsylvania	766	2
45. Mississippi	752	2
46. Michigan	728	1
47. Ohio	721	1
48. Indiana	690	0
49. West Virginia	680	0
50. Rhode Island	667	0

Fortune 500 Companies

DOING THE MATH

American business is dominated by the *Fortune* 500, those companies identified by *Fortune* magazine as having the largest sales volumes in the nation. The list includes all of corporate America's most familiar names, such as Eastman Kodak, IBM, and Xerox. This category counts the number of *Fortune* 500 powerhouses headquartered in each state, converting the figure to a rate per 1 million residents.

BEST STATES

No state has a greater concentration of major corporate headquarters than Connecticut, the home of 28 *Fortune* 500 companies. Its rate is 8.5 headquarters per 1 million residents. The only entry that comes close is Delaware at 6.0.

WORST STATES

Ten states are totally without *Fortune* 500 headquarters. Six of those states are from the West, two each from the East and Midwest.

REGIONAL WINNERS

East—Connecticut
South—Texas
Midwest—Illinois
West—Colorado, Oregon

BIGGEST SURPRISE

New York has always topped the nation in the raw total of *Fortune* 500 companies; it currently has 56. But that impressive number does not translate into an equally impressive rate. New York does no better than sixth place in this category.

THE BOTTOM LINE

America's corporate center is solidly in the East, which placed seven states in the top 11. The other four leaders are all from the Midwest.

342 *Fortune* 500 Companies

State	*Fortune* 500 Headquarters Per Million Residents	Points
1. Connecticut	8.5	100
2. Delaware	6.0	100
3. Illinois	4.0	67
Rhode Island	4.0	67
5. Minnesota	3.7	61
6. Ohio	3.1	52
New York	3.1	52
8. Pennsylvania	2.9	48
9. New Jersey	2.8	47
10. Massachusetts	2.5	41
Wisconsin	2.5	41
12. Missouri	2.3	39
Texas	2.3	39
14. Michigan	2.2	36
15. Virginia	2.1	35
16. Indiana	2.0	33
17. Nebraska	1.9	32
18. Colorado	1.8	30
New Hampshire	1.8	30
Iowa	1.8	30
Oregon	1.8	30
22. Arkansas	1.7	28
Georgia	1.7	28
24. California	1.5	25
25. Oklahoma	1.3	21
26. Alabama	1.2	21
27. South Carolina	1.1	19
West Virginia	1.1	19
29. Washington	1.0	17
Idaho	1.0	17
31. Louisiana	0.9	16
32. Maryland	0.8	14
Kansas	0.8	14
North Carolina	0.8	14
35. Utah	0.6	10
36. Arizona	0.5	9
Kentucky	0.5	9
Florida	0.5	9
39. Tennessee	0.4	7
Mississippi	0.4	7
41. Alaska	0.0	0
Hawaii	0.0	0
Maine	0.0	0
Montana	0.0	0
Nevada	0.0	0
New Mexico	0.0	0
North Dakota	0.0	0
South Dakota	0.0	0
Vermont	0.0	0
Wyoming	0.0	0

Student Migration

DOING THE MATH

Selecting a college can be the most important choice in your life. Which school you attend might determine whom you marry or where you get a job. This category measures the drawing power of each state's universities, comparing the influx of undergraduates from other states with the outflow of the state's own college-bound students. The resulting balance of migration is expressed as a rate per 1,000 home-state students.

BEST STATES

Rhode Island benefits from America's strongest influx of young talent. It annually pulls in 4,800 more undergraduates than it loses. That equals a net addition of 593 students to every original group of 1,000 Rhode Island college students. Second place belongs to Vermont.

WORST STATES

Undergraduates from Alaska can't wait to go to college on the mainland. Its out-migration is 455 students per 1,000. New Jersey is next to last.

REGIONAL WINNERS

East—Rhode Island
South—Alabama
Midwest—North Dakota
West—Utah

BIGGEST SURPRISE

West Virginia is not commonly considered an educational magnet. But its state university has a solid reputation, contributing to America's seventh-highest student in-migration rate.

THE BOTTOM LINE

Eastern colleges remain attractive to students from other parts of the country. Six of the top 10 states are eastern. The West, on the other hand, holds five of 11 slots at the bottom of the list.

344 Student Migration

State	Net Migration of College Students Per 1,000 Home State Students	Points
1. Rhode Island	593	100
2. Vermont	468	100
3. Utah	398	91
4. Idaho	329	82
5. Delaware	297	78
6. New York	249	72
7. West Virginia	206	67
8. New Hampshire	193	65
9. North Dakota	190	65
10. Indiana	177	63
11. Alabama	172	63
12. Massachusetts	169	62
13. North Carolina	153	60
14. Virginia	144	59
15. Oregon	122	56
16. Arizona	112	55
17. South Carolina	109	55
18. Kansas	91	52
19. Missouri	78	51
20. Tennessee	77	51
21. Pennsylvania	73	50
22. Michigan	72	50
23. Florida	65	49
24. Iowa	62	49
25. Mississippi	61	48
26. California	54	48
27. Wisconsin	50	47
Wyoming	50	47
29. Louisiana	46	47
30. Washington	38	46
31. Kentucky	33	45
32. Georgia	32	45
33. Texas	26	44
Colorado	26	44
35. Minnesota	20	43
36. Arkansas	18	43
37. Ohio	10	42
South Dakota	10	42
39. Nebraska	–10	40
40. Oklahoma	–17	39
Maine	–17	39
42. New Mexico	–25	38
43. Nevada	–31	37
44. Illinois	–74	31
45. Maryland	–99	28
46. Hawaii	–126	25
47. Montana	–153	21
48. Connecticut	–203	15
49. New Jersey	–322	0
50. Alaska	–455	0

National Relations: Scores and Grades

BEST STATE

Delaware, no. 1 in this section, is the state with the strongest connections to the rest of the country. Its residents have family ties throughout America; almost half of them were born in other states. Delaware's rate of national corporate power is virtually unmatched; only Connecticut has a higher concentration of *Fortune* 500 headquarters. And just four states are more successful than Delaware at attracting out-of-state students to its colleges.

RUNNERS-UP

Second place is shared by Nevada and Virginia. Nevada maintains its national relations the easy way, getting the rest of America to come to it. No state can top Nevada's record of luring new residents and tourists from other states. Virginia's strength is its ability to pull in federal funding; only three states receive larger shares of the national wealth.

WORST STATES

Kentucky attracted immigrants from throughout the United States in the early 19th century, but no longer. It is now America's most isolated state, drawing only 21.9 percent of its residents from elsewhere. Eight other states received F's.

REGIONAL WINNERS

East—Delaware
South—Virginia
Midwest—Missouri
West—Nevada

REGIONAL AVERAGES

East—54 (C)
South—31 (D)
Midwest—23 (D–)
West—62 (B–)

346 BIGGEST SURPRISE

It is difficult to maintain strong national relations when you're physically separated from the other states, but Alaska and Hawaii manage to do it. Both earned grades of B+ in this section.

THE BOTTOM LINE

Western states have the strongest connections with the rest of America; five are in the top 10. The most isolated region is the Midwest, with six states in the bottom 10.

National Relations: Scores and Grades

State	Score	Grade
1. Delaware	100	A+
2. Nevada	94	A
Virginia	94	A
4. Rhode Island	86	A
5. Alaska	79	B+
6. Florida	78	B+
Hawaii	78	B+
8. Colorado	75	B+
9. New Mexico	71	B
10. Maryland	70	B
11. Connecticut	67	B
Idaho	67	B
13. Arizona	64	B–
14. Wyoming	61	B–
15. New Hampshire	60	B–
16. Massachusetts	57	C+
17. Oregon	52	C
Vermont	52	C
19. Washington	49	C
20. New York	48	C
Missouri	48	C
22. California	47	C
23. North Dakota	39	D+
24. Utah	38	D+
25. Alabama	33	D
South Carolina	33	D
27. Kansas	31	D
28. Georgia	30	D
Pennsylvania	30	D
30. Montana	28	D
31. Maine	25	D
New Jersey	25	D
33. Oklahoma	24	D–
Illinois	24	D–
Minnesota	24	D–
36. Arkansas	23	D–
Nebraska	23	D–
Texas	23	D–
39. Tennessee	22	D–
West Virginia	22	D–
41. Ohio	20	D–
42. Indiana	18	F
43. Mississippi	17	F
44. South Dakota	14	F
45. North Carolina	13	F
46. Iowa	12	F
47. Michigan	10	F
48. Louisiana	8	F
Wisconsin	8	F
50. Kentucky	0	F

24

International Relations

The Big Question

Which state has the strongest connections with the rest of the world?

The Categories

1. Foreign Employers
2. Export-Related Jobs
3. Foreign Born
4. Agricultural Exports
5. Overseas Population

Foreign Employers

DOING THE MATH

Alarmists would have us believe that foreigners, particularly the Japanese, are buying all of America. It isn't true. Foreign employers control just 4 percent of U.S. jobs. Their presence, in fact, is usually beneficial, providing states with economic links to the rest of the world. This category expresses the number of foreign-controlled jobs in each state as a rate per 100,000 employees of all companies.

BEST STATES

Foreign employers oversee roughly 35,200 of Delaware's 273,600 employees. That's a rate of 12,860 foreign-controlled jobs per 100,000 total jobs, easily the highest rate in the nation. Hawaii is in second place at 7,213.

WORST STATES

South Dakota's economy has had little exposure to the outside world. The state has 1,489 foreign-controlled jobs, which works out to 795 per 100,000. Neighboring North Dakota is next to last.

REGIONAL WINNERS

East—Delaware
South—South Carolina
Midwest—Illinois
West—Hawaii

BIGGEST SURPRISE

South Carolina historically has resisted outside influences. It, after all, was the state that started the Civil War. But times have changed, and South Carolina ranks no. 3 in this category.

THE BOTTOM LINE

Foreign employers have been most readily welcomed in the East, which has five states in the top 10. The region attracting the least foreign capital is the Midwest, with six states in the bottom 10.

350 Foreign Employers

State	Employees of Foreign-Owned Companies Per 100,000 Employees of All Companies	Points
1. Delaware	12,860	100
2. Hawaii	7,213	100
3. South Carolina	5,896	79
4. New Jersey	5,755	77
5. North Carolina	5,680	76
6. West Virginia	5,629	75
7. Maine	5,375	71
8. Georgia	4,980	65
9. New York	4,942	64
10. Alaska	4,635	59
11. Tennessee	4,456	57
12. Arizona	4,355	55
13. Louisiana	4,313	54
14. New Hampshire	4,171	52
15. Virginia	4,056	50
16. Texas	4,012	50
17. Pennsylvania	3,925	48
18. Connecticut	3,817	46
19. California	3,725	45
20. Illinois	3,712	45
21. New Mexico	3,637	44
22. Kentucky	3,572	43
23. Massachusetts	3,326	39
24. Ohio	3,314	39
25. Maryland	3,239	37
26. Oklahoma	3,205	37
27. Indiana	3,194	37
28. Wisconsin	3,183	37
29. Vermont	3,061	35
30. Arkansas	3,057	35
31. Alabama	2,955	33
32. Michigan	2,940	33
33. Washington	2,896	32
34. Colorado	2,789	30
35. Wyoming	2,774	30
36. Rhode Island	2,765	30
37. Oregon	2,760	30
38. Missouri	2,693	29
39. Florida	2,645	28
40. Mississippi	2,567	27
41. Utah	2,291	22
42. Nevada	2,288	22
43. Iowa	2,137	20
44. Minnesota	2,108	20
45. Kansas	2,096	19
46. Idaho	1,776	14
47. Montana	1,492	10
48. Nebraska	1,391	8
49. North Dakota	865	0
50. South Dakota	795	0

Export-Related Jobs

DOING THE MATH

The United States has negotiated free trade agreements with Canada and Mexico in recent years, emphasizing the increasing role played in the American economy by exports. The Census Bureau estimates that 6 million jobs are directly tied to the manufacture and shipping of exported goods. This category determines each state's number of export-related jobs, converting it to a rate per 100,000 residents.

BEST STATES

Washington is ideally located for trade with Canada and the Pacific Rim. That helps to explain why it leads the nation with 4,140 export-related jobs per 100,000 residents. Connecticut is the top exporter on the other coast, with a rate of 3,915.

WORST STATES

International trade is surprisingly unimportant to the economy of Hawaii, which has just 894 jobs tied to manufactured exports per 100,000 residents. Nevada is the only other state below 1,000.

REGIONAL WINNERS

East—Connecticut
South—North Carolina
Midwest—Indiana
West—Washington

BIGGEST SURPRISE

Hawaii would seem to be perfectly situated for trade with Asia, but instead it holds last place in this category. That's because Hawaii's manufacturing sector is exceptionally weak, producing few goods for export.

THE BOTTOM LINE

It's a tie between the East and Midwest. Each placed four states among the 10 leaders. The West, on the other hand, includes the category's five worst states.

352 Export-Related Jobs

State	Jobs Related to Manufactured Exports Per 100,000 Residents	Points
1. Washington	4,140	100
2. Connecticut	3,915	100
3. Rhode Island	3,370	82
4. Massachusetts	3,253	78
5. Vermont	3,233	77
6. Indiana	3,220	77
7. Ohio	3,036	71
8. Michigan	2,998	70
9. Minnesota	2,983	69
10. Oregon	2,977	69
11. North Carolina	2,880	66
12. South Carolina	2,876	66
13. Wisconsin	2,866	65
14. Illinois	2,715	60
15. New Hampshire	2,687	59
16. Delaware	2,643	58
17. California	2,589	56
18. New Jersey	2,581	56
19. Pennsylvania	2,447	51
20. Iowa	2,384	49
21. Maine	2,345	48
22. Tennessee	2,338	48
23. Kansas	2,312	47
24. Alabama	2,230	44
25. Texas	2,221	44
26. Arkansas	2,208	43
27. New York	2,204	43
28. Idaho	2,185	43
29. Alaska	2,145	41
30. Missouri	2,118	40
31. Kentucky	2,022	37
32. Georgia	1,988	36
33. Colorado	1,985	36
34. Arizona	1,965	35
35. Mississippi	1,932	34
36. Nebraska	1,876	32
37. Virginia	1,741	28
38. West Virginia	1,723	27
39. Oklahoma	1,713	27
40. Utah	1,683	26
41. Florida	1,666	25
42. South Dakota	1,638	25
43. Louisiana	1,514	20
44. Maryland	1,491	20
45. North Dakota	1,455	18
46. Wyoming	1,233	11
47. Montana	1,214	10
48. New Mexico	1,083	6
49. Nevada	899	0
50. Hawaii	894	0

Foreign Born

DOING THE MATH

There was a time when foreign languages were more commonly heard than English on the streets of major American cities. That's no longer the case, but the nation's immigrant population still keeps America in touch with other cultures. More than 21 million U.S. residents were born in foreign lands; many still follow the customs of their native countries. We calculated the percentage of each state's residents who were born outside of the United States.

BEST STATES

California is the promised land for immigrants from Mexico, Latin America, and Asia. Fully 21.7 percent of California's residents were born in other countries, the highest rate in the nation. Four other states are above 10 percent: New York, Hawaii, Florida, and New Jersey.

WORST STATES

Few immigrants are drawn to Mississippi, where just 0.8 percent of all residents were born on foreign soil. Also below 1 percent are West Virginia and Kentucky.

REGIONAL WINNERS

East—New York
South—Florida
Midwest—Illinois
West—California

BIGGEST SURPRISE

New Jersey has the reputation of being a homogeneous, suburban state. It actually includes a surprising diversity of cultures, earning fifth place in this category.

THE BOTTOM LINE

The East, with five states in the top 10, still has the largest foreign-born population. The South includes six of the 11 lowest-ranked states, while the Midwest has four.

354 Foreign Born

State	Residents Born in Another Country	Points
1. California	21.7%	100
2. New York	15.9	100
3. Hawaii	14.7	92
4. Florida	12.9	80
5. New Jersey	12.5	77
6. Massachusetts	9.5	57
Rhode Island	9.5	57
8. Texas	9.0	54
9. Nevada	8.7	52
10. Connecticut	8.5	51
11. Illinois	8.3	49
12. Arizona	7.6	45
13. Maryland	6.6	38
Washington	6.6	38
15. New Mexico	5.3	29
16. Virginia	5.0	27
17. Oregon	4.9	27
18. Alaska	4.5	24
19. Colorado	4.3	23
20. Michigan	3.8	19
21. New Hampshire	3.7	19
22. Utah	3.4	17
23. Delaware	3.3	16
24. Pennsylvania	3.1	15
Vermont	3.1	15
26. Maine	3.0	14
27. Idaho	2.9	13
28. Georgia	2.7	12
29. Minnesota	2.6	11
30. Kansas	2.5	11
Wisconsin	2.5	11
32. Ohio	2.4	10
33. Louisiana	2.1	8
Oklahoma	2.1	8
35. Nebraska	1.8	6
36. Indiana	1.7	5
Montana	1.7	5
North Carolina	1.7	5
Wyoming	1.7	5
40. Iowa	1.6	5
Missouri	1.6	5
42. North Dakota	1.5	4
43. South Carolina	1.4	3
44. Tennessee	1.2	2
45. Alabama	1.1	1
Arkansas	1.1	1
South Dakota	1.1	1
48. Kentucky	0.9	0
West Virginia	0.9	0
50. Mississippi	0.8	0

Agricultural Exports

DOING THE MATH

Exporting involves more than shipping manufactured goods overseas. The rest of the world also demands fruit and farm products from the United States. And America responds, selling more than $37 billion of agricultural commodities to foreign countries each year. This category finds each state's share of that total, translating it into a rate per 1,000 square miles of land area.

BEST STATES

Iowa is America's leading exporter of feed grains ($1.3 billion a year) and is second in international sales of soybeans ($792 million). Its total agricultural exports of $2.8 billion equal $50,195,973 per 1,000 square miles, the best rate in America. Illinois is the second-most productive exporter.

WORST STATES

A short growing season keeps Alaska's farmers from having an impact on the world market. Alaska's agricultural exports amount to just $351 per 1,000 square miles. Nevada is the only other state below $100,000.

REGIONAL WINNERS

East—Delaware
South—Kentucky
Midwest—Iowa
West—California

BIGGEST SURPRISE

Tiny Delaware ranks no. 4, surrounded by well-known farm states such as Iowa, Illinois, Indiana, and Nebraska. Delaware is one of the nation's leading exporters of poultry.

THE BOTTOM LINE

No surprise here. America's heartland, the Midwest, holds seven of the top 10 slots. The bottom 10 is evenly split between the East and West.

356 Agricultural Exports

State	Agricultural Exports Per 1,000 Square Miles	Points
1. Iowa	$50,195,973	100
2. Illinois	46,379,940	100
3. Indiana	36,099,805	78
4. Delaware	30,895,141	67
5. Nebraska	30,656,365	66
6. California	29,617,947	64
7. Ohio	24,840,671	54
8. Kansas	24,522,445	53
9. Kentucky	22,739,857	49
10. Minnesota	22,539,156	49
11. North Carolina	20,661,768	44
12. Arkansas	19,237,638	41
13. Maryland	15,805,627	34
14. Washington	15,789,553	34
15. Florida	15,204,548	33
16. Wisconsin	14,563,464	31
17. Mississippi	13,725,114	30
18. Michigan	12,968,016	28
19. Missouri	12,881,361	28
20. North Dakota	12,469,200	27
21. Connecticut	12,094,943	26
22. Louisiana	10,834,137	23
23. Texas	9,717,694	21
24. South Dakota	9,361,248	20
25. Georgia	9,300,920	20
26. Hawaii	8,749,805	19
27. Tennessee	7,962,154	17
28. South Carolina	7,067,185	15
29. Virginia	6,949,846	15
30. Pennsylvania	6,822,847	15
31. New Jersey	6,523,790	14
32. Idaho	6,352,793	14
33. Colorado	6,239,275	13
34. Alabama	5,700,493	12
35. New York	5,664,493	12
36. Oklahoma	5,193,727	11
37. Oregon	4,786,309	10
38. Massachusetts	3,470,273	7
39. Arizona	3,349,114	7
40. Montana	1,566,407	3
41. Utah	1,049,070	2
42. Rhode Island	861,244	2
43. New Mexico	684,711	1
44. Maine	362,871	1
45. Wyoming	348,077	1
46. Vermont	335,171	1
47. West Virginia	244,945	0
48. New Hampshire	100,346	0
49. Nevada	41,892	0
50. Alaska	351	0

Overseas Population

DOING THE MATH

The best way to learn about another part of the world is to live there. That's exactly what more than 920,000 federal government employees are doing, as they handle overseas assignments for branches as diverse as the armed forces and the Library of Congress. This category expresses each state's number of overseas residents as a rate per 100,000 persons living at home.

BEST STATES

Slightly more than 7,000 citizens of Hawaii are working in foreign lands for the federal government. That means there are 636 Hawaiians living overseas for every 100,000 within the state. Montana and South Dakota are the only other states with rates above 550.

WORST STATES

Massachusetts has the proportionately smallest presence in America's overseas contingent, just 210 persons per 100,000 residents at home. New Jersey is next to last.

REGIONAL WINNERS

East—West Virginia
South—South Carolina, Alabama
Midwest—South Dakota
West—Hawaii

BIGGEST SURPRISE

Several small, supposedly unworldly states are near the top of this list. Montana, South Dakota, South Carolina, and Alabama are all in the top five.

THE BOTTOM LINE

The South is the region most likely to have citizens working overseas for the armed services and other branches of the federal government. Five of the 10 leading states are southern. Five of the bottom 10 states are eastern.

358 Overseas Population

State	Overseas Population Per 100,000 Residents	Points
1. Hawaii	636	100
2. Montana	574	100
South Dakota	574	100
4. South Carolina	545	91
Alabama	545	91
6. Wyoming	526	86
7. Idaho	520	84
8. Mississippi	514	82
9. Florida	506	80
10. Arkansas	490	75
11. Virginia	472	70
12. Georgia	466	68
13. West Virginia	454	64
14. New Mexico	443	61
15. North Carolina	437	59
Washington	437	59
17. Louisiana	432	58
18. Texas	431	57
Maine	431	57
20. New Hampshire	420	54
21. Colorado	410	51
22. Missouri	405	50
23. Oregon	402	49
24. North Dakota	401	48
25. Tennessee	399	48
26. Nebraska	395	47
27. Vermont	392	46
28. Iowa	384	43
29. Oklahoma	382	43
30. Delaware	380	42
31. Kentucky	371	39
Ohio	371	39
33. Pennsylvania	362	37
Indiana	362	37
35. Michigan	360	36
36. Nevada	359	36
Maryland	359	36
38. Arizona	348	33
39. Alaska	346	32
40. Kansas	324	25
41. Illinois	316	23
42. Wisconsin	306	20
43. New York	300	18
44. Utah	286	14
45. Minnesota	273	10
46. California	266	8
47. Connecticut	260	6
48. Rhode Island	251	4
49. New Jersey	239	0
50. Massachusetts	210	0

International Relations: Scores and Grades

BEST STATE

Hawaii, half an ocean removed from the rest of America, does the best job of keeping in touch with the outside world. No state has a larger proportion of citizens living and working overseas; only Delaware benefits from a more significant array of foreign employers within its borders. Hawaii also has a daily reminder of the world's diversity: 14.7 percent of its residents were born in other countries.

RUNNERS-UP

Delaware, no. 2 in this section, has close relationships with overseas corporations. Fully 12,860 of every 100,000 jobs in the state are controlled by foreign companies, America's highest rate. Delaware also ranks fourth in agricultural exports. Two other states earned A's: Illinois and California.

WORST STATES

Utah holds the rest of the world at arm's length. It has a below-average record in exporting manufactured goods and does even worse with farm products. Only six states have fewer citizens living overseas. Also receiving F's were North Dakota and Nevada.

REGIONAL WINNERS

East—Delaware
South—South Carolina
Midwest—Illinois
West—Hawaii

REGIONAL AVERAGES

East—51 (C)
South—50 (C)
Midwest—43 (C–)
West—41 (C–)

BIGGEST SURPRISE

New York, which considers itself the most worldly of the 50 states, does no better than ninth here, behind Delaware and both Carolinas.

360 THE BOTTOM LINE

The East has the highest regional average, but the West and South lead the way with three states each in the section's top 10. The West dominates the bottom of the list, holding six of the 10 worst slots.

International Relations: Scores and Grades

State	Score	Grade
1. Hawaii	100	A+
2. Delaware	88	A
3. Illinois	85	A
4. California	83	A–
5. Washington	79	B+
6. South Carolina	75	B+
7. North Carolina	73	B
8. Florida	72	B
9. New York	68	B
10. Indiana	67	B
11. Connecticut	64	B–
12. Texas	63	B–
13. New Jersey	62	B–
14. Iowa	59	C+
15. Ohio	57	C+
16. Georgia	52	C
17. Arkansas	50	C
18. Maine	48	C
19. Virginia	47	C
20. Michigan	46	C
21. Oregon	45	C
New Hampshire	45	C
23. Alabama	43	C–
Massachusetts	43	C–
25. Arizona	41	C–
Rhode Island	41	C–
27. Vermont	40	C–
Mississippi	40	C–
Tennessee	40	C–
30. Idaho	38	D+
Kentucky	38	D+
32. Pennsylvania	37	D+
West Virginia	37	D+
Maryland	37	D+
35. Wisconsin	36	D+
Louisiana	36	D+
37. Minnesota	34	D
Nebraska	34	D
39. Alaska	33	D
40. Kansas	32	D
41. Colorado	31	D
Missouri	31	D
43. South Dakota	28	D
44. New Mexico	26	D
45. Wyoming	23	D–
46. Montana	20	D–
Oklahoma	20	D–
48. Nevada	13	F
49. North Dakota	7	F
50. Utah	0	F

25

Future

The Big Question

Which state faces the brightest future, in terms of demographics, economics, and politics?

The Categories

1. Population Density
2. Projected Population Growth
3. Projected Job Growth
4. Projected Income Growth
5. Future Political Power

Population Density

DOING THE MATH

It's common sense that future growth requires open space. This category assesses the available room in each state by measuring its population density, the number of persons per square mile. The lower its density, the more comfortably a state can absorb future expansion without losing its quality of life.

BEST STATES

No state has more open space than Alaska. Its 550,000 residents are spread out across 570,000 square miles, which rounds off to a density of one person per square mile. The most sparsely populated state on the mainland is Wyoming, with five people per mile.

WORST STATES

The suburbs of New York City and Philadelphia have clogged New Jersey's 7,400 square miles with 7.73 million residents. That works out to the nation's highest population density, 1,042 persons per square mile. Next to last is Rhode Island at 960.

REGIONAL WINNERS

East—Maine
South—Arkansas
Midwest—South Dakota, North Dakota
West—Alaska

BIGGEST SURPRISE

America's two smallest states in land area, Delaware and Rhode Island, are also among the most densely populated. Both are in the bottom seven in this category.

THE BOTTOM LINE

It's no surprise that the West, with its wide, open spaces, is the leader here. It placed seven states among the top 10. The East, on the other hand, includes eight of the 10 worst states.

364 Population Density

State	Persons Per Square Mile	Points
1. Alaska	1	100
2. Wyoming	5	100
3. Montana	6	100
4. South Dakota	9	100
North Dakota	9	100
6. Nevada	11	99
7. Idaho	12	99
8. New Mexico	13	99
9. Nebraska	21	98
Utah	21	98
11. Oregon	30	97
Kansas	30	97
13. Colorado	32	97
Arizona	32	97
15. Maine	40	96
16. Arkansas	45	96
17. Oklahoma	46	96
18. Iowa	50	95
19. Mississippi	55	95
Minnesota	55	95
21. Vermont	61	94
22. Texas	65	94
23. Washington	73	93
24. Missouri	74	93
25. West Virginia	75	93
26. Alabama	80	92
27. Wisconsin	90	91
28. Kentucky	93	91
29. Louisiana	97	90
30. Georgia	112	89
31. South Carolina	116	88
32. Tennessee	118	88
33. New Hampshire	124	88
34. North Carolina	136	86
35. Indiana	155	84
36. Virginia	156	84
37. Michigan	164	83
38. Hawaii	173	82
39. California	191	81
40. Illinois	206	79
41. Florida	240	75
42. Ohio	265	73
Pennsylvania	265	73
44. Delaware	341	65
45. New York	381	61
46. Maryland	489	49
47. Connecticut	678	29
48. Massachusetts	768	20
49. Rhode Island	960	0
50. New Jersey	1,042	0

Projected Population Growth

DOING THE MATH

No one really can foresee the future, but the U.S. Bureau of Economic Analysis takes its best shot. It produces population estimates for decades far down the road; it has already issued figures for 2040. This category calculates the difference between each state's actual population in 1988 and the bureau's projections for 2020.

BEST STATES

The Bureau of Economic Analysis expects Nevada to be America's fastest-growing state in the early 21st century. Its projected 2020 population is 1.66 million, up 58 percent from 1.05 million in 1988. A neighboring desert state, Arizona, holds second place at 44.4 percent.

WORST STATES

The bureau anticipates little difference between present-day Wyoming and the same state in 2020. Its projected growth rate is just 1 percent. The only other state below 5 percent is Louisiana.

REGIONAL WINNERS

East—Delaware
South—Florida
Midwest—Minnesota
West—Nevada

BIGGEST SURPRISE

It's commonly assumed that the entire Sunbelt is enjoying a population boom. But two southern states—Alabama and Louisiana—are among only six in the nation that expect less than 10 percent growth by 2020.

THE BOTTOM LINE

Future growth will be concentrated in the West, which has six of this category's 10 best entries. The South includes some of America's fastest-growing states, such as Florida and Virginia, but it also has five of the 10 slowest.

366 Projected Population Growth

State	Projected Population Change, 1988–2020	Points
1. Nevada	58.0%	100
2. Arizona	44.4	100
3. Florida	40.1	90
4. Hawaii	36.0	80
5. California	33.7	75
6. Utah	30.2	67
7. Delaware	29.5	65
8. Colorado	29.3	65
9. Virginia	28.9	64
10. New Hampshire	28.3	62
11. Washington	27.6	61
12. Georgia	24.9	54
13. New Mexico	24.4	53
14. Oregon	23.2	50
15. Maryland	22.9	50
16. New Jersey	21.3	46
17. Vermont	21.0	45
18. Tennessee	20.6	44
19. Rhode Island	18.7	40
Maine	18.7	40
21. North Carolina	18.4	39
22. Massachusetts	17.7	38
23. Connecticut	17.6	37
24. Minnesota	17.2	36
25. Idaho	16.6	35
26. Illinois	14.9	31
Texas	14.9	31
28. South Carolina	14.7	31
29. Indiana	14.5	30
30. Wisconsin	14.4	30
31. Missouri	14.0	29
32. Arkansas	13.5	28
33. Michigan	13.3	27
34. Iowa	13.0	27
35. Nebraska	12.9	26
36. Pennsylvania	12.5	25
37. South Dakota	11.9	24
38. Kansas	11.8	24
39. North Dakota	11.4	23
40. Alaska	10.9	22
41. Kentucky	10.7	21
42. Oklahoma	10.5	21
Mississippi	10.5	21
44. Ohio	10.4	21
45. Alabama	9.6	19
46. New York	8.4	16
47. Montana	8.3	16
48. West Virginia	5.2	8
49. Louisiana	1.6	0
50. Wyoming	1.0	0

Projected Job Growth

DOING THE MATH

Population growth depends on job growth. Or is it the other way around? The Bureau of Economic Analysis covers both ends of this chicken-and-egg equation by also estimating future employment totals. This category calculates the increase between each state's actual number of jobs in 1988 and its projected total in 2020.

BEST STATES

Nevada, the top state in future population growth, unsurprisingly is also no. 1 here. It is projected to have 951,600 jobs in 2020, a 47.7 percent increase from its 1988 total of 644,400. Arizona, with an expected employment gain of 41.4 percent, is in second place.

WORST STATES

The Bureau of Economic Analysis foresees scant economic progress in Wyoming, projecting job growth of only 0.4 percent by 2020. Tied for next to last are West Virginia and Louisiana, each with an expected increase of 2.2 percent.

REGIONAL WINNERS

East—New Hampshire
South—Florida
Midwest—Minnesota
West—Nevada

BIGGEST SURPRISE

Most states show a direct correlation between projected population growth and projected job growth. Not Delaware, which was no. 7 in the former category, but is only no. 13 in this one.

THE BOTTOM LINE

It's nearly a clean sweep for the West, which holds eight of the top 10 slots. The other two belong to the South.

368 Projected Job Growth

State	Projected Employment Change, 1988–2020	Points
1. Nevada	47.7%	100
2. Arizona	41.4	100
3. Utah	33.1	79
4. Florida	32.9	78
5. California	30.5	72
6. Hawaii	27.2	64
7. Colorado	26.7	62
8. New Mexico	24.1	56
9. Washington	23.9	55
10. Virginia	23.2	54
11. Georgia	22.7	52
12. New Hampshire	21.1	48
13. Delaware	20.9	48
14. Maryland	19.2	43
15. Tennessee	18.8	42
16. Oregon	18.2	41
17. Idaho	17.9	40
18. New Jersey	16.4	36
19. Minnesota	16.2	36
20. Texas	15.4	34
21. Vermont	15.1	33
22. Indiana	14.9	32
Rhode Island	14.9	32
Illinois	14.9	32
25. Massachusetts	14.0	30
Michigan	14.0	30
27. North Carolina	13.8	30
28. Wisconsin	13.3	28
29. South Carolina	13.0	28
30. Connecticut	12.9	27
31. Maine	12.7	27
32. Oklahoma	12.5	26
33. Missouri	12.4	26
Iowa	12.4	26
35. Alaska	12.0	25
36. Arkansas	11.9	25
37. Nebraska	11.7	24
38. Kentucky	11.2	23
39. Mississippi	11.0	23
40. South Dakota	10.8	22
41. Pennsylvania	10.4	21
42. Kansas	10.0	20
43. Ohio	9.9	20
44. Alabama	9.6	19
45. North Dakota	9.0	17
46. Montana	7.0	12
47. New York	6.9	12
48. West Virginia	2.2	0
Louisiana	2.2	0
50. Wyoming	0.4	0

Projected Income Growth

DOING THE MATH

It's easy to find out about a state's current standard of living. But will it improve or deteriorate in the future? The Bureau of Economic Analysis answers that question with its income projections. We looked at the difference between each state's 1988 per capita income and its projected 2020 figure. Numbers for both years have been converted to 1982 dollars, eliminating inflation as a factor.

BEST STATES

The bureau predicts that Oklahoma's per capita income (in 1982 dollars) will reach $15,368 by 2020. That would be a 43.6 percent increase from 1988, the biggest jump in America. North Dakota ranks no. 2.

WORST STATES

Rapid economic expansion was the rule in Connecticut during the 1980s, but don't expect that trend to continue. The bureau estimates that Connecticut will have the nation's smallest income growth rate by 2020, just 23 percent. Next to last is Delaware.

REGIONAL WINNERS

East—West Virginia
South—Oklahoma
Midwest—North Dakota
West—Idaho

BIGGEST SURPRISE

Connecticut currently has the nation's highest per capita income, which is why it's surprising to find it at the very bottom of this list.

THE BOTTOM LINE

Three regions did almost equally well in this category. The West has four states in the top 10, while the South and Midwest have three each. And the East? Six of its states are in the bottom 10.

370 Projected Income Growth

State	Projected Per Capita Income Change, 1988–2020	Points
1. Oklahoma	43.6%	100
2. North Dakota	42.9	100
3. Idaho	42.7	99
4. Montana	42.4	97
5. South Dakota	41.5	92
6. New Mexico	41.4	92
7. Mississippi	41.3	91
8. Utah	41.1	90
9. Nebraska	40.0	84
10. Louisiana	39.8	83
11. Alabama	39.1	79
South Carolina	39.1	79
13. Kentucky	38.8	77
14. Texas	38.7	77
Wyoming	38.7	77
16. Arkansas	38.6	76
17. Tennessee	38.5	76
18. Kansas	37.5	70
19. Missouri	36.9	66
20. West Virginia	36.8	66
21. Iowa	36.7	65
22. North Carolina	36.4	63
23. Indiana	36.1	62
24. Georgia	35.6	59
25. Wisconsin	35.2	57
26. Colorado	34.9	55
27. Oregon	34.7	54
Ohio	34.7	54
29. Pennsylvania	34.5	53
30. Maine	34.4	52
31. Arizona	34.2	52
Washington	34.2	52
33. Florida	34.1	51
34. Vermont	34.0	50
35. Minnesota	33.5	47
36. Michigan	33.2	46
37. New York	32.8	43
38. Virginia	32.7	43
39. Rhode Island	31.7	37
40. Illinois	30.3	30
41. California	30.2	29
42. Hawaii	29.1	23
43. Nevada	28.2	18
44. Maryland	27.7	15
45. New Hampshire	27.1	12
46. New Jersey	25.8	4
47. Massachusetts	25.3	2
48. Alaska	25.1	1
49. Delaware	25.0	0
50. Connecticut	23.0	0

Future Political Power

DOING THE MATH

Which states will wield the most political clout in the future? The best clue comes from the Electoral College, which officially elects the president every four years. A state's number of electoral votes is equal to its number of senators and congressmen. We used the population projections of the Bureau of Economic Analysis to predict each state's electoral vote total in 2020.

BEST STATES

California, with 54 electoral votes, is already America's political giant. But its total is expected to balloon to 58 by 2020, the largest Electoral College delegation for a single state in the nation's history. New York and Texas will be tied for second with 31 votes each.

WORST STATES

The fewest number of electoral votes a state can have is three. Seven states are predicted to be at that level in 2020. Three are western, and two each are eastern and midwestern.

REGIONAL WINNERS

East—New York
South—Texas
Midwest—Illinois
West—California

BIGGEST SURPRISE

New York historically was the biggest prize in presidential elections, dominating the Electoral College until 1972. The surprise is how quickly California has passed it by; it will almost double New York's vote total by 2020.

THE BOTTOM LINE

The South placed four states among the 11 leaders in this category. The East and Midwest each hold three of the top slots.

372 Future Political Power

State	Projected Number of Electoral Votes, 2020	Points
1. California	58	100
2. New York	31	100
Texas	31	100
4. Florida	28	89
5. Pennsylvania	22	68
Illinois	22	68
7. Ohio	20	61
8. Michigan	18	54
9. New Jersey	16	46
10. Georgia	14	39
Virginia	14	39
12. North Carolina	13	36
13. Massachusetts	12	32
14. Indiana	11	29
Washington	11	29
Tennessee	11	29
Missouri	11	29
18. Maryland	10	25
Wisconsin	10	25
20. Minnesota	9	21
Arizona	9	21
Alabama	9	21
Louisiana	9	21
24. Colorado	8	18
Kentucky	8	18
South Carolina	8	18
Connecticut	8	18
28. Oklahoma	7	14
Oregon	7	14
Iowa	7	14
31. Mississippi	6	11
Kansas	6	11
Arkansas	6	11
34. Utah	5	7
West Virginia	5	7
New Mexico	5	7
Nebraska	5	7
38. Nevada	4	4
Hawaii	4	4
Maine	4	4
New Hampshire	4	4
Rhode Island	4	4
Idaho	4	4
44. Montana	3	0
Delaware	3	0
South Dakota	3	0
North Dakota	3	0
Vermont	3	0
Alaska	3	0
Wyoming	3	0

Future: Scores and Grades

BEST STATE

The future is brightest in Florida. It's among just three states that anticipate population growth of more than 40 percent by 2020, and it ranks no. 4 in projected job growth. Florida also is becoming one of America's political powers. It will have 28 electoral votes in 2020, putting it behind only California, New York, and Texas.

RUNNERS-UP

Arizona, with just 32 persons per square mile, has plenty of room to grow. And plenty of people want to go there, which is why Arizona ranks no. 2 in projections of population and job growth—and no. 2 in this section as a whole. Three other states earned grades in the A range: California, Utah, and Texas.

WORST STATES

The future is bleak in Connecticut. No state has a lower rate of projected income growth; just three states are more densely populated. Three other eastern states received F's—Rhode Island, Massachusetts, and New Jersey—along with Alaska.

REGIONAL WINNERS

East—Pennsylvania
South—Florida
Midwest—Missouri
West—Arizona

REGIONAL AVERAGES

East—25 (D)
South—57 (C+)
Midwest—46 (C)
West—61 (B–)

374 BIGGEST SURPRISE

The West is America's hottest region. But two of its states are not expected to share in its future prosperity. Wyoming earned a D– in this section, Alaska an F.

THE BOTTOM LINE

The future belongs to the West. It has seven of the top 10 scores; the South has the remaining three. The East, on the other hand, includes four of the five states with F's.

Future: Scores and Grades

State	Score	Grade
1. Florida	100	A+
2. Arizona	95	A
3. California	90	A
4. Utah	85	A
5. Texas	83	A–
6. Nevada	77	B+
7. New Mexico	72	B
8. Colorado	68	B
9. Georgia	67	B
10. Washington	65	B
11. Virginia	64	B–
12. Tennessee	62	B–
13. Idaho	61	B–
14. Oklahoma	54	C
15. Oregon	53	C
North Carolina	53	C
17. Hawaii	52	C
18. South Carolina	49	C
Missouri	49	C
20. Mississippi	48	C
21. Illinois	47	C
Michigan	47	C
North Dakota	47	C
Pennsylvania	47	C
Nebraska	47	C
South Dakota	47	C
27. Indiana	46	C
Arkansas	46	C
Minnesota	46	C
30. New York	44	C–
Wisconsin	44	C–
Alabama	44	C–
Kentucky	44	C–
34. Ohio	43	C–
Iowa	43	C–
36. Montana	42	C–
37. Kansas	41	C–
Vermont	41	C–
39. Maine	40	C–
40. New Hampshire	38	D+
41. Louisiana	31	D
42. Maryland	26	D
43. Delaware	25	D
44. Wyoming	24	D–
45. West Virginia	23	D–
46. Alaska	14	F
47. New Jersey	8	F
48. Massachusetts	4	F
49. Rhode Island	1	F
50. Connecticut	0	F

Conclusion: States of the Union

We have come to the end of the line.

Our statistical journey began with a study of history, then meandered through almost every aspect of present-day life, and finally wrapped up with a glimpse into the future. We have identified the outstanding states in all 25 sections, thereby answering that long series of questions posed in the introduction to this book.

But the most important question remains: Which of the 50 states offers the best *overall* quality of life?

We will determine the answer by using the final formula outlined in the introduction. This formula takes all 25 section scores for each state into account, giving extra weight to 10 sections of particular importance.

The envelope, please.

National Results

"Vermont has smooth and gentle dulcet hills—yes," wrote John Gunther in *Inside U.S.A.* "But underneath is slate, marble, granite. This granite is solid in the state character. Hit a man with an ax; he will practically chip off like a block of stone."

Much has changed since Gunther visited in the mid-1940s. The stereotypical Vermont Yankee—taciturn, frugal, conservative, and very definitely Republican—now shares the state with a younger, more worldly, more liberal generation. Refugees from northeastern metropolitan areas have arrived in search of simpler lifestyles. The current governor, Howard Dean, a native New Yorker and a Democrat, is a symbol of this new Vermont.

Yet there still is much that Gunther would find familiar: the quiet beauty of the Green Mountains, the lingering sunsets over Lake Champlain, the villages with well-kept greens and white-spired churches, the blaze of color every autumn, and the spirit of self-reliance and community involvement that is matched by few places in America.

This blend of new and old fascinated Gunther's self-appointed successors, Neal Peirce and Jerry Hagstrom, who traveled the country in the early 1980s doing research for *The Book of America.* They sensed the quiet pride shared by these generations that otherwise are so different. "Vermonters love Vermont," they wrote, "and with good reason."

Now we can add another reason to the list.

Our final calculations show that Vermont currently offers the best quality of life in America. It earned a final score of 666 points, making it no. 1 among the 50 states as well as the only state to earn an overall grade of A+.

Vermont has a broad base of excellence. It received A's in nine sections, B's in another four. No state topped it in the Resource Conservation or Female Equality sections. Only New Hampshire fared better in Children and Families; only Alaska scored higher in Recreation.

Vermont did especially well in what we might call the basic sections, those that received extra weight in the final formula because they deal with the essentials of modern life. It earned straight A's in the Environment and Public Safety sections, grades of A– in Education and Business.

None of this would have surprised Gunther very much. He predicted 50 years ago that Vermont would become more diverse, perhaps even to the extent of voting Democratic someday. But he also believed in the lasting qualities of that granite strain he detected in the state's character. "Vermonters," he wrote in 1947, "are really something quite special and unique."

But Vermont is not the only one of the United States to offer a superior quality of life in the 1990s. Nine other states earned overall grades of A:

Hawaii (no. 2, 660 points) led the nation in the Terrain, Racial Equality, and International Relations sections. It came close to another victory in Transportation, placing second. Hawaii received A's in 10 sections all told.

Perhaps the outstanding place to make money in America is **Connecticut** (no. 3, 647 points), which had grades of A+ in the Business and Personal Finances sections. It also earned the nation's top score in Communications.

A rich heritage and a wealth of brain power are the strengths of **Massachusetts** (no. 4, 641 points). It finished first in History and Applied Intelligence.

The best setting for family life can be found in **New Hampshire** (no. 5, 639 points), the no. 1 state in the Children and Families section. It was also a close no. 2 in Resource Conservation.

Amateur and professional athletics thrive in **Colorado** (no. 6, 616 points), which received an A+ in Sports. Another of its strengths was the Environment section, where it earned an A.

The residents of **Minnesota** (no. 7, 608 points) are a hardy breed. Their state topped the rest of the country in the Health section. It also had straight A's in Education, as well as Children and Families.

Maryland (no. 8, 608 points) has strengths you might not expect in a medium-sized eastern state. Perhaps the most surprising were its grades of A in Natural Resources and A– in Resource Conservation.

One of the nation's most open and responsive political systems can be found in **Washington** (no. 9, 601 points), which received an A in Politics. Its mountains and beaches earned it an A– in the Terrain section.

California (no. 10, 601 points) finished a strong no. 2 in Natural Resources. Other A's came in the Resource Conservation, Politics, and Future sections.

The other 40 states sifted out this way: 18 earned B's (including pluses and minuses), 13 received C's, six got D's, and three were hit with F's. All grades were determined by the same system used throughout this book. Each state's overall score was converted to the familiar 100-point scale, allowing a simple match with our standard grade chart.

We encountered one problem in compiling the final rankings. There were three ties in total points. You probably noticed two of them above: Minnesota-Maryland and Washington-California. The other was Georgia-Michigan, for 38th place.

Each tie was broken in head-to-head competition, with the higher ranking going to the state that won the most sections. Minnesota, for example, outscored Maryland in 13 sections, while Maryland was tops in the other 12. That's why Minnesota is ranked no. 7 and Maryland no. 8.

There is, of course, one final detail that deserves our attention. The ghost of H. L. Mencken would never forgive us if we didn't look closely at the three states that received overall grades of F:

Alabama (no. 48, 303 points) earned F's in 10 of the 25 sections. Its worst performance was in Recreation, where it received a single point.

Mississippi (no. 49, 268 points) finished last in six sections: Children and Families, Education, Arts, Communications, Sports, and Recreation. It had 12 F's overall.

Louisiana (no. 50, 239 points) received F's in 11 sections, including last-place finishes in Health, Female Equality, and Personal Finances. The state had above-average grades in only two sections: Natural Resources and Housing.

It is interesting to note that some things have changed very little since Mencken put together his pioneering ratings more than 60 years ago. His best state, Massachusetts, is no. 4 in our rankings, earning a straight A on its overall report card. And his last-place state, Mississippi, still gets failing marks today, finishing 49th among the 50 states.

Total Scores and Grades

State	Score	Scale	Grade
1. Vermont	666	100	A+
2. Hawaii	660	99	A
3. Connecticut	647	95	A
4. Massachusetts	641	94	A
5. New Hampshire	639	94	A
6. Colorado	616	88	A
7. Minnesota	608	86	A
8. Maryland	608	86	A
9. Washington	601	85	A
10. California	601	85	A
11. New York	573	78	B+
12. Maine	567	77	B+
13. Virginia	560	75	B+
14. Utah	559	75	B+
15. Wisconsin	558	75	B+
16. New Jersey	552	73	B
17. Delaware	544	71	B
18. Wyoming	539	70	B
19. Rhode Island	528	68	B
20. Nebraska	526	67	B
21. Iowa	523	67	B
22. Idaho	521	66	B
23. Oregon	518	65	B
24. Pennsylvania	517	65	B
25. Nevada	507	63	B–
26. Illinois	505	62	B–
27. North Dakota	504	62	B–
28. Alaska	498	61	B–
29. Montana	488	58	C+
30. Florida	483	57	C+
31. South Dakota	476	56	C+
32. Kansas	466	53	C
33. North Carolina	457	51	C
34. Arizona	455	50	C
35. Ohio	453	50	C
36. Indiana	438	47	C
37. Missouri	427	44	C–
38. Georgia	426	44	C–
39. Michigan	426	44	C–
40. Texas	416	41	C–
41. New Mexico	413	41	C–
42. Tennessee	386	34	D
43. South Carolina	359	28	D
44. Kentucky	357	28	D
45. West Virginia	349	26	D
46. Oklahoma	341	24	D–
47. Arkansas	323	20	D–
48. Alabama	303	15	F
49. Mississippi	268	7	F
50. Louisiana	239	0	F

Regional Results

Vermont is no. 1 on our overall list, but that might be of little interest to you. Perhaps you live in the South, and you have no use for cold weather. Or you're a westerner, and you plan to stay that way. Why should you care about some state on the other end of the continent?

Fair enough. Most of the great rivalries between states stem from proximity. It's only natural to be primarily concerned about how your state ranks against its neighbors.

Such comparisons are easy to make. We grouped the states into four regions, then ranked them according to overall scores. Here's what we found:

East—Guess who is no. 1 in the East? Vermont, of course. The other states at the top of the regional list are equally familiar, since the East had four of the nation's five best scores. Hawaii was the only outsider to join Vermont, Connecticut, Massachusetts, and New Hampshire in the nation's highest echelon.

Quality of life is consistently above average in the East. Five of the region's 12 states earned A's (including pluses and minuses), and another six received B's. The only disappointment was West Virginia, 45th nationally with a D.

It certainly is no surprise that the East had the nation's highest regional score, figured by averaging its individual state scores. The typical eastern state earned 569 points, worth a B+.

South—It is just the opposite story in the South. Not a single state from the region finished in the top 10, while the bottom of the national list has a distinctly southern flavor.

Virginia is the star of the region, finishing 13th nationally and earning an overall grade of B+. But it requires a long trip down to 30th place to find the next southern entry, Florida. The five states with the worst quality of life, including the three saddled with F's, are all in the South.

These poor showings by individual states, naturally enough, translated into a low regional score. The average southern state earned 378 points, equal to a D. That's 114 points less than any other region.

Midwest—The Midwest truly is the home of middle America—the heartland, if you will. Just check its state scores if you aren't convinced.

Minnesota finished seventh nationally, stamping it as one of the country's leaders in quality of life. The other 11 midwestern states settled comfortably in the middle range of the national standings. All of them—from no. 15 Wisconsin to no. 39 Michigan—earned B's and C's. Not a below-average mark in the bunch.

So what grade would you expect such a region to get as a whole? Something around the middle of the scale, of course, and the Midwest doesn't disappoint. Its typical state received 492 points, good for a C+. That's 77 points fewer than the top-rated East, but 114 ahead of the last-place South.

West—Any easterner instinctively knows which region would be the East's closest rival in the quality-of-life sweepstakes. Those guys on the Left Coast. You know, the West. It's the New York–California rivalry carried to its regional extreme.

The West has an impressive array of high-class states, led by Hawaii, which finished only six points behind Vermont to rank no. 2 nationally. Three other western states earned A's: Colorado, Washington, and California. The rest of the region received six B's and three C's. Nothing lower.

This solid performance brings the West close to its cross-country nemesis, but not close enough. The West's regional score of 536 was good enough for a grade of B. But the East stayed just a step ahead—33 points ahead, to be exact.

East: Top to Bottom

State (National Rank)	Score	Grade
1. Vermont (1)	666	A+
2. Connecticut (3)	647	A
3. Massachusetts (4)	641	A
4. New Hampshire (5)	639	A
5. Maryland (8)	608	A
6. New York (11)	573	B+
7. Maine (12)	567	B+
8. New Jersey (16)	552	B
9. Delaware (17)	544	B
10. Rhode Island (19)	528	B
11. Pennsylvania (24)	517	B
12. West Virginia (45)	349	D

South: Top to Bottom

State (National Rank)	Score	Grade
1. Virginia (13)	560	B+
2. Florida (30)	483	C+
3. North Carolina (33)	457	C
4. Georgia (38)	426	C–
5. Texas (40)	416	C–
6. Tennessee (42)	386	D
7. South Carolina (43)	359	D
8. Kentucky (44)	357	D
9. Oklahoma (46)	341	D–
10. Arkansas (47)	323	D–
11. Alabama (48)	303	F
12. Mississippi (49)	268	F
13. Louisiana (50)	239	F

Midwest: Top to Bottom

State (National Rank)	Score	Grade
1. Minnesota (7)	608	A
2. Wisconsin (15)	558	B+
3. Nebraska (20)	526	B
4. Iowa (21)	523	B
5. Illinois (26)	505	B–
6. North Dakota (27)	504	B–
7. South Dakota (31)	476	C+
8. Kansas (32)	466	C
9. Ohio (35)	453	C
10. Indiana (36)	438	C
11. Missouri (37)	427	C–
12. Michigan (39)	426	C–

West: Top to Bottom

State (National Rank)	Score	Grade
1. Hawaii (2)	660	A
2. Colorado (6)	616	A
3. Washington (9)	601	A
4. California (10)	601	A
5. Utah (14)	559	B+
6. Wyoming (18)	539	B
7. Idaho (22)	521	B
8. Oregon (23)	518	B
9. Nevada (25)	507	B–
10. Alaska (28)	498	B–
11. Montana (29)	488	C+
12. Arizona (34)	455	C
13. New Mexico (41)	413	C–

Size Group Results

The bigger the better. That's what Americans think. We are impressed by tall buildings, large salaries, and big cars. Size, to many of us, is the equivalent of quality.

But even a cursory glance at our ratings proves that size and quality are not always linked. Some big states did well, to be sure: California earned an A, New York a B+. But Vermont and Hawaii, the nation's two best states, aren't exactly giants.

That brings to mind the old saying that you can find good and bad in everything. It's a cliche, of course, but it also has the element of truth that is at the center of most cliches. Quality of life is good in some large states, bad in others. The same goes for small states. There shouldn't be anything surprising about that.

The important question is which size group is of interest to you. You might prefer a big, urban state, or a quaint, rural one, or perhaps something in between. Here are the overall rankings for all three size classes:

Large—Massachusetts is no. 4 of all 50 states in quality of life, but it's no. 1 among the 13 large states, those that have more than 6 million residents. California was the only other large state to earn an A.

The rest of this group was divided almost equally: five B's (including pluses and minuses) and six C's. New York and Virginia, each with a grade of B+, were the best of these runners-up. Texas, ranked 40th nationally, had the lowest score among large states.

Quality of life is just a bit above the norm in the typical large state. The average score for this class was 508, which works out to a B–.

Medium—The competition was much more intense among the 20 medium-size states with populations between 2 million and 6 million. Five of America's 10 best states are in this group.

Connecticut, which finished no. 3 overall, took the top position in the medium class. Also earning A's were Colorado, Minnesota, Maryland, and Washington. They were followed by three states with B's and four with C's.

The problem is that the competition was equally fierce at the bottom of this group. Eight of the nation's 10 worst quality-of-life scores were registered by medium-size states, including the only three with F's: Alabama, Mississippi, and Louisiana.

The crowding at both ends of the scale naturally resulted in a class score that settled right in the middle. The typical medium-size state had 452 points, a C.

Small—We already know the two best small states. Vermont and Hawaii ran a close one-two race in the nation as a whole. New Hampshire earned the only other A in this class, which includes 17 states that have fewer than 2 million residents.

Most small states had grades in the B range. There were two B-pluses

(Maine and Utah), five B's, and three B-minuses. They were trailed by three states with C's, as well as West Virginia, which earned a D.

Small states, as a group, offer the best quality of life in America. The average state in this class had a score of 528 points, good for a straight B.

Large States: Top to Bottom

State (National Rank)	Score	Grade
1. Massachusetts (4)	641	A
2. California (10)	601	A
3. New York (11)	573	B+
4. Virginia (13)	560	B+
5. New Jersey (16)	552	B
6. Pennsylvania (24)	517	B
7. Illinois (26)	505	B–
8. Florida (30)	483	C+
9. North Carolina (33)	457	C
10. Ohio (35)	453	C
11. Georgia (38)	426	C–
12. Michigan (39)	426	C–
13. Texas (40)	416	C–

Medium States: Top to Bottom

State (National Rank)	Score	Grade
1. Connecticut (3)	647	A
2. Colorado (6)	616	A
3. Minnesota (7)	608	A
4. Maryland (8)	608	A
5. Washington (9)	601	A
6. Wisconsin (15)	558	B+
7. Iowa (21)	523	B
8. Oregon (23)	518	B
9. Kansas (32)	466	C
10. Arizona (34)	455	C
11. Indiana (36)	438	C
12. Missouri (37)	427	C–
13. Tennessee (42)	386	D
14. South Carolina (43)	359	D
15. Kentucky (44)	357	D
16. Oklahoma (46)	341	D–
17. Arkansas (47)	323	D–
18. Alabama (48)	303	F
19. Mississippi (49)	268	F
20. Louisiana (50)	239	F

Small States: Top to Bottom

State (National Rank)	Score	Grade
1. Vermont (1)	666	A+
2. Hawaii (2)	660	A
3. New Hampshire (5)	639	A
4. Maine (12)	567	B+
5. Utah (14)	559	B+
6. Delaware (17)	544	B
7. Wyoming (18)	539	B
8. Rhode Island (19)	528	B
9. Nebraska (20)	526	B
10. Idaho (22)	521	B
11. Nevada (25)	507	B–
12. North Dakota (27)	504	B–
13. Alaska (28)	498	B–
14. Montana (29)	488	C+
15. South Dakota (31)	476	C+
16. New Mexico (41)	413	C–
17. West Virginia (45)	349	D

The Report Cards

We have compiled a mountain of data about each state, covering everything from per capita income and water usage to arts funding and voter turnout. Now is the time to tie it all together. The rest of this book consists of detailed report cards for the 50 states. Think of each as a one-stop center that contains all the basic facts about quality of life in a particular state.

Each package begins with an examination of a state's strengths and weaknesses. This text is followed by five charts. Let's do a quick run-through, using New York as an example.

1. General Information—A brief summary of how the state did in our ratings, including total points, overall grade, and national and regional ranks. This chart also lists population and land area figures, as well as the names of the state's capital and largest city.

We see that New York's score of 573 points earned it an overall grade of B+, good for 11th place in the national rankings and sixth place in the East.

2. Report Card—A list of the state's scores and grades in all 25 sections.

New York started with 75 points and a grade of B+ in the History section, then got a 54 and a C in Terrain, and so on. Its highest score was 100 in the Arts section; its lowest was a zero for Housing.

3. Record with Neighboring States—Head-to-head comparisons of the state and its neighbors, based on their overall scores. The winner of each pairing is listed, along with the margin of victory. The state's overall record against its neighbors is in parentheses at the top of the chart.

New York has a 2–3 record, beating New Jersey and Pennsylvania, but losing to Connecticut, Massachusetts, and Vermont. The last was its worst defeat, with Vermont winning by 93 points.

4. Category Scores of 100—A list of all categories in which the state received a perfect score. The total number of 100's is in parentheses at the top of the chart.

New York earned 10 perfect scores, beginning with the Presidential Candidates category in the History section.

5. Category Scores of 0—A list of all categories in which the state had the lowest possible score. The total number again is in parentheses.

New York received zeros in six categories. Its first strikeout came in the Rangeland category of the Terrain section.

These report cards, as you can see, provide a quick, yet thorough, summary of conditions in each state. They direct you to categories and sections that deserve your closer attention. They point you to those states that best fit your needs and interests.

The 50 state packages are printed in the order of our quality-of-life rankings, beginning with no. 1 Vermont and ending with no. 50 Louisiana. Check the Total Scores and Grades chart near the beginning of this chapter to figure out where to find your state. Or just start browsing. You might be surprised by what you find.

1. Vermont (A+)

FINAL STANDINGS

Vermont is no. 1 in quality of life, no matter how you look at it: no. 1 nationally, no. 1 in the East, no. 1 among small states. It earned A's in nine sections and B's in four—but only one F.

BEST SECTIONS

Resource Conservation (100 points)—Vermont ranks no. 1 in this section, largely because of its efficient use of water and natural gas.

Female Equality (100)—Another first-place finish. No state offers better employment opportunities for women; only two states have higher ratios of women-owned businesses.

Children and Families (98)—Utah is the only state with an infant mortality rate lower than Vermont's.

WORST SECTIONS

Transportation (14 points)—Vermont gives you few alternatives when you're trying to get from place to place. Airline service is spotty, and public transit is virtually nonexistent.

Housing (29)—Property taxes are high, and housing stock is old. Only Massachusetts has a higher percentage of homes built before World War II.

History (37)—Vermont never has had its own presidential candidate. And you thought that being in New England was an automatic guarantee of history.

NEIGHBORS

Who could beat the no. 1 state? Nobody, of course. Vermont's three neighbors all earned grades of B+ or better, but each loses in head-to-head competition.

BIGGEST SURPRISE

You wouldn't expect the state with the nation's smallest minority population (just 1.9 percent) to do so well in the Racial Equality section. But Vermont earned an A–.

THE BOTTOM LINE

Vermont offers the highest quality of life of any of the 50 states, bar none.

VERMONT

General Information

Total Points: 666
Overall Grade: A+

National Rank: 1 of 50
Regional Rank: 1 of 12 (East)

Population: 563,000
Capital: Montpelier

Land Area: 9,249 square miles
Largest City: Burlington

Report Card

Section	Score	Grade
1. History	37	D+
2. Terrain	56	C+
3. Natural Resources	50	C
4. Resource Conservation	100	A+
5. Environment	89	A
6. Health	74	B
7. Children and Families	98	A
8. Female Equality	100	A+
9. Racial Equality	84	A–
10. Housing	29	D
11. Education	81	A–
12. Applied Intelligence	58	C+
13. Arts	79	B+
14. Communications	58	C+
15. Sports	60	B–
16. Recreation	96	A
17. Business	83	A–
18. Personal Finances	53	C
19. Public Safety	85	A
20. Transportation	14	F
21. Politics	54	C
22. Government	60	B–
23. National Relations	52	C
24. International Relations	40	C–
25. Future	41	C–
Overall	666	A+

Record with Neighboring States (3–0)

Neighbor	Neighbor's Score	Winner
Massachusetts	641	Vermont by 25
New Hampshire	639	Vermont by 27
New York	573	Vermont by 93

Category Scores of 100 (13)

Section	Category
Resource Conservation	Water Usage
Environment	Toxic Emissions
Children and Families	Infant Mortality
Female Equality	Employment Opportunities
Racial Equality	Minority College Graduates
Arts	Museums and Galleries
Sports	Olympic Athletes
Recreation	Fitness Centers
Recreation	Shopping
Business	Service Sector Strength
Public Safety	Violent Crimes
Government	State Constitution Length
National Relations	Student Migration

Category Scores of 0 (12)

Section	Category
History	Presidential Candidates
Terrain	Ocean Shoreline
Terrain	Rangeland
Natural Resources	Crude Oil Reserves
Natural Resources	Coal Reserves
Racial Equality	Minority Population
Housing	Housing Age
Sports	Professional Champions
Sports	Spectator Seats
Politics	Electoral Votes
National Relations	*Fortune* 500 Companies
Future	Future Political Power

2. Hawaii (A)

FINAL STANDINGS

Hawaii deserves its reputation as an island paradise. It finished in second place nationally, just six points behind Vermont. It is no. 1 in the West, no. 2 among small states.

BEST SECTIONS

Terrain (100 points)—No state has a more varied landscape. Hawaii has everything from ocean beaches and mountains to dense forests and rangeland.

Racial Equality (100)—It's no surprise that minority groups have more clout in Hawaii than anywhere else. Minorities actually are in the majority, with persons of Asian heritage outnumbering whites by about two to one.

International Relations (100)—Hawaii, the gateway to the Pacific Rim, is comfortable in a global setting. No state has a higher ratio of persons living overseas.

WORST SECTIONS

History (0 points)—Hawaii has two strikes against it in this section. It is our newest state, and it does not share the mainland's Eurocentric heritage.

Housing (16)—Housing costs are outrageously high in Hawaii. No state has higher purchase prices; only California has higher rents.

Sports (18)—Hawaii has no major-league teams, and athletic participation at the high-school level is fairly low.

NEIGHBORS

Our only island state has no neighbors.

BIGGEST SURPRISE

It would seem that Hawaii has an unlimited future, but it earned only a C in the Future section. Its biggest problem is a projected rate of income growth that is well below the national average.

THE BOTTOM LINE

Hawaii has been a state for less than 40 years, but it already is superior to nearly all of its more-established rivals.

HAWAII

General Information

Total Points: 660
Overall Grade: A

National Rank: 2 of 50
Regional Rank: 1 of 13 (West)

Population: 1,108,000
Capital: Honolulu

Land Area: 6,423 square miles
Largest City: Honolulu

Report Card

Section	Score	Grade
1. History	0	F
2. Terrain	100	A+
3. Natural Resources	55	C+
4. Resource Conservation	75	B+
5. Environment	86	A
6. Health	87	A
7. Children and Families	89	A
8. Female Equality	67	B
9. Racial Equality	100	A+
10. Housing	16	F
11. Education	61	B–
12. Applied Intelligence	21	D–
13. Arts	76	B+
14. Communications	91	A
15. Sports	18	F
16. Recreation	89	A
17. Business	65	B
18. Personal Finances	83	A–
19. Public Safety	60	B–
20. Transportation	97	A
21. Politics	44	C–
22. Government	34	D
23. National Relations	78	B+
24. International Relations	100	A+
25. Future	52	C
Overall	660	A

Record with Neighboring States (0–0)

Neighbor	Neighbor's Score	Winner
(None)		

Category Scores of 100 (20)

Section	Category
Terrain	Inland Water
Resource Conservation	Natural Gas Consumption
Environment	Toxic Emissions
Health	Life Expectancy
Female Equality	Women in Poverty
Racial Equality	Minority Population
Racial Equality	Income Disparity
Racial Equality	Minority Businesses
Arts	Arts Funding
Communications	Cable Television
Recreation	Shopping
Recreation	Restaurants and Bars
Business	Retail Trade
Personal Finances	Income Growth
Personal Finances	Unemployment
Transportation	Airline Service
Government	Government Units
National Relations	Domestic Travel
International Relations	Foreign Employers
International Relations	Overseas Population

Category Scores of 0 (14)

Section	Category
History	Statehood
History	Presidential Candidates
Natural Resources	Crude Oil Reserves
Natural Resources	Coal Reserves
Housing	Housing Costs
Housing	Rent
Applied Intelligence	MacArthur Fellows
Sports	Professional Champions
Sports	Spectator Seats
Business	Manufacturing Productivity
Transportation	Road Mileage
Government	State Taxes
National Relations	*Fortune* 500 Companies
International Relations	Export-Related Jobs

3. Connecticut (A)

FINAL STANDINGS

Connecticut finished no. 3 nationally and no. 2 in the East. But its real distinction is its no. 1 ranking among medium states, those with populations between 2 million and 6 million.

BEST SECTIONS

Communications (100 points)—No state has a better overall system for disseminating information. Only Alaska spends more than Connecticut on libraries; just two states have better telephone networks.

Business (100)—Connecticut is among the nation's strongest states in both the manufacturing and service sectors. Its gross state product is second only to Alaska's.

Personal Finances (100)—This is where the money is. Connecticut has America's highest per capita income, as well as the highest ratio of people earning more than $200,000 a year.

WORST SECTIONS

Future (0 points)—Connecticut residents had better enjoy the present. Their state took last place in this section. Its biggest problems are high population density and an anticipated slowdown in income growth.

Housing (19)—Property taxes in Connecticut are among the nation's highest. So are purchase prices.

Sports (21)—Connecticut has only one major-league team, and its college teams have not had much success on the national level.

NEIGHBORS

A clean sweep. Connecticut beats all three of its neighbors in quality-of-life showdowns.

BIGGEST SURPRISE

Nobody expects Connecticut to be a future growth center, but who would put it at the bottom of the list? There it is, dead last in the Future section.

THE BOTTOM LINE

Vermont is no. 1 in New England, but Connecticut has nothing to be ashamed of. It, too, is one of America's truly superior states.

CONNECTICUT

General Information

Total Points: 647
Overall Grade: A

National Rank: 3 of 50
Regional Rank: 2 of 12 (East)

Population: 3,287,000
Capital: Hartford

Land Area: 4,845 square miles
Largest City: Bridgeport

Report Card

Section	Score	Grade
1. History	72	B
2. Terrain	48	C
3. Natural Resources	73	B
4. Resource Conservation	89	A
5. Environment	61	B–
6. Health	63	B–
7. Children and Families	82	A–
8. Female Equality	75	B+
9. Racial Equality	36	D+
10. Housing	19	F
11. Education	68	B
12. Applied Intelligence	86	A
13. Arts	63	B–
14. Communications	100	A+
15. Sports	21	D–
16. Recreation	55	C+
17. Business	100	A+
18. Personal Finances	100	A+
19. Public Safety	67	B
20. Transportation	66	B
21. Politics	76	B+
22. Government	64	B–
23. National Relations	67	B
24. International Relations	64	B–
25. Future	0	F
Overall	647	A

Record with Neighboring States (3–0)

Neighbor	Neighbor's Score	Winner
Massachusetts	641	Connecticut by 6
New York	573	Connecticut by 74
Rhode Island	528	Connecticut by 119

Category Scores of 100 (10)

Section	Category
Children and Families	Children in Poverty
Applied Intelligence	College Graduates
Applied Intelligence	Patents
Communications	Library Spending
Business	Gross State Product
Personal Finances	Per Capita Income
Personal Finances	Poverty
Personal Finances	Upper Incomes
National Relations	*Fortune* 500 Companies
International Relations	Export-Related Jobs

Category Scores of 0 (6)

Section	Category
History	Presidential Candidates
Terrain	Rangeland
Natural Resources	Crude Oil Reserves
Natural Resources	Coal Reserves
Sports	Professional Champions
Future	Projected Income Growth

4. Massachusetts (A)

FINAL STANDINGS

Massachusetts is no. 4 in the entire country, but only no. 3 in the East, trailing two of its neighbors, Vermont and Connecticut. Its best performance is among large states, where it ranks first.

BEST SECTIONS

History (100 points)—Not too surprising. The birthplace of the American Revolution holds first place in this section.

Applied Intelligence (100)—Another first-place finish. No state surpasses Massachusetts' ratios of college graduates, MacArthur fellows, or holders of doctorates.

Communications (97)—Massachusetts has the most thorough telephone network in the country. Only Colorado has higher newspaper readership.

WORST SECTIONS

Housing (2 points)—Massachusetts has the oldest housing stock in the nation. It also is among the five worst states when it comes to housing costs and rent.

Future (4)—The state with the best history faces one of the dimmest futures. Job growth is projected to be moderate at best; income growth is expected to be slow.

Environment (40)—Massachusetts has a higher ratio of Superfund sites than all but three states.

NEIGHBORS

Massachusetts may be one of the nation's quality-of-life leaders, but competition is fierce in New England. The state wins contests with three of its neighbors, but loses to Vermont and Connecticut.

BIGGEST SURPRISE

Massachusetts spawned the American Revolution and was later the home of several leaders of the anti-slavery movement—all of which makes it surprising that the state today earns only a C– in the Racial Equality section.

THE BOTTOM LINE

Even an average performance in the Housing and Future sections would have earned Massachusetts the nation's no. 1 ranking. But there's nothing wrong with being no. 4.

MASSACHUSETTS

General Information

Total Points: 641
Overall Grade: A

National Rank: 4 of 50
Regional Rank: 3 of 12 (East)

Population: 6,016,000
Capital: Boston

Land Area: 7,838 square miles
Largest City: Boston

Report Card

Section	Score	Grade
1. History	100	A+
2. Terrain	66	B
3. Natural Resources	65	B
4. Resource Conservation	86	A
5. Environment	40	C–
6. Health	57	C+
7. Children and Families	92	A
8. Female Equality	74	B
9. Racial Equality	43	C–
10. Housing	2	F
11. Education	75	B+
12. Applied Intelligence	100	A+
13. Arts	63	B–
14. Communications	97	A
15. Sports	78	B+
16. Recreation	61	B–
17. Business	83	A–
18. Personal Finances	76	B+
19. Public Safety	64	B–
20. Transportation	85	A
21. Politics	63	B–
22. Government	59	C+
23. National Relations	57	C+
24. International Relations	43	C–
25. Future	4	F
Overall	641	A

Record with Neighboring States (3–2)

Neighbor	Neighbor's Score	Winner
Connecticut	647	Connecticut by 6
New Hampshire	639	Massachusetts by 2
New York	573	Massachusetts by 68
Rhode Island	528	Massachusetts by 113
Vermont	666	Vermont by 25

Category Scores of 100 (11)

Section	Category
History	Historic Places
History	Historic Natives
Health	Specialists
Education	College Students
Applied Intelligence	College Graduates
Applied Intelligence	Doctoral Degrees
Applied Intelligence	MacArthur Fellows
Communications	Telephone Service
Communications	Newspaper Circulation
Sports	Professional Champions
Transportation	Motor Vehicle Deaths

Category Scores of 0 (6)

Section	Category
Terrain	Rangeland
Natural Resources	Crude Oil Reserves
Natural Resources	Coal Reserves
Health	Family Doctors
Housing	Housing Age
International Relations	Overseas Population

5. New Hampshire (A)

FINAL STANDINGS

Another New England state makes the national top five. New Hampshire also is no. 4 in the East and no. 3 among small states.

BEST SECTIONS

Children and Families (100 points)—New Hampshire is the best place in America to raise a family. Its percentage of children living in poverty is by far the lowest in the nation.

Resource Conservation (96)—New Hampshire is among the country's most efficient users of natural gas. It also gets 20 percent of its energy from renewable sources.

Business (94)—No state economy grew faster during the 1980s than New Hampshire's. Only Hawaii has higher retail sales per household.

WORST SECTIONS

Housing (8 points)—It's the typical New England story once again. New Hampshire's housing stock is old and its property taxes are high.

Transportation (11)—Driving in New Hampshire can be unpleasant. It has the nation's highest percentage of roads in poor condition.

Sports (26)—There are no major-league teams in New Hampshire, and its college teams rarely win national glory, either.

NEIGHBORS

New Hampshire's 1–2 record is deceiving. It is adjacent to two of the nation's top four states.

BIGGEST SURPRISE

You might expect women to fare poorly in a small state that honors tradition. But New Hampshire earned an A in the Female Equality section. Only four states have higher percentages of women in their legislatures.

THE BOTTOM LINE

You could look at the dark side: New Hampshire is only the fourth best state in New England. Or you could choose the bright side: It's still better than 45 other states.

NEW HAMPSHIRE

General Information

Total Points: 639
Overall Grade: A

National Rank: 5 of 50
Regional Rank: 4 of 12 (East)

Population: 1,109,000
Capital: Concord

Land Area: 8,969 square miles
Largest City: Manchester

Report Card

Section	Score	Grade
1. History	52	C
2. Terrain	62	B–
3. Natural Resources	42	C–
4. Resource Conservation	96	A
5. Environment	61	B–
6. Health	63	B–
7. Children and Families	100	A+
8. Female Equality	90	A
9. Racial Equality	79	B+
10. Housing	8	F
11. Education	68	B
12. Applied Intelligence	55	C+
13. Arts	56	C+
14. Communications	76	B+
15. Sports	26	D
16. Recreation	91	A
17. Business	94	A
18. Personal Finances	66	B
19. Public Safety	89	A
20. Transportation	11	F
21. Politics	68	B
22. Government	80	A–
23. National Relations	60	B–
24. International Relations	45	C
25. Future	38	D+
Overall	639	A

Record with Neighboring States (1–2)

Neighbor	Neighbor's Score	Winner
Maine	567	New Hampshire by 72
Massachusetts	641	Massachusetts by 2
Vermont	666	Vermont by 27

Category Scores of 100 (14)

Section	Category
Terrain	Forests
Natural Resources	Timberland
Children and Families	Birth Weight
Children and Families	Births to Single Teens
Children and Families	Children in Poverty
Female Equality	Women in Poverty
Racial Equality	Minority College Graduates
Business	Economic Growth
Business	Retail Trade
Personal Finances	Poverty
Public Safety	Violent Crimes
Government	State Taxes
Government	Government Employees
Government	State Constitution Length

Category Scores of 0 (8)

Section	Category
Terrain	Rangeland
Natural Resources	Crude Oil Reserves
Natural Resources	Coal Reserves
Housing	Property Taxes
Sports	Professional Champions
Sports	Spectator Seats
Transportation	Pavement Condition
International Relations	Agricultural Exports

6. Colorado (A)

FINAL STANDINGS

Colorado is in sixth place, putting it right in the middle of the nine states that earned straight A's. It has identical no. 2 rankings in the West and among medium-size states.

BEST SECTIONS

Sports (100 points)—Colorado is America's most sports-crazy state, with the highest ratio of available seats at professional games. It is second to Vermont as a home of Olympic athletes.

Environment (85)—Colorado is among the five states with the lowest toxic emissions and cleanest drinking water.

Education (82)—Only Alaska and Utah have higher percentages of high school graduates than Colorado. It also is in the national top 10 when it comes to standardized test results.

Communications (82)—This is a state that keeps up with current events. Colorado leads the nation in newspaper readership.

WORST SECTIONS

History (5 points)—The first permanent European settlement in what is now Colorado was established in 1858. Only two states were settled later.

Natural Resources (18)—Colorado has coal, oil, and timber, but not enough of any to be an outstanding producer.

International Relations (31)—Colorado is below the national norms for exports of manufactured goods and agricultural products.

NEIGHBORS

Few states have more neighbors than Colorado, and it beats every one of them. A perfect record: 7–0.

BIGGEST SURPRISE

Think of the West, and you think of an unlimited storehouse of natural treasures. That isn't exactly the case in Colorado, which received an F in the Natural Resources section.

THE BOTTOM LINE

Colorado is no. 1 in the continental West. The only state in the region with a better score, Hawaii, is an island.

COLORADO

General Information

Total Points: 616
Overall Grade: A

National Rank: 6 of 50
Regional Rank: 2 of 13 (West)

Population: 3,294,000
Capital: Denver

Land Area: 103,730 square miles
Largest City: Denver

Report Card

Section	Score	Grade
1. History	5	F
2. Terrain	49	C
3. Natural Resources	18	F
4. Resource Conservation	76	B+
5. Environment	85	A
6. Health	75	B+
7. Children and Families	54	C
8. Female Equality	80	A–
9. Racial Equality	43	C–
10. Housing	71	B
11. Education	82	A–
12. Applied Intelligence	69	B
13. Arts	37	D+
14. Communications	82	A–
15. Sports	100	A+
16. Recreation	63	B–
17. Business	57	C+
18. Personal Finances	42	C–
19. Public Safety	47	C
20. Transportation	68	B
21. Politics	72	B
22. Government	70	B
23. National Relations	75	B+
24. International Relations	31	D
25. Future	68	B
Overall	616	A

Record with Neighboring States (7–0)

Neighbor	Neighbor's Score	Winner
Arizona	455	Colorado by 161
Kansas	466	Colorado by 150
Nebraska	526	Colorado by 90
New Mexico	413	Colorado by 203
Oklahoma	341	Colorado by 275
Utah	559	Colorado by 57
Wyoming	539	Colorado by 77

Category Scores of 100 (5)

Section	Category
Female Equality	Women in Business
Communications	Newspaper Circulation
Sports	Olympic Athletes
Sports	Spectator Seats
Business	Service Sector Strength

Category Scores of 0 (4)

Section	Category
History	European Settlement
History	Historic Natives
History	Presidential Candidates
Terrain	Ocean Shoreline

7. Minnesota (A)

FINAL STANDINGS

Minnesota finished in seventh place overall, but it ranks no. 1 in the Midwest. It also is in third place among all medium-size states.

BEST SECTIONS

Health (100 points)—Minnesota is America's healthiest state. In no other state are family doctors as easily available; only Hawaii has a longer average life expectancy.

Education (90)—Minnesota is no. 2 in this section. Its high school dropout rate is the nation's second lowest.

Children and Families (89)—Minnesota is among the 10 states with the lowest percentages of infant deaths and births to single teens.

WORST SECTIONS

History (16 points)—Many have tried, but no Minnesota resident has ever been elected president. Remember Hubert Humphrey, Eugene McCarthy, and Walter Mondale?

National Relations (24)—The federal government spends less money per capita in Minnesota than anywhere but Wisconsin and Indiana.

International Relations (34)—Minnesota is a bit isolated from the outside world. It trails most of the nation in jobs offered by foreign companies and residents living overseas.

NEIGHBORS

Minnesota is the top state in the Midwest, so naturally it is superior to all four of its neighbors.

BIGGEST SURPRISE

One of the nation's coldest states also is the healthiest state. Who would expect frigid Minnesota to lead the Health section? But it does. The average Minnesotan lives two years longer than the typical resident of sunny Florida.

THE BOTTOM LINE

An emphasis on the basics—health, education, children—has earned Minnesota one of the nation's highest quality-of-life scores.

MINNESOTA

General Information

Total Points: 608
Overall Grade: A

National Rank: 7 of 50
Regional Rank: 1 of 12 (Midwest)

Population: 4,375,000
Capital: St. Paul

Land Area: 79,617 square miles
Largest City: Minneapolis

Report Card

Section	Score	Grade
1. History	16	F
2. Terrain	38	D+
3. Natural Resources	49	C
4. Resource Conservation	82	A–
5. Environment	62	B–
6. Health	100	A+
7. Children and Families	89	A
8. Female Equality	80	A–
9. Racial Equality	37	D+
10. Housing	55	C+
11. Education	90	A
12. Applied Intelligence	49	C
13. Arts	51	C
14. Communications	56	C+
15. Sports	86	A
16. Recreation	47	C
17. Business	58	C+
18. Personal Finances	50	C
19. Public Safety	66	B
20. Transportation	56	C+
21. Politics	82	A–
22. Government	72	B
23. National Relations	24	D–
24. International Relations	34	D
25. Future	46	C
Overall	608	A

Record with Neighboring States (4–0)

Neighbor	Neighbor's Score	Winner
Iowa	523	Minnesota by 85
North Dakota	504	Minnesota by 104
South Dakota	476	Minnesota by 132
Wisconsin	558	Minnesota by 50

Category Scores of 100 (8)

Section	Category
Health	Life Expectancy
Health	Family Doctors
Female Equality	Employment Opportunities
Education	High School Dropouts
Communications	Telephone Service
Public Safety	Prison Population
Politics	Voter Turnout
Government	State Constitution Length

Category Scores of 0 (4)

Section	Category
History	Historic Natives
Terrain	Ocean Shoreline
Natural Resources	Crude Oil Reserves
Natural Resources	Coal Reserves

414 8. Maryland (A)

FINAL STANDINGS

Maryland, no. 8 nationally, is the fifth eastern state to make the national top 10. It also ranks fourth among the 20 medium-size states.

BEST SECTIONS

Natural Resources (94 points)—A solid third-place finish in this section. Maryland leads the nation in nonfuel mining and is no. 4 in farm marketings per square mile.

Transportation (92)—Only four states have public transit systems that are more heavily used than Maryland's. Its roads also are among the best in America: 78 percent are in good-to-excellent shape.

Resource Conservation (84)—Maryland is one of the nation's most efficient states in using water and petroleum products.

WORST SECTIONS

Future (26 points)—Future development will be difficult, since Maryland already is one of the most crowded states. Income growth is expected to be slow over the next quarter-century.

Politics (30)—Maryland does not have a competitive political system. Few races are close, and most state legislators stay in office as long as they like.

International Relations (37)—Maryland has a weak record when it comes to exporting manufactured goods.

NEIGHBORS

Maryland has a perfect 4-0 record in quality-of-life showdowns with its neighbors. Not one is even close.

BIGGEST SURPRISE

Maryland's image is that of a small, urban state, but it earned an A in the Natural Resources section. Its prowess in nonfuel mining is particularly surprising. No state has a higher mineral yield per square mile.

THE BOTTOM LINE

Maryland offers the best quality of life in the mid-Atlantic portion of the East.

MARYLAND

General Information

Total Points: 608
Overall Grade: A

National Rank: 8 of 50
Regional Rank: 5 of 12 (East)

Population: 4,781,000
Capital: Annapolis

Land Area: 9,775 square miles
Largest City: Baltimore

Report Card

Section	Score	Grade
1. History	51	C
2. Terrain	73	B
3. Natural Resources	94	A
4. Resource Conservation	84	A–
5. Environment	69	B
6. Health	59	C+
7. Children and Families	72	B
8. Female Equality	57	C+
9. Racial Equality	53	C
10. Housing	72	B
11. Education	62	B–
12. Applied Intelligence	80	A–
13. Arts	38	D+
14. Communications	49	C
15. Sports	67	B
16. Recreation	45	C
17. Business	55	C+
18. Personal Finances	72	B
19. Public Safety	41	C–
20. Transportation	92	A
21. Politics	30	D
22. Government	70	B
23. National Relations	70	B
24. International Relations	37	D+
25. Future	26	D
Overall	608	A

Record with Neighboring States (4–0)

Neighbor	Neighbor's Score	Winner
Delaware	544	Maryland by 64
Pennsylvania	517	Maryland by 91
Virginia	560	Maryland by 48
West Virginia	349	Maryland by 259

Category Scores of 100 (7)

Section	Category
Terrain	Ocean Shoreline
Natural Resources	Nonfuel Mining
Housing	Housing Size
Applied Intelligence	Research and Development
Sports	Professional Champions
Government	Government Units
National Relations	Federal Spending

Category Scores of 0 (4)

Section	Category
History	Presidential Candidates
Terrain	Rangeland
Natural Resources	Crude Oil Reserves
Communications	Newspaper Circulation

9. Washington (A)

FINAL STANDINGS

Washington took ninth place away from California on a tie-breaker. It also is no. 3 in the West and no. 5 among medium-size states.

BEST SECTIONS

Politics (91 points)—Washington voters believe in regular house cleanings. No other state changes the composition of its legislature more often. Elections, as you might expect, are generally close.

Terrain (84)—Washington has everything from soaring mountains to ocean beaches. Just two states have a larger difference in elevation between their highest and lowest points.

Resource Conservation (80)—This is the nation's leader in using energy that can be reused. More than half of Washington's power is from renewable sources.

Communications (80)—Only Alaska and Connecticut spend more on libraries than Washington does.

WORST SECTIONS

History (8 points)—It's the typical western story. Washington was late in being settled, late in becoming a state, and is still trying to catch up.

Natural Resources (32)—Washington produces no oil and very little coal. Its farm marketings are nothing spectacular, either.

Arts (33)—Washington doesn't willingly open its purse for the arts. State appropriations are well below the national norm.

NEIGHBORS

Washington is tucked in the northwestern corner of the nation, so it has only two neighbors, Idaho and Oregon. It defeats both easily.

BIGGEST SURPRISE

Think of Washington, and you think of the outdoors: mountains, beaches, pristine forests. That's why its grade of C in the Environment section is so surprising—and disappointing.

418 THE BOTTOM LINE

Washington offers a grade A alternative for people who want to be on the Pacific coast, but don't want to live in California.

WASHINGTON

General Information

Total Points: 601
Overall Grade: A

National Rank: 9 of 50
Regional Rank: 3 of 13 (West)

Population: 4,867,000
Capital: Olympia

Land Area: 66,582 square miles
Largest City: Seattle

Report Card

Section	Score	Grade
1. History	8	F
2. Terrain	84	A–
3. Natural Resources	32	D
4. Resource Conservation	80	A–
5. Environment	48	C
6. Health	65	B
7. Children and Families	73	B
8. Female Equality	65	B
9. Racial Equality	70	B
10. Housing	58	C+
11. Education	75	B+
12. Applied Intelligence	45	C
13. Arts	33	D
14. Communications	80	A–
15. Sports	60	B–
16. Recreation	73	B
17. Business	51	C
18. Personal Finances	44	C–
19. Public Safety	40	C–
20. Transportation	71	B
21. Politics	91	A
22. Government	65	B
23. National Relations	49	C
24. International Relations	79	B+
25. Future	65	B
Overall	601	A

Record with Neighboring States (2–0)

Neighbor	Neighbor's Score	Winner
Idaho	521	Washington by 80
Oregon	518	Washington by 83

Category Scores of 100 (6)

Section	Category
Resource Conservation	Renewable Energy
Female Equality	Women in Government
Racial Equality	Housing Disparity
Education	Standardized Tests
Politics	State Legislature Turnover
International Relations	Export-Related Jobs

Category Scores of 0 (5)

Section	Category
History	Historic Natives
History	Presidential Candidates
Natural Resources	Crude Oil Reserves
Resource Conservation	Electricity Consumption
Public Safety	Police Presence

10. California (A)

FINAL STANDINGS

California rounds out the national top 10. It is second to Massachusetts among the 13 large states, and it is no. 4 in the West.

BEST SECTIONS

Natural Resources (99 points)—California truly is the Golden State in terms of natural gifts. It has the nation's richest oil reserves per square mile. It is no. 6 in farm marketings.

Resource Conservation (91)—Only Rhode Island is more efficient than California in the use of electricity.

Future (90)—Just four states are expected to outpace California in population and job growth over the next quarter-century. It will be politically dominant by 2020, with 27 more electoral votes than any other state.

WORST SECTIONS

Housing (4 points)—The house of your dreams carries a large price tag in California. Only Hawaii has higher purchase prices; no state has higher rents.

Public Safety (18)—Crime is a deadly problem in California. Florida and New York are the only states with higher violent crime rates.

Recreation (39)—It might be hard to believe, but California suffers from a leisure shortage. It is below the national norms for fitness centers, movie theaters, and large stores.

NEIGHBORS

No contest. California's quality of life is far superior to all three of its neighbors.

BIGGEST SURPRISE

California supposedly is one of America's most cosmopolitan states, the national center for the visual arts. But it earned only a B– in the Arts section, largely because of shortages of dancers, museums, and galleries.

THE BOTTOM LINE

The distinction of being America's largest state carries some negative baggage—crime, pollution, high housing costs—but California still deserves an A for overall quality of life.

CALIFORNIA

General Information

Total Points: 601
Overall Grade: A

National Rank: 10 of 50
Regional Rank: 4 of 13 (West)

Population: 29,760,000
Capital: Sacramento

Land Area: 155,973 square miles
Largest City: Los Angeles

Report Card

Section	Score	Grade
1. History	42	C–
2. Terrain	78	B+
3. Natural Resources	99	A
4. Resource Conservation	91	A
5. Environment	54	C
6. Health	53	C
7. Children and Families	65	B
8. Female Equality	63	B–
9. Racial Equality	63	B–
10. Housing	4	F
11. Education	54	C
12. Applied Intelligence	66	B
13. Arts	62	B–
14. Communications	53	C
15. Sports	68	B
16. Recreation	39	D+
17. Business	72	B
18. Personal Finances	49	C
19. Public Safety	18	F
20. Transportation	51	C
21. Politics	85	A
22. Government	78	B+
23. National Relations	47	C
24. International Relations	83	A–
25. Future	90	A
Overall	601	A

Record with Neighboring States (3–0)

Neighbor	Neighbor's Score	Winner
Arizona	455	California by 146
Nevada	507	California by 94
Oregon	518	California by 83

Category Scores of 100 (8)

Section	Category
History	Presidential Candidates
Terrain	Elevation Variation
Natural Resources	Crude Oil Reserves
Resource Conservation	Electricity Consumption
Arts	Entertainers
Politics	Electoral Votes
International Relations	Foreign Born
Future	Future Political Power

Category Scores of 0 (6)

Section	Category
History	Historic Natives
Natural Resources	Coal Reserves
Environment	Waste Generation
Housing	Housing Costs
Housing	Rent
Communications	Broadcasting Stations

11. New York (B+)

FINAL STANDINGS

New York falls just short of grade A territory. It is no. 11 nationally, no. 6 in the East, and no. 3 among large states.

BEST SECTIONS

Arts (100 points)—Broadway and all of New York's orchestras and museums would settle for nothing less than first place. No state has a more vibrant theater community; only Hawaii spends more government money on the arts.

Resource Conservation (95)—New York is among America's most efficient consumers of petroleum products and electricity.

Transportation (92)—No state even comes close to New York in the use of public transit.

WORST SECTIONS

Housing (0 points)—Last place. It goes without saying that housing is expensive in New York. Property taxes are extremely high, and the housing stock is among the oldest in the country.

Government (18)—New York's government is costly and overstaffed. It is also verbose: The state's 80,000-word constitution is America's second longest.

Recreation (19)—Believe it or not, New York has the nation's second-worst ratio of large retail outlets.

NEIGHBORS

New York's neighbors, especially no. 1 Vermont, offer some high-powered competition. That's the main reason for its 2–3 record.

BIGGEST SURPRISE

The home state of such current or former champions as the New York Yankees, Mets, Knicks, Rangers, Islanders, and the Buffalo Bills is not such a great place for athletics. New York earned a D+ in the Sports section.

THE BOTTOM LINE

No. 11 isn't bad at all, but it must be galling for New York to be one position behind its national archrival, California.

NEW YORK

General Information

Total Points: 573
Overall Grade: B+

National Rank: 11 of 50
Regional Rank: 6 of 12 (East)

Population: 17,990,000
Capital: Albany

Land Area: 47,224 square miles
Largest City: New York City

Report Card

Section	Score	Grade
1. History	75	B+
2. Terrain	54	C
3. Natural Resources	54	C
4. Resource Conservation	95	A
5. Environment	62	B–
6. Health	52	C
7. Children and Families	56	C+
8. Female Equality	56	C+
9. Racial Equality	59	C+
10. Housing	0	F
11. Education	65	B
12. Applied Intelligence	71	B
13. Arts	100	A+
14. Communications	69	B
15. Sports	39	D+
16. Recreation	19	F
17. Business	63	B–
18. Personal Finances	72	B
19. Public Safety	31	D
20. Transportation	92	A
21. Politics	87	A
22. Government	18	F
23. National Relations	48	C
24. International Relations	68	B
25. Future	44	C–
Overall	573	B+

Record with Neighboring States (2–3)

Neighbor	Neighbor's Score	Winner
Connecticut	647	Connecticut by 74
Massachusetts	641	Massachusetts by 68
New Jersey	552	New York by 21
Pennsylvania	517	New York by 56
Vermont	666	Vermont by 93

Category Scores of 100 (10)

Section	Category
History	Presidential Candidates
Health	Specialists
Racial Equality	Housing Disparity
Applied Intelligence	MacArthur Fellows
Arts	Arts Funding
Arts	Theater
Transportation	Public Transit Usage
Politics	Electoral Votes
International Relations	Foreign Born
Future	Future Political Power

Category Scores of 0 (6)

Section	Category
Terrain	Rangeland
Natural Resources	Crude Oil Reserves
Natural Resources	Coal Reserves
Recreation	Shopping
Public Safety	Violent Crimes
Government	State Constitution Length

12. Maine (B+)

FINAL STANDINGS

Maine ranks below most of New England, but no. 12 is a respectable showing, nonetheless. It is no. 7 in the East and no. 4 among small states.

BEST SECTIONS

Resource Conservation (91 points)—Only Hawaii is more efficient in the use of natural gas. Maine also is among the national leaders in renewable energy, getting 27 percent of its power from such sources.

Children and Families (85)—Maine is among the four states with the fewest infant deaths and low-weight births.

Female Equality (85)—Women hold more than 30 percent of the legislative seats in just seven states. Maine is one of them.

Politics (85)—Maine residents believe in democracy. Only Minnesota has higher voter turnout.

WORST SECTIONS

Applied Intelligence (9 points)—Colleges in Maine award few doctoral degrees, and the state has never had a MacArthur fellow. Research and development funds also are hard to come by.

Housing (24)—It's the tired New England refrain: Housing in Maine is old and fairly expensive.

Sports (24)—Maine has no major-league franchises, and its college teams rarely are competitive at the national level.

NEIGHBORS

Maine loses the matchup with its only American neighbor, New Hampshire.

BIGGEST SURPRISE

Most New England states earned above-average grades in the Education section, but Maine settled for a C. Its chief drawback is that too many of its high school graduates must head out of state for college.

THE BOTTOM LINE

Maine is safe, clean, and well-governed. It deserves its position among the upper 25 percent of states.

MAINE

General Information

Total Points: 567
Overall Grade: B+

National Rank: 12 of 50
Regional Rank: 7 of 12 (East)

Population: 1,228,000
Capital: Augusta

Land Area: 30,865 square miles
Largest City: Portland

Report Card

Section	Score	Grade
1. History	41	C–
2. Terrain	79	B+
3. Natural Resources	36	D+
4. Resource Conservation	91	A
5. Environment	84	A–
6. Health	50	C
7. Children and Families	85	A
8. Female Equality	85	A
9. Racial Equality	63	B–
10. Housing	24	D–
11. Education	54	C
12. Applied Intelligence	9	F
13. Arts	47	C
14. Communications	62	B–
15. Sports	24	D–
16. Recreation	58	C+
17. Business	65	B
18. Personal Finances	46	C
19. Public Safety	82	A–
20. Transportation	35	D+
21. Politics	85	A
22. Government	71	B
23. National Relations	25	D
24. International Relations	48	C
25. Future	40	C–
Overall	567	B+

Record with Neighboring States (0–1)

Neighbor	Neighbor's Score	Winner
New Hampshire	639	New Hampshire by 72

Category Scores of 100 (7)

Section	Category
Terrain	Inland Water
Terrain	Forests
Natural Resources	Timberland
Resource Conservation	Natural Gas Consumption
Environment	Drinking Water
Racial Equality	Income Disparity
Politics	Voter Turnout

Category Scores of 0 (8)

Section	Category
Terrain	Rangeland
Natural Resources	Crude Oil Reserves
Natural Resources	Coal Reserves
Racial Equality	Minority Population
Applied Intelligence	MacArthur Fellows
Sports	Professional Champions
Sports	Spectator Seats
National Relations	*Fortune* 500 Companies

13. Virginia (B+)

FINAL STANDINGS

Virginia finds itself at no. 13, but it can take solace from its no. 1 ranking in the South. It also is no. 4 among large states.

BEST SECTIONS

National Relations (94 points)—The Pentagon is in Virginia, as is one of the navy's largest bases. So it's no surprise that the federal government spends more money per capita in Virginia than in all but three states.

Government (87)—Virginia has a streamlined system. Only Hawaii has a smaller ratio of governmental units. Taxes are below the national norm.

Resource Conservation (81)—Virginia is respectably efficient in its use of water and natural gas.

WORST SECTIONS

Sports (14 points)—High school sports participation is low, and the state turns out few Olympic athletes. Nor does it have any major-league teams.

Racial Equality (32)—Virginia elected a black governor, but that's the exception to the rule. Blacks have not made much economic progress.

Environment (35)—Only two states generate more waste per person than Virginia does.

Arts (35)—Theater, entertainment groups, museums, and galleries are all underrepresented in Virginia.

NEIGHBORS

Virginia borders three southern states; it defeats them all, as well as West Virginia. Its only loss is to an eastern neighbor, Maryland.

BIGGEST SURPRISE

Virginia was the home of such giants as Washington, Jefferson, and Lee. Why did it get only a C+ in the History section? Because it didn't maintain its momentum: Virginia has turned out few national leaders since the Civil War.

THE BOTTOM LINE

Virginia still has much to learn about treating all of its people equally, but it nonetheless offers the best quality of life in the old Confederacy.

VIRGINIA

General Information

Total Points: 560
Overall Grade: B+

National Rank: 13 of 50
Regional Rank: 1 of 13 (South)

Population: 6,187,000
Capital: Richmond

Land Area: 39,598 square miles
Largest City: Virginia Beach

Report Card

Section	Score	Grade
1. History	58	C+
2. Terrain	62	B–
3. Natural Resources	51	C
4. Resource Conservation	81	A–
5. Environment	35	D+
6. Health	49	C
7. Children and Families	65	B
8. Female Equality	40	C–
9. Racial Equality	32	D
10. Housing	74	B
11. Education	55	C+
12. Applied Intelligence	46	C
13. Arts	35	D+
14. Communications	51	C
15. Sports	14	F
16. Recreation	41	C–
17. Business	67	B
18. Personal Finances	57	C+
19. Public Safety	72	B
20. Transportation	54	C
21. Politics	40	C–
22. Government	87	A
23. National Relations	94	A
24. International Relations	47	C
25. Future	64	B–
Overall	560	B+

Record with Neighboring States (4–1)

Neighbor	Neighbor's Score	Winner
Kentucky	357	Virginia by 203
Maryland	608	Maryland by 48
North Carolina	457	Virginia by 103
Tennessee	386	Virginia by 174
West Virginia	349	Virginia by 211

Category Scores of 100 (2)

Section	Category
History	European Settlement
Government	Government Units

Category Scores of 0 (4)

Section	Category
Terrain	Rangeland
Natural Resources	Crude Oil Reserves
Sports	Professional Champions
Sports	Spectator Seats

14. Utah (B+)

FINAL STANDINGS

Utah is no. 14 on the national list. It has identical no. 5 rankings in the West and among the nation's small states.

BEST SECTIONS

Housing (100 points)—Utah has a higher proportion of large families than any other state, which is why it also has the best supply of large houses. Only four states have lower rents.

Government (91)—Taxes are considerably below the national average, as is the level of government employment.

Children and Families (90)—Utah has America's lowest rates of infant mortality and births to single teens.

WORST SECTIONS

International Relations (0 points)—Utah is isolated in the continental West. Relatively few foreign employers have located there, and the state has a weak record in exporting.

History (4)—Most of the famous people in Utah's past were born elsewhere. The state has never had a presidential candidate.

Natural Resources (21)—Utah is near the bottom of the national production rankings for farm products and timber.

NEIGHBORS

Utah is superior in quality of life to five of its six neighbors. The exception is Colorado, no. 6 nationally.

BIGGEST SURPRISE

Sports is not the first word that pops into mind when Utah is mentioned. But no state has a higher ratio of champions in college athletics. That helps to explain Utah's grade of A– in the Sports section.

THE BOTTOM LINE

Utah is out of the mainstream, one of the nation's best-kept secrets. But it earned a solid overall grade of B+.

UTAH

General Information

Total Points: 559
Overall Grade: B+

National Rank: 14 of 50
Regional Rank: 5 of 13 (West)

Population: 1,723,000
Capital: Salt Lake City

Land Area: 82,168 square miles
Largest City: Salt Lake City

Report Card

Section	Score	Grade
1. History	4	F
2. Terrain	85	A
3. Natural Resources	21	D–
4. Resource Conservation	78	B+
5. Environment	37	D+
6. Health	51	C
7. Children and Families	90	A
8. Female Equality	37	D+
9. Racial Equality	38	D+
10. Housing	100	A+
11. Education	83	A–
12. Applied Intelligence	58	C+
13. Arts	55	C+
14. Communications	34	D
15. Sports	84	A–
16. Recreation	43	C–
17. Business	22	D–
18. Personal Finances	33	D
19. Public Safety	50	C
20. Transportation	63	B–
21. Politics	83	A–
22. Government	91	A
23. National Relations	38	D+
24. International Relations	0	F
25. Future	85	A
Overall	559	B+

Record with Neighboring States (5–1)

Neighbor	Neighbor's Score	Winner
Arizona	455	Utah by 104
Colorado	616	Colorado by 57
Idaho	521	Utah by 38
Nevada	507	Utah by 52
New Mexico	413	Utah by 146
Wyoming	539	Utah by 20

Category Scores of 100 (6)

Section	Category
Health	Major Causes of Death
Children and Families	Infant Mortality
Children and Families	Births to Single Teens
Housing	Housing Size
Education	High School Graduates
Sports	College Champions

Category Scores of 0 (6)

Section	Category
History	Historic Natives
History	Presidential Candidates
Terrain	Ocean Shoreline
Environment	Toxic Emissions
Health	Hospital Costs
Communications	Cable Television

15. Wisconsin (B+)

FINAL STANDINGS

Wisconsin is no. 15 on the national scale, but a strong no. 2 in the Midwest. It is in sixth place among the nation's 20 medium-size states.

BEST SECTIONS

Politics (100 points)—Wisconsin has America's most responsive political system. Voter turnout is among the highest in the nation, and elections almost always are competitive.

Environment (88)—Just four states generate proportionately less waste than Wisconsin does. Spending on environmental programs is reasonably high.

Education (82)—Wisconsin's students tied with Iowa and Washington for the nation's highest standardized test scores. The high school dropout rate is low.

WORST SECTIONS

National Relations (8 points)—This was an isolationist state before the two world wars, and it retains some of that character today. Only four states have smaller percentages of residents born in other states.

Racial Equality (11)—Wisconsin is among the six states that have the worst racial income disparities and the fewest minority-owned businesses.

History (20)—Wisconsin has never produced a major-party nominee for president.

NEIGHBORS

Wisconsin borders the Midwest's best state, Minnesota. But it wins its three other matchups.

BIGGEST SURPRISE

This is one of America's most liberal states, proud of its progressive tradition. That makes all the more stunning—and disappointing—the F it received in the Racial Equality section.

THE BOTTOM LINE

Wisconsin can be proud of its success in the basics, such as the Environment and Education sections. But it could improve its B+ overall grade by extending opportunities to everyone.

WISCONSIN

General Information

Total Points: 558
Overall Grade: B+

National Rank: 15 of 50
Regional Rank: 2 of 12 (Midwest)

Population: 4,892,000
Capital: Madison

Land Area: 54,314 square miles
Largest City: Milwaukee

Report Card

Section	Score	Grade
1. History	20	D–
2. Terrain	41	C–
3. Natural Resources	40	C–
4. Resource Conservation	81	A–
5. Environment	88	A
6. Health	61	B–
7. Children and Families	73	B
8. Female Equality	65	B
9. Racial Equality	11	F
10. Housing	52	C
11. Education	82	A–
12. Applied Intelligence	34	D
13. Arts	34	D
14. Communications	63	B–
15. Sports	79	B+
16. Recreation	28	D
17. Business	50	C
18. Personal Finances	40	C–
19. Public Safety	76	B+
20. Transportation	69	B
21. Politics	100	A+
22. Government	76	B+
23. National Relations	8	F
24. International Relations	36	D+
25. Future	44	C–
Overall	558	B+

Record with Neighboring States (3–1)

Neighbor	Neighbor's Score	Winner
Illinois	505	Wisconsin by 53
Iowa	523	Wisconsin by 35
Michigan	426	Wisconsin by 132
Minnesota	608	Minnesota by 50

Category Scores of 100 (3)

Section	Category
Resource Conservation	Petroleum Consumption
Education	Standardized Tests
Transportation	Pavement Condition

Category Scores of 0 (5)

Section	Category
Terrain	Ocean Shoreline
Terrain	Rangeland
Natural Resources	Crude Oil Reserves
Natural Resources	Coal Reserves
National Relations	Federal Spending

16. New Jersey (B)

FINAL STANDINGS

New Jersey is in the top third of all states, ranking no. 16 overall. But it's in the second division in the East, where it is eighth of 12 states. It also is no. 5 among large states.

BEST SECTIONS

Personal Finances (96 points)—The suburban spillover from New York City and Philadelphia has brought great wealth to New Jersey. Only Connecticut has a higher per capita income or a larger share of people earning more than $200,000 a year.

Business (90)—New Jersey is in the national top 10 in retail trade and service sector strength.

Transportation (87)—Roads are safe in New Jersey, which has the third-lowest rate of motor vehicle deaths. Public transit is well-used.

WORST SECTIONS

Environment (0 points)—The stereotype is correct: New Jersey carries a deadly environmental burden, including the nation's heaviest concentration of Superfund sites and most serious drinking-water problems.

Future (8)—There isn't much room for future growth. New Jersey is America's most densely populated state.

Housing (22)—Only Alaska and New Hampshire have property taxes higher than New Jersey's.

NEIGHBORS

New Jersey has a record of 2–1 against its neighbors. The margin is close in all three showdowns.

BIGGEST SURPRISE

An affluent state so close to two major urban centers should offer an outstanding range of leisure activities, right? Not New Jersey, which earned a D– in the Recreation section. It has the nation's lowest concentration of movie theaters and video rental stores.

440 THE BOTTOM LINE

New Jersey remains in New York's shadow, losing their quality-of-life matchup by 21 points. But that shouldn't obscure New Jersey's fine record, evidenced by its overall grade of B.

NEW JERSEY

General Information

Total Points: 552
Overall Grade: B

National Rank: 16 of 50
Regional Rank: 8 of 12 (East)

Population: 7,730,000
Capital: Trenton

Land Area: 7,419 square miles
Largest City: Newark

Report Card

Section	Score	Grade
1. History	61	B–
2. Terrain	48	C
3. Natural Resources	78	B+
4. Resource Conservation	80	A–
5. Environment	0	F
6. Health	51	C
7. Children and Families	73	B
8. Female Equality	62	B–
9. Racial Equality	43	C–
10. Housing	22	D–
11. Education	55	C+
12. Applied Intelligence	66	B
13. Arts	57	C+
14. Communications	67	B
15. Sports	25	D
16. Recreation	23	D–
17. Business	90	A
18. Personal Finances	96	A
19. Public Safety	71	B
20. Transportation	87	A
21. Politics	69	B
22. Government	65	B
23. National Relations	25	D
24. International Relations	62	B–
25. Future	8	F
Overall	552	B

Record with Neighboring States (2–1)

Neighbor	Neighbor's Score	Winner
Delaware	544	New Jersey by 8
New York	573	New York by 21
Pennsylvania	517	New Jersey by 35

Category Scores of 100 (7)

Section	Category
History	Statehood
Natural Resources	Nonfuel Mining
Health	Hospital Costs
Arts	Dance
Personal Finances	Per Capita Income
Personal Finances	Upper Incomes
Public Safety	Police Presence

Category Scores of 0 (12)

Section	Category
Terrain	Rangeland
Natural Resources	Crude Oil Reserves
Natural Resources	Coal Reserves
Environment	Superfund Sites
Environment	Drinking Water
Housing	Property Taxes
Communications	Broadcasting Stations
Recreation	Movies and Videos
Transportation	Road Mileage
National Relations	Student Migration
International Relations	Overseas Population
Future	Population Density

17. Delaware (B)

FINAL STANDINGS

Delaware is a step behind neighboring New Jersey in two classifications: It is no. 17 overall and no. 9 in the East. It also finished in sixth place among the 17 small states.

BEST SECTIONS

National Relations (100 points)—The home state of an industrial giant such as DuPont naturally has strong coast-to-coast ties. Only Connecticut has a greater concentration of *Fortune* 500 companies. Delaware also is a magnet for out-of-state college students.

International Relations (88)—Delaware has the nation's highest proportion of jobs controlled by foreign companies. The state also is a strong agricultural exporter.

Business (86)—Delaware is among America's 10 best states in manufacturing and retail trade.

WORST SECTIONS

Sports (21 points)—Delaware is shut out from major-league sports. It is below the national norms for Olympic athletes and college champions.

Future (25)—Future economic news is not good. Only Connecticut is projected to have a slower rate of income growth than Delaware.

Environment (26)—Industrial prowess has a price. Delaware has a higher proportion of Superfund sites than all states but Rhode Island and New Jersey.

NEIGHBORS

Tiny Delaware has a split record with its two large neighbors, beating Pennsylvania, but losing to New Jersey. It also loses to Maryland, a medium-size state.

BIGGEST SURPRISE

Delaware has the image of a rural, quiet state. But it's not rural: Two of its three counties are metropolitan areas. Nor is it as quiet as you might expect, doing no better than a C in the Public Safety section.

444 THE BOTTOM LINE

Delaware, the original ratifier of the Constitution, likes to call itself the First State. It settles for being the 17th state in our rankings.

DELAWARE

General Information

Total Points: 544
Overall Grade: B

National Rank: 17 of 50
Regional Rank: 9 of 12 (East)

Population: 666,000
Capital: Dover

Land Area: 1,955 square miles
Largest City: Wilmington

Report Card

Section	Score	Grade
1. History	65	B
2. Terrain	52	C
3. Natural Resources	62	B–
4. Resource Conservation	66	B
5. Environment	26	D
6. Health	29	D
7. Children and Families	39	D+
8. Female Equality	42	C–
9. Racial Equality	28	D
10. Housing	79	B+
11. Education	68	B
12. Applied Intelligence	65	B
13. Arts	67	B
14. Communications	66	B
15. Sports	21	D–
16. Recreation	69	B
17. Business	86	A
18. Personal Finances	66	B
19. Public Safety	50	C
20. Transportation	30	D
21. Politics	40	C–
22. Government	36	D+
23. National Relations	100	A+
24. International Relations	88	A
25. Future	25	D
Overall	544	B

Record with Neighboring States (1–2)

Neighbor	Neighbor's Score	Winner
Maryland	608	Maryland by 64
New Jersey	552	New Jersey by 8
Pennsylvania	517	Delaware by 27

Category Scores of 100 (8)

Section	Category
History	Statehood
Natural Resources	Farm Marketings
Resource Conservation	Water Usage
Applied Intelligence	Patents
Communications	Cable Television
Public Safety	Public Safety Spending
National Relations	*Fortune* 500 Companies
International Relations	Foreign Employers

Category Scores of 0 (14)

Section	Category
History	Presidential Candidates
Terrain	Rangeland
Terrain	Elevation Variation
Natural Resources	Crude Oil Reserves
Natural Resources	Coal Reserves
Children and Families	Infant Mortality
Female Equality	Violence Against Women
Sports	Professional Champions
Sports	Spectator Seats
Transportation	Airline Service
Politics	Electoral Votes
Government	State Debt
Future	Projected Income Growth
Future	Future Political Power

18. Wyoming (B)

FINAL STANDINGS

Wyoming ranks no. 18 among the 50 states in quality of life. It also is no. 6 in the West and no. 7 among small states.

BEST SECTIONS

Environment (100 points)—Wyoming is a clean state that is working to keep it that way. It generates a small amount of waste and has just 0.3 Superfund sites per 10,000 square miles. Only Alaska spends more on environmental programs.

Education (100)—Another first-place finish. Wyoming is among the five states with the lowest dropout rates, highest high school graduation rates, and heaviest education spending.

Communications (97)—Wyoming has America's strongest concentration of broadcasting stations.

WORST SECTIONS

Resource Conservation (0 points)—Wyoming's fine environmental record doesn't extend to its consumption habits. No state uses more electricity per person; only Idaho uses more water.

History (5)—Wyoming is a typical state of the interior West, with hardly any historic figures it can call its own.

Applied Intelligence (22)—Relatively few Wyoming residents get patents. None has ever been a MacArthur fellow.

Government (22)—No state has a higher proportion of government employees than Wyoming.

NEIGHBORS

Wyoming holds its own against its six larger neighbors, defeating four in quality-of-life showdowns.

BIGGEST SURPRISE

Wyoming is so sparsely settled that you would expect news to travel slowly. But it is actually among the national leaders in cable television, broadcasting, and libraries, earning it an A in the Communications section.

448 THE BOTTOM LINE

Lonely Wyoming is last among all 50 states in population and alphabetical order, but it does substantially better in our rankings, finishing a respectable 18th.

WYOMING

General Information

Total Points: 539
Overall Grade: B

National Rank: 18 of 50
Regional Rank: 6 of 13 (West)

Population: 454,000
Capital: Cheyenne

Land Area: 97,105 square miles
Largest City: Cheyenne

Report Card

Section	Score	Grade
1. History	5	F
2. Terrain	84	A–
3. Natural Resources	42	C–
4. Resource Conservation	0	F
5. Environment	100	A+
6. Health	70	B
7. Children and Families	57	C+
8. Female Equality	66	B
9. Racial Equality	37	D+
10. Housing	76	B+
11. Education	100	A+
12. Applied Intelligence	22	D–
13. Arts	36	D+
14. Communications	97	A
15. Sports	35	D+
16. Recreation	91	A
17. Business	32	D
18. Personal Finances	32	D
19. Public Safety	84	A–
20. Transportation	67	B
21. Politics	65	B
22. Government	22	D–
23. National Relations	61	B–
24. International Relations	23	D–
25. Future	24	D–
Overall	539	B

Record with Neighboring States (4–2)

Neighbor	Neighbor's Score	Winner
Colorado	616	Colorado by 77
Idaho	521	Wyoming by 18
Montana	488	Wyoming by 51
Nebraska	526	Wyoming by 13
South Dakota	476	Wyoming by 63
Utah	559	Utah by 20

Category Scores of 100 (11)

Section	Category
Terrain	Rangeland
Environment	Superfund Sites
Environment	Environmental Spending
Housing	Rent
Education	Education Spending
Communications	Broadcasting Stations
Recreation	Park Visitors
Recreation	Movies and Videos
Public Safety	Police Presence
Transportation	Pavement Condition
Future	Population Density

Category Scores of 0 (18)

Section	Category
History	Historic Places
History	Historic Natives
History	Presidential Candidates
Terrain	Ocean Shoreline
Resource Conservation	Water Usage
Resource Conservation	Electricity Consumption
Racial Equality	Minority College Graduates
Applied Intelligence	MacArthur Fellows
Arts	Entertainers
Sports	Professional Champions
Sports	Spectator Seats
Business	Economic Growth
Politics	Electoral Votes
Government	Government Employees
National Relations	*Fortune* 500 Companies
Future	Projected Population Growth
Future	Projected Job Growth
Future	Future Political Power

19. Rhode Island (B)

FINAL STANDINGS

Rhode Island ranks a respectable no. 19 nationally, but it is only no. 10 among the 12 eastern states, ahead of Pennsylvania and West Virginia. It holds eighth place among small states.

BEST SECTIONS

Resource Conservation (93 points)—Rhode Island sets an example for the rest of America to follow. It is the most efficient state in the use of water or electricity.

History (87)—Rhode Island has the nation's highest density of designated historic places. It is second to Massachusetts in the proportion of native historic figures.

National Relations (86)—Out-of-state students are drawn to Rhode Island in great numbers. No state has a more favorable college migration ratio.

WORST SECTIONS

Housing (0 points)—A last-place tie with New York. Housing in Rhode Island is expensive, old, small, and fairly heavily taxed.

Future (1)—Future development will be difficult because of crowded conditions. Rhode Island is second only to New Jersey in population density.

Environment (8)—Rhode Island again is just behind New Jersey in a negative way. It has the nation's second-highest concentration of Superfund sites.

NEIGHBORS

Rhode Island has just two neighbors, Massachusetts and Connecticut, and it is far behind both in quality-of-life scores.

BIGGEST SURPRISE

History buffs flock to other Atlantic Seaboard states, such as Massachusetts, New York, and Virginia. But they also should pay attention to Rhode Island, which finished second in the History section, earning an A.

THE BOTTOM LINE

The other five New England states are among the top 12 in our national rankings. Rhode Island is the exception to the regional rule, finishing 19th.

RHODE ISLAND

General Information

Total Points: 528
Overall Grade: B

National Rank: 19 of 50
Regional Rank: 10 of 12 (East)

Population: 1,003,000
Capital: Providence

Land Area: 1,045 square miles
Largest City: Providence

Report Card

Section	Score	Grade
1. History	87	A
2. Terrain	73	B
3. Natural Resources	54	C
4. Resource Conservation	93	A
5. Environment	8	F
6. Health	37	D+
7. Children and Families	73	B
8. Female Equality	64	B–
9. Racial Equality	29	D
10. Housing	0	F
11. Education	58	C+
12. Applied Intelligence	74	B
13. Arts	71	B
14. Communications	81	A–
15. Sports	21	D–
16. Recreation	45	C
17. Business	55	C+
18. Personal Finances	55	C+
19. Public Safety	71	B
20. Transportation	56	C+
21. Politics	57	C+
22. Government	67	B
23. National Relations	86	A
24. International Relations	41	C–
25. Future	1	F
Overall	528	B

Record with Neighboring States (0–2)

Neighbor	Neighbor's Score	Winner
Connecticut	647	Connecticut by 119
Massachusetts	641	Massachusetts by 113

Category Scores of 100 (10)

Section	Category
History	Historic Places
History	Historic Natives
Terrain	Ocean Shoreline
Resource Conservation	Water Usage
Resource Conservation	Electricity Consumption
Education	College Students
Applied Intelligence	Doctoral Degrees
Arts	Dance
Transportation	Motor Vehicle Deaths
National Relations	Student Migration

Category Scores of 0 (11)

Section	Category
History	Presidential Candidates
Terrain	Rangeland
Natural Resources	Crude Oil Reserves
Natural Resources	Coal Reserves
Environment	Superfund Sites
Health	Family Doctors
Sports	College Champions
Sports	Professional Champions
Sports	Spectator Seats
National Relations	Domestic Travel
Future	Population Density

20. Nebraska (B)

FINAL STANDINGS

Nebraska is only the third midwestern entry in the national top 20. It ranks right in the middle of America's small states, ninth among 17.

BEST SECTIONS

Education (84 points)—Nebraska is among the 10 states with the lowest dropout rates, best high school graduation rates, and highest scores on standardized tests.

Communications (82)—This is a state that believes in the printed word. Only Colorado and Massachusetts have higher newspaper circulation rates.

Children and Families (79)—Nebraska's ratios of children in poverty, births to single teens, and infant deaths all are lower than the national averages.

WORST SECTIONS

Natural Resources (14 points)—The plains are not a great storehouse of resources. Nebraska is virtually devoid of timber. It has no coal and a scarcity of other minerals.

History (15)—Nebraska has one of America's lowest concentrations of designated historic places.

Applied Intelligence (18)—Only three states receive a smaller share of federal research and development funds than Nebraska.

NEIGHBORS

Nebraska loses to its two western neighbors, Colorado and Wyoming. But it defeats all four adjacent midwestern states.

BIGGEST SURPRISE

You would think a state with an A– in the Education section also would do well in Applied Intelligence. But Nebraska isn't able to keep its native brain power at home. It was hit with an F in the latter section.

THE BOTTOM LINE

Nebraska has the highest quality-of-life ranking of the six midwestern states located wholly west of the Mississippi River.

NEBRASKA

General Information

Total Points: 526
Overall Grade: B

National Rank: 20 of 50
Regional Rank: 3 of 12 (Midwest)

Population: 1,578,000
Capital: Lincoln

Land Area: 76,878 square miles
Largest City: Omaha

Report Card

Section	Score	Grade
1. History	15	F
2. Terrain	45	C
3. Natural Resources	14	F
4. Resource Conservation	62	B–
5. Environment	76	B+
6. Health	71	B
7. Children and Families	79	B+
8. Female Equality	65	B
9. Racial Equality	26	D
10. Housing	62	B–
11. Education	84	A–
12. Applied Intelligence	18	F
13. Arts	48	C
14. Communications	82	A–
15. Sports	31	D
16. Recreation	45	C
17. Business	40	C–
18. Personal Finances	52	C
19. Public Safety	69	B
20. Transportation	58	C+
21. Politics	60	B–
22. Government	51	C
23. National Relations	23	D–
24. International Relations	34	D
25. Future	47	C
Overall	526	B

Record with Neighboring States (4–2)

Neighbor	Neighbor's Score	Winner
Colorado	616	Colorado by 90
Iowa	523	Nebraska by 3
Kansas	466	Nebraska by 60
Missouri	427	Nebraska by 99
South Dakota	476	Nebraska by 50
Wyoming	539	Wyoming by 13

Category Scores of 100 (2)

Section	Category
Environment	Drinking Water
Personal Finances	Unemployment

Category Scores of 0 (9)

Section	Category
History	Historic Natives
Terrain	Ocean Shoreline
Terrain	Forests
Natural Resources	Timberland
Natural Resources	Coal Reserves
Applied Intelligence	MacArthur Fellows
Sports	Olympic Athletes
Sports	Professional Champions
Sports	Spectator Seats

21. Iowa (B)

FINAL STANDINGS

Iowa is just three points and one place behind neighboring Nebraska. It is no. 21 nationally, no. 4 in the Midwest, and no. 7 among medium-size states.

BEST SECTIONS

Education (83 points)—Iowa students know how to take exams. They tied Wisconsin and Washington with America's best standardized test scores. Only two states have lower dropout rates than Iowa.

Children and Families (81)—Iowa is among the 10 states with the smallest percentages of low-weight births.

Resource Conservation (77)—This state is respectably efficient in its consumption of water and petroleum products.

Government (77)—The heartland does not believe in owing money. Iowa's government has accumulated the seventh-smallest debt of the 50 states.

WORST SECTIONS

Terrain (5 points)—Don't expect variety in the landscape. You will find rolling hills in Iowa, but no mountains, oceans, or large lakes.

National Relations (12)—Iowa is a bit out of the national mainstream. Only three states have smaller proportions of residents born in other states.

History (18)—No Iowa resident has ever been nominated for president by a major party.

NEIGHBORS

Iowa has a 3–3 record. It just happens to border the only three midwestern states with better scores.

BIGGEST SURPRISE

Iowa is somewhat isolated, as shown by its F in the National Relations section. Who would expect it to have closer ties with the rest of the world? But it earns a C+ in International Relations, largely because of its strength as an exporter of farm products.

THE BOTTOM LINE

Iowa might be only 21st overall, but it is attractive for its region. It is one of only four midwestern states to finish in the top half of the national rankings.

IOWA

General Information

Total Points: 523
Overall Grade: B

National Rank: 21 of 50
Regional Rank: 4 of 12 (Midwest)

Population: 2,777,000
Capital: Des Moines

Land Area: 55,875 square miles
Largest City: Des Moines

Report Card

Section	Score	Grade
1. History	18	F
2. Terrain	5	F
3. Natural Resources	46	C
4. Resource Conservation	77	B+
5. Environment	62	B–
6. Health	57	C+
7. Children and Families	81	A–
8. Female Equality	61	B–
9. Racial Equality	32	D
10. Housing	66	B
11. Education	83	A–
12. Applied Intelligence	37	D+
13. Arts	38	D+
14. Communications	75	B+
15. Sports	43	C–
16. Recreation	35	D+
17. Business	40	C–
18. Personal Finances	38	D+
19. Public Safety	69	B
20. Transportation	37	D+
21. Politics	71	B
22. Government	77	B+
23. National Relations	12	F
24. International Relations	59	C+
25. Future	43	C–
Overall	523	B

Record with Neighboring States (3–3)

Neighbor	Neighbor's Score	Winner
Illinois	505	Iowa by 18
Minnesota	608	Minnesota by 85
Missouri	427	Iowa by 96
Nebraska	526	Nebraska by 3
South Dakota	476	Iowa by 47
Wisconsin	558	Wisconsin by 35

Category Scores of 100 (6)

Section	Category
Natural Resources	Farm Marketings
Housing	Housing Costs
Housing	Rent
Education	Standardized Tests
Sports	High School Athletes
International Relations	Agricultural Exports

Category Scores of 0 (5)

Section	Category
Terrain	Ocean Shoreline
Terrain	Rangeland
Natural Resources	Crude Oil Reserves
Sports	Professional Champions
Sports	Spectator Seats

22. Idaho (B)

FINAL STANDINGS

Idaho is no. 22 nationally, earning a straight B. It is also no. 7 in the West and no. 10 among America's small states.

BEST SECTIONS

Housing (93 points)—Idaho is one of the cheapest places in America in which to rent. It also has the benefit of property taxes that are substantially below the national average.

Politics (83)—Idaho is among the top 10 states in voter turnout. Most elections are competitive.

Terrain (79)—The difference between Idaho's highest and lowest points is 11,952 feet; only six states have sharper variations. Idaho is also blessed with an abundance of rangeland.

WORST SECTIONS

History (5 points)—Only three states have had fewer historic native sons and daughters than Idaho. It never has been home to a presidential nominee.

Natural Resources (12)—Idaho has no oil and little coal. Nor is it a strong agricultural state; the mountains and rangeland don't leave much room for farms.

Business (21)—This state is not an economic powerhouse. Idaho is among America's five lowest states in gross state product and retail trade.

NEIGHBORS

It's a draw. Idaho defeats three of its neighbors, including a narrow, three-point win over Oregon. But it also loses to three.

BIGGEST SURPRISE

Idaho, a mountain fortress in the northwestern corner of the country, would seem an ideal candidate for a low grade in the National Relations section. But it actually earns a B. Only three states attract a higher proportion of out-of-state college students.

THE BOTTOM LINE

Idaho didn't receive a perfect score in any of our 125 categories, but it did well enough to finish in the top half of the overall national rankings.

IDAHO

General Information

Total Points: 521
Overall Grade: B

National Rank: 22 of 50
Regional Rank: 7 of 13 (West)

Population: 1,007,000
Capital: Boise

Land Area: 82,751 square miles
Largest City: Boise

Report Card

Section	Score	Grade
1. History	5	F
2. Terrain	79	B+
3. Natural Resources	12	F
4. Resource Conservation	60	B–
5. Environment	71	B
6. Health	56	C+
7. Children and Families	74	B
8. Female Equality	67	B
9. Racial Equality	30	D
10. Housing	93	A
11. Education	50	C
12. Applied Intelligence	25	D
13. Arts	23	D–
14. Communications	57	C+
15. Sports	24	D–
16. Recreation	57	C+
17. Business	21	D–
18. Personal Finances	32	D
19. Public Safety	73	B
20. Transportation	40	C–
21. Politics	83	A–
22. Government	68	B
23. National Relations	67	B
24. International Relations	38	D+
25. Future	61	B–
Overall	521	B

Record with Neighboring States (3–3)

Neighbor	Neighbor's Score	Winner
Montana	488	Idaho by 33
Nevada	507	Idaho by 14
Oregon	518	Idaho by 3
Utah	559	Utah by 38
Washington	601	Washington by 80
Wyoming	539	Wyoming by 18

Category Scores of 100 (0)

Section	Category
(None)	

Category Scores of 0 (11)

Section	Category
History	Historic Natives
History	Presidential Candidates
Terrain	Ocean Shoreline
Natural Resources	Crude Oil Reserves
Natural Resources	Coal Reserves
Resource Conservation	Water Usage
Health	Specialists
Applied Intelligence	MacArthur Fellows
Sports	College Champions
Sports	Professional Champions
Sports	Spectator Seats

23. Oregon (B)

FINAL STANDINGS

Oregon is hot on the heels of its neighbor, no. 22 Idaho. It is one position behind at no. 23 nationally and no. 8 in the West. It also holds eighth place among the 20 medium states.

BEST SECTIONS

Resource Conservation (91 points)—Oregon understands the importance of conservation. Almost 48 percent of its energy comes from renewable sources; only Washington does better.

Recreation (80)—Oregon has a diversity of recreational options. It is among America's 10 best states in terms of park visitors; the same is true when it comes to the availability of movie theaters and large stores.

Terrain (79)—Oregon has it all, from mountains and high plains to a rugged ocean shoreline.

WORST SECTIONS

Natural Resources (10 points)—Relatively few farmers make a go of it in Oregon; the yield is low. The same is true for mining. And forget about oil: Oregon has no reserves.

History (12)—The Oregon Trail made the history books, but that wasn't the case for the people who hiked it. Oregon has had relatively few historic figures.

Arts (34)—Arts appropriations from the state government are low. So is the number of dancers.

NEIGHBORS

Oregon has four neighbors, but beats only Nevada in quality-of-life matchups.

BIGGEST SURPRISE

You would assume that a coastal state with broad valleys and high plains would be blessed with an abundance of resources. But that isn't the story in Oregon. It earned an F in the Natural Resources section.

THE BOTTOM LINE

Oregon has the reputation for offering a high quality of life. But it doesn't quite deliver on the promise, settling in the middle of the national pack.

OREGON

General Information

Total Points: 518
Overall Grade: B

National Rank: 23 of 50
Regional Rank: 8 of 13 (West)

Population: 2,842,000
Capital: Salem

Land Area: 96,003 square miles
Largest City: Portland

Report Card

Section	Score	Grade
1. History	12	F
2. Terrain	79	B+
3. Natural Resources	10	F
4. Resource Conservation	91	A
5. Environment	58	C+
6. Health	42	C–
7. Children and Families	65	B
8. Female Equality	45	C
9. Racial Equality	46	C
10. Housing	39	D+
11. Education	65	B
12. Applied Intelligence	36	D+
13. Arts	34	D
14. Communications	63	B–
15. Sports	52	C
16. Recreation	80	A–
17. Business	45	C
18. Personal Finances	38	D+
19. Public Safety	41	C–
20. Transportation	49	C
21. Politics	76	B+
22. Government	68	B
23. National Relations	52	C
24. International Relations	45	C
25. Future	53	C
Overall	518	B

Record with Neighboring States (1–3)

Neighbor	Neighbor's Score	Winner
California	601	California by 83
Idaho	521	Idaho by 3
Nevada	507	Oregon by 11
Washington	601	Washington by 83

Category Scores of 100 (1)

Section	Category
Resource Conservation	Renewable Energy

Category Scores of 0 (6)

Section	Category
History	Historic Natives
History	Presidential Candidates
Natural Resources	Crude Oil Reserves
Natural Resources	Coal Reserves
Female Equality	Employment Opportunities
Public Safety	Police Presence

468 24. Pennsylvania (B)

FINAL STANDINGS

It all depends on whether you look at Pennsylvania from a national or regional perspective. It did moderately well in the overall rankings, no. 24 of 50. But it's near the bottom in the East, no. 11 of 12. It also is sixth among large states.

BEST SECTIONS

Natural Resources (94 points)—Pennsylvania, while not the mining power it once was, is still well above the national average. It is no. 6 in coal reserves and no. 11 in nonfuel mining.

Government (90)—The state government is lean. Pennsylvania has America's lowest proportion of government employees.

Politics (85)—Pennsylvania is responsive to national trends. Only four states more closely mirror the results of presidential elections.

WORST SECTIONS

Racial Equality (16 points)—Pennsylvania has a substantial minority population, but it does not treat nonwhites well. No state has a greater gap in the value of homes owned by whites and minorities.

Terrain (22)—Water is the key: Pennsylvania doesn't have enough. Its access to the Atlantic Ocean is only through bays, and it has relatively few lakes.

Recreation (23)—Pennsylvania is next to last in the availability of movie theaters and video rental stores.

NEIGHBORS

Pennsylvania is 2–4. It defeats West Virginia, the only eastern state with a lower score, and Ohio.

BIGGEST SURPRISE

Pennsylvania, the home of Independence Hall and the Liberty Bell, getting only a C in the History section? That's right. Its golden era was the republic's early days; there have been relatively few famous Pennsylvanians in recent history.

THE BOTTOM LINE

Pennsylvania is in the middle of the pack. It needs to improve its economic climate and the way it treats women and minorities if it wants to move up.

PENNSYLVANIA

General Information

Total Points: 517
Overall Grade: B

National Rank: 24 of 50
Regional Rank: 11 of 12 (East)

Population: 11,882,000
Capital: Harrisburg

Land Area: 44,820 square miles
Largest City: Philadelphia

Report Card

Section	Score	Grade
1. History	50	C
2. Terrain	22	D–
3. Natural Resources	94	A
4. Resource Conservation	81	A–
5. Environment	58	C+
6. Health	35	D+
7. Children and Families	57	C+
8. Female Equality	49	C
9. Racial Equality	16	F
10. Housing	55	C+
11. Education	44	C–
12. Applied Intelligence	34	D
13. Arts	32	D
14. Communications	67	B
15. Sports	53	C
16. Recreation	23	D–
17. Business	42	C–
18. Personal Finances	49	C
19. Public Safety	73	B
20. Transportation	56	C+
21. Politics	85	A
22. Government	90	A
23. National Relations	30	D
24. International Relations	37	D+
25. Future	47	C
Overall	517	B

Record with Neighboring States (2–4)

Neighbor	Neighbor's Score	Winner
Delaware	544	Delaware by 27
Maryland	608	Maryland by 91
New Jersey	552	New Jersey by 35
New York	573	New York by 56
Ohio	453	Pennsylvania by 64
West Virginia	349	Pennsylvania by 168

Category Scores of 100 (2)

Section	Category
History	Statehood
Government	Government Employees

Category Scores of 0 (5)

Section	Category
Terrain	Rangeland
Health	Major Causes of Death
Racial Equality	Housing Disparity
Recreation	Movies and Videos
National Relations	Population Influx

25. Nevada (B–)

FINAL STANDINGS

Nevada is no. 25 nationally, no. 9 in the West, and no. 11 among America's small states.

BEST SECTIONS

National Relations (94 points)—Its casinos attract tourists from across the country, bringing Nevada the nation's highest revenues from domestic travel. No state has a bigger percentage of residents born in other states.

Children and Families (85)—The infant mortality rate is low, and relatively few children live in poverty. Nevada also gets an artificial boost in this section from its booming business in instant weddings.

Terrain (83)—Nevada has America's most extensive rangeland; it also has peaks higher than 13,000 feet.

Government (83)—The state government is relatively trim, with fewer employees per 100,000 residents than the national average.

WORST SECTIONS

History (8 points)—Old-timers might disagree, but Nevada's modern history really dates only to 1931, when gambling was legalized.

Health (8)—Life expectancy in Nevada is near the bottom of the national rankings. So is the state's ratio of medical specialists.

Applied Intelligence (10)—Only Alaska turns out fewer candidates for doctoral degrees; only four states have fewer adults with bachelor's degrees.

NEIGHBORS

Nevada is on the short end of four quality-of-life pairings. The only neighbor it defeats is Arizona.

BIGGEST SURPRISE

Nevada, the state of nightlife and high rollers, received an A in the Children and Families section. One factor is the state's artificially high score in the Marriage Stability category, but a bigger reason is its generally favorable conditions for children.

THE BOTTOM LINE

Those who think of Nevada as nothing but casinos and desert will be surprised. The state offers quality of life that is above average.

NEVADA

General Information

Total Points: 507
Overall Grade: B–

National Rank: 25 of 50
Regional Rank: 9 of 13 (West)

Population: 1,202,000
Capital: Carson City

Land Area: 109,806 square miles
Largest City: Las Vegas

Report Card

Section	Score	Grade
1. History	8	F
2. Terrain	83	A–
3. Natural Resources	19	F
4. Resource Conservation	65	B
5. Environment	76	B+
6. Health	8	F
7. Children and Families	85	A
8. Female Equality	61	B–
9. Racial Equality	44	C–
10. Housing	49	C
11. Education	31	D
12. Applied Intelligence	10	F
13. Arts	59	C+
14. Communications	74	B
15. Sports	19	F
16. Recreation	57	C+
17. Business	56	C+
18. Personal Finances	52	C
19. Public Safety	26	D
20. Transportation	62	B–
21. Politics	46	C
22. Government	83	A–
23. National Relations	94	A
24. International Relations	13	F
25. Future	77	B+
Overall	507	B–

Record with Neighboring States (1–4)

Neighbor	Neighbor's Score	Winner
Arizona	455	Nevada by 52
California	601	California by 94
Idaho	521	Idaho by 14
Oregon	518	Oregon by 11
Utah	559	Utah by 52

Category Scores of 100 (11)

Section	Category
Terrain	Rangeland
Environment	Superfund Sites
Children and Families	Marriage Stability
Housing	Housing Age
Arts	Theater
Arts	Entertainers
Transportation	Airline Service
National Relations	Population Influx
National Relations	Domestic Travel
Future	Projected Population Growth
Future	Projected Job Growth

Category Scores of 0 (18)

Section	Category
History	Historic Places
History	Historic Natives
History	Presidential Candidates
Terrain	Ocean Shoreline
Natural Resources	Farm Marketings
Natural Resources	Timberland
Natural Resources	Crude Oil Reserves
Natural Resources	Coal Reserves
Education	High School Dropouts
Applied Intelligence	Doctoral Degrees
Applied Intelligence	MacArthur Fellows
Sports	Professional Champions
Sports	Spectator Seats
Business	Manufacturing Productivity
Public Safety	Prison Population
National Relations	*Fortune* 500 Companies
International Relations	Export-Related Jobs
International Relations	Agricultural Exports

26. Illinois (B-)

FINAL STANDINGS

The bottom half of the national list begins with Illinois, which is no. 26 overall. Its other rankings sound more impressive: no. 5 in the Midwest, no. 7 among large states.

BEST SECTIONS

Natural Resources (100 points)—Illinois has been blessed with the nation's widest array of resources. It is among the leaders in farming and coal mining, and it has surprisingly large reserves of oil.

Transportation (100)—Another first-place finish. Illinois is second to New York in the use of public transit. It is no. 10 in airline service.

International Relations (85)—Illinois is comfortable with the outside world. Only Iowa is stronger in the field of agricultural exports.

WORST SECTIONS

Terrain (14 points)—They don't call it the Prairie State for nothing. No oceans or mountains, few lakes or forests.

National Relations (24)—The federal government spends relatively little in Illinois. The state has a net out-migration of college students.

Public Safety (29)—Only California, New York, and Florida have violent crime rates higher than that of Illinois.

NEIGHBORS

Illinois has a 3–2 record. Its two losses, both by reasonably close margins, are to Iowa and Wisconsin.

BIGGEST SURPRISE

A quick glance reveals an apparently barren state. A few rolling hills, a few trees, not much else. Illinois actually has soil that is so fertile and so dense with minerals that it earned first place and a grade of A+ in the Natural Resources section.

THE BOTTOM LINE

Illinois is the Midwest's population center, but not its quality-of-life leader. That honor has migrated northwest to Minnesota.

ILLINOIS

General Information

Total Points: 505
Overall Grade: B–

National Rank: 26 of 50
Regional Rank: 5 of 12 (Midwest)

Population: 11,431,000
Capital: Springfield

Land Area: 55,593 square miles
Largest City: Chicago

Report Card

Section	Score	Grade
1. History	39	D+
2. Terrain	14	F
3. Natural Resources	100	A+
4. Resource Conservation	78	B+
5. Environment	39	D+
6. Health	35	D+
7. Children and Families	40	C–
8. Female Equality	56	C+
9. Racial Equality	34	D
10. Housing	43	C–
11. Education	50	C
12. Applied Intelligence	51	C
13. Arts	33	D
14. Communications	54	C
15. Sports	33	D
16. Recreation	30	D
17. Business	55	C+
18. Personal Finances	52	C
19. Public Safety	29	D
20. Transportation	100	A+
21. Politics	77	B+
22. Government	82	A–
23. National Relations	24	D–
24. International Relations	85	A
25. Future	47	C
Overall	505	B–

Record with Neighboring States (3–2)

Neighbor	Neighbor's Score	Winner
Indiana	438	Illinois by 67
Iowa	523	Iowa by 18
Kentucky	357	Illinois by 148
Missouri	427	Illinois by 78
Wisconsin	558	Wisconsin by 53

Category Scores of 100 (4)

Section	Category
Natural Resources	Coal Reserves
Transportation	Public Transit Usage
Politics	Presidential Election Trends
International Relations	Agricultural Exports

Category Scores of 0 (3)

Section	Category
Terrain	Ocean Shoreline
Terrain	Rangeland
Politics	State Legislature Turnover

27. North Dakota (B–)

FINAL STANDINGS

Look for North Dakota in the middle of the pack. It's No. 27 of the 50 states, no. 6 of the 12 midwestern states, and no. 12 among the 17 small states.

BEST SECTIONS

Public Safety (100 points)—Quiet, rural North Dakota is America's safest place. No state has a lower violent crime rate or a smaller prison population.

Environment (85)—Mississippi is the only state that generates less waste per person than North Dakota; Nevada and Alaska are the only ones with a smaller concentration of Superfund sites.

Communications (83)—Newspapers are widely read in North Dakota. It ranks no. 4 nationally in circulation rates.

WORST SECTIONS

Natural Resources (3 points)—North Dakota's array of resources is as bleak as its landscape. It is the nation's least-productive state in nonfuel mining, and it has less timber than any state but Nevada.

International Relations (7)—North Dakota is one of the weaker states in exporting manufactured goods. The only state where foreign companies offer fewer jobs is South Dakota.

History (8)—There never has been a major-party presidential nominee from North Dakota.

NEIGHBORS

North Dakota is trounced by Minnesota in their matchup, but it wins its other two against Montana and South Dakota.

BIGGEST SURPRISE

You might think that North Dakota, being a rural state, would have a poorly developed communications system. That's hardly the case. It's among the national leaders in newspaper readership and concentration of broadcasting stations, earning an A– in the Communications section.

THE BOTTOM LINE

It might be difficult for outsiders to detect, but there is a difference between the Dakotas. North Dakota is the better of the two states.

NORTH DAKOTA

General Information

Total Points: 504
Overall Grade: B–

National Rank: 27 of 50
Regional Rank: 6 of 12 (Midwest)

Population: 639,000
Capital: Bismarck

Land Area: 68,994 square miles
Largest City: Fargo

Report Card

Section	Score	Grade
1. History	8	F
2. Terrain	42	C–
3. Natural Resources	3	F
4. Resource Conservation	71	B
5. Environment	85	A
6. Health	77	B+
7. Children and Families	76	B+
8. Female Equality	57	C+
9. Racial Equality	14	F
10. Housing	77	B+
11. Education	75	B+
12. Applied Intelligence	17	F
13. Arts	22	D–
14. Communications	83	A–
15. Sports	46	C
16. Recreation	46	C
17. Business	16	F
18. Personal Finances	29	D
19. Public Safety	100	A+
20. Transportation	45	C
21. Politics	63	B–
22. Government	41	C–
23. National Relations	39	D+
24. International Relations	7	F
25. Future	47	C
Overall	504	B–

Record with Neighboring States (2–1)

Neighbor	Neighbor's Score	Winner
Minnesota	608	Minnesota by 104
Montana	488	North Dakota by 16
South Dakota	476	North Dakota by 28

Category Scores of 100 (11)

Section	Category
Environment	Superfund Sites
Environment	Waste Generation
Female Equality	Violence Against Women
Education	High School Dropouts
Recreation	Fitness Centers
Public Safety	All Crimes
Public Safety	Violent Crimes
Public Safety	Prison Population
Transportation	Road Mileage
Future	Population Density
Future	Projected Income Growth

Category Scores of 0 (18)

Section	Category
History	Historic Places
History	Historic Natives
History	Presidential Candidates
Terrain	Ocean Shoreline
Terrain	Forests
Natural Resources	Timberland
Natural Resources	Nonfuel Mining
Applied Intelligence	MacArthur Fellows
Arts	Dance
Sports	Professional Champions
Sports	Spectator Seats
Public Safety	Public Safety Spending
Transportation	Pavement Condition
Politics	Electoral Votes
Government	Government Units
National Relations	*Fortune* 500 Companies
International Relations	Foreign Employers
Future	Future Political Power

28. Alaska (B–)

FINAL STANDINGS

Our northernmost state ranks no. 28 in quality of life. It also is in tenth place in the West and thirteenth place among small states.

BEST SECTIONS

Recreation (100 points)—Hard to believe, but true. Alaska offers the nation's best range of recreational opportunities. Only Wyoming has more park visitors or proportionately more movie theaters and video rental stores; only Hawaii has a better ratio of restaurants and bars.

Terrain (95)—The Alaskan landscape is breathtaking, ranging from America's highest mountains to its coldest oceans.

Communications (86)—No state spends more per person on its libraries than Alaska does.

WORST SECTIONS

History (0 points)—Our 49th state has barely made a dent in American history. Not a single native of Alaska is profiled in the *Dictionary of American Biography.*

Government (0)—Welcome to the home of the nation's highest state taxes and highest state debt. Only Wyoming keeps Alaska from also having the highest level of government employment.

Natural Resources (5)—The mountains and tundra yield little. Alaska unsurprisingly is America's weakest farm state. Only North Dakota is less productive in nonfuel mining.

NEIGHBORS

Alaska doesn't border any state. And we didn't figure quality-of-life scores for its neighbors, Siberia and the Yukon.

BIGGEST SURPRISE

Alaska is a state of many surprises. Take your pick: A+ in Recreation, A in Communications, B+ in Arts, B+ in Education, B+ in Children and Families. None fits Alaska's image as an untamed, unforgiving wilderness.

THE BOTTOM LINE

Alaska is beginning to fulfill its great potential. It was the last state to receive an overall grade that was above average.

ALASKA

General Information

Total Points: 498
Overall Grade: B–

National Rank: 28 of 50
Regional Rank: 10 of 13 (West)

Population: 550,000
Capital: Juneau

Land Area: 570,374 square miles
Largest City: Anchorage

Report Card

Section	Score	Grade
1. History	0	F
2. Terrain	95	A
3. Natural Resources	5	F
4. Resource Conservation	36	D+
5. Environment	57	C+
6. Health	23	D–
7. Children and Families	76	B+
8. Female Equality	70	B
9. Racial Equality	44	C–
10. Housing	46	C
11. Education	75	B+
12. Applied Intelligence	16	F
13. Arts	76	B+
14. Communications	86	A
15. Sports	61	B–
16. Recreation	100	A+
17. Business	63	B–
18. Personal Finances	24	D–
19. Public Safety	54	C
20. Transportation	45	C
21. Politics	83	A–
22. Government	0	F
23. National Relations	79	B+
24. International Relations	33	D
25. Future	14	F
Overall	498	B–

Record with Neighboring States (0–0)

Neighbor	Neighbor's Score	Winner
(None)		

Category Scores of 100 (22)

Section	Category
Terrain	Inland Water
Terrain	Elevation Variation
Environment	Superfund Sites
Environment	Environmental Spending
Health	Major Causes of Death
Children and Families	Birth Weight
Female Equality	Women in Business
Racial Equality	Minority Businesses
Housing	Housing Age
Education	High School Graduates
Education	Education Spending
Communications	Broadcasting Stations
Communications	Library Spending
Sports	High School Athletes
Recreation	Park Visitors
Recreation	Movies and Videos
Recreation	Restaurants and Bars
Business	Gross State Product
Public Safety	Public Safety Spending
Politics	Political Party Competition
National Relations	Federal Spending
Future	Population Density

Category Scores of 0 (26)

Section	Category
History	Statehood
History	Historic Places
History	Historic Natives
History	Presidential Candidates
Natural Resources	Farm Marketings
Natural Resources	Nonfuel Mining
Resource Conservation	Petroleum Consumption
Resource Conservation	Natural Gas Consumption
Health	Specialists
Female Equality	Violence Against Women
Housing	Property Taxes
Applied Intelligence	Doctoral Degrees
Applied Intelligence	MacArthur Fellows
Communications	Cable Television
Sports	College Champions
Sports	Professional Champions
Sports	Spectator Seats
Personal Finances	Income Growth
Politics	Electoral Votes
Government	State Taxes
Government	State Debt
Government	Government Employees
National Relations	*Fortune* 500 Companies
National Relations	Student Migration
International Relations	Agricultural Exports
Future	Future Political Power

29. Montana (C+)

FINAL STANDINGS

Montana tops the states that have grades in the C range. It is no. 29 nationally, no. 11 in the West, and no. 14 among small states.

BEST SECTIONS

Politics (92 points)—Montana residents believe in political participation; only Minnesota has a higher voter turnout rate. Legislature membership is rotated more frequently here than in most states.

Public Safety (90)—This certainly is not the wild West. Montana has the nation's fifth-lowest violent crime rate.

Recreation (88)—Montana is one of the best places to experience the great outdoors or see a film. That's because it's among the top five states for park visitors and the availability of movie theaters and video rental stores.

WORST SECTIONS

History (8 points)—Montana never has been home to a presidential nominee. It joins Alaska and Arizona in having the fewest native sons and daughters in the history books.

Business (15)—Montana is one of the weakest states in manufacturing and retail trade. Its rate of economic growth is well below average.

Racial Equality (18)—There are wide economic and educational gaps between whites and minorities in Montana.

NEIGHBORS

South Dakota is the only neighbor that Montana defeats in quality-of-life showdowns. It loses to Idaho, North Dakota, and Wyoming.

BIGGEST SURPRISE

Montana has carefully cultivated its image as a state of unspoiled wilderness. But the reality is that it did no better than a C in the Environment section. Utah and Louisiana are the only states with higher rates of toxic emissions.

THE BOTTOM LINE

Montana has room to grow—and room for improvement. High priority should be given to cleaning the environment, bettering conditions for minorities, and upgrading the economic climate.

MONTANA

General Information

Total Points: 488
Overall Grade: C+

National Rank: 29 of 50
Regional Rank: 11 of 13 (West)

Population: 799,000
Capital: Helena

Land Area: 145,556 square miles
Largest City: Billings

Report Card

Section	Score	Grade
1. History	8	F
2. Terrain	78	B+
3. Natural Resources	31	D
4. Resource Conservation	49	C
5. Environment	47	C
6. Health	62	B–
7. Children and Families	57	C+
8. Female Equality	63	B–
9. Racial Equality	18	F
10. Housing	61	B–
11. Education	69	B
12. Applied Intelligence	25	D
13. Arts	46	C
14. Communications	62	B–
15. Sports	35	D+
16. Recreation	88	A
17. Business	15	F
18. Personal Finances	22	D–
19. Public Safety	90	A
20. Transportation	49	C
21. Politics	92	A
22. Government	50	C
23. National Relations	28	D
24. International Relations	20	D–
25. Future	42	C–
Overall	488	C+

Record with Neighboring States (1–3)

Neighbor	Neighbor's Score	Winner
Idaho	521	Idaho by 33
North Dakota	504	North Dakota by 16
South Dakota	476	Montana by 12
Wyoming	539	Wyoming by 51

Category Scores of 100 (5)

Section	Category
Environment	Superfund Sites
Female Equality	Violence Against Women
Politics	Voter Turnout
International Relations	Overseas Population
Future	Population Density

Category Scores of 0 (9)

Section	Category
History	Historic Natives
History	Presidential Candidates
Terrain	Ocean Shoreline
Sports	Professional Champions
Sports	Spectator Seats
Personal Finances	Upper Incomes
Politics	Electoral Votes
National Relations	*Fortune* 500 Companies
Future	Future Political Power

30. Florida (C+)

FINAL STANDINGS

Florida is just no. 30 on the national scale, but it is second only to Virginia in the South. It also is no. 8 among the 13 large states.

BEST SECTIONS

Future (100 points)—No state faces a brighter future than Florida, the leader in this section. It is projected to be third among the 50 states in population growth and fourth in job growth between now and 2020.

Government (92)—Florida's administration is streamlined. Only Hawaii and Virginia have smaller ratios of governmental units.

Natural Resources (82)—Florida is an agricultural powerhouse, one of 10 states with farm marketings of more than $100,000 per square mile.

WORST SECTIONS

Public Safety (0 points)—The violence in Miami is well-known, but the problem isn't confined to that single city. Florida has America's highest rates of violent crimes and all crimes.

Applied Intelligence (19)—Florida is below the national average for college graduates. It trains fewer doctoral candidates than most states.

Health (21)—An elderly population is the main reason that Florida has the nation's third-highest death rate from heart disease, cancer, and strokes.

NEIGHBORS

Florida's most prominent neighbors are the Atlantic Ocean and the Gulf of Mexico. It easily defeats the two states it borders, Alabama and Georgia.

BIGGEST SURPRISE

Millions flock to Florida for sun and fun every year, especially every winter. But the state isn't quite as fun as most people expect. It did no better than a grade of D in the Recreation section.

THE BOTTOM LINE

Florida already is a quality-of-life leader in the South, but it has a great deal of work to do if it wants the same status on the national level.

FLORIDA

General Information

Total Points: 483
Overall Grade: C+

National Rank: 30 of 50
Regional Rank: 2 of 13 (South)

Population: 12,938,000
Capital: Tallahassee

Land Area: 53,997 square miles
Largest City: Jacksonville

Report Card

Section	Score	Grade
1. History	34	D
2. Terrain	60	B–
3. Natural Resources	82	A–
4. Resource Conservation	81	A–
5. Environment	38	D+
6. Health	21	D–
7. Children and Families	43	C–
8. Female Equality	37	D+
9. Racial Equality	41	C–
10. Housing	30	D
11. Education	22	D–
12. Applied Intelligence	19	F
13. Arts	45	C
14. Communications	59	C+
15. Sports	28	D
16. Recreation	34	D
17. Business	53	C
18. Personal Finances	52	C
19. Public Safety	0	F
20. Transportation	55	C+
21. Politics	54	C
22. Government	92	A
23. National Relations	78	B+
24. International Relations	72	B
25. Future	100	A+
Overall	483	C+

Record with Neighboring States (2–0)

Neighbor	Neighbor's Score	Winner
Alabama	303	Florida by 180
Georgia	426	Florida by 57

Category Scores of 100 (4)

Section	Category
History	European Settlement
Business	Economic Growth
Government	Government Units
National Relations	Population Influx

Category Scores of 0 (10)

Section	Category
History	Historic Natives
History	Presidential Candidates
Terrain	Elevation Variation
Natural Resources	Coal Reserves
Health	Major Causes of Death
Housing	Housing Size
Sports	High School Athletes
Public Safety	All Crimes
Public Safety	Violent Crimes
Politics	Political Party Competition

31. South Dakota (C+)

FINAL STANDINGS

South Dakota is no. 31 nationally, no. 7 in the Midwest, and no. 15 among America's small states.

BEST SECTIONS

Resource Conservation (95 points)—Waste not, want not. That's the rule in South Dakota, which ranks fourth in America in the use of renewable energy.

Public Safety (83)—Only West Virginia and North Dakota have total crime rates that are better than South Dakota's. The state also has the sixth-lowest violent crime rate.

Transportation (76)—This is the place for anyone in love with the open road. It is second only to North Dakota in road mileage per 100,000 residents.

WORST SECTIONS

Natural Resources (0 points)—Last place. South Dakota's landscape is stark, some would say bleak. That also is true of its inventory of resources. It has very little timber, coal, or oil.

Racial Equality (0)—South Dakota has America's smallest concentration of minority-owned businesses. Mississippi and Louisiana are the only states with wider income gaps between whites and nonwhites.

History (4)—George McGovern probably received more acclaim than any other South Dakota resident in this century. And you know what happened to him.

NEIGHBORS

South Dakota loses the all-important battle with North Dakota. It also loses to everyone else. Its record is 0–6.

BIGGEST SURPRISE

Any state this far north is supposed to be free of prejudice. So goes the stereotype. But South Dakota actually is one of America's most intolerant states, earning an F in the Racial Equality section and a D+ in Female Equality.

THE BOTTOM LINE

There is nowhere to go but up. South Dakota is surrounded by states that offer a superior quality of life.

SOUTH DAKOTA

General Information

Total Points: 476
Overall Grade: C+

National Rank: 31 of 50
Regional Rank: 7 of 12 (Midwest)

Population: 696,000
Capital: Pierre

Land Area: 75,898 square miles
Largest City: Sioux Falls

Report Card

Section	Score	Grade
1. History	4	F
2. Terrain	59	C+
3. Natural Resources	0	F
4. Resource Conservation	95	A
5. Environment	45	C
6. Health	68	B
7. Children and Families	73	B
8. Female Equality	38	D+
9. Racial Equality	0	F
10. Housing	70	B
11. Education	53	C
12. Applied Intelligence	21	D–
13. Arts	39	D+
14. Communications	70	B
15. Sports	22	D–
16. Recreation	57	C+
17. Business	18	F
18. Personal Finances	48	C
19. Public Safety	83	A–
20. Transportation	76	B+
21. Politics	56	C+
22. Government	44	C–
23. National Relations	14	F
24. International Relations	28	D
25. Future	47	C
Overall	476	C+

Record with Neighboring States (0–6)

Neighbor	Neighbor's Score	Winner
Iowa	523	Iowa by 47
Minnesota	608	Minnesota by 132
Montana	488	Montana by 12
Nebraska	526	Nebraska by 50
North Dakota	504	North Dakota by 28
Wyoming	539	Wyoming by 63

Category Scores of 100 (9)

Section	Category
Environment	Superfund Sites
Health	Family Doctors
Health	Hospital Costs
Arts	Museums and Galleries
Personal Finances	Unemployment
Transportation	Road Mileage
Government	State Taxes
International Relations	Overseas Population
Future	Population Density

Category Scores of 0 (18)

Section	Category
History	European Settlement
History	Historic Natives
Terrain	Ocean Shoreline
Natural Resources	Crude Oil Reserves
Natural Resources	Coal Reserves
Health	Specialists
Racial Equality	Minority Businesses
Applied Intelligence	Patents
Applied Intelligence	Research and Development
Sports	College Champions
Sports	Professional Champions
Sports	Spectator Seats
Transportation	Public Transit Usage
Politics	Electoral Votes
Government	Government Units
National Relations	*Fortune* 500 Companies
International Relations	Foreign Employers
Future	Future Political Power

32. Kansas (C)

FINAL STANDINGS

Kansas is truly average, the first state with a straight C. It ranks 32nd among the 50 states, no. 8 in the Midwest, and no. 9 on the list of medium-size states.

BEST SECTIONS

Politics (75 points)—Just six states have higher frequencies of competitive elections. Voter turnout in Kansas is substantially above the national average.

Education (72)—Kansas is among the 10 states with the best graduation rates for high schoolers.

Housing (68)—It's easy to find a bargain in Kansas. Its housing costs are the third-lowest in America, behind only Iowa and Indiana.

WORST SECTIONS

Natural Resources (19 points)—Farm marketings are reasonably healthy, but the story otherwise is a familiar one on the plains. There is some timber, coal, and oil in Kansas, but not all that much.

History (20)—The dispute over "Bloody Kansas" hastened the start of the Civil War. Things have been much quieter ever since.

Sports (22)—Kansas has no major-league teams and few college champions.

NEIGHBORS

It's a draw. Kansas wins its quality-of-life showdowns with Missouri and Oklahoma, but loses to Colorado and Nebraska.

BIGGEST SURPRISE

You would think that a largely rural, medium-size state like Kansas would be one of the safest places in America. But it earned just a C in the Public Safety section. That doesn't make it one of the nation's crime capitals, but it isn't a haven, either.

THE BOTTOM LINE

Kansas has room to improve in whatever field you choose. It didn't receive an A in any of the 25 sections.

KANSAS

General Information

Total Points: 466
Overall Grade: C

National Rank: 32 of 50
Regional Rank: 8 of 12 (Midwest)

Population: 2,478,000
Capital: Topeka

Land Area: 81,823 square miles
Largest City: Wichita

Report Card

Section	Score	Grade
1. History	20	D–
2. Terrain	28	D
3. Natural Resources	19	F
4. Resource Conservation	61	B–
5. Environment	36	D+
6. Health	63	B–
7. Children and Families	62	B–
8. Female Equality	61	B–
9. Racial Equality	29	D
10. Housing	68	B
11. Education	72	B
12. Applied Intelligence	30	D
13. Arts	37	D+
14. Communications	51	C
15. Sports	22	D–
16. Recreation	38	D+
17. Business	41	C–
18. Personal Finances	47	C
19. Public Safety	53	C
20. Transportation	45	C
21. Politics	75	B+
22. Government	64	B–
23. National Relations	31	D
24. International Relations	32	D
25. Future	41	C–
Overall	466	C

Record with Neighboring States (2–2)

Neighbor	Neighbor's Score	Winner
Colorado	616	Colorado by 150
Missouri	427	Kansas by 39
Nebraska	526	Nebraska by 60
Oklahoma	341	Kansas by 125

Category Scores of 100 (1)

Section	Category
Government	State Debt

Category Scores of 0 (7)

Section	Category
History	Historic Natives
History	Presidential Candidates
Terrain	Ocean Shoreline
Resource Conservation	Renewable Energy
Sports	Professional Champions
Sports	Spectator Seats
Recreation	Park Visitors

33. North Carolina (C)

FINAL STANDINGS

Threes are wild for North Carolina: It is no. 33 nationally and no. 3 in the South. It also holds ninth place among large states.

BEST SECTIONS

Government (93 points)—The state government keeps a close watch on its finances. North Carolina carries less debt than all states but Kansas and Texas.

Resource Conservation (79)—North Carolina is among the 12 states that are most efficient in the use of natural gas and petroleum products.

Housing (74)—Rents are reasonable, property taxes are fairly low, and the housing stock is relatively new.

WORST SECTIONS

Sports (9 points)—North Carolina is the hotbed of college basketball, isn't it? Well, yes, but that's about all. Participation in high school sports is low, and only six states turn out fewer Olympic athletes.

National Relations (13)—The federal government spends less money per person in North Carolina than in all but three states. State corporations have little clout on the national scene.

Education (14)—North Carolina students do worse on standardized tests than their counterparts in 48 states; only Mississippi has a lower average score.

NEIGHBORS

North Carolina had to settle for an overall grade of C, but that's still better than most of its neighbors. Its head-to-head record is 3–1.

BIGGEST SURPRISE

North Carolina is considered a progressive, enlightened state, a model for the rest of the South. But the image isn't supported by its grades: C– in Female Equality, D in Children and Families, D in Racial Equality, F in Education.

THE BOTTOM LINE

North Carolina needs to hit the books. An improved educational system is its best hope for improving its quality of life.

NORTH CAROLINA

General Information

Total Points: 457
Overall Grade: C

National Rank: 33 of 50
Regional Rank: 3 of 13 (South)

Population: 6,629,000
Capital: Raleigh

Land Area: 48,718 square miles
Largest City: Charlotte

Report Card

Section	Score	Grade
1. History	39	D+
2. Terrain	64	B–
3. Natural Resources	62	B–
4. Resource Conservation	79	B+
5. Environment	58	C+
6. Health	27	D
7. Children and Families	26	D
8. Female Equality	43	C–
9. Racial Equality	26	D
10. Housing	74	B
11. Education	14	F
12. Applied Intelligence	30	D
13. Arts	33	D
14. Communications	41	C–
15. Sports	9	F
16. Recreation	36	D+
17. Business	58	C+
18. Personal Finances	44	C–
19. Public Safety	39	D+
20. Transportation	53	C
21. Politics	49	C
22. Government	93	A
23. National Relations	13	F
24. International Relations	73	B
25. Future	53	C
Overall	457	C

Record with Neighboring States (3–1)

Neighbor	Neighbor's Score	Winner
Georgia	426	North Carolina by 31
South Carolina	359	North Carolina by 98
Tennessee	386	North Carolina by 71
Virginia	560	Virginia by 103

Category Scores of 100 (2)

Section	Category
Business	Manufacturing Productivity
Transportation	Pavement Condition

Category Scores of 0 (6)

Section	Category
History	Presidential Candidates
Terrain	Rangeland
Natural Resources	Crude Oil Reserves
Natural Resources	Coal Reserves
Education	Standardized Tests
Sports	Professional Champions

34. Arizona (C)

FINAL STANDINGS

Arizona is no. 34 nationally, right in the middle of the five states with C's. It also is no. 12 in the West and no. 10 among medium-size states.

BEST SECTIONS

Future (95 points)—Arizona's strength lies in what is yet to come. A low population density leaves plenty of room for expansion. Arizona is projected to have the nation's second-fastest rate of population growth until 2020.

Government (84)—The state debt is relatively low, and the state government has a lean work force.

Resource Conservation (82)—Arizona uses less petroleum per capita than any other state.

WORST SECTIONS

History (9 points)—Arizona, admitted to the Union in 1912, was America's youngest state until Alaska and Hawaii came along.

Personal Finances (20)—Per capita income is low, and it increased at a disappointingly slow pace in the late 1980s and early 1990s. Only Alaska had a slower rate of income growth.

Public Safety (24)—Texas and Florida are the only states with total crime rates higher than Arizona's. Police are understaffed.

NEIGHBORS

Arizona is outclassed by four neighbors. Its only victory comes over no. 41 New Mexico.

BIGGEST SURPRISE

Arizona is a rapidly growing state that always has plenty of construction. Housing must be excellent, right? Wrong. Renting is expensive in Arizona, and housing units are small by national standards. The result is a grade of C in the Housing section.

THE BOTTOM LINE

The Arizona sun will continue to attract thousands of northern settlers each year, but many are bound to be unhappy with the state's undistinguished quality of life.

ARIZONA

General Information

Total Points: 455
Overall Grade: C

National Rank: 34 of 50
Regional Rank: 12 of 13

Population: 3,665,000
Capital: Phoenix

Land Area: 113,642 square miles
Largest City: Phoenix

Report Card

Section	Score	Grade
1. History	9	F
2. Terrain	57	C+
3. Natural Resources	35	D+
4. Resource Conservation	82	A–
5. Environment	40	C–
6. Health	26	D
7. Children and Families	41	C–
8. Female Equality	70	B
9. Racial Equality	33	D
10. Housing	45	C
11. Education	53	C
12. Applied Intelligence	46	C
13. Arts	28	D
14. Communications	36	D+
15. Sports	32	D
16. Recreation	34	D
17. Business	41	C–
18. Personal Finances	20	D–
19. Public Safety	24	D–
20. Transportation	34	D
21. Politics	60	B–
22. Government	84	A–
23. National Relations	64	B–
24. International Relations	41	C–
25. Future	95	A
Overall	455	C

Record with Neighboring States (1–4)

Neighbor	Neighbor's Score	Winner
California	601	California by 146
Colorado	616	Colorado by 161
Nevada	507	Nevada by 52
New Mexico	413	Arizona by 42
Utah	559	Utah by 104

Category Scores of 100 (4)

Section	Category
Resource Conservation	Petroleum Consumption
Female Equality	Women in Government
Future	Projected Population Growth
Future	Projected Job Growth

Category Scores of 0 (9)

Section	Category
History	Historic Natives
Terrain	Ocean Shoreline
Terrain	Inland Water
Natural Resources	Crude Oil Reserves
Natural Resources	Coal Reserves
Environment	Drinking Water
Health	Hospital Costs
Education	High School Dropouts
Personal Finances	Income Growth

35. Ohio (C)

FINAL STANDINGS

Ohio is in the bottom half of all three rankings. It is no. 35 overall, no. 9 in the Midwest, and no. 10 among large states.

BEST SECTIONS

Government (82 points)—Ohio's government is a fairly tight ship. It has America's eighth-lowest ratio of government employees. State taxes and debt are less than the national averages.

Politics (77)—Ohio once prided itself on being the birthplace of presidents. It now contents itself with mirroring the results of presidential elections more consistently than all but five states.

Resource Conservation (72)—This is one of the 10 most efficient states in the use of petroleum products.

WORST SECTIONS

National Relations (20 points)—Ohio doesn't have much contact with outsiders. More than three-quarters of its residents were born in the state. Domestic travel spending in Ohio is among the lowest in the country.

Health (21)—Ohio is below the national averages for availability of both family doctors and specialists.

Racial Equality (21)—There are large income and housing gaps between whites and minorities.

NEIGHBORS

Ohio is one of the lower-ranked states, but it's still better than most of its neighbors. It has a 4–1 record in quality-of-life showdowns. Its only loss is to Pennsylvania.

BIGGEST SURPRISE

A state with more than 10 million residents certainly would have tremendous national connections, right? Not Ohio. It attracts relatively few tourists and scant federal spending per person. The result was a D– in the National Relations section.

THE BOTTOM LINE

Ohio needs improvement across the board. It received only one A and four B's in the 25 sections.

510 OHIO

General Information

Total Points: 453
Overall Grade: C

National Rank: 35 of 50
Regional Rank: 9 of 12 (Midwest)

Population: 10,847,000
Capital: Columbus

Land Area: 40,953 square miles
Largest City: Columbus

Report Card

Section	Score	Grade
1. History	51	C
2. Terrain	27	D
3. Natural Resources	71	B
4. Resource Conservation	72	B
5. Environment	31	D
6. Health	21	D–
7. Children and Families	45	C
8. Female Equality	43	C–
9. Racial Equality	21	D–
10. Housing	70	B
11. Education	53	C
12. Applied Intelligence	31	D
13. Arts	33	D
14. Communications	58	C+
15. Sports	42	C–
16. Recreation	35	D+
17. Business	45	C
18. Personal Finances	28	D
19. Public Safety	38	D+
20. Transportation	41	C–
21. Politics	77	B+
22. Government	82	A–
23. National Relations	20	D–
24. International Relations	57	C+
25. Future	43	C–
Overall	453	C

Record with Neighboring States (4–1)

Neighbor	Neighbor's Score	Winner
Indiana	438	Ohio by 15
Kentucky	357	Ohio by 96
Michigan	426	Ohio by 27
Pennsylvania	517	Pennsylvania by 64
West Virginia	349	Ohio by 104

Category Scores of 100 (0)

Section	Category
(None)	

Category Scores of 0 (2)

Section	Category
Terrain	Ocean Shoreline
Terrain	Rangeland

36. Indiana (C)

FINAL STANDINGS

Indiana is right behind neighboring Ohio, ranking no. 36 overall and no. 10 in the Midwest. It also is no. 11 among the 20 medium-size states.

BEST SECTIONS

Government (90 points)—Indiana's founders believed in brevity; only Vermont and New Hampshire have shorter constitutions. State taxes and debt are below the national averages.

Housing (72)—Affordable is the word that best describes housing in Indiana. Its average purchase price is lower than all states but Iowa; its average rent is below all but three states.

International Relations (67)—Indiana is in the national top 10 in exports of both manufactured goods and agricultural products.

WORST SECTIONS

Terrain (0 points)—Indiana will never be called scenic. It has few forests or lakes and no mountains.

National Relations (18)—The federal government spends less money per person in Indiana than anywhere else. Only two states have lower revenues from domestic travel.

Racial Equality (23)—There are serious income and housing disparities between white and black residents of Indiana.

NEIGHBORS

It's a draw. Indiana defeats Kentucky and Michigan, but loses to Illinois and Ohio.

BIGGEST SURPRISE

Indiana is supposed to be a state that retains good midwestern family values, but it did no better than a C– in the Children and Families section. A higher percentage of marriages end in divorce in Indiana than anywhere but Oklahoma.

THE BOTTOM LINE

Indiana just barely made it to the middle range of the national rankings. It was the final state to earn a straight C.

INDIANA

General Information

Total Points: 438
Overall Grade: C

National Rank: 36 of 50
Regional Rank: 10 of 12 (Midwest)

Population: 5,544,000
Capital: Indianapolis

Land Area: 35,870 square miles
Largest City: Indianapolis

Report Card

Section	Score	Grade
1. History	32	D
2. Terrain	0	F
3. Natural Resources	61	B–
4. Resource Conservation	64	B–
5. Environment	42	C–
6. Health	32	D
7. Children and Families	43	C–
8. Female Equality	52	C
9. Racial Equality	23	D–
10. Housing	72	B
11. Education	35	D+
12. Applied Intelligence	31	D
13. Arts	26	D
14. Communications	66	B
15. Sports	26	D
16. Recreation	39	D+
17. Business	46	C
18. Personal Finances	35	D+
19. Public Safety	47	C
20. Transportation	38	D+
21. Politics	51	C
22. Government	90	A
23. National Relations	18	F
24. International Relations	67	B
25. Future	46	C
Overall	438	C

Record with Neighboring States (2–2)

Neighbor	Neighbor's Score	Winner
Illinois	505	Illinois by 67
Kentucky	357	Indiana by 81
Michigan	426	Indiana by 12
Ohio	453	Ohio by 15

Category Scores of 100 (3)

Section	Category
Housing	Housing Costs
Business	Manufacturing Productivity
Government	State Constitution Length

Category Scores of 0 (6)

Section	Category
Terrain	Ocean Shoreline
Terrain	Inland Water
Terrain	Rangeland
Children and Families	Marriage Stability
National Relations	Federal Spending
National Relations	Domestic Travel

37. Missouri (C–)

FINAL STANDINGS

Missouri is no. 37 nationally, no. 11 in the Midwest, and no. 12 among medium-size states.

BEST SECTIONS

Resource Conservation (79 points)—Missouri does better than the average state when it comes to conserving water, petroleum products, and natural gas.

Government (76)—Missouri is among the 10 states that have the lowest taxes and the smallest ratios of government employees.

Sports (72)—This is a great state for fans of major-league sports. Only Colorado has more spectator seats available at professional games; only Massachusetts and Maryland have had larger proportions of pro champions.

WORST SECTIONS

Health (16 points)—Just four states have higher rates of death from heart disease, cancer, and strokes. Missouri has one of the nation's lowest availability rates for family doctors.

Terrain (17)—This is a state with great rivers, the Mississippi and the Missouri. But it has relatively few lakes or forests, and the Ozark Mountains aren't as high as they sound.

Applied Intelligence (26)—Missouri residents receive fewer patents than you would expect.

NEIGHBORS

Missouri has no shortage of neighbors, eight in all. It defeats four in quality-of-life pairings and loses to the other four.

BIGGEST SURPRISE

This is a state with a large, respected public university and two major metropolitan areas, St. Louis and Kansas City. You would expect Missouri to have a substantial amount of brain power as a result, but it earned just a D in the Applied Intelligence section.

THE BOTTOM LINE

Missouri is known as the Show Me state, but its residents won't be happy when shown the bottom line of their report card: 37th place, C–.

MISSOURI

General Information

Total Points: 427
Overall Grade: C–

National Rank: 37 of 50
Regional Rank: 11 of 12 (Midwest)

Population: 5,117,000
Capital: Jefferson City

Land Area: 68,898 square miles
Largest City: Kansas City

Report Card

Section	Score	Grade
1. History	29	D
2. Terrain	17	F
3. Natural Resources	38	D+
4. Resource Conservation	79	B+
5. Environment	27	D
6. Health	16	F
7. Children and Families	43	C–
8. Female Equality	53	C
9. Racial Equality	29	D
10. Housing	70	B
11. Education	37	D+
12. Applied Intelligence	26	D
13. Arts	41	C–
14. Communications	39	D+
15. Sports	72	B
16. Recreation	42	C–
17. Business	49	C
18. Personal Finances	33	D
19. Public Safety	27	D
20. Transportation	33	D
21. Politics	62	B–
22. Government	76	B+
23. National Relations	48	C
24. International Relations	31	D
25. Future	49	C
Overall	427	C–

Record with Neighboring States (4–4)

Neighbor	Neighbor's Score	Winner
Arkansas	323	Missouri by 104
Illinois	505	Illinois by 78
Iowa	523	Iowa by 96
Kansas	466	Kansas by 39
Kentucky	357	Missouri by 70
Nebraska	526	Nebraska by 99
Oklahoma	341	Missouri by 86
Tennessee	386	Missouri by 41

Category Scores of 100 (1)

Section	Category
Sports	Spectator Seats

Category Scores of 0 (4)

Section	Category
Terrain	Ocean Shoreline
Terrain	Rangeland
Natural Resources	Crude Oil Reserves
Environment	Waste Generation

38. Georgia (C–)

FINAL STANDINGS

Georgia does no better than no. 38 nationally and no. 11 among the 13 large states, but it still stands tall in its home region. It is no. 4 in the South.

BEST SECTIONS

Natural Resources (82 points)—Georgia is among the nation's leaders in timber reserves and nonfuel mining. It also is a moderate success in agriculture and has just a bit of coal.

Government (82)—Georgia has the fifth-lowest state debt in the country. Its taxes also are below the national average.

Resource Conservation (81)—Georgia gets more than 15 percent of its energy from renewable sources. Only 11 other states can say that.

WORST SECTIONS

Education (5 points)—Just three states have standardized test scores that are worse than Georgia's; just four states have higher dropout rates.

Politics (10)—Apathy is the watchword in Georgia. South Carolina is the only state with a lower voter turnout rate.

Health (18)—Average life expectancy in Georgia is less than in 46 states. There are relatively few family doctors.

Children and Families (18)—Only Delaware has a worse infant mortality rate than Georgia.

NEIGHBORS

Georgia has the quality-of-life edge on three of its neighbors. It loses to Florida and North Carolina.

BIGGEST SURPRISE

Several southern states are known for their laxity in enforcing environmental regulations. Georgia is an exception, earning an A– in the Environment section. It generates less waste per person than all but two states.

THE BOTTOM LINE

Georgia is emerging as a national power, but it still is far behind most other major states when it comes to quality of life.

GEORGIA

General Information

Total Points: 426
Overall Grade: C-

National Rank: 38 of 50
Regional Rank: 4 of 13 (South)

Population: 6,478,000
Capital: Atlanta

Land Area: 57,919 square miles
Largest City: Atlanta

Report Card

Section	Score	Grade
1. History	35	D+
2. Terrain	48	C
3. Natural Resources	82	A–
4. Resource Conservation	81	A–
5. Environment	80	A–
6. Health	18	F
7. Children and Families	18	F
8. Female Equality	29	D
9. Racial Equality	27	D
10. Housing	69	B
11. Education	5	F
12. Applied Intelligence	20	D–
13. Arts	25	D
14. Communications	21	D–
15. Sports	25	D
16. Recreation	32	D
17. Business	58	C+
18. Personal Finances	39	D+
19. Public Safety	34	D
20. Transportation	56	C+
21. Politics	10	F
22. Government	82	A–
23. National Relations	30	D
24. International Relations	52	C
25. Future	67	B
Overall	426	C–

Record with Neighboring States (3–2)

Neighbor	Neighbor's Score	Winner
Alabama	303	Georgia by 123
Florida	483	Florida by 57
North Carolina	457	North Carolina by 31
South Carolina	359	Georgia by 67
Tennessee	386	Georgia by 40

Category Scores of 100 (0)

Section	Category
(None)	

Category Scores of 0 (5)

Section	Category
Terrain	Rangeland
Natural Resources	Crude Oil Reserves
Natural Resources	Coal Reserves
Children and Families	Infant Mortality
Politics	Voter Turnout

39. Michigan (C-)

FINAL STANDINGS

Michigan loses a tie-breaker with Georgia to end up no. 39 overall. It also is 12th (and last) in the Midwest and 12th (and next to last) among the nation's large states.

BEST SECTIONS

Government (84 points)—Michigan does better than most states when it comes to controlling its debt and maintaining a lean government work force. State taxes are below the national average.

Resource Conservation (83)—An unexpected irony in this automobile-producing state: Michigan consumes less petroleum per capita than any state but Arizona. It also is efficient in its use of electricity.

Politics (77)—Voter turnout is better than the national average, and most elections in Michigan are competitive.

WORST SECTIONS

National Relations (10 points)—Outsiders are not particularly welcome in Michigan. Just 22.2 percent of its residents were born out of state. Only four states take in less per capita revenue from domestic travel.

Racial Equality (13)—Michigan has the nation's second-worst disparity in housing values. Pennsylvania is the lone state with a wider gap between the value of homes owned by whites and those owned by minorities.

Personal Finances (19)—Only three states had income growth slower than Michigan's in the late 1980s and early 1990s; just two states had worse unemployment.

NEIGHBORS

A strikeout. Michigan loses quality-of-life showdowns with all three of its American neighbors.

BIGGEST SURPRISE

You would expect an industrial giant such as Michigan to have strong clout and connections across the country. But it actually is isolated and lacks influence, which is why it earned an F in the National Relations section.

522 THE BOTTOM LINE

Michigan is the worst state in the Midwest. Major improvements are needed in its economic climate, its health-care system, and the way it treats women and minorities.

MICHIGAN

General Information

Total Points: 426
Overall Grade: C–

National Rank: 39 of 50
Regional Rank: 12 of 12 (Midwest)

Population: 9,295,000
Capital: Lansing

Land Area: 56,809 square miles
Largest City: Detroit

Report Card

Section	Score	Grade
1. History	34	D
2. Terrain	45	C
3. Natural Resources	71	B
4. Resource Conservation	83	A–
5. Environment	45	C
6. Health	21	D–
7. Children and Families	44	C–
8. Female Equality	27	D
9. Racial Equality	13	F
10. Housing	56	C+
11. Education	62	B–
12. Applied Intelligence	37	D+
13. Arts	24	D–
14. Communications	54	C
15. Sports	37	D+
16. Recreation	24	D–
17. Business	45	C
18. Personal Finances	19	F
19. Public Safety	22	D–
20. Transportation	29	D
21. Politics	77	B+
22. Government	84	A–
23. National Relations	10	F
24. International Relations	46	C
25. Future	47	C
Overall	426	C–

Record with Neighboring States (0–3)

Neighbor	Neighbor's Score	Winner
Indiana	438	Indiana by 12
Ohio	453	Ohio by 27
Wisconsin	558	Wisconsin by 132

Category Scores of 100 (3)

Section	Category
Terrain	Inland Water
Resource Conservation	Petroleum Consumption
Environment	Drinking Water

Category Scores of 0 (4)

Section	Category
Terrain	Ocean Shoreline
Terrain	Rangeland
Natural Resources	Coal Reserves
Racial Equality	Housing Disparity

40. Texas (C–)

FINAL STANDINGS

Texas is no. 40 on the national list. Its other rankings are wildly different: It is a respectable no. 5 of the 13 southern states, but it is dead last among the 13 large states.

BEST SECTIONS

Future (83 points)—Low population density means there still is plenty of room for growth. Texas is expected to tie New York with the nation's second-largest number of electoral votes by 2020.

Government (70)—Kansas is the only state that carries less debt than Texas. Only three states have lower taxes.

Terrain (64)—Texas truly is a home on the range; more than 57 percent of the state is rangeland. But it also has ocean beaches and mountains as high as 8,700 feet.

WORST SECTIONS

Public Safety (8 points)—Only Florida has a worse total crime rate than Texas. The violent crime rate also is among America's 10 worst. Police departments in Texas are understaffed.

Communications (11)—Cable television penetration is weak, library spending is low, and the telephone network misses almost 9 percent of all homes.

Recreation (18)—Just two states have lower concentrations of movie theaters and video rental stores.

NEIGHBORS

Texas might be no. 40 overall, but it still beats all four of its neighbors in quality-of-life pairings.

BIGGEST SURPRISE

Texas is supposed to be a hotbed for athletics, especially football. So why does it get just a C– in the Sports section? Because it turns out very few Olympic athletes, and its professional teams rarely win championships.

526 THE BOTTOM LINE

Texans are prone to bragging, but their state really doesn't have much to brag about. Its quality of life is inferior to that of any other state with at least 6 million residents.

TEXAS

General Information

Total Points: 416
Overall Grade: C–

National Rank: 40 of 50
Regional Rank: 5 of 13 (South)

Population: 16,987,000
Capital: Austin

Land Area: 261,914 square miles
Largest City: Houston

Report Card

Section	Score	Grade
1. History	38	D+
2. Terrain	64	B–
3. Natural Resources	57	C+
4. Resource Conservation	39	D+
5. Environment	43	C–
6. Health	29	D
7. Children and Families	60	B–
8. Female Equality	32	D
9. Racial Equality	42	C–
10. Housing	55	C+
11. Education	31	D
12. Applied Intelligence	35	D+
13. Arts	26	D
14. Communications	11	F
15. Sports	43	C–
16. Recreation	18	F
17. Business	39	D+
18. Personal Finances	25	D
19. Public Safety	8	F
20. Transportation	45	C
21. Politics	62	B–
22. Government	70	B
23. National Relations	23	D–
24. International Relations	63	B–
25. Future	83	A–
Overall	416	C–

Record with Neighboring States (4–0)

Neighbor	Neighbor's Score	Winner
Arkansas	323	Texas by 93
Louisiana	239	Texas by 177
New Mexico	413	Texas by 3
Oklahoma	341	Texas by 75

Category Scores of 100 (3)

Section	Category
Natural Resources	Crude Oil Reserves
Government	State Debt
Future	Future Political Power

Category Scores of 0 (5)

Section	Category
History	Historic Natives
Resource Conservation	Renewable Energy
Arts	Arts Funding
Recreation	Park Visitors
Public Safety	All Crimes

41. New Mexico (C–)

FINAL STANDINGS

New Mexico is no. 41 nationally. Its other rankings are at or near the bottom: no. 13 of 13 western states and no. 16 of 17 small states.

BEST SECTIONS

Politics (82 points)—As goes New Mexico, so goes the nation. The state has correctly matched the national result in 20 of the past 21 presidential elections. It also leads the nation with its high percentage of competitive statewide races.

Future (72)—New Mexico is projected to be among the 10 fastest-growing states over the next quarter-century in terms of incomes and jobs.

National Relations (71)—Alaska and Maryland are the only states that receive more federal spending per person than New Mexico.

WORST SECTIONS

Personal Finances (1 point)—New Mexico has the nation's fifth-lowest per capita income. It has a larger percentage of families below the poverty level than any state but Mississippi and Louisiana.

Business (8)—New Mexico's manufacturing and retail sectors both are among the six weakest in the country.

Transportation (9)—Drive defensively in New Mexico. It has the nation's highest rate of deaths in motor vehicle accidents.

NEIGHBORS

New Mexico wins over Oklahoma and barely loses to Texas. Its three other defeats are by substantial margins.

BIGGEST SURPRISE

New Mexico received a C– in the Education section, so you wouldn't expect it to do well in Applied Intelligence. But it did, earning a B. No state gets a larger share of federal research and development funding.

THE BOTTOM LINE

New Mexico is at the bottom of the West's quality-of-life list. It does poorly in the basics, including the Health, Business, Personal Finances, and Public Safety sections.

NEW MEXICO

General Information

Total Points: 413
Overall Grade: C–

National Rank: 41 of 50
Regional Rank: 13 of 13 (West)

Population: 1,515,000
Capital: Santa Fe

Land Area: 121,365 square miles
Largest City: Albuquerque

Report Card

Section	Score	Grade
1. History	24	D–
2. Terrain	63	B–
3. Natural Resources	10	F
4. Resource Conservation	67	B
5. Environment	58	C+
6. Health	37	D+
7. Children and Families	32	D
8. Female Equality	36	D+
9. Racial Equality	55	C+
10. Housing	58	C+
11. Education	43	C–
12. Applied Intelligence	69	B
13. Arts	34	D
14. Communications	26	D
15. Sports	11	F
16. Recreation	44	C–
17. Business	8	F
18. Personal Finances	1	F
19. Public Safety	36	D+
20. Transportation	9	F
21. Politics	82	A–
22. Government	60	B–
23. National Relations	71	B
24. International Relations	26	D
25. Future	72	B
Overall	413	C–

Record with Neighboring States (1–4)

Neighbor	Neighbor's Score	Winner
Arizona	455	Arizona by 42
Colorado	616	Colorado by 203
Oklahoma	341	New Mexico by 72
Texas	416	Texas by 3
Utah	559	Utah by 146

Category Scores of 100 (5)

Section	Category
Racial Equality	Minority Population
Housing	Property Taxes
Applied Intelligence	Research and Development
Politics	Presidential Election Trends
Politics	Political Party Competition

Category Scores of 0 (10)

Section	Category
History	Historic Natives
History	Presidential Candidates
Terrain	Ocean Shoreline
Communications	Telephone Service
Sports	College Champions
Sports	Professional Champions
Sports	Spectator Seats
Personal Finances	Upper Incomes
Transportation	Motor Vehicle Deaths
National Relations	*Fortune* 500 Companies

42. Tennessee (D)

FINAL STANDINGS

Tennessee is no. 42 on the national scale, but it still is in the upper half on the southern list: no. 6 out of 13 states. It also is no. 13 among medium-size states.

BEST SECTIONS

Government (100 points)—First place in the country. Tennessee's government levies the nation's third-lowest taxes, carries little debt, has a lean work force, and is responsible for a relatively small number of governmental units.

Housing (78)—Housing costs are below the national average, and Tennessee is among the 10 states that have the lowest property taxes.

Resource Conservation (70)—Tennessee is reasonably efficient in its use of natural gas and petroleum products.

WORST SECTIONS

Sports (1 point)—The problem begins at an early age: Participation in high school sports is below normal. Tennessee produces very few Olympic athletes, and it has no major-league teams at all.

Education (4)—No state spends less on education than Tennessee. It is among the six states with the largest high school dropout rates and the smallest proportions of college students.

Applied Intelligence (14)—Tennessee is well below average with its ratios of doctoral candidates and patents received.

NEIGHBORS

Tennessee is in competition with eight neighbors, including seven southern states and Missouri. Its overall record is 4–4.

BIGGEST SURPRISE

Tennessee is a state plagued by many problems, which makes it surprising that it finished no. 1 with an A+ in the Government section. Perhaps the explanation is that its government values efficiency above solutions.

THE BOTTOM LINE

Tennessee is the first state to earn a D, a well-deserved grade. It received D's or F's in 16 of the 25 sections.

TENNESSEE

General Information

Total Points: 386
Overall Grade: D

National Rank: 42 of 50
Regional Rank: 6 of 13 (South)

Population: 4,877,000
Capital: Nashville

Land Area: 41,220 square miles
Largest City: Memphis

Report Card

Section	Score	Grade
1. History	35	D+
2. Terrain	39	D+
3. Natural Resources	47	C
4. Resource Conservation	70	B
5. Environment	34	D
6. Health	24	D–
7. Children and Families	34	D
8. Female Equality	28	D
9. Racial Equality	26	D
10. Housing	78	B+
11. Education	4	F
12. Applied Intelligence	14	F
13. Arts	48	C
14. Communications	27	D
15. Sports	1	F
16. Recreation	34	D
17. Business	45	C
18. Personal Finances	32	D
19. Public Safety	48	C
20. Transportation	24	D–
21. Politics	25	D
22. Government	100	A+
23. National Relations	22	D–
24. International Relations	40	C–
25. Future	62	B–
Overall	386	D

Record with Neighboring States (4–4)

Neighbor	Neighbor's Score	Winner
Alabama	303	Tennessee by 83
Arkansas	323	Tennessee by 63
Georgia	426	Georgia by 40
Kentucky	357	Tennessee by 29
Mississippi	268	Tennessee by 118
Missouri	427	Missouri by 41
North Carolina	457	North Carolina by 71
Virginia	560	Virginia by 174

Category Scores of 100 (0)

Section	Category
(None)	

Category Scores of 0 (6)

Section	Category
Terrain	Ocean Shoreline
Terrain	Rangeland
Natural Resources	Crude Oil Reserves
Education	Education Spending
Sports	Professional Champions
Sports	Spectator Seats

43. South Carolina (D)

FINAL STANDINGS

South Carolina is no. 43 nationally, no. 7 in the South, and no. 14 among America's 20 medium-size states.

BEST SECTIONS

Government (80 points)—State taxes and debt both are lower than the national averages. South Carolina has the country's 15th-lowest ratio of governmental units.

Housing (77)—South Carolina is among the 10 states with the lowest rents and the newest housing stocks.

International Relations (75)—Foreign companies control a larger proportion of jobs in South Carolina than anywhere but Delaware and Hawaii. This is a surprisingly strong state in exports of manufactured goods.

WORST SECTIONS

Sports (2 points)—There are no major-league teams in South Carolina, its college teams rarely win championships, and participation in high school athletics is weak.

Public Safety (10)—South Carolina has the nation's largest ratio of prisoners. Only four states have higher rates of violent crimes.

Applied Intelligence (11)—Research and development funding is hard to come by. South Carolina has never had a MacArthur fellow.

Transportation (11)—Only New Mexico has a higher motor vehicle death rate than South Carolina.

NEIGHBORS

South Carolina loses decisively to both of its neighbors, North Carolina and Georgia.

BIGGEST SURPRISE

A medium-size, southern state seems an unlikely candidate to have strong ties with the rest of the world. But South Carolina has exactly such connections, earning a B+ in the International Relations section.

THE BOTTOM LINE

In some respects, South Carolina is lucky to have an overall grade as high as D. It received F's in more than a quarter of all sections (seven of 25).

SOUTH CAROLINA

General Information

Total Points: 359
Overall Grade: D

National Rank: 43 of 50
Regional Rank: 7 of 13 (South)

Population: 3,487,000
Capital: Columbia

Land Area: 30,111 square miles
Largest City: Columbia

Report Card

Section	Score	Grade
1. History	40	C
2. Terrain	59	C+
3. Natural Resources	48	C
4. Resource Conservation	70	B
5. Environment	41	C
6. Health	17	F
7. Children and Families	36	D+
8. Female Equality	21	D
9. Racial Equality	22	D
10. Housing	77	B+
11. Education	12	F
12. Applied Intelligence	11	F
13. Arts	33	D
14. Communications	21	D
15. Sports	2	F
16. Recreation	25	D
17. Business	43	C
18. Personal Finances	33	D
19. Public Safety	10	F
20. Transportation	11	F
21. Politics	13	F
22. Government	80	A
23. National Relations	33	D
24. International Relations	75	B+
25. Future	49	C
Overall	359	D

Record with Neighboring States (0–2)

Neighbor	Neighbor's Score	Winner
Georgia	426	Georgia by 67
North Carolina	457	North Carolina by 98

Category Scores of 100 (1)

Section	Category
Children and Families	Marriage Stability

Category Scores of 0 (11)

Section	Category
Terrain	Rangeland
Natural Resources	Crude Oil Reserves
Natural Resources	Coal Reserves
Health	Life Expectancy
Racial Equality	Minority College Graduates
Applied Intelligence	MacArthur Fellows
Sports	Professional Champions
Sports	Spectator Seats
Public Safety	Prison Population
Transportation	Motor Vehicle Deaths
Politics	Voter Turnout

44. Kentucky (D)

FINAL STANDINGS

Kentucky is two slots behind neighboring Tennessee in all three rankings. It is no. 44 overall, no. 8 in the South, and no. 15 among medium states.

BEST SECTIONS

Housing (77 points)—You will find property taxes lower than Kentucky's in only three states. Housing costs also are below the national average.

Natural Resources (74)—Kentucky is one of the country's leading coal states. It also is in the upper half of the national rankings for farm marketings and timber reserves. There is even a small amount of oil under the bluegrass.

Public Safety (72)—Kentucky has America's fourth-lowest total crime rate. Its police departments are adequately staffed.

WORST SECTIONS

Education (0 points)—Tied with Mississippi for last place in this section. Only Tennessee spends less on education than Kentucky; only Mississippi has a worse graduation rate for high school students.

National Relations (0)—Kentucky is insular. Just five states have smaller percentages of residents who were born out of state. Kentucky corporations have little clout on a national basis.

Applied Intelligence (1)—No state gets a smaller share of federal research and development funding than Kentucky.

NEIGHBORS

The trend is unmistakable. Most of Kentucky's seven neighbors offer a superior quality of life. West Virginia is the only adjacent state it defeats.

BIGGEST SURPRISE

Kentucky once was in the national mainstream. Settlers and trade goods passed through the Cumberland Gap or down the Ohio River on their way west. But modern Kentucky is much more isolated, earning an F in the National Relations section.

THE BOTTOM LINE

Last in the Education section, next to last in Applied Intelligence, Kentucky needs to concentrate on improving its brain power.

KENTUCKY

General Information

Total Points: 357
Overall Grade: D

National Rank: 44 of 50
Regional Rank: 8 of 13 (South)

Population: 3,685,000
Capital: Frankfort

Land Area: 39,732 square miles
Largest City: Louisville

Report Card

Section	Score	Grade
1. History	33	D
2. Terrain	32	D
3. Natural Resources	74	B
4. Resource Conservation	63	B
5. Environment	55	C+
6. Health	23	D
7. Children and Families	52	C
8. Female Equality	23	D
9. Racial Equality	19	F
10. Housing	77	B+
11. Education	0	F
12. Applied Intelligence	1	F
13. Arts	28	D
14. Communications	24	D
15. Sports	12	F
16. Recreation	22	D
17. Business	31	D
18. Personal Finances	22	D
19. Public Safety	72	B
20. Transportation	8	F
21. Politics	27	D
22. Government	71	B
23. National Relations	0	F
24. International Relations	38	D+
25. Future	44	C
Overall	357	D

Record with Neighboring States (1–6)

Neighbor	Neighbor's Score	Winner
Illinois	505	Illinois by 148
Indiana	438	Indiana by 81
Missouri	427	Missouri by 70
Ohio	453	Ohio by 96
Tennessee	386	Tennessee by 29
Virginia	560	Virginia by 203
West Virginia	349	Kentucky by 8

Category Scores of 100 (0)

Section	Category
(None)	

Category Scores of 0 (10)

Section	Category
Terrain	Ocean Shoreline
Terrain	Rangeland
Female Equality	Women in Government
Education	High School Graduates
Education	Education Spending
Applied Intelligence	Research and Development
Sports	High School Athletes
Sports	Spectator Seats
Recreation	Fitness Centers
International Relations	Foreign Born

45. West Virginia (D)

FINAL STANDINGS

West Virginia, no. 45 overall, is at the bottom in the East, far behind next-to-last Pennsylvania. It also ranks last among the 17 small states.

BEST SECTIONS

Public Safety (98 points)—There is no reason to fear for your safety in West Virginia. It has the nation's lowest total crime rate. The level of police staffing is excellent.

Natural Resources (89)—Everyone knows that West Virginia is America's greatest coal state. But few are aware that it also has substantial reserves of timber, ranking no. 3 in that category.

Government (74)—West Virginia has a lean government work force, with a much smaller ratio of state employees than the national average.

WORST SECTIONS

Applied Intelligence (0 points)—Only 12.3 percent of West Virginia's adults have college degrees, the lowest figure in the country. The state turns out few doctoral candidates, and it has never had a MacArthur fellow.

Business (0)—Another last-place finish. West Virginia has the nation's weakest retail sector. Only Mississippi has a smaller gross state product.

Transportation (0)—Last again. Airline service is poor, public transit is virtually nonexistent, and the motor vehicle death rate is high.

NEIGHBORS

A clean sweep, in a bad way. West Virginia loses to all five neighbors

BIGGEST SURPRISE

Coal-mining states supposedly are lawless and polluted. But West Virginia defies the stereotype. It earned an A in the Public Safety section and a C in Environment.

THE BOTTOM LINE

West Virginia is the worst state in the East. It received D's or F's in 16 of the 25 sections, including three last-place finishes.

544 WEST VIRGINIA

General Information

Total Points: 349
Overall Grade: D

National Rank: 45 of 50
Regional Rank: 12 of 12 (East)

Population: 1,793,000
Capital: Charleston

Land Area: 24,087 square miles
Largest City: Charleston

Report Card

Section	Score	Grade
1. History	23	D–
2. Terrain	30	D
3. Natural Resources	89	A
4. Resource Conservation	61	B–
5. Environment	51	C
6. Health	11	F
7. Children and Families	30	D
8. Female Equality	45	C
9. Racial Equality	21	D
10. Housing	70	B
11. Education	7	F
12. Applied Intelligence	0	F
13. Arts	15	F
14. Communications	41	C–
15. Sports	21	D–
16. Recreation	19	F
17. Business	0	F
18. Personal Finances	2	F
19. Public Safety	98	A
20. Transportation	0	F
21. Politics	73	B
22. Government	74	B
23. National Relations	22	D–
24. International Relations	37	D+
25. Future	23	D–
Overall	349	D

Record with Neighboring States (0–5)

Neighbor	Neighbor's Score	Winner
Kentucky	357	Kentucky by 8
Maryland	608	Maryland by 259
Ohio	453	Ohio by 104
Pennsylvania	517	Pennsylvania by 168
Virginia	560	Virginia by 211

Category Scores of 100 (3)

Section	Category
Natural Resources	Coal Reserves
Public Safety	All Crimes
Politics	State Legislature Turnover

Category Scores of 0 (23)

Section	Category
Terrain	Ocean Shoreline
Terrain	Inland Water
Terrain	Rangeland
Health	Major Causes of Death
Education	College Students
Applied Intelligence	College Graduates
Applied Intelligence	MacArthur Fellows
Arts	Entertainers
Arts	Museums and Galleries
Communications	Library Spending
Sports	Professional Champions
Sports	Spectator Seats
Recreation	Restaurants and Bars
Business	Gross State Product
Business	Retail Trade
Personal Finances	Per Capita Income
Personal Finances	Unemployment
Public Safety	Public Safety Spending
Transportation	Airline Service
National Relations	Domestic Travel
International Relations	Foreign Born
International Relations	Agricultural Exports
Future	Projected Job Growth

46. Oklahoma (D-)

FINAL STANDINGS

Oklahoma is on the next-to-last rung of the grade ladder, D–. It is no. 46 nationally, no. 9 in the South, and no. 16 of the 20 medium-size states.

BEST SECTIONS

Housing (68 points)—Oklahoma is among the seven states that have the smallest housing costs and the lowest property taxes. The housing stock is considerably younger than in most of America.

Politics (67)—Oklahoma voters believe in new blood. Just nine states have faster rates of legislative turnover.

Resource Conservation (60)—Much of Oklahoma is dry and dusty, so its residents know the value of water. Only six states are better than Oklahoma at water conservation.

WORST SECTIONS

History (1 point)—This was the last state to be permanently settled by people of European descent, 30 years behind South Dakota, the next youngest. Oklahoma has never had a major-party nominee for president.

Business (12)—Oklahoma had one of the nation's slowest economic growth rates in the 1980s. Its retail sector is weak, and its manufacturing and service sectors aren't much better.

Health (13)—Oklahoma is among the 10 states with the highest rates of death from heart disease, cancer, and strokes. Medical specialists are relatively scarce.

NEIGHBORS

Oklahoma defeats Arkansas in a quality-of-life showdown, but it loses to everyone else. Its overall record is 1–5.

BIGGEST SURPRISE

Oklahoma received above-average grades in only three sections. The surprise is that one was a B– in the Resource Conservation section. You wouldn't expect an oil-rich and water-poor state to be so willing to conserve.

THE BOTTOM LINE

Oklahoma is one of the nation's five worst states in terms of quality of life. It is particularly hampered by a weak economy and a poor educational system.

OKLAHOMA

General Information

Total Points: 341
Overall Grade: D–

National Rank: 46 of 50
Regional Rank: 9 of 13 (South)

Population: 3,146,000
Capital: Oklahoma City

Land Area: 68,679 square miles
Largest City: Oklahoma City

Report Card

Section	Score	Grade
1. History	1	F
2. Terrain	46	C
3. Natural Resources	27	D
4. Resource Conservation	60	B–
5. Environment	50	C
6. Health	13	F
7. Children and Families	35	D+
8. Female Equality	37	D+
9. Racial Equality	30	D
10. Housing	68	B
11. Education	36	D+
12. Applied Intelligence	23	D–
13. Arts	24	D–
14. Communications	33	D
15. Sports	15	F
16. Recreation	26	D
17. Business	12	F
18. Personal Finances	17	F
19. Public Safety	31	D
20. Transportation	41	C–
21. Politics	67	B
22. Government	45	C
23. National Relations	24	D–
24. International Relations	20	D–
25. Future	54	C
Overall	341	D–

Record with Neighboring States (1-5)

Neighbor	Neighbor's Score	Winner
Arkansas	323	Oklahoma by 18
Colorado	616	Colorado by 275
Kansas	466	Kansas by 125
Missouri	427	Missouri by 86
New Mexico	413	New Mexico by 72
Texas	416	Texas by 75

Category Scores of 100 (1)

Section	Category
Future	Projected Income Growth

Category Scores of 0 (8)

Section	Category
History	European Settlement
History	Historic Natives
History	Presidential Candidates
Terrain	Ocean Shoreline
Environment	Environmental Spending
Children and Families	Marriage Stability
Sports	Professional Champions
Sports	Spectator Seats

47. Arkansas (D-)

FINAL STANDINGS

Arkansas is three from the bottom on all of its lists: no. 47 overall, no. 10 in the South, and no. 17 among medium-size states.

BEST SECTIONS

Resource Conservation (77 points)—Arkansas has America's 10th best record in using renewable energy, getting 16.3 percent of its power from such sources. It also is reasonably efficient in its use of petroleum.

Government (75)—Arkansas is one of nine states with per capita tax loads below $1,000. It also carries the ninth-lowest state debt.

Housing (72)—Housing costs are low, and the inventory includes a good proportion of new homes. Only Alabama and New Mexico have lighter property taxes.

WORST SECTIONS

Politics (0 points)—Arkansas has America's least-responsive political system. Elections are rarely close, and membership in the state legislature changes at a glacial pace.

Applied Intelligence (1)—Only West Virginia has a smaller percentage of college graduates; just two states get smaller shares of federal research and development funding.

Education (5)—Arkansas spends less on schools than everyone but Kentucky and Tennessee. It is among the seven states with the worst high school graduation rates and standardized test scores.

NEIGHBORS

Only three states are ranked below Arkansas, but two are neighbors. That's why it ends up with a semi-respectable 2–4 record.

BIGGEST SURPRISE

Arkansas produced the current president of the United States, but it still ranked 50th in the Politics section with an F. Just two states have had less success matching the national results in presidential elections.

THE BOTTOM LINE

Arkansas needs drastic improvement in many areas, especially in the way it educates its young and the way it treats women and minorities.

ARKANSAS

General Information

Total Points: 323
Overall Grade: D–

National Rank: 47 of 50
Regional Rank: 10 of 13 (South)

Population: 2,351,000
Capital: Little Rock

Land Area: 52,075 square miles
Largest City: Little Rock

Report Card

Section	Score	Grade
1. History	32	D
2. Terrain	42	C–
3. Natural Resources	43	C–
4. Resource Conservation	77	B+
5. Environment	55	C+
6. Health	29	D
7. Children and Families	22	D–
8. Female Equality	19	F
9. Racial Equality	14	F
10. Housing	72	B
11. Education	5	F
12. Applied Intelligence	1	F
13. Arts	17	F
14. Communications	20	D–
15. Sports	43	C–
16. Recreation	14	F
17. Business	24	D–
18. Personal Finances	13	F
19. Public Safety	33	D
20. Transportation	13	F
21. Politics	0	F
22. Government	75	B+
23. National Relations	23	D–
24. International Relations	50	C
25. Future	46	C
Overall	323	D–

Record with Neighboring States (2–4)

Neighbor	Neighbor's Score	Winner
Louisiana	239	Arkansas by 84
Mississippi	268	Arkansas by 55
Missouri	427	Missouri by 104
Oklahoma	341	Oklahoma by 18
Tennessee	386	Tennessee by 63
Texas	416	Texas by 93

Category Scores of 100 (1)

Section	Category
Sports	College Champions

Category Scores of 0 (13)

Section	Category
History	Historic Natives
Terrain	Ocean Shoreline
Housing	Housing Size
Education	College Students
Education	Education Spending
Applied Intelligence	College Graduates
Applied Intelligence	Research and Development
Communications	Library Spending
Sports	Professional Champions
Sports	Spectator Seats
Recreation	Restaurants and Bars
Transportation	Public Transit Usage
Politics	State Legislature Turnover

48. Alabama (F)

FINAL STANDINGS

Alabama is the first state to receive an F. It is no. 48 nationally, no. 11 in the South, and no. 18 among medium-size states.

BEST SECTIONS

Housing (89 points)—This is a tax haven; no state has lighter property taxes than Alabama. Rents are the lowest in the country. The housing stock is fairly young.

Resource Conservation (72)—Only nine states get more than 17 percent of their energy from renewable sources. Alabama is among them.

Natural Resources (59)—Alabama has surprisingly large reserves of timber, ranking fifth of the 50 states. It also has small amounts of coal and oil.

WORST SECTIONS

Recreation (1 point)—Looking for fitness centers, movie theaters, restaurants, or large stores? All are in short supply in Alabama. The parks are not heavily used, either.

Sports (5)—There are no major-league teams. Only Mississippi and Nebraska turn out fewer Olympic athletes than Alabama.

Health (8)—The death rate from heart disease, cancer, and strokes is much higher than normal. Alabamans live shorter lives, on average, than people in 44 states.

Politics (8)—Elections are hardly ever close. Alabama matches the national results in presidential elections only half the time, which is the worst percentage in the country.

NEIGHBORS

Thank God for Mississippi. It provides the one victory in Alabama's 1–3 record.

BIGGEST SURPRISE

Alabama received only two above-average grades, so its A in the Housing section truly stands out on its report card. Its residents are blessed with rents and taxes that are exceptionally low.

THE BOTTOM LINE

The quality of life in Alabama is consistently poor. It earned eight D's and 10 F's in the 25 sections.

ALABAMA

General Information

Total Points: 303
Overall Grade: F

National Rank: 48 of 50
Regional Rank: 11 of 13 (South)

Population: 4,041,000
Capital: Montgomery

Land Area: 50,750 square miles
Largest City: Birmingham

Report Card

Section	Score	Grade
1. History	30	D
2. Terrain	47	C
3. Natural Resources	59	C+
4. Resource Conservation	72	B
5. Environment	28	D
6. Health	8	F
7. Children and Families	17	F
8. Female Equality	10	F
9. Racial Equality	18	F
10. Housing	89	A
11. Education	15	F
12. Applied Intelligence	18	F
13. Arts	24	D–
14. Communications	23	D–
15. Sports	5	F
16. Recreation	1	F
17. Business	26	D
18. Personal Finances	19	F
19. Public Safety	23	D–
20. Transportation	24	D–
21. Politics	8	F
22. Government	53	C
23. National Relations	33	D
24. International Relations	43	C–
25. Future	44	C–
Overall	303	F

Record with Neighboring States (1-3)

Neighbor	Neighbor's Score	Winner
Florida	483	Florida by 180
Georgia	426	Georgia by 123
Mississippi	268	Alabama by 35
Tennessee	386	Tennessee by 83

Category Scores of 100 (2)

Section	Category
Housing	Rent
Housing	Property Taxes

Category Scores of 0 (11)

Section	Category
Terrain	Rangeland
Environment	Environmental Spending
Female Equality	Women in Business
Female Equality	Women in Government
Racial Equality	Minority Businesses
Sports	Professional Champions
Sports	Spectator Seats
Business	Service Sector Strength
Politics	Presidential Election Trends
Politics	Political Party Competition
Government	State Constitution Length

49. Mississippi (F)

FINAL STANDINGS

Mississippi is next to last across the board: no. 49 overall, no. 12 in the South, and no. 19 of the 20 medium-size states.

BEST SECTIONS

Government (83 points)—Mississippi is among the five states with the lowest taxes and the smallest debts. It also has fewer governmental units than most states.

Housing (78)—The light tax load makes Mississippi's housing attractive. Its inventory of homes is one of the nation's 10 youngest.

Resource Conservation (74)—Mississippi ranks 11th in the use of renewable energy. It also has a respectable record of water conservation.

WORST SECTIONS

Children and Families (0 points)—This is the first of six last-place finishes. Mississippi has the nation's highest percentages of low-weight births, births to single teens, and children in poverty.

Education (0)—No state does worse on standardized tests or has fewer high school graduates.

Arts (0)—The arts community in Mississippi is tiny. The state finished 49th or 50th in all five categories in this section.

Communications (0)—Mississippi spends less on libraries than any other state. Almost 13 percent of all homes are without phones.

Sports (0)—There are no major-league teams, and participation at other levels is very low.

Recreation (0)—Mississippi has America's lowest ratios of fitness centers, large stores, and restaurants.

NEIGHBORS

Mississippi ekes out a win over last-place Louisiana, but loses to its three other neighbors.

BIGGEST SURPRISE

Mississippi has serious problems, as evidenced by its five D's and 12 F's. That's why its A– in the Government section is so surprising. The state administration apparently is more concerned with financial management than quality of life.

THE BOTTOM LINE

You call this progress? H. L. Mencken called Mississippi the nation's worst state in 1931. Now it's next to worst.

MISSISSIPPI

General Information

Total Points: 268
Overall Grade: F

National Rank: 49 of 50
Regional Rank: 12 of 13 (South)

Population: 2,573,000
Capital: Jackson

Land Area: 46,914 square miles
Largest City: Jackson

Report Card

Section	Score	Grade
1. History	30	D
2. Terrain	41	C–
3. Natural Resources	39	D+
4. Resource Conservation	74	B
5. Environment	47	C
6. Health	5	F
7. Children and Families	0	F
8. Female Equality	4	F
9. Racial Equality	23	D–
10. Housing	78	B+
11. Education	0	F
12. Applied Intelligence	9	F
13. Arts	0	F
14. Communications	0	F
15. Sports	0	F
16. Recreation	0	F
17. Business	13	F
18. Personal Finances	4	F
19. Public Safety	42	C–
20. Transportation	21	D–
21. Politics	31	D
22. Government	83	A–
23. National Relations	17	F
24. International Relations	40	C–
25. Future	48	C
Overall	268	F

Record with Neighboring States (1–3)

Neighbor	Neighbor's Score	Winner
Alabama	303	Alabama by 35
Arkansas	323	Arkansas by 55
Louisiana	239	Mississippi by 29
Tennessee	386	Tennessee by 118

Category Scores of 100 (3)

Section	Category
Environment	Superfund Sites
Environment	Waste Generation
Personal Finances	Income Growth

Category Scores of 0 (34)

Section	Category
History	Presidential Candidates
Terrain	Rangeland
Natural Resources	Coal Reserves
Children and Families	Birth Weight
Children and Families	Births to Single Teens
Children and Families	Children in Poverty
Female Equality	Women in Poverty
Female Equality	Women in Business
Racial Equality	Income Disparity
Education	High School Graduates
Education	Standardized Tests
Applied Intelligence	Patents
Arts	Arts Funding
Arts	Theater
Arts	Dance
Arts	Entertainers
Arts	Museums and Galleries
Communications	Telephone Service
Communications	Newspaper Circulation
Communications	Library Spending
Sports	Olympic Athletes
Sports	Professional Champions
Sports	Spectator Seats
Recreation	Fitness Centers
Recreation	Shopping
Recreation	Restaurants and Bars
Business	Gross State Product
Business	Retail Trade
Business	Service Sector Strength
Personal Finances	Per Capita Income
Personal Finances	Poverty
Personal Finances	Upper Incomes
Politics	Presidential Election Trends
International Relations	Foreign Born

50. Louisiana (F)

FINAL STANDINGS

All of Louisiana's rankings translate to last place: no. 50 nationally, no. 13 in the South, and no. 20 among medium-size states.

BEST SECTIONS

Housing (64 points)—Just five states have property taxes lower than Louisiana's. The housing stock is relatively young, with fewer than 11 percent of all current units built prior to World War II.

Natural Resources (62)—Louisiana has the nation's third-richest oil reserves, behind only California and Texas. It also has surprisingly large amounts of timber.

Terrain (59)—Louisiana offers exceptional variety for anyone seeking access to water, ranging from ocean beaches to bayous to lakes.

WORST SECTIONS

Health (0 points)—Louisiana has the lowest life expectancy in America; its typical resident dies more than five years before his contemporaries in top-rated Hawaii. Hospital costs are among the nation's highest.

Female Equality (0)—Louisiana is a bastion of male chauvinism. No state offers fewer job opportunities for women; only Alabama and Kentucky have fewer women in their state legislatures.

Personal Finances (0)—This is the worst place in America to make money. West Virginia is the only state with higher unemployment; Mississippi is the only one with more families living below the poverty level.

NEIGHBORS

Last place means last place. Louisiana loses to all three of its neighbors.

BIGGEST SURPRISE

Louisiana is a poor state economically, but it is surprisingly rich in resources, particularly oil and timber. That's why it earned a grade of B– in the Natural Resources section.

THE BOTTOM LINE

Louisiana offers the worst quality of life in America. Just look at its report card: There are only two above-average grades—and 10 D's, 11 F's.

LOUISIANA

General Information

Total Points: 239
Overall Grade: F

National Rank: 50 of 50
Regional Rank: 13 of 13 (South)

Population: 4,220,000
Capital: Baton Rouge

Land Area: 43,566 square miles
Largest City: New Orleans

Report Card

Section	Score	Grade
1. History	32	D
2. Terrain	59	C+
3. Natural Resources	62	B–
4. Resource Conservation	15	F
5. Environment	33	D
6. Health	0	F
7. Children and Families	11	F
8. Female Equality	0	F
9. Racial Equality	23	D–
10. Housing	64	B–
11. Education	9	F
12. Applied Intelligence	16	F
13. Arts	17	F
14. Communications	25	D
15. Sports	34	D
16. Recreation	5	F
17. Business	21	D–
18. Personal Finances	0	F
19. Public Safety	7	F
20. Transportation	24	D–
21. Politics	33	D
22. Government	55	C+
23. National Relations	8	F
24. International Relations	36	D+
25. Future	31	D
Overall	239	F

Record with Neighboring States (0–3)

Neighbor	Neighbor's Score	Winner
Arkansas	323	Arkansas by 84
Mississippi	268	Mississippi by 29
Texas	416	Texas by 177

Category Scores of 100 (0)

Section	Category
(None)	

Category Scores of 0 (18)

Section	Category
Resource Conservation	Petroleum Consumption
Resource Conservation	Natural Gas Consumption
Environment	Toxic Emissions
Health	Life Expectancy
Children and Families	Birth Weight
Children and Families	Births to Single Teens
Children and Families	Children in Poverty
Female Equality	Women in Poverty
Female Equality	Employment Opportunities
Racial Equality	Income Disparity
Arts	Theater
Recreation	Park Visitors
Business	Economic Growth
Personal Finances	Unemployment
Personal Finances	Poverty
National Relations	Population Influx
Future	Projected Population Growth
Future	Projected Job Growth

Sources

A quality-of-life rating is much like a snapshot. It captures a single, specific moment. Click the shutter a minute earlier or later, and you might get a different picture. Only slightly different, perhaps, but different nonetheless. It all depends on when you make that click.

We took our snapshot on May 1, 1993. All statistics in this book were the latest figures publicly available from the federal government and other sources on that date. Almost all the publications and reports listed below were printed between 1991 and 1993, though one dates to 1975. Much of our data, of course, was compiled by the 1990 census, which has been published in stages since 1991 and which won't be outdated until the federal government conducts its next head count at the turn of the century.

Don't expect to find the exact same figures in this book and in the reports cited below. Our statistics generally are rates or percentages based on raw numbers from the original sources. Example: We express petroleum, natural gas, and electricity consumption on a per capita basis. The U.S. Department of Energy only provides total consumption figures for entire states, which we then divided by each state's population.

The source listings on the following pages include the author—whether a person, private company, or government agency—and the title of the book or report. There are two exceptions: No author is cited when an almanac, dictionary, magazine, or newspaper is the source. And three standard works printed by the U.S. Census Bureau are listed only by abbreviated title, as indicated in parentheses:

- *1990 Census of Population and Housing* (*1990 Census*)
- *State and Metropolitan Area Data Book* (*State Data Book)*
- *Statistical Abstract of the United States* (*Statistical Abstract*)

Each source listing is followed by two numbers in brackets. The first number is the date the publication or report was printed, followed by the year to which its statistics apply. Example: [1993, 1991] means that the source was published in 1993 and contains statistics for 1991. If the category involves statistics from several years, such as unemployment rates from 1983 through 1992, the second number in brackets is the final year of the series.

1. History

European Settlement: *World Almanac* [1993, 1993]

Statehood: *Statistical Abstract* [1992, 1992]

Historic Places: National Conference of State Historic Preservation Officers, National Park Service, and American Association for State and Local History, *National Register of Historic Places* [1989, 1989]

Historic Natives: *Dictionary of American Biography, Comprehensive Index* [1990, 1990]

Presidential Candidates: G. Scott Thomas, *The Pursuit of the White House* [1987, 1984] (The book's figures were updated to include the 1988 and 1992 elections.)

2. Terrain

Ocean Shoreline: National Oceanic and Atmospheric Administration, *The Coastline of the United States* [1975, 1975]

Inland Water, Elevation Variation: *State Data Book* [1991, 1990]

Forests, Rangeland: U.S. Forest Service, *An Analysis of the Land Base Situation in the United States: 1989–2040* [1989, 1989]

3. Natural Resources

Farm Marketings: U.S. Department of Agriculture, *Economic Indicators of the Farm Sector: State Financial Summary* [1991, 1990]

Timberland: *State Data Book* [1991, 1987]

Nonfuel Mining: U.S. Bureau of Mines, *State Commodity Summaries* [1993, 1992]

Crude Oil Reserves: U.S. Department of Energy, *U.S. Crude Oil, Natural Gas, and Natural Gas Liquids Reserves* [1991, 1990]

Coal Reserves: U.S. Department of Energy, *Coal Production* [1990, 1990]

4. Resource Conservation

Water Usage: *Statistical Abstract* [1992, 1985]

Petroleum Consumption, Natural Gas Consumption, Electricity Consumption: U.S. Department of Energy, *State Energy Data Report* [1992, 1990]

Renewable Energy: Bob Hall and Mary Lee Kerr, *1991–1992 Green Index* [1991, 1990]; *Information Please Environmental Almanac* [1993, 1990]

5. Environment

Superfund Sites: *Information Please Environmental Almanac* [1993, 1992]

Toxic Emissions: *Information Please Environmental Almanac* [1993, 1990]

Drinking Water: Bob Hall and Mary Lee Kerr, *1991–1992 Green Index* [1991, 1987]

Waste Generation: *BioCycle* [April 1992, 1991]

Environmental Spending: U.S. Census Bureau, *Government Finances: 1989–90* [1991, 1990]

6. Health

Life Expectancy: National Center for Health Statistics, *U.S. Decennial Life Tables for 1979–81, State Life Tables* [1985, 1981]

Major Causes of Death: National Center for Health Statistics, *Monthly Vital Statistics Report* [January 7, 1993, 1990]

Family Doctors, Specialists: American Medical Association, *Physician Characteristics and Distribution in the United States* [1992, 1990]

Hospital Costs: *Statistical Abstract* [1992, 1990]

7. Children and Families

Birth Weight, Births to Single Teens: Annie E. Casey Foundation and Center for the Study of Social Policy, *Kids Count Data Book* [1993, 1990]

Infant Mortality: National Center for Health Statistics, *Monthly Vital Statistics Report* [September 30, 1992, 1991]

Children in Poverty: *1990 Census* [1991–1993, 1989]

Marriage Stability: U.S. Department of Health and Human Services, *Vital Statistics of the United States, Volume III: Marriage and Divorce* [1991, 1987] (Louisiana's statistics are from 1985, the latest year in which complete figures are available for that state)

8. Female Equality

Women in Poverty: U.S. Census Bureau, *Poverty Statistics for Family and Female Headed Households* (CPH-L-108) [1993, 1989]

Employment Opportunities: U.S. Bureau of Labor Statistics, *Geographic Profile of Employment and Unemployment* [1992, 1991]

Women in Business: U.S. Census Bureau, *Women-Owned Businesses* [1990, 1987]

Women in Government: Center for the American Woman and Politics (Rutgers University), *Fact Sheet: Women in State Legislatures 1993* [1993, 1993]

Violence Against Women: Federal Bureau of Investigation, *Uniform Crime Reports: Crime in the United States* [1992, 1991]

9. Racial Equality

Minority Population: U.S. Census Bureau, Press Release: CB91-282 [1991, 1990]

Income Disparity: U.S. Census Bureau, *1990 Census Minority Economic Profile* (CPH-L-92/95) [1992, 1989]

Comparisons were made between whites and the largest minority group in each state.

Blacks are the leading minority in 30 states.

Hispanics form the largest minority group in 14 states: Arizona, California, Colorado, Idaho, Maine, Nevada, New Hampshire, New Mexico, Oregon, Rhode Island, Texas, Utah, Vermont, and Wyoming.

American Indians, Eskimos, or Aleuts are the top minority in four states: Alaska, Montana, North Dakota, and South Dakota.

Asians or Pacific Islanders are the leading non-white group in two states: Hawaii and Washington.

Housing Disparity: *1990 Census* [1991–1993, 1990] (comparisons were made between non-Hispanic white households and the minority groups included in the Income Disparity category)

Minority College Graduates: U.S. Census Bureau, *1990 Census Minority Economic Profile* (CPH-L-92/95) [1992, 1990]

Minority Businesses: U.S. Census Bureau, *Survey of Minority-Owned Business Enterprises* [1991, 1987]

10. Housing

Housing Costs, Rent, Housing Age, Housing Size: *1990 Census* [1991–1993, 1990]

Property Taxes: U.S. Census Bureau, *Government Finances: 1989–90* [1991, 1990]

11. Education

High School Dropouts, High School Graduates, College Students: *1990 Census* [1991–1993, 1990]

Standardized Tests: U.S. Department of Education, *State Education Performance Chart* [1990, 1989]; National Center for Education Statistics, *Digest of Education Statistics* [1992, 1989]

Education Spending: U.S. Census Bureau, *Government Finances: 1989–90* [1991, 1990]

12. Applied Intelligence

College Graduates: *1990 Census* [1991–1993, 1990]

Doctoral Degrees: National Research Council, *Doctorate Recipients from United States Universities* [1991, 1990]

Patents: *Statistical Abstract* [1992, 1990]

Research and Development: National Science Foundation, *Federal Funds for Research and Development: Fiscal Years 1989, 1990, and 1991* [1991, 1989]

MacArthur Fellows: The John D. and Catherine T. MacArthur Foundation, *MacArthur Fellows 1978–1992* [1992, 1992]

13. Arts

Arts Funding: *Statistical Abstract* [1992, 1991]

Theater, Dance, Entertainers, Museums and Galleries: U.S. Census Bureau, *County Business Patterns* [1992–1993, 1990]

14. Communications

Telephone Service: *1990 Census* [1991–1993, 1990]

Cable Television: Warren Publishing Inc., *TV & Cable Factbook* [1993, 1992] (Delaware's statistics are from 1991; the 1992 cable household count for that state was discarded because it exceeded the total number of households in Delaware.)

Broadcasting Stations: *State Data Book* [1991, 1990]

Newspaper Circulation: Editor & Publisher Co., *Editor & Publisher Year Book* [1992, 1991]

State totals in this category do not include circulation figures for national newspapers. Example: *Editor & Publisher Year Book* gave Virginia credit for the entire national circulation of *USA Today,* which is based in Arlington, Virginia. But this category subtracted the *USA Today* figure, counting only the circulation for local dailies in Virginia.

Library Spending: U.S. Census Bureau, *Government Finances: 1989–90* [1991, 1990]

15. Sports

High School Athletes: National Federation of State High School Associations, *1992 Sports Participation Survey* [1992, 1992]

College Champions, Professional Champions, Spectator Seats: *Information Please Sports Almanac* [1993, 1992] (additional information for the College Champions category was provided by the National Collegiate Athletic Association)

Olympic Athletes: *USA Today* [February 25 and July 24, 1992, 1992]

16. Recreation

Park Visitors: *Statistical Abstract* [1992, 1990]; U.S. Forest Service, *Report of the Forest Service* [1991, 1990]; National Park Service, *National Park Service Statistical Abstract* [1991, 1990]

Fitness Centers, Movies and Videos, Shopping, Restaurants and Bars: U.S. Census Bureau, *County Business Patterns* [1992–1993, 1990]

17. Business

Gross State Product, Economic Growth: U.S. Bureau of Economic Analysis, *Survey of Current Business* [December 1991, 1989]

Manufacturing Productivity: U.S. Census Bureau, *Annual Survey of Manufactures* [1992, 1990]

Retail Trade: *Statistical Abstract* [1992, 1990]

Service Sector Strength: U.S. Census Bureau, *County Business Patterns* [1992–1993, 1990]

18. Personal Finances

Per Capita Income, Income Growth: U.S. Bureau of Economic Analysis, *Survey of Current Business* [August 1992, 1991]

Unemployment: U.S. Bureau of Labor Statistics, *Employment and Earnings* [1983–1992, 1991]

Poverty: *1990 Census* [1991–1993, 1990]

Upper Incomes: Internal Revenue Service, *Statistics of Income Bulletin* [Summer 1992, 1990]

19. Public Safety

All Crimes, Violent Crimes, Police Presence: Federal Bureau of Investigation, *Uniform Crime Reports: Crime in the United States* [1992, 1991]

Public Safety Spending: U.S. Census Bureau, *State Government Finances* [1992, 1991]

Prison Population: *Statistical Abstract* [1992, 1990]

20. Transportation

Road Mileage, Pavement Condition: Federal Highway Administration, *Highway Statistics* [1991, 1990]

Motor Vehicle Deaths: *Statistical Abstract* [1992, 1990]

Public Transit Usage: *1990 Census* [1991–1993, 1990]

Airline Service: Federal Aviation Administration, *FAA Statistical Handbook of Aviation* [1991, 1990]

21. Politics

Voter Turnout: Institute for Southern Studies, Press Release: "Voter Turnout Among Adults, 1980 to 1992" [January 10, 1993, 1992]

Electoral Votes: *Congressional Quarterly Weekly Report* [November 7, 1992, 1992]

Presidential Election Trends: G. Scott Thomas, *The Pursuit of the White House* [1987, 1984] (The book's figures were updated to include the 1988 and 1992 elections.)

Political Party Competition: Richard Scammon and Alice McGillivray, *America Votes* [1991, 1990]; *The Washington Post* [November 5, 1992, 1992]

State Legislature Turnover: Council of State Governments, *The Book of the States* [1992, 1989]

22. Government

State Taxes, State Debt: U.S. Census Bureau, *State Government Finances* [1992, 1991]

Government Employees: U.S. Census Bureau, *Public Employment* [1992, 1991]

Government Units: U.S. Census Bureau, Press Release: CB93-25 [1993, 1992]

State Constitution Length: Council of State Governments, *The Book of the States* [1992, 1992]

23. National Relations

Federal Spending: U.S. Census Bureau, *Federal Expenditures by State for Fiscal Year 1992* [1993, 1992]

Population Influx: *1990 Census* [1991–1993, 1990]

Domestic Travel: U.S. Travel Data Center, *Impact of Travel on State Economies* [1992, 1990]

***Fortune* 500 Companies:** *Fortune* [April 20, 1992, 1991]

Student Migration: National Center for Education Statistics, *Digest of Education Statistics* [1992, 1988]

24. International Relations

Foreign Employers: U.S. Bureau of Economic Analysis, *Survey of Current Business* [October 1992, 1987]

Export-Related Jobs: U.S. Census Bureau, *Exports From Manufacturing Establishments* [1992, 1989]

Foreign Born: *1990 Census* [1991–1993, 1990]

Agricultural Exports: U.S. Department of Agriculture, *Foreign Agricultural Trade of the United States* [May/June 1992, 1991] (The Department of Agriculture's Economic Research Service provided unpublished estimates for Alaska, New Hampshire and Rhode Island, which were not included in the main report.)

Overseas Population: U.S. Census Bureau, Press Release: CB91-07 [1991, 1990]

25. Future

Population Density: *1990 Census* [1991–1993, 1990]

Projected Population Growth, Projected Job Growth, Projected Income

Growth: U.S. Bureau of Economic Analysis, *BEA Regional Projections to 2040, Volume 1: States* [1990, 2020]

Future Political Power: *Congressional Quarterly Weekly Report* [November 7, 1992, 1992]; U.S. Bureau of Economic Analysis, *BEA Regional Projections to 2040, Volume 1: States* [1990, 2020]